Praise for Time's Enemy
Saturn Society, Book One

"I could not put it down. The characters were clear and well-drawn. The popping in and out of eras and changes in the surroundings in Dayton, Ohio, a place I have lived, failed to confuse me. That says a lot for the skill of the author."
– Maggie, Reviewer for Coffee Time Romance and More

"*Time's Enemy* is not your typical time travel romance. It takes this general premise and gives it a science fiction edge, taking the reader on a page turning journey... take *The Butterfly Effect*, mix in *The Time Traveler's Wife,* and sprinkle it with *Somewhere in Time*, and you'll get this amazing book."
– Lori Reader & Writer, The Otherworld Diner

"...so many little historical touches that I began to wonder if the author could describe them so well because she had slipped back into the past herself."
– Michele Stegman, author of *Mr. Right's Baby* and *Fortune's Pride*

"...a wonderfully-paced book that brings all the best parts of *Inception*, *Jumpers*, and old-school time-travel romances... a well-researched, exciting adventure through time in Dayton, Ohio, and a fascinating, unputdownable story rich in action, romance, and history."
– Athena Grayson, author of *Forever Material*

Other books by Jennette Marie Powell
Time's Enemy
Hangar 18: Legacy (Forthcoming)

Time's Fugitive

Jennette Marie Powell

Mythical Press

MYTHICAL PRESS ✶ DAYTON, OHIO

MYTHICAL PRESS ✷ DAYTON, OHIO
www.mythicalpress.com

Time's Fugitive

Editing by Sheri L. McGathy
Text design, cover, and prehistoric village photo by Jennette Marie Powell
Other photos used under license via www.istockphoto.com

This story is a work of fiction. Names, characters, places, and incidents are either products of the author's imagination or are used fictitiously. Any resemblance to actual events, locales, business establishments, media titles, or persons living or dead, is entirely coincidental.

Print ISBN 978-0-9839097-4-3
Digital ISBN 978-0-9839097-3-6
Library of Congress Control Number: 2012937010

Acknowledgements

Like most novels, it might have taken only one person to bring *Time's Fugitive* to life, but it took a village to make it something others might want to read. Of course, it would have never gotten to that point without the support of my family and writing friends, not only those in the Ohio Valley Romance Writers of America, but people on various email lists, and bloggers who don't even know me, but whose advice has been invaluable.

Specifically, I'd like to thank my three first readers, Carey Corp, Athena Grayson, and Michele Stegman, for your quick reads and thoughtful critique. As always, many thanks to my editor, cousin, and fellow author Sheri McGathy for your eagle eye and thorough review that always remains true to my story and vision. Finally, I'd be remiss if I failed to mention my very first critiquer, Linda Chalk. All of your input helped me take what was (hopefully!) a good book and make it better.

And last, but far from least, I'd like to thank the readers who enjoyed *Time's Enemy*, and asked (sometimes multiple times) when this book would be available. You're the reason authors continue to create stories, and knowing that I've been able to provide you with a few hours' entertainment is what makes it all worthwhile!

One

Violet Sinclair might have stayed home if she'd known she'd end her dream date running for her life. It would have been a tough choice. Tony Solomon, the man she'd pined for for years, had asked her out.

Tony slowed to navigate a curve on the dark, deserted street, and her belly fluttered with excitement.

A traffic jam on the way to the opera had forced them to take back roads. The snow that had started that afternoon was beginning to stick and get slippery, slowing them further.

Tony shot her a wan smile that she could barely see by the dashboard lights. "Looks like we're going to be late."

"It's all right." The opera didn't matter, even if it was never performed in Dayton again. She doubted she'd remember it afterward anyway—

The car jerked, throwing her forward.

"What the hell?" Tony whirled around.

Violet twisted to see out the back window. A black SUV—a big, military-styled one—closed in on them. "Did he hit ice?"

"*I* didn't." The truck's headlights glimmered in Tony's glasses and magnified his round eyes. The SUV drew close again. Violet doubled over as it impacted with a grating crunch.

Tony swore and dug into his pocket as the truck pushed them for several yards. He jabbed at his cell phone. The car bumped and jounced as it went off the right shoulder of the road and slowed to a stop. "What do you mean, no service?" He tossed the phone down.

Outside Violet's window, a thin, red light slashed the night. "What was that?"

Something burned through the Buick's roof with a sizzle. "Holy fuck!" Tony ducked as a line of red light speared through the hole. *Laser.*

A man leaned out of the SUV's passenger window and pointed a narrow object at them. A red beam burst from its end, and the back window shattered.

Violet grabbed the door handle. "That shopping center we just passed! It should be on the other side of the woods, he won't expect—"

"Get out!" Tony threw open his car door and tumbled out. Violet did the same.

Behind them, car doors clicked open. Violet stumbled down the road's shoulder and bolted into the trees. A red beam sliced the air inches from her head. She looked back as two men hopped out of the truck. One raised a weapon. The other man staggered into him and both crashed to the ground. Violet turned and ran. Muffled curses punctuated the night behind the crunch of her and Tony's footfalls in the frozen vegetation.

He panted as he glanced behind them. Before Violet could follow his gaze, he shoved her in the back, slamming her into the snowy leaves face first. Beside her, a red beam sizzled into a tree trunk, smoking where it struck.

Violet slowly raised her head. Her heartbeat thudded in her throat.

Tony grabbed her arm. "Come on!"

He dashed to a clump of bushes a few yards away. Violet's sharp puffs of breath rasped in her ears. She scurried after him, her pumps sticking in the frozen leaf cover, until something tripped her and she tumbled to the ground.

Snapping branches and crackling undergrowth heralded their pursuers' closing distance. She clawed her hair out of her face, then fought to free her foot from a root. Tony hurried back and pulled her up. "You go that way, I'll go..." He dropped her hand and darted for a stand of bushes to his left. Violet clambered up a rise toward where the strip mall should be, her legs already growing leaden. She gulped in the numbing, cold February air. *Tomorrow.* She'd start exercising— and get back on her diet. *If I'm alive.* Nothing like running from maniacal killers to drive home the danger of being overweight and out of shape.

She fled for the other end of the gully, branches slapping her face. A laser shot singed the earth near her feet. The crisp smell of burnt vegetation stung her nose. Though the moon was full, she could barely see. She inhaled as if she'd been gagged and bound, and each breath made her bonds tighter. Where was the shopping center? She feared her trembling legs wouldn't hold her much longer.

Behind her, something crashed to the ground. She risked a backward glance. The tree that the men had shot had fallen. A shouted curse, the snapping of branches, and crashing in the leaves told her one of the gunmen had been caught in the fallout.

She pushed onward, her lungs burning, her stomach churning. Even if she lost the men, they'd see her footprints in the snow. After an eternity, a building appeared at the gully's edge. She stumbled onto a strip of snow-covered, crumbled asphalt and the bottomed-out feeling in her belly lifted.

She dashed under a rust-stained, unlit sign on a high pole that read Paradise Motel. Not a strip mall, but the kind of place she'd seen on television, where people took prostitutes and conducted drug deals. Despite its seedy appearance, it would be a welcome haven.

When she topped the rise and beheld the building, her belly turned to stone.

Holes gaped where doors and windows had once been. Moonlight filtered through the long-gone ceiling to reveal a snow-dusted carpet of leaves on the rooms' floors. Black charred the walls, and soot had settled into the etched date—1958—of a once-white cornerstone.

Laser fire whizzed behind her. Violet bolted for the nearest door. As she tumbled through, a red blaze missed her leg by inches. She slipped on a mat of leaves and pitched forward, but before she hit the ground strong hands gripped her arms and yanked her upright. She screamed. A hand clamped over her mouth.

"Violet! It's me!"

She drew back.

Tony released her. "Are you okay?" The moon lit his concerned face.

"I- I think so." Though she was sweating, she trembled.

Tony leaned against the wall and panted. The impression of his fingers lingered on her arm. The acrid smell of something burnt broke through the motel's musty scent. Violet looked down, then jerked straight. A charred slash rent her black dress's hem.

In the distance, a man shouted. Tony pressed his back into the wall, palms flat. Fear crashed over Violet in waves, suffocating, drowning.

There was no place to run. If they'd stayed in the car, they'd be dead. If they'd kept running, they'd be dead. If they ran now, they'd be dead. By ducking into the motel, they'd only delayed the inevitable.

The shouts grew louder. She inched closer to Tony. She had to do one thing before she died. "Tony, there's something I have to tell you—"

"Not now. Maybe we can get out of this alive." He clamped a hand around her arm, then turned her to face him. "These guys are after me, not you." Violet drew back, stiffening. "Turn around. Don't look at me. If I disappear—"

"Disappear? Like you did in Mexico?"

His jaw tightened. "Yeah. Now turn around."

"But—" With a hand on both her shoulders, he spun her so her back was to him, then released her. "1959," he mumbled. "1959..."

Violet's fear solidified. What on earth was he doing? What had he done to draw those men's wrath? How would he make himself disappear? She started to turn, but he held her shoulders. "Stay there. Don't look at me for... a slow count to ten. It's our only chance, okay?"

"Are you sure... those men are after you?"

"Positive. Now turn around."

She wet her lips. Why would those men be after him? What if he was wrong?

Trust him. She didn't know where that came from, but—

"Violet?"

"All right."

"When you turn around, I'll be gone—"

"How?"

"Do it!"

The shouts and footsteps drew nearer. Tony let go of her. "When I'm gone, they'll know you're alone. You'll be safe. God, I hate this, but there's no other way. Okay, count."

She tried not to consider the possibility he was wrong. Or crazy. *One Mississippi, two Mississippi, three—*

Vertigo blasted through her, and she stumbled backward into Tony. She barely felt him catch her through the dizziness and the sense of the ground beneath her disappearing. Even the dizzy spells she'd had earlier that day hadn't been as strong. She grabbed Tony, but instead of steadying her, the dizziness intensified. *1959.* A year after the motel was built. Why had he said that?

"Violet!" He tried to shove her away.

"No!" She clutched harder, pulled at his coat with both hands, the vertigo so bad it was like her head spun on a dozen different axes. Then the world faded to black.

The first thing Tony noticed when the dizziness wore off was the smell of vinyl.

And warmth.

The blackness faded from his vision. A vertical crack of light bisected a curtained picture window. All he could make out were the hulking shapes of a bed, a dresser, and a small, square table with two chairs.

The motel. Before it burned. He'd made it! He pushed himself off the cool, tile floor—

"Tony?"

His blood froze as his warp-befuddled mind registered warmth and pressure against his side. "Violet?" *No way. No way. No way.*

She moved away. Her voice trembled. "What happened? Where are—"

"Oh my God... How did— you shouldn't be—"

"Where are we? Where are those men—"

"Gone. We're safe for now." Holy hell, what had he done? How had she come with him? He lurched to his feet and walked to the door, his footsteps clacking on the floor.

She pushed herself up, then straightened her dress with a sharp tug. When she spoke, her voice regained its firmness. "Where on earth—"

"The Paradise Motel." He gave a wry half-laugh. "Look." He yanked open the door. The sign in the parking lot glowed brightly. Beneath it, a pink neon "Vacancy" welcomed them.

"Oh my word." Violet drew up beside him. "What—? How...?"

Crisp stripes marked parking spaces in the smooth, black asphalt. In a few of the spaces sat cars with huge fins and bulging headlights. She blinked.

"Welcome to 1959," Tony said. *Shit, shit, shit!*

"Ninetee— Good heavens! Do you mean to tell me we've traveled back in time?" She leaned on the doorframe, and touched two shaking fingers to her lower lip. "It's—surely I'm dreaming." She pinched the back of her hand, then jerked her fingers away. "Ouch!"

"'Fraid not." Dread gripped Tony in a bear hug. Months ago he'd sworn he was through with time travel. Never again. Yet here he was.

Though there was no snow, a chill breeze blew dry leaves between the cars and chased them back inside. He shut the door.

"What are we going to do?" Violet fumbled with a lock of her blond hair. "Where are those men? Will they find us here?" Her voice rose with each question. "Who are—"

"I don't know." Tony moved closer, laying a hand on her elbow. "I have no idea why they're chasing us, but there's not much chance they'll find us here, *now*."

"But... are we stuck here?" Her words came fast. "I don't want to be in 1959! What will—"

"It's okay." Tony pulled her into his arms. "We'll be able to go home once we get the Pull—when our mental energy builds back up. But that probably won't happen for a few days."

"What about..." She rolled her lower lip in and bit it. "...when we go back? Will those men be there?"

He shook his head. "I don't know. You warp in time, but stay in the same physical location. All I can think of is to jump home from someplace else. And pray they're elsewhere—else*when*." He stroked her hair.

"What will people at home think? This is what happened when you disappeared, wasn't it? Mercy, I can't afford to lose my job—"

"I'll talk to Keith." Tony rubbed her back. She calmed, though she still trembled. "I do have a little pull around there, you know. As for the rest..."

What would he tell his daughter? Or his parents? Last time, he'd told them he went on a cruise and he'd never had a chance to call home. He'd hated to say it, the lie burning his mouth, but the truth was too strange.

Thankfully, Keith, his boss and CEO of the company, had accepted Tony's claim of not remembering where he'd been, but would he force Tony to go on leave of absence again? "We'll figure out something," Tony said. "I'm not thrilled to be here either, but it beats the alternative."

Violet covered her face with her hands. "I'm sorry, it's not like me to prattle on so—"

"It's okay." He pulled her closer, trying to give—and take— comfort in her nearness. "I'd worry if you *weren't* freaked out."

Guilt blanketed him. When six months went by with no sign of the snipers, he'd thought it was okay to go back to work, to resume normal life, never mind the flashes of death he'd seen, felt, lived, ever since he'd jumped back three years in time to make Bethany leave that party. *Just hallucinations.* Nightmares. Memories of being shot, stabbed, beaten to death. Memories. That never happened. He'd spent his leave of absence working out, building his strength. He'd bought a gun, learned to shoot, and re-learned martial arts, hoping he'd never need any of it.

Too bad he'd left his gun at home; then again, a lot of good it would do in the dark, against futuristic laser weapons.

Bad enough those guys had shot at Violet, too, forcing Tony to do something he never wanted to do again: jump into the past to escape. But how the hell had she come along? Was physical contact all it took? Or what if—

She could time-travel too? Because she was Charlotte? Charlotte had been able to—

It's impossible to travel into one's future. And Charlotte was dead. Violet must have come with him because she'd grabbed him as he warped. Simple proximity.

She slumped against him. "I'm... exhausted. Not just from running, but..."

"Recovery." Tony was growing fatigued, too. "Once it kicks in, nothing will keep you awake. It's like being in a coma."

"What's—"

He walked her to the bed. "Lie down. Once recovery hits, you can't fight it." She sank onto the bed, then struggled to shrug off her coat and purse. He grabbed them and dropped them on one of the padded vinyl chairs, then his gut dropped.

There was only one bed.

It doesn't matter. Not when neither would have the energy to move, much less take advantage of the situation.

Violet slouched against the headboard, oblivious to the cleavage her black, v-neck dress revealed.

Tony snatched his glasses off, then rubbed them with his shirt-tail. He wasn't typically attracted to big girls, yet there was something about her. Something had made him ask her out, and not just her resemblance to Charlotte.

He jammed his glasses on. She'd be attractive even if she didn't look so much like Charlotte, she could be her older, heavier, blonder twin. Not model-gorgeous, but with an inner grace that transcended society's definition of beauty, just like Charlotte. She carried herself with the same quiet confidence Charlotte had. Even her voice bore the huskiness of a longtime smoker—like Charlotte.

And Charlotte had been able to travel in time. The Saturn Society insisted it was impossible to jump into one's own future, but what if they were wrong?

Tony's heart curled in on itself at the memory of the woman from the past he'd loved more than he'd thought possible.

She's. Not. Charlotte.

Charlotte died in 1933. Why had he tortured himself by asking her modern double on a date?

Because he liked Violet. Still, her words were Charlotte's. *Mercy. Good Heavens. What on earth.* Too much coincidence—

"Tony?" Her voice jerked him out of a past better forgotten. "What if someone comes in here while we're... sleeping?"

"Damn, you're right. I guess I'd better go check us in before I drop." He grabbed his wallet. Bills and loose change plinged onto the dresser, along with business cards and a joke from his friend Bernie—a condom. *Shit.* It wasn't funny now. He crammed it back into his wallet, hoping Violet didn't think he'd asked her out expecting to get laid.

Her gaze flicked from the offending item to the money. "Surely that's plenty—" Her eyes fixed on a ten with the twenty-first century, large portrait. "Oh, dear, that won't work, will it?" She stifled a yawn. "Hand me my purse, I have a bunch of singles. Maybe together we'll have enough."

Tony gave a rueful snort. "Hope no one notices the dates."

They came up with twenty-six dollars in ones and older fives. Tony slipped the money back into his wallet. When he reached for the business cards, his hand paused.

On top was Chad Everly's Saturn Society card. Tony grabbed it and shoved it into his wallet, a chill rushing through his body.

He wasn't exactly on good terms with the time travelers' organization. The last time he'd spoken with Everly, six months ago, Everly had left in an uneasy truce.

In 1959, Theodore Pippin would be running the Dayton Saturn Society House. It was unlikely that Pippin's vendetta against those he

considered Enemies of Time had diminished—and one of those enemies was Tony. Yet with recovery setting in, there wasn't a damn
thing he could do.

"Tony?" Violet called as he gripped the doorknob. "What's the
Saturn Society?"

"Forty hours?" Violet repeated as she dropped the bag of food on
the motel room's little square table. "We slept for almost two whole
days?" Her fingers twirled on the burger's paper wrapper.

Tony shrugged and looked away. "That's nothing." He took a bite
of hamburger, the sound of his chewing oddly loud in the motel room,
even though he wasn't eating impolitely. "Go back further, and you
could sleep for weeks."

"Goodness! But how?" Even as she voiced the question, the
knowledge felt familiar. But she had to keep up a good front.

Tony gave a half-shrug as he reached for the fries. "They say it's
sort of like animals in hibernation. All I know is I'm glad you went
for food." Luckily, two dollars and forty-five cents was more than
enough to buy a couple of burgers and fries from the motel restaurant. The woman who'd taken her order had stared at Violet like she'd
grown a second head when she'd ordered a Diet Coke, belatedly
realizing it didn't exist in 1959.

She and Tony both focused on their food, though it could have
been greased paper for all Violet tasted. This was all her fault. Those
men—whoever they were—were after her, and she had no idea why.
All she knew, was that after six years, her unknown past had finally
caught up with her. It only surprised her that the gunmen hadn't
come after her sooner.

Apprehension fell over her body like a bucket of chilled water.
Right before they'd reached the motel, Tony had pushed her away and
run in another direction. Why on earth had he done such a thing?

Then she remembered. Tony thought those men were after him,

he'd told her that, when they'd first run into the derelict motel. But why? "Tony? Who were those men who were shooting at us?"

"I don't know," he choked out, his face in a funny twist.

He was lying. Did he know about her past? "And why were they chasing us?"

"You wouldn't believe—"

"Try me." Violet squeezed a fistful of her dress.

"They're from the future. Our future."

Violet wrinkled her nose. "What?"

"I told you you wouldn't believe me."

Fear cooled into firm resolve. Her logical mind slipped around the concept and found no purchase. It went against every fiber of her being, yet...

She let go of her dress. She and Tony had somehow jumped back to 1959. As illogical as it seemed, the evidence was hard to dismiss. So why couldn't others come back from the future, too? Tony's face had gone slack. He wasn't lying now. Maybe all those times he'd disappeared, he'd gotten mixed up with something bad.

She tried to avoid looking at the bed in which they'd both slept. Her belly twitched. She should have had the propriety to lie on the floor—or ask Tony to.

Nothing happened. She wouldn't have, even if she hadn't slept like the dead. They might have shared a bed, but as much as she longed to, they hadn't touched.

She yearned to find out if the reality lived up to her dreams. She knew exactly how he'd feel in her arms. The way he'd feel as he moved inside her when they made love—

Her face heated. *Violet! For shame! On a first date, for crying out loud!*

She cast an abashed glance at him, but he was engrossed in his food. She was not that kind of woman. She might not remember her past, but this she knew. Never mind that other women, including her roommate Stephanie, took men to their beds all the time and few thought the worse of them.

She still couldn't believe Tony Solomon, the man every unattached woman in the office wanted, the man who never dated, had asked her out. She'd wondered if he'd kiss her goodnight afterward, had wondered if she'd have the nerve to invite him in. Tony had said she looked fantastic when he'd come to pick her up, and the way his eyes lingered on her told her he'd meant it. She'd wondered if perhaps there would be more than a goodnight kiss.

Only to wind up sharing a motel room with him—in 1959.

(crazy)

Yet she knew it wasn't.

She dabbed her mouth with a napkin. "Mercy, I don't think I've ever been so hungry."

"Recovery'll do that to you."

"Recovery from what?"

"Time travel." He wadded his napkin into a tight ball. "You haven't done this before, have you?"

She stared at the edge of the table, squeezing her napkin. A sensation of doom settled over her, heavy enough to push her through the floor, and realization trickled over her skin in a cold sweat. The familiar dizzy spells. She'd always known that they were something frightening, so much that every time one hit, she gripped the chair, her desk, the wall, anything, to stay grounded. Because she *had* traveled in time—*before*. Before that day six years ago.

The day something terrible happened. Something so terrible she had no memory of it. Something to do with Tony. And there was no way on earth she could tell him. Not when there was a good chance she'd killed someone.

"No." She wiped her mouth, though it was already clean. "But... how did this happen? How did we go back in time?"

"We thought about it. For people with this... ability, that's all it takes."

Her head spun. Not like the time travel dizzy spell, but like she'd climbed on an amusement park ride that was spiraling out of control. A high-pitched roar filled her head.

Because she knew this.

She forced herself to speak. *Sound surprised.* "When—how...

have you always been able to travel in time?"

"No." He rose and paced to the door, but didn't open it. "Last year. When I fell, in Mexico. I died. Or almost did." He faced her, his head canted to the side. "You ever heard about people having near death experiences?" She nodded. "Well, that's what happened to me. I saw my dau—people I knew who'd died. Then something pulled me back. That's how you get the ability. If you're near death and someone who can time-travel touches you."

It hit her like a blow to the ribs. She'd been there, thanks to winning a spot on the executives' company trip a year ago. She'd touched him, when he'd fallen and almost died.

Then he'd disappeared, only to reappear a half hour later, and still near death.

She'd done this to him. And now someone was after her for reasons she couldn't remember, and because of her, they were after Tony, too.

The food in her mouth solidified.

He couldn't know. If he did, wouldn't he have contacted the authorities?

He turned around and wiped a hand through his short, spiky dark hair. "You must think I'm insane—"

"Then I am, too." She stood and met his eyes. "Because I believe you." The cars in the parking lot made it hard to refute. So did the old-fashioned telephone beside her (with a dial!), and the news she'd heard on the ancient-looking radio at the restaurant.

But most of all, it was the way the knowledge had clicked into place. Picture a bygone era to go there, focus on the present to stay put. The knowledge, the dizzy spells, the fatigue—all familiar. From *before*. Just like that planet Saturn with the three stars on that business card in Tony's wallet. Some guy he'd met in the parking garage, he'd told her. She'd sensed there was a lot more to it, but she'd fallen into recovery by the time he'd returned from checking in.

She forced herself to breathe. *Inhale. Exhale.* One thing at a time. First, they had to figure out how they'd live while in 1959, then—

"All I wanted was a nice, normal night out." Tony stared at his hands.

"It's not your fault." His stricken expression made her try to inject some levity. "Unless you'd planned for us to get run off the road and shot at."

He gave a mirthless laugh. "Sure, that's all it was, a fancy scheme to give me an excuse to bring you to a dumpy motel in 1959 and..." He swallowed. His expression changed to the strange look she'd often seen when he passed her in the hall at work. The same way he'd looked at her last summer when she'd visited him in the hospital, after he'd disappeared *(time traveled?)* for three weeks. An expression of pain, sadness, and something else.

Flutters battered her ribcage. She'd never been able to identify *what* else but it came to her now. Yearning.

The setting sun's light coming in through the window brought out the hollows in his face. Could he think of her the same way she had about him for so long?

He paced back to the window and the expression faded.

If it had been there at all. She joined him at the window. He rested his forehead against the glass. "Jeez, I'm sorry."

"I'm the one who grabbed you. And," she took a deep breath, "I have no family. No one will miss me except my roommate Stephanie. And work, of course." She pressed her lips together. It wouldn't be hard for a potential employer to check her background and find she had none. All she had was the faked birth certificate and Social Security card Stephanie's ex-husband had obtained for her. "What we need to do now is make the best of this crazy situation and figure out how we'll eat for the next few days. And where we'll sleep." She squared her shoulders. "Is there any way to find... others like you? Someone we could explain our situation to, who might be able to help—"

"No."

She drew back. "You don't know any—"

"Not in this time."

Her eyes flicked to the dresser where he'd emptied his wallet. She'd seen the symbol on that business card before. The words meant nothing, but words never did. Even Tony's name hadn't.

But when she first saw him, his face had made her belly leap in recognition. The logo of the planet Saturn and three stars did the same.

That symbol had meant something to her in her old life. Something important. Something she needed to find out.

Something Tony wasn't willing to share. If that Saturn organization was part of her past and she asked him about it, she'd raise suspicion.

Outside, the Paradise Motel sign flickered to life in the deepening twilight. Tony moved away from the window, shaking his head. "I wasn't ever going to do this again. And now I've dragged you into it—"

"We'll manage. Tomorrow I'll ask if they could use help with the cleaning. Or in the restaurant." She stared down at herself. Though modestly long, her filthy dress with its laser-burnt hem would hardly impress a would-be boss.

Tony started to say something, but she dropped her hand to his arm, silencing him. "Don't blame yourself."

Her gaze climbed his body until it reached his eyes. The sign illuminated him in a spectral glow, making him appear not quite real, but more the stuff of dreams.

His arm slid around her back, and he traced his fingers up her shoulder blade. Her skin tightened in the line he touched.

He tilted his head, his gaze a caress. "You're an amazing person. Anyone else... my ex-wife would be hysterical if she went back in time. Hell, the first time I did, I spent half the time trying to convince myself I was imagining it. But you..." He slipped his other arm around her waist. "You just accept it all, crazy as it must sound."

Her insides were a quivering pile of jelly. She gave a jerky nod behind her. "All of this is pretty convincing."

He pulled her closer.

She barely dared to breathe. A lightness swelled in her chest. Lost in the light of his eyes, she moved into the heat his body radiated, the ache to mold herself to him overpowering.

He lowered his face toward hers.

Her stomach bottomed with desire. He was going to kiss her.

She stretched up, and her lips met his, moved with his. Her eyes drifted half-closed. Heat flooded her as their mouths moved together, the reality as heavenly as she'd known it would be. She slid her arms around him, reveling in his solidness, his taste, the roughness of his day-old beard, the gentle pressure of his tongue meeting hers...

He pulled away. "God, I'm sorry. I don't know what came over me." He dragged a hand over his face.

Violet's mouth moved wordlessly. She ached for his touch. The same constant ache that plagued her whenever she saw him, worse now that she'd tasted what she'd been missing. "Don't be sorry," she whispered. "I didn't try to stop you."

She should leave. It was the proper thing to do.

But she had no money, no place to go.

Hang it all, she was tired of being proper. A doctor's exam had confirmed that she was no innocent. But it had been years since she'd lain with a man—and whenever it had been, she had no memory of it. Or him.

Tony's gaze roved around like he feared he was doing something dishonest.

She would allay those fears. Stephanie said men liked it when a woman let them know what she wanted.

Violet thirsted for Tony's arms around her, for the knowledge, for the answer to the question that had haunted her since the first time she saw him.

What had he meant to her in her forgotten past?

She slipped her arms around his waist. His hands trailed down her sides, then slipped around her back. The heavens opened, drenching her body in a deluge of sparks. He drew her against him, crushing her breasts to his chest as he once again lowered his face to hers and their lips met in a searing join.

This was what she'd been missing. Two years of having to be content to talk to him on the phone when he called the helpdesk, or passed her in the hallway and said hello.

His mouth never leaving hers, he ran his hand up and down her back, then slowly moved it around her side. Her skin prickled in jittery delight at his touch, her dress the only thing between them. Heaven help her, but she wished it wasn't.

Mercy, he could kiss her forever. His hand brushed the side of her breast. She gasped.

He snatched his hand away. "Oh hell, I—"

"Don't." Her voice was firm. She was not going to let him apologize. She didn't want him to be sorry.

"I was going to say, I need a shower," he said. "A cold one," he added under his breath.

Violet's strength sapped, she sank onto the bed. She looked at her dirty dress. "I'm... a bit worse for the wear myself." She met his gaze, her breath ragged.

"You can go first." He backed toward the table.

Not what she wanted to hear. The words she longed to say lodged in her throat. She had to know now, or never know.

Need nagged her in Stephanie's voice. *Be bold. Men like it when the woman makes the first move.*

"I- I'm usually not this forward, but..." Violet met his gaze and gave him her best demure smile. "We could share."

His shoulders flattened, and his voice was strained, as if he was choking. "Violet, we're both under a lot of stress. I don't want to do anything we'll regret."

If she let him go, she might never have another chance to gain the knowledge she craved. To experience heaven.

He'd kissed her with fervor and passion. She'd seen enough, heard enough around the office to know Tony Solomon never said anything he didn't mean. He wanted her as much as she wanted him.

And it might be her only chance to be with him, and find out what he'd been to her *before.*

It's not proper! her inner voice shouted.

But she wasn't a woman of the fifties. Propriety was overrated. And she needed to know him, now. She rose and crossed the room, then stopped at the bathroom door. "I won't regret it." She began to unbutton her dress.

Two

CHARLOTTE... TONY MOVED TOWARD HER.

What the hell are you doing? Logic faded in the clamor of desire. He was lost. Lost in the triangle of creamy skin she was slowly revealing. Lost in his need.

He slid his arms around her back and pulled her against him. She tipped her face up and ran her tongue along her upper lip, not in a flirty way, but as if her mouth had gone dry. He lowered his face to hers and reveled in the soft, moist heat of her kisses.

He needed her warmth, her closeness. Even while he was married, loneliness had ruled his life. Violet offered escape. He hadn't realized how empty his existence was until his brief sojourn with Charlotte.

He tipped his head to the side and his tongue wrangled with hers. Her tentative explorations warmed him like a fiery hearth on a winter day.

She was so like Charlotte. The way she walked. The way she held her cigarette in the office smoking area. Her eyes, the color of golden honey. Her voice, low and throaty. The way she caught herself when she'd started to freak.

So much like Charlotte and yet... He drew back, breaking the kiss. *She's not Charlotte!*

Question and hunger filled Violet's eyes. "Tony?"

"I don't think this is a good idea."

She gripped his elbow and drew him into the tiny bathroom. "I do." She slid her hands up his chest in a tantalizing, light touch.

When she loosened his tie and began to unbutton his shirt, he struggled to remember why it wasn't a good idea.

She paused, eying the scar above his heart, the one from the Mayan priest's knife when Tony's first, unintentional trip back in time had taken him a thousand years into the past. She traced the raised line. Tony inhaled through his teeth. She looked up. "I'm sorry."

"It's okay, it doesn't hurt, I just don't like—"

"This happened while you were... gone, didn't it?"

"Yeah." He steeled himself while she ran her hand over the scar again, then her gaze lit on the one ringing his neck.

Where the ancient Mayans had beheaded him, and he'd hurtled back into the present upon his death. "That one, too," he said.

She leaned up to press a kiss to his lips, then resumed unbuttoning his shirt. She reached for his belt buckle, but he captured her hands, brought them to his mouth, brushed his lips over her smooth fingertips. *She's not Charlotte.* Surely her skin couldn't be as soft.

He pushed her unbuttoned dress down and brushed his fingertips over her satiny shoulders. *Wrong.* She closed her eyes and lifted her face, and her soft sigh almost made Tony come undone. *So like Charlotte.*

But she wasn't Charlotte, and this wasn't fair to either of them. Violet deserved better.

He closed his hands over her wrists. "Violet... we can't."

Her head jerked up. "Why?"

Her drawn face, brows pressed inward, the little vertical crease between them was so Charlotte, it cut like the ancient Mayan priest plunging a dagger into Tony's heart all over again.

But he couldn't tell her about Charlotte.

"I'm not ready for a relationship." The truth. Because Violet sure as hell didn't strike him as a woman who went for one-night stands.

She drew away, her back stiff. "Who said anything about a relationship?"

"You're not the kind of—"

"No strings." Her voice was firm. Charlotte's don't-argue-with-me voice. "Just tonight. That's all I ask."

Hell. He combed his mind for another excuse, but couldn't keep his gaze from drifting to the lacy edge of her bra and the round tops of her breasts. Her shoulders drooped, the dejection on her face as clear as the motel's neon sign.

Realization settled over him like a lead curtain. She thought this was about her weight.

He didn't care about that. She was curvy and soft and powerful, beautiful in a way beyond guy-talk at the bar, or the media's notion that only thin-and-willowy could be attractive.

Hell and damnation. He brushed his lips across hers. "Go start the water." He dashed to the dresser and dug into his wallet for the condom.

He ran his thumb over the foil wrapper. *No strings,* she'd said.

She'd just stepped into the shower when he got there. Fog already obscured the mirror, the air hot and damp. "Tony?" Her voice came out like a squeak as she drew back the shower curtain. Beads of water glistened on her smooth shoulders. He wanted to lick them dry, wanted to—

He held up the condom.

Violet exhaled, touching her fingertips to a spot above her cleavage. "Good heavens, I'd forgotten..." Her voice died away as he set the package on the sink and slipped his shirt off. Mercy, he was handsome—not overly bulked up, but lean and strong. Just right. Her knees ready to give out, Violet leaned against the shower wall to steady herself. Had she been wearing a blouse, she'd have sworn it was suddenly too tight when he dropped his slacks, then pushed his drawers down. She finally collected her wits enough to realize she was staring and withdrew behind the shower curtain.

When he slipped into the shower, the sensation of the water beating on her skin faded. The absence of his glasses bared more than his lack of clothing, and his face held the same look of pain she'd seen in the hospital. Haunted. Yearning.

She folded him into her arms and pressed herself against him. Whatever hurt he bore, she'd do anything to wash it away. He leaned down and took her mouth with his. She sighed into his kiss, the water sealing their bodies together.

His hand slid over her back, up and down, around the sides, over her shoulders. With every touch, he brushed away her fears. He rubbed her back in a light, feathery caress and heat blazed between her thighs. Oh, Lord have mercy, she'd wanted this for so long. At last, all those questions she'd never dared to ask would be answered.

Her body thrilled as his hand glided up and down her back. She realized he'd grabbed the soap when he started lathering her spine then drew his hands over her shoulder blades. Her skin prickled at his every touch—heavens, she'd never known her back was an erogenous zone. He soaped up her sides, then slid his hands around the contours of her breasts. She arched into him. He turned her around so she faced the showerhead, her back against his chest.

The water massaged her breasts as he ran his soapy hands over them. Tingles mingled with chills when he rubbed his fingers over her nipples, so taut they could cut glass. The warmth below flared into fire.

They had done this before. It was all familiar. His hands cupping her bottom. The splashing water. His hands skittering over her body with the soap. Not a familiarity that bred boredom and discontent, but comfort, security, and *knowing*.

He dropped the soap with a clunk on the tub's edge. "I think you're clean enough." He yanked the shower curtain aside and leaned out to grab the condom.

"But you haven't washed..." Violet trailed off at a sense of familiarity so strong it stole her breath. *Before*. She seized the soap and twirled it in her hands. His face stretched into a grin, igniting a warmth in the center of her body that spread outward.

He flung the condom onto the soap dish. Starting with his back, she rubbed all over his body. The feel of his slippery skin beneath her hands confirmed the knowledge that she'd savored this sweet torture before. Her fingers explored his chest, splayed through the delightful texture of hair on muscle, then moved lower, to his stomach—

Another scar? "My goodness, you—"

"Never mind that." His voice came out a low growl. He took the soap from her and tossed it onto the soap dish.

He massaged her shoulders, trailed down her breasts, glided his hands over her belly. Then lower. He slipped a finger into the fire between her legs, and explored the soft folds of her skin. Her insides tensed. Then he rubbed over the spot where her flesh burned hottest. Her thighs clenched. "Tony..." she whimpered.

He grabbed the condom and tore it open. Seconds later, he gripped her hips and guided her onto him.

She moaned as he slid inside. Her dreams, reality. But the dreams were a dim comparison, like watching television wearing sunglasses, or viewing a solar eclipse through smoked glass.

This was foregoing the safety of the darkened lens and risking the burn. A risk she'd never be sorry she'd taken.

They moved together endlessly, as past, present, and future condensed into one. She barely noticed goose bumps forming on her arms as the water grew cold, until Tony reached around her to shut off the taps, then jerked the shower curtain open. "I say we finish in bed."

In half a minute, she lay beneath him and he was back inside her. She barely noticed his weight, noticed nothing but his clean, soapy scent, their mouths joined, their bodies touching in every way possible. She lifted her hips to match his rhythm, a celebration of pleasure and love.

She did love him. She wouldn't say it—how she wanted to, but she'd heard enough from Stephanie to know that word was guaranteed to send a man running. Being with Tony now was heaven enough to last her a lifetime. Lightness swelled inside her like a hot air balloon.

He whispered in her ear, his breath ticklish and hot. She couldn't hear his words, but words didn't matter. He licked a line down the side of her neck, and chills coursed through her. Down low, she constricted around him as he moved faster, and she tightened until she was sure she would force him out. Then her body squeezed and pulsated. Shards of pleasure burst through her.

She shouted his name, and he pumped faster. His body went rigid as he reached completion. "Charlotte!"

Violet's soaring, balloon-y feeling popped. *Charlotte?*

It *was* her.

Tony gripped the bathroom sink, as if it would settle his turbulent thoughts.

The feel of her body moving beneath his. The way she traced down his chest in a light touch that drove him crazy. Her cries of passion, her whimpers of desire, her sighs of satisfaction. After he'd returned from 1933, he'd concluded Violet's resemblance to Charlotte was pure coincidence. Supposedly everyone had a double.

Too much coincidence.

His eyes burned, his body wound so tight he could snap. Why had she deceived him? And how? Had Everly lied about jumping into the future, or had Charlotte discovered some trick no one knew? What if she hadn't meant to kill him that night in the river, and her true intention was to ensure he didn't escape Pippin? Or had she come forward in time to bring him to justice?

He couldn't shake the image of her curling into the blanket after he'd called her Charlotte, her eyes shining with unshed tears, the quaver in her voice as she said it was all a big mistake and ran to the bathroom to grab her clothes.

But why the false identity?

Or was it? Had he hurt a wonderful woman he'd long cared for as a friend?

He pressed his palms to the wall and leaned over the sink.

He felt as if a stack of weights pressed down on his chest. He had to do something. Say something. Try to ease her hurt.

But there was nothing he could do, nothing he could say.

He sniffled and blinked in tight squeezes. *Ironic.* A mere thought could take him back in time decades, even centuries, but he couldn't go back five minutes. It didn't work that way.

His ears pricked at the sound of Violet's voice. He straightened, listening, but couldn't make out the words. Who was she talking to?

With a sigh, he went about getting rid of the condom, but as he reached for it, his stomach dropped to his toes.

God, no. Weight pressed in on him from all sides, sucking the air from the tiny bathroom, his throat trapped in a giant hand's choking grasp. *Oh shit oh shit oh shit!*

The rubber had broken.

His mind turned to molasses. "Yes, thank you, operator," Violet said from the main room.

Her voice kicked him back into reality. He pitched the condom and snatched his underwear off the floor.

He yanked his slacks on. He'd have to tell her. As if getting shot at and being forced to warp back over fifty years wasn't enough. He threw on his shirt and fumbled with his belt. How could he face her? With this, after what he'd done?

His fingers slipped on this belt buckle as he tried to force it closed, until he failed for the third time to slide the prong into the hole. *Fuck it.* He dropped the damn thing, the clang of the buckle striking the tile surprisingly loud. He'd ask Violet—*Charlotte*—if she had something to tell him. See if she'd admit her subterfuge, now that he knew.

He tucked his shirt in, then untucked it and wiped his glasses on the shirttail.

He was healthy, he'd gotten checked out after he'd caught his wife Dora running around on him. Since his divorce there had been no one but Charlotte.

Who'd claimed she couldn't have children. Tony shoved his glasses on and jammed his shirt into his waistband. Even if Violet wasn't Charlotte with her female problems, the odds she'd get pregnant were slim. No point in asking for trouble. The weight lifted, if only a little. He straightened his shirt, slipped into his shoes, and opened the door.

Violet perched on the bed, disheveled but dressed. "Yes, I'll do that." Smoke drifted up from the cigarette she held in one shaking hand while she gripped the phone in the other. "Thank you, Mr.

Pippin."

Tony couldn't move. Couldn't speak. Couldn't think.

She looked up. The nightstand lamp's dim light shone in her wide, red-rimmed eyes as she tossed the phone onto its cradle as if it had suddenly grown hot.

Tony's brain kicked in as a burn rose up his throat. "What the hell are you doing?"

Violet shrank away from him. "The symbol. On that card." She glanced at Everly's business card, which had fallen out of Tony's wallet when he'd retrieved the condom. "I- I've seen it somewhere before, and I thought maybe they could help—"

"I should have known." Tony's mind drained of all other thought.

She straightened. "Known what?"

She'd betrayed him again. "You planned this all along."

"Planned what? Tony, what are you talking about?"

"Like you don't know!"

"I only wanted to get help!"

"Yeah, help doing me in!" Reason slammed him like a sledge-hammer to his skull. He had to get out. Fast, before Pippin arrived.

He shoved his shock, his fear, his hurt to the back of his mind as he grabbed his coat and bolted for the door. As he yanked it open, he turned to her, unable to ignore the knife in his heart. "If you have a shred of decency left, don't come after me. Don't tell him—"

"Tell who? What? Tony, I—" She jumped up and moved toward him, but he dashed out, slamming the door in her face.

He was barely conscious of his feet slapping the asphalt. He almost collided with a parked car. "Tony!" He ignored her and kept running. His eyes stung. He blamed the cold and wind, though he hardly felt either. All that mattered was getting away. Away from Charlotte and her treachery.

He ran beneath the Paradise Motel sign, the neon *Vacancy* buzz-ing as if it was about to burn out. He ran across the parking lot and onto grass, the frosty blades crackling beneath his feet. He was dimly aware of stepping onto pavement again and took off down the road, slowing only when he noticed the rough asphalt had become a concrete sidewalk.

He scanned the homes lining the road, typical fifties-era Cape Cod houses, like the one his mom had lived in as a kid. She'd driven him by it a few times when he was growing up, and it wasn't far from the motel, if he remembered correctly.

That's it. He'd go to his grandparents, tell them he was Grandma's brother Bob, who'd disappeared when his mom was ten.

With the plan solidified, his mind raced back to Charlotte.

How could she? She'd worked at LCT for over three years. *Why now, after all this time?*

How had she managed to jump into the future, and when? How had she obtained a drivers' license, gotten a job?

It didn't matter. All that mattered was getting away before Pippin showed up, and pray that the obsessed, Society nut case didn't find him.

Violet stood numbly by the motel room's door. *Charlotte.* Was that her real name? Words and names never evoked any memories—Tony's hadn't, only his picture had—but the stricken look on his face, the hurled accusations—of what, she had no idea—she'd seen him like that, he'd yelled at her like that, *before.*

What had happened? What had she done, on that long-ago day she didn't remember, when she'd been Charlotte? Whatever it was, it must have been as terrible as she'd feared,

(killed someone)

considering the blood all over her that day, when she'd woken in Stephanie's garage—

Someone knocked on the motel room's door.

Violet jumped. Wiping her eyes, she hurried to the window and peeked around the curtains.

A colored man in a staid, black suit waited at the door, a fringe of curly, white hair showing beneath his fedora. Mr. Pippin.

Exactly how she'd pictured him when she'd heard his smooth, cultured voice. "Just a minute!" She ran to the bathroom and splashed water on her face, trying not to look at Tony's belt on the floor.

Before they'd jumped in time, she'd almost told him she loved him. *Fool.* Thank heavens he'd stopped her.

When she opened the door, the man's teeth flashed white in his dark, shadowed face. Like Tony's taut, angered expression, Mr. Pippin's smile settled into her mind as something she'd seen *before.* "Miss Sinclair, I presume?"

"Yes." Somehow, his smile made everything a little less horrible, and her belly unknotted. She tried to smile back.

The man extended a hand. "I'm Theodore Pippin. May I come—"

"Oh! Of course." She stepped aside.

He walked in, his steady stride belying his white hair and lined face. "You said there was also a man?"

"Yes, but..." Violet gripped a wad of dress. "He left. He didn't want to take charity from your Society." Her belly re-knotted, but she forced herself to let go of her dress. *Charlotte. My name is Charlotte.*

But she couldn't say it. Not when she still hadn't an inkling of what she'd done. Not with her suspicion that Mr. Pippin was a friend, but he was also a threat, someone else she might have wronged.

She motioned at the table. "Please, sit down." Her misgivings at Tony's reaction to Mr. Pippin's name warred with a sense that Mr. Pippin was kind and good. Because like Tony, she knew him—from *before.* She took the other chair.

"Tell me, Miss Sinclair, where—or I should say, when—are you from?"

Violet grabbed her purse and fingered the strap. "I- I can't believe I'm saying this..." *Charlotte.* Was that her name? Did Mr. Pippin know?

"Relax," he said in a soothing voice. "The Saturn Society is here to help."

"That's what I was hoping. I... I'm from the early twenty-first century. I have money, but I doubt it would be accepted here. I mean, now. So until I can go back..." She turned up her hands.

Mr. Pippin gave her a gentle smile. "My dear, that's what the Society's for. No matter where you are—or when, the Society can provide lodging, food, and clean, appropriate clothing."

Violet stole a glance at her laser-fire-torn dress.

"When you return home, your contemporary Society will help you explain why you've been away. They can help if financial difficulties result from your absence."

"I've no doubt they will, as I fully expect to be unemployed when I return." This Society sounded like a godsend. The man's promises aside, her intuition—or buried memories—told her she had nothing to fear and much to gain, making Tony's reaction to her contacting the Society even more of a mystery.

Her stomach growled loudly. Violet clapped a hand over it. Mercy, it hadn't been that long since she'd eaten!

Mr. Pippin's gaze dropped to her belly. "Why don't we go back to the House, and get you some supper? My housekeeper prepared a roast, if that suits your tastes."

"That would be wonderful." Violet let go of her belly.

Mr. Pippin stood. "Shall we, then? Perhaps we'll run into your friend along the way." Violet rose, snatched her coat off her chair, then followed him outdoors.

An old-fashioned car—from the thirties, Violet guessed, and also eerily familiar—gleamed dark red

(like blood)

in the neon sign's pink flicker. Mr. Pippin opened the passenger door and motioned her inside.

Have you no more sense than to get into a car with a stranger? her logical side warned. *For all you know he could be a serial killer—*

She met his eyes. Kind. Trustworthy.

He was no stranger.

Another knot in her belly loosened.

But the familiarity Mr. Pippin exuded was not what she felt with Tony. She and Tony had been lovers. This man was more like a favored uncle, a revered teacher, a friend. "Mr. Pippin? I have to ask...

do you know anyone... like us, named Charlotte?"

Mr. Pippin's lips pressed together tightly before he answered. "No. Someone you know?"

Violet mimicked his actions. "No. Just... heard about."

Was her intuition wrong, and she hadn't known Mr. Pippin before? Or had Tony simply called her by another woman's name?

Her heart plummeted at the thought. If she wasn't Charlotte, then who—

"Miss Sinclair?"

She climbed into the car. *Are you crazy? Are you sure you know him?*

The certainty slipped over her like a warm coat. "Thank you, sir."

He shut her door then slid behind the wheel. Her stomach let out another loud grumble.

"Supper is but a short drive away." He chuckled. "The Society takes care of its own, and you're one of us."

"It sounds too good to be true. What's the catch?"

"Catch? There is none, my dear. All we ask is that you abide by the Society Code." He started the car.

She picked at her coat hem. "What's that?"

"The rules are simple, Sh- Miss Sinclair. Never discuss the Society, and our gift, with linears."

Her heart caught in her throat. "What did you say?"

"Linears. Those who lack our gift. Normal folk."

"You- you started to call me something else." *Like Charlotte.*

"A slip of the tongue, my dear."

Or was he lying to her?

But why would he do that? she argued with herself.

He turned onto a street lined with small brick and frame houses, some with warm lights glowing in dormer windows. Ordinary houses—one even had a white picket fence—for an ordinary world where there was no such thing as time travel or a Saturn Society.

She chewed her lip as Mr. Pippin shifted gears, then pointed into the air. "Secondly, you must attempt to blend in to the prevailing culture as much as possible, by appearance, word and deed. Every

Society House keeps a variety of contemporary clothing, so our visitors don't draw undue attention."

"What's the third rule?"

He braked at a stop sign, peering sideways at her. The dim glow of a streetlamp caught the whites of his eyes. "Never, *ever*, change the past. Especially for personal gain."

Fear cast an anchor down her throat. "But how do you know if you're changing something? What if it's unavoidable?"

"That's one thing. But intentionally changing the past can have severe ramifications. And in some time periods, using your knowledge of the future to change things bears harsh punishment."

Though the car's interior was warm, a chill washed over Violet, and when she thought about Tony her unease grew into jittery, jumpy feelings that portended nothing good.

Far ahead, a figure—a man—passed beneath a streetlight at a fast walk. Despite the darkness and distance, she couldn't mistake his stance or his hurried stride. Tony!

Mr. Pippin punched the accelerator, and Tony's parting words struck her. *If you have a shred of decency, don't come after me.* What was he talking about? What did he think Mr. Pippin would do?

Tony didn't know how far he'd run, and he'd lost his sense of direction in the near darkness. The gibbous moon lent no familiarity to the street or the cookie-cutter houses, or the nineteen-fifties cars that parked along the curb. Clouds obscured all but a few stars.

He stopped at an intersection. Which way led toward his grandparents' house on Fairmeyer Avenue?

What the hell. He turned right and continued down the deserted sidewalk. A picket fence bordered the yard he strode past. From somewhere behind him, brakes squealed as a car slowed to turn the corner.

He tried to empty his mind, but his thoughts wouldn't leave.

Is she Charlotte, or isn't she?

They both smoked.

So do a lot of people.

Charlotte had had brown hair—

Violet's not a natural blonde.

He'd seen that in the shower. *Violet's heavier—*

Which made sense she'd come from a life where she walked everywhere, in a time where there was no such thing as fast food—

Charlotte had a gap between her front teeth.

Easily fixed.

Violet's older—

But how long had she lived in Tony's time?

You can't jump into the future.

Another intersection. Tony stopped to think. Wasn't Fairmeyer Avenue farther to the west? In the present, I-75 would be just past the road the motel was on, and he remembered his mom driving a little ways when they got off the highway, so yeah...

He turned to cross the street. An engine revved, and he whirled around as a pair of blazing headlights bore down on him.

Three

Violet screamed. Mr. Pippin stomped on the brake. Tires squealed. Too late. In the instant before her head slammed into the dash, Violet saw Tony go down, crumpling like a paper doll.

Ignoring her sore head, Violet jumped out. "Tony!" As she bent to peer beneath the vehicle, a fierce wave of dizziness stole her balance and she crashed to the ground.

The vertigo subsided. She pushed herself up, and crouched low, searching for Tony, even though somehow, she knew he wouldn't be there. How she knew this—and why she'd think something so illogical—she hadn't the foggiest idea, but this, too, was something she was certain she'd seen before.

On the pavement in front of the car, only a dark splatter on the road's surface indicated Tony had been there, been hit, been hurt. "What on earth?" Something sparkled in the light of the car's headlamps.

"Your companion has returned to his own time," Mr. Pippin said from behind her.

The gap beneath the car loomed in her vision, threatening to swallow her, a yawning empty space that shouldn't be.

His glasses. That's what was sparkling. She reached for them—

"Miss Sinclair?"

She grabbed Tony's glasses and tore her gaze from the street. "Y-yes?"

Mr. Pippin tipped his head to the side, though his posture remained stiff, straight, mechanical. "Perhaps we should get out of the road, lest we meet the same fate—"

"Where did he go?" Hysteria bubbled up inside Violet. Her head whipped back and forth between Mr. Pippin and the splash of Tony's blood. "You- you've killed him! You—"

"I did no such thing. Please, let me explain." He held out a hand, motioning Violet to the car.

She didn't know why, but she felt compelled to obey. Slipping the glasses into her coat pocket, she followed him to the car's passenger door.

Time travel. Tony's accusations. Now, his disappearance. Her life had become a thousand-piece jigsaw puzzle, its pieces scattered, several missing.

Pull yourself together. Maybe she could at least assemble the puzzle's edges. "Mr. Pippin, what's going on here? What happened? Where did Tony go?"

"His death has returned him to his own time, alive."

"But how?"

His eyes closed, then opened, a slow blink. "How can one die before one is born?"

Violet stared at the road as if Tony might magically reappear. In an odd way, Mr. Pippin's words made sense.

As much sense as any of this bizarre time travel did. A bubbly, queasy feeling rose in her belly, and she feared she might vomit.

"Miss Sinclair? There's nothing you can do for your friend. Please... get in the car."

How could he be so glib? Yet the knowledge clicked into place that the man spoke the truth. Logic agreed, and her swirling thoughts settled. With no body, there was nothing she could do. She climbed into the car, swallowing a sob.

Mr. Pippin drove away. "You mustn't worry over your friend, my dear. I'm sure he's fine in his own time."

"How do you know?"

"Recovery does more than restore the mental energies drained when you jump, it also heals physically. His contemporaries will care for him if they reach him first, otherwise he may be taken to a hospital where he'll sleep for a few days, and the doctors will be unable to find anything wrong."

Just like the other times Tony had disappeared. She stared at her lap, then an idea struck her. If death returned one to the present, why couldn't she join Tony?

She needed to explain. Needed to make him see that in calling Mr. Pippin, she'd meant no harm. All she needed now was a quick, unmessy way to die.

Her belly twitched. "Mr. Pippin? Do you park in a garage?"

"Yes, why?"

"I- I appreciate your offer of hospitality, but... I want to go home. Now. Perhaps you could leave the car running. With me in it. Will that—"

"Out of the question." He spoke sharply. "Suicide is permanent. Yes, you'll go back. Dead. Is that what you want?"

Violet rubbed her skirt. "Of course not—"

"Then unless something unfortunate sends you back—and not by your own hand—you are indeed stuck here, at least until the Pull takes you."

"What's... the Pull?" Tony had mentioned that.

"It's the force connecting us to our own present, that automatically returns us there, once our temporal energy has replenished itself."

Of course one wouldn't stay in the past indefinitely. As the concept filtered through her brain, she realized she knew this, too. "But what about Tony? He's hurt! What if no one finds him until morning?" Would he lie on the road all night? Heavens, what a horrible thought! And what if the gunmen were still in the area?

Mr. Pippin's mouth twisted at the corners. "He'll be fine."

"But..." How could he be so certain?

Tony woke to warmth, starched sheets, and a squawking TV

somewhere in the distance.

Unease trickled over him like sprinkled sand. Where the hell— His gaze flicked to a blank, white ceiling. White sheets. White sunlight blazing through the windows opposite him, so bright he had to look away.

Hospital.

Squinting, he took another look around. No TV, but a window facing him, through which he could barely make out barren treetops without his glasses.

But what kind of hospital didn't have TV in the rooms? And now that he thought about it, no smell of antiseptic or ambiguous, institutional meat-and-vegetable mush?

Tony half-coughed, his mouth suddenly dry. *Not a hospital.* The fucking Saturn Society House, in present-day Dayton.

At least he didn't feel half bad, considering he'd been roadkill, last he remembered.

Blood rushed in his ears. Pippin. He'd been driving that car, and Violet had been beside him, in the passenger seat. He'd hit Tony, undoubtedly not to kill, but only to disable him, so he could take him back to the Society House and make him like—

"Hhhnnnnnnnggggg!" The low moan came from beyond the recovery room's open door as if on cue. Tony's fingers scrubbed at the sheets as dread wrapped his chest in a tightening noose. Fred. The brain-damaged guy who'd suffered the Treatment at Pippin's hands. "Arrrnhhh!"

The Treatment Pippin gave to his so-called enemies of time... like Tony.

Tony's breathing rasped in his ears, loud even over the tinny laugh track on that distant TV. Another groan came from the hallway. Nearer. "Haarrrrrnnnng!"

One thought tunneled through the haze of recovery. He had to get out of there—

"Uhhhhhhnnnnnngg?" A hunched-over old man lurched into the room and stumbled toward Tony. Clumps of gray hair lay in a greasy comb-over on the man's balding crown, but not enough to hide the scar crossing his forehead.

(lobotomy)

"Uh…" Tony began.

"Chill out, Fred." Chad Everly, Pippin's modern-day counterpart, called from down the hall. "Come on, dinner'll be ready soon."

Though the room was spacious, the walls contracted, yet the window remained a mile away. No escape. Tony's leaden fingers clawed at the sheet, still weak. What if Everly and that assistant of his were just waiting until he recovered before they took him into that basement room Charlotte had told him about, to do terrible things to him and leave him a mindless zombie like Fred?

But Everly insisted they didn't do that anymore.

"Uh?" Fred turned and lumbered back out the door, and the room again became just a room, with innocuous white walls and a faint scent of food—baked chicken, maybe. Tony's mouth watered. Maybe he could—

An image assaulted him, of a thin, willowy blonde standing over him, gripping a pillow, and shoving it over his face. He struggled… too weak, just come out of recovery from death in the past… no oxygen, couldn't breathe, no one could hear his muffled scream as he fought to suck in a breath—

"Hey, you're awake," a woman said in an overly loud voice.

The memory—or so it felt like—fled as a black-clad blur flounced into the room. Without his glasses, Tony could barely see her chopped, dark ponytails against the recovery room's bare, white walls.

Taylor Gressman, Everly's young assistant. Who'd been dating Tony's nephew Danny for almost a year now.

He tried to speak, but nothing came out. A year ago he'd been a new and unwilling time traveler. It was Taylor who'd initiated him into the Society by trapping him in the House's conference room, with warping into a danger-filled past his only escape. "You!" His voice came out a croak.

"Nice way to greet someone who's taken care of your ass for the past three days." She snorted. "Oh, and you're welcome."

Dim memories slipped into place. Damn, she had, with Everly's help. "Thanks," he said through a dry cough.

She held a glass of water to his lips, leaning close enough he could see only kindness in the eyes behind her Ben Franklin glasses. "Here, take a drink. It's easy to get dehydrated during recovery."

He drained the water and let his head flop back onto the pillow, lessening his unrealized tension. She set the glass aside. "You gotta stop dying on us like this, you know. Supposedly there's a limit to how many times you can die in the past and come back. No one knows what it is, but I wouldn't want to be the one to find out."

His strength returning, Tony pushed himself up. His gaze flitted around the room. Someone lay in the bed two down from his.

Surprising, but not important. Not when he had to figure out how the hell to get out of there. The recovery room was on the second story. Taylor Gressman's gaze remained on him, and he looked down. All that covered his ass was a t-shirt and... he felt around his waist. Boxer shorts.

Not a good recipe for escape. From somewhere down the hall drifted Fred's nonsensical, mindless grunts. Tony forced himself to let go of the wad of sheet in his fist. *They don't do that anymore.*

He groped at the nightstand. "What'cha need?" Taylor asked.

"My glasses?"

"You weren't wearing them when we found you."

They must've flown off when Pippin's car hit him in 1959. But— "Found me? How'd I get here?"

The girl half-shrugged. "Someone rang the doorbell the other night, and there you were on the front porch, a bloody mess." She held up her hands. "We looked around, but whoever left you'd already split—"

Footsteps rang on the hardwood floor and Everly appeared in the doorway, his constant smile splitting his black goatee. "Hey Tony, how're you doing?"

Did the guy have to be so damned cheerful? Tony felt his face curl into a snarl but stopped it. "Okay, I guess, considering I've been shot at, hit by a car, died, and I have no idea how the hell I got here."

He fought back his unease.

Everly's eyebrows went up. "Shot at?"

"Whoa," Taylor said.

Tony crossed his arms over his chest. "How many people have warped into this time around here in, oh, the past week or so?"

"Just you and her." Everly tipped his head toward the other occupied bed. "Why?"

"Because the people who shot at me weren't from around here—or *now*."

Everly's vacuous smile disappeared. "How do you know?"

"They had laser weapons. Like something out of *Star Wars*."

Everly drew back. "That's a major breach of the Saturn Society Code."

"Maybe things have changed." Tony traced a wrinkle in the sheet.

"I know for a fact they haven't. Or won't." Everly glanced at the other bed.

Tony's gut twitched. The baked chicken taunted him—man, he was starving—and the Society was supposed to provide for him, but he couldn't push away his old fears. "Where are my clothes?"

Everly's mouth tightened. "They weren't exactly fit to be worn. I laid out a change of clothing there." He jerked a hand toward the bed beside Tony's. Tony kept his eyes on Everly, barely aware that he kept smoothing the sheet.

Everly's grin stretched back into existence and he held his hands up, palms out. "Look, I'm not going to do anything to you, okay?"

Tony's gaze flitted to the doorway. *Try telling that to that Fred guy.*

Taylor drew up beside him. "Yeah, if we were going to, y'know it would've been easy to off you during recovery."

Tony regarded them through narrowed eyes, then forced himself to relax. Taylor was right. It wasn't like he could go to the cops. If he described the shooters' laser weapons, chances were they'd toss him into a rubber room.

Everly moved toward the door. "I'll go put dinner on the table. Come downstairs when you're ready, and you can fill me in on what happened." He and Taylor left.

Tony threw off the sheet and started to remove the t-shirt, but stopped when he remembered he wasn't alone.

He reached for his glasses to clean them, but *(Duh!)* they weren't there. Rational thought returned, and his gaze went back to the woman. Not Violet. This woman was too slender.

He heaved himself to his feet and crept to her bed. He leaned over, but couldn't see her face, as it was half-buried in her pillow, the other half obscured in a blur of shimmering, blond hair. His heart jumped. The woman who'd tried to smother him in that weird, waking dream—

Don't be ridiculous. His gaze swept her motionless form. Something about that lustrous fall of hair reminded him of someone. Someone important.

His stomach growled. He'd come back later. He snatched the clothes off the next bed and withdrew into the adjoining bathroom.

As he dressed, memories filtered through his mind. 1959. Violet. No, *Charlotte*. It had to be her. His guts felt like curling in on themselves. The way she'd felt in his arms, even though she'd gained weight. Like an afterimage that lingered when he shut his eyes on a bright day, he could still feel her silken skin beneath his hands as he'd caressed her back. Could still hear the soft sounds she made—

Fuck her.

Thank God her plan had backfired when Pippin's car hit him. But how the hell had he gotten to the Society House, miles away?

A strange image struck him. Keith Lynch, his boss, hauling him out of the street onto a snowy embankment. The pressure of Keith's grip under his armpits, Tony's feet dragging across the asphalt. The cold, sinking through his skin. Every part of his body shrieking in pain, even through the haze of recovery.

Tony shook his head to clear the detritus. Though mostly healed, the broken bones, cuts and scrapes had all been real—he had the faded bruises and scabbed-over lacerations to prove it.

He must have dreamed the part about Keith. How would his boss have known where to find him? Why would he have carted him off to the Society House, instead of calling an ambulance?

The smell of the chicken now maddening, Tony hurried downstairs.

In the foyer, he found Taylor at the desk, her granny-boot-clad feet propped up, with her nose in a romance novel. Just like the first time he'd come to the House, soon after his mishap in Mexico had left him with the time travel affliction, and he didn't know how to keep it from happening.

Nothing had changed since that day almost a year ago. Same burgundy and green striped wallpaper, same antique mahogany desk with oddly incongruous computer beside the banker's lamp. Same Taylor Gressman, with her frilly, black dress and red and white striped socks. "Chad's in there." She jerked a thumb to her right without looking up.

In the dining room, Everly was already seated at the elegant, dark wood table. He motioned Tony to a chair. "Sit, eat."

Tony hesitated. "What about..." He glanced upward.

"Fred? He usually eats in his room. He never comes out when *Friends* is on, or *Seinfeld*, which comes on next."

Tony gave a sharp nod and sat. The sight of the meal fit for Thanksgiving quelled his urge to bolt for the door.

"Go ahead, help yourself." Everly flashed Tony his ubiquitous grin—did the guy ever stop smiling?—and waited for Tony to fill his plate. "Okay, tell me about these people who came after you. What did they do, did they say anything..." His chair creaked as he tipped it back.

"Chad!" Taylor flounced into the room in a flurry of black skirts, and grabbed a plate. "You're going to ruin those chairs!" Everly dropped his chair with a thud.

As Taylor filled her plate, Tony related his story between succulent bites of the feast he learned she'd cooked, stopping only when Everly interrupted him for clarification. As he talked, his jumpiness subsided. Maybe he could trust the Society.

Or maybe it was just the food. "So, do you know these people?"

Everly rubbed his goatee. "I know *of* them. Our other guest is from two hundred years in the future. She's visited before."

"Who is she?" Something niggled in the back of Tony's mind.

"Her name's Jennifer Warren Alpha," Taylor said.

"Jennifer..." Tony jerked straight. "The dog lady!"

Everly's face twisted. "The who?"

"She's always walking a dog when I see her—or carrying one. But she always disappears before I can talk to her. When's she from? What's she doing here, in this time?"

"She hasn't told us much," Everly said. "That would go against the Society Code—but in her time, the Society's going through an upheaval. And most of it not good." He leaned back in his chair, more slowly so it didn't squeak, and clasped his hands across his waist. "There's a group within the Society that's splintered off. They call themselves the Order of Titan. They think the Code's interpreted too loosely, and want to reinstate the Black Book and the Treatment." A corner of his mouth twitched.

Though the room was warm, goose bumps formed on Tony's arms. Everly's smile disappeared. "Alpha—the woman upstairs—says some of them have gone so far as to hunt down their so-called enemies in the distant past."

Tony squeezed his spoon. "And they're after me."

"We don't know enough about these guys to be sure they're the people who shot at you, but..." Everly turned up his hands.

It sounded like a gang war. Would Tony be shot down as soon as he left the sanctuary of the House? "Where are they now?"

Everly shook his head. "No idea. I sensed several people jumping into this time Friday, but no one showed up here. Must've been them coming in."

The food curdled in Tony's stomach, the lingering smell of dinner suddenly foul. The Society House could be the first place they looked. He had to get out of there. "My shoes. Do you—"

"Under the bed where you recovered."

Tony dashed upstairs. His shoes had escaped all but a few drops of dried blood. As he shoved them on, his gaze lit on the recovering woman from the future. *The dog lady!* Finally, he was near enough to talk to her, and here she was, in recovery sleep.

He moved to her side and his gaze drifted over her body and her face, angelic and peaceful. His guardian angel.

When he was a kid, she'd plucked him at knifepoint from a park where he was playing, fifteen minutes before a tornado had ripped through, obliterating the park and half the town. She'd returned him home, unharmed.

Years later, she'd cut Tony off in traffic, making him miss a plane—one that went down in rural Missouri with no survivors.

He didn't realize he'd been watching her sleep, until footsteps approached behind him.

"She won't wake for several days," Everly said.

Tony looked up. "Call me when she does. We have a lot to talk about."

Had she deliberately changed the past to save him? And gotten away with breaking the Society's highest law?

Four

NASEA THREATENED AS VIOLET LAID THE SCREWDRIVER ON THE BENCH beside the computer with the DVD drive she'd just replaced. After two weeks in 1959, she'd been amazed to return to the present and find she still had a job. Her good fortune had ended the other day, a month later, when she'd confirmed that her queasiness wasn't due to an onset of the flu, but morning sickness.

Sit still, wait it out... Her stomach settled as the woman on the helpdesk phone informed Violet that her computer had restarted. "All right, try printing now." Violet stifled a yawn and glanced at her computer clock. Only seven oh-two. Another hour until she could go home.

"It's fixed," the woman snapped, and hung up.

Violet tossed her headset to her desk. *Ungrateful shrew.* At least the call had taken her mind off Tony for five minutes. She should be glad they had the San Diego office. With a baby on the way, she needed all the overtime she could get. She tried to focus on the I.T. lab's bare, white walls, the torn-apart computer on her workbench, the status bar on another computer running an extended virus scan. Nothing helped.

She entered a record of the helpdesk call. Deshawna, the other evening I.T. Support tech, looked up with a wide-eyed stare, and only then did Violet realize how hard she was pounding the keys. "Sorry," she muttered.

"Get a crabby one?" Deshawna asked.

Violet tried to press her mouth into a smile. "Usually they roll right off me, but..." Ever since her ill-fated date with Tony, the smallest things set her off.

"Hormones, girl. They done me like that with both my kids. One minute you wanna cry, the next you want to throw stuff at anyone who looks at you."

"But I've always wanted a baby." At least she had for the few years she could remember.

"Don't matter. 'Specially when the daddy ain't around to help you deal with it." Deshawna turned back to the call log she was updating.

Violet had told no one who her baby's father was, although her roommate had figured it out.

She had to tell him. She'd put it off long enough.

Of all the bad luck. A year ago, her female problems would have prevented her from getting pregnant. But she'd gone for treatment, hoping to put an end to the horrible cramps that made her miss work almost every month. Then one time with a man, and boom. Once the baby came, she'd be lucky if she only missed one day of work a month.

She'd looked up Tony's address and phone number in the company database the day after she got the news, but a week later, she had yet to work up the nerve to speak to him.

He'd been so horrible to her when she'd taken his glasses to his office soon after her return to the present. He'd been wearing another pair—of course, he'd have a spare—but he'd refused to so much as look up from his computer screen. "Put them on the desk," he'd said in short, clipped words.

She trembled as she did as he asked. "Tony... whatever I've done... I'm sorry." She took a deep breath and swallowed, trying not to cry.

"Sorry won't cut it. Now get out. And don't come back." He'd started typing, dismissing her.

Violet leaned her head on her hands, the tools on her workbench blurring until she blinked back the tears. That had been over a month ago, before she learned about the baby. She hadn't seen Tony since. He'd called one of the other techs to reset his password, and he must have started eating lunch at his desk or going out, as she hadn't seen him in the cafeteria. The vomiting, the fatigue and the constant running to the washroom were minor problems when she had yet to tell him.

She'd picked up the phone on a dozen occasions, and put it down every time. She'd walked past his office door, but it was always shut. She doubted she could bring herself to tell him at work anyway.

But she had to tell him. Even if he wanted nothing to do with her or the baby. Her eyes burned as if she'd just peeled a whole bag of onions.

She slid the DVD drive back into its slot on the computer, then picked up her screwdriver to bolt it in, each twist an effort.

The clock changed to seven oh-four. She fought the urge to lay her head on her desk. If she hadn't used all her sick days, she wouldn't have to work late to make up the time she missed due to her doctor's appointment.

The flip-flops in her belly wouldn't go away. How would time travel affect the baby? What would happen if she unintentionally jumped? *Call Mr. Everly,* she scribbled on a sticky note. The kind Society man and his assistant had cared for her and patiently answered her questions when she'd finally jumped home from 1959. He'd even offered her a room at the House if she had problems with a landlord, but luckily, Stephanie and Timmy were just glad she was back. Besides, there was no way she could live at the House with that horrid Fred fellow there. Taylor and Mr. Everly had assured her that the brain-damaged man was harmless, but as soon as they left the room, he'd thrown himself at Violet, clawing at her face as if trying to tear it from her skull. Even though she didn't get the same sense of familiarity she had with Tony and Mr. Pippin, she feared she knew Fred from before, too.

Nausea threatened again. Deshawna was almost due for a smoke break—one thing Violet missed since she quit when she found out she was pregnant. Violet would ask her to grab her a pack of crackers from the vending machine, and while Deshawna was away, maybe she could work up the nerve to call Tony.

Her stomach rebelled at the idea. "Deshawna! I'm going to the ladies' room!"

"Again?"

Violet grabbed her purse and bolted down the hall.

She stumbled when she ran into a janitor's cart—*since when did they clean on Friday night?*—as she careened around a corner, but made it to the washroom before she lost her dinner.

She brushed her teeth to get the taste out of her mouth, then gripped the sink to catch her breath. The fluorescent light above the sink flickered and buzzed in a visual death throe, highlighting the pallor of her face.

The door squealed. "Deshawna?" Besides the two of them, the area was deserted. They weren't supposed to leave the helpdesk unattended—

A man appeared around the corner. The fluorescent light twinkled on his glasses, and the scar around his neck shone. "Tony?" she breathed.

He grinned. Her heart leaped.

How could it be? Why was Tony here now, and in the ladies' room of all places?

She took two hesitant steps toward him. His coiled stance, his leering grin, the scent of cigar smoke that rolled off him…

(All wrong)

The man laughed and lunged at her. With a shriek, she crashed to the ground, her breath cut off by his arm across her throat.

His weight bore down on her, pressing her spine into the floor. She tried to scream, but only a squeak came out. Panic burst through her as she struggled to take in air. She kicked, connecting with the man's leg.

"Damnation!" the man said. His gravelly voice bore a British accent. His smoke-laden breath made Violet gag. Toothbrush still in hand, she jabbed it into his belly. His grip loosened. She screamed and leaped up, but before she could get away he clapped a hand over her mouth and shoved her down, face first.

Gripping her hair, he jerked her head back. Tears filled her eyes.

"Guess what, ye little tart?" His hands clamped around her neck. "Yer gonna die tonight."

This isn't happening! She was imagining it, transferring her worry about telling Tony—

The man shoved her face into the floor. Pain blossomed in her nose and forehead, bringing reality back in a rush. She tried to kick him again, but he'd shifted so that his legs pinned hers. Her heart pounded so hard her chest hurt. He squeezed harder. "Ye don't know what pleasure it gives me, feeling yer wretched life slip away in my hands."

Her body was going numb, from lack of oxygen or something else, she didn't know. She twisted, but his chokehold tightened. Her throat was killing her. Dark spots clouded her vision—

No! If she died now, she'd never get to see her baby. Never get to hold her baby. Never get to love her baby—

The door squealed. "Violet?"

Deshawna! With the last of her breath, Violet forced out a muffled squeak. The man's hands twisted on her neck. Her vision swam. Her eyes felt about to pop out—

"Violet? You oka— Oh my God!"

Swearing, the man slammed Violet's head down and bolted into the wheelchair stall.

Violet tried to push herself up, dimly aware of receding, running footsteps and her coworker screaming for security.

The lines in the tiled floor blurred together. She put one palm down, then the other, and slowly sat up.

The room spun. She keeled over as dizziness hit, then subsided.

The door flew open. Deshawna burst in with a security guard, their footsteps painfully loud in the echoey room. They crouched beside Violet. "Are you all right?" her coworker asked.

Violet touched her neck. "H- hurt."

"Can you get up?" the guard asked. She managed a nod. They helped her stand. She painstakingly unfolded each limb as if she'd aged to twice her thirty-five years—or so she guessed. "Where'd the guy go?" the security guard said.

Violet pointed at the large stall. "Gone," she choked out.

"But no one came outta here," Deshawna said.

The guard pushed the door open as Deshawna held onto Violet. The stall was empty.

Tony trudged across the parking lot to his apartment, fingering the handgun in his pocket. His accuracy at the shooting range had been his best yet, no doubt due to his increased attendance since returning from 1959. The week before, he'd obtained his concealed carry permit.

Probably none too soon, as someone had been attacked at the office the other night. Of course, when he'd heard it was one of the I.T. techs, he'd immediately thought of Violet

(Charlotte)

but dismissed the notion, since it happened at night and she worked days.

Fuck her.

Unease rose in him as he walked past the rental office and crossed the street to his apartment. *It's nothing.* As he'd passed on his way out that afternoon, he'd had another one of those weird hallucinations, the most vivid one yet. This time, someone had sneaked up behind him and locked him in a chokehold. Then Danny'd opened the rental office door to step out and greet Tony, dispelling the gruesome image.

Tony was thankful he'd hired his nineteen-year-old nephew to man the office on the weekends, but why were all the lights on? And why was Danny's car still there, when he should have closed the office two hours ago?

Tony started to walk across the street to see what was going on when his cell phone rang from inside the apartment, where he'd left it on the charger, having forgotten the night before.

The burglar alarm chirped when he opened the door. He frowned at the keypad's green light. He'd been running late for his reserved time at the gun range, and must have forgotten to arm the system.

His steps lightened as he hurried inside. Bethany was coming tomorrow, and that was probably her on the phone. But when he grabbed it, it stopped ringing. The number on the display was unidentified. The battery was still low, so he replaced it on the charger. He'd grab a bite to eat, then call Bethany to make sure she was still coming. His seventeen-year-old daughter's weekend stays were all that made him smile, more so since he'd loved—and lost—Charlotte.

He squeezed the gun tighter as a ball formed beneath his ribs. *Don't go there.* He'd called Everly, and made sure Violet was all right. And on Keith's suggestion, he'd taken another leave of absence from work, which was just as well.

Tony set the gun on an end table and took off his jacket. As he hung it up, he thought he heard a cough from his bedroom.

Senses heightened, he grabbed the gun and crept across the carpeted living room. "Who's there?"

No answer. Tony fingered the gun's handgrip. All that time at the shooting range was making him paranoid. Not to mention the attack at the office. He couldn't imagine that had anything to do with him, but still... "Hello?" *Idiot.* Probably a car backfiring on the main road.

He stretched and massaged his neck, trying to relieve the tension. Damn, he was tired. He'd gone to a drop-in class at the martial arts center after he'd left the shooting range, and the instructor had worked him hard, but Tony was already slipping into the routine, the disciplined thought, and the controlled strength that had drawn him to karate in junior high.

He wandered into the bedroom and flipped on the TV. He'd hit the gym hard the day before, too. He'd be sore tomorrow. But the workouts, training and target practice kept him busy and made him feel he was doing something proactive in case the snipers returned.

He stashed the gun in the nightstand drawer, then kicked off his shoes. Sniffing, he paused. Was that cigarette smoke?

He frowned and sniffed again. He wasn't imagining it. But where was it coming from?

The shirt he'd worn last time he'd gone to Bernie's house had probably gotten kicked under his bed, and like everything else after an afternoon with his sports-watching buddy, reeked of smoke. Too tired to look for the damn thing, he started to unbutton his jeans.

The closet door flew open and something whacked Tony's back, slamming him to the floor face-first. "What the fu—" Hands clamped around his neck with inhuman strength.

Tony froze at visions of the Mayan priests and the huge stone battle-axe that had left the pencil-thick scar around his neck. The assailant took advantage of Tony's hesitation to let go with one hand and punch his head. Tony's ears rang, jerking him back to reality.

He twisted, trying to squirm from beneath the guy, but the assailant squeezed tighter, cutting off Tony's breath. Tony clawed at the man's hands, then jammed his elbow backward, trying to connect with his opponent's stomach. The attacker anticipated the move and half-rolled to the side, his grip on Tony's neck unyielding. His knees pressed into Tony's back as he ground Tony's face into the carpet. Tony flailed for the nightstand, but couldn't reach the drawer pull.

The man laughed. "Lotta good yer gun'll do ya," he said in a thick British accent, his breath reeking of cigar smoke. "Yer neighbor's out. And I've taken care of the boy in the office."

Danny! Tony struggled, trying to donkey-kick the guy while clawing at his iron hands. Karate hadn't prepared him for this.

"Such a delight to squeeze the soft flesh of the boy's neck," the attacker said. "To watch his eyes bulge, feel his young life leave him in my hands. Just like yours soon will."

Tony bucked beneath him, but could barely move with the guy's weight pressing him down. He tried to speak but only a choked grunt came out.

The hands on his throat tightened, and the man slammed Tony's head against the floor. Tony saw stars. Where the hell was the dog lady now? Everly had called when she woke from recovery, but by the time Tony got to the House, she'd disappeared, surprising Everly and Taylor as much as Tony.

The man squeezed harder. Panicked, Tony's mind ran over a dozen escape scenarios in a second and discarded all but one. *Warp!*

Damn! The one time he wanted to, he couldn't. It couldn't be done in view of others. Not unless he was in the past, and got killed.

His strength flagging, Tony gave up trying to pry the man's hands loose and pummeled his sides.

The attacker's weight shifted enough for Tony to roll over, but the man regained his hold. "Don't think ta get away," he growled. Tony reached for the guy's neck. Maybe—

Oh. My. God. Tony's hand slipped on his assailant's leather jacket. The world stopped.

It was like looking in a mirror. Even his glasses were identical to Tony's.

Even the scar ringing his neck.

The attacker laughed and squeezed harder. Tony gagged, trying to suck in a breath. "Guess who'll be blamed for the killing across the way?" The man tightened his grip on Tony's throat. Tony's vision darkened. "No need to worry 'bout that. 'Cause yer about to join him."

Violet's heart raced as she plodded up the sidewalk to Tony's apartment Monday after work. Yellow caution tape strung across the door into the rental office—*what on earth happened?*—bore a stark contrast to the tidy flowerbeds, the tarp-covered swimming pool behind a slatted fence, the sun striking a shiny spot on the carport roof. Dozens of apartments, and Tony owned them all, according to the public real estate records.

Even if he never returned to work, the baby wouldn't have to worry about money, though Violet would accept it only if she had to.

Her feet dragged as if she trudged through mud, the sunshine and warm breeze a stark contrast to her inner dreariness. *Get out. And don't come back.* Her chest felt as though her new bra was too tight, making it an effort to draw in a breath. *If you'd had some sense instead of lying on your back—*

She swallowed what felt like a mouthful of rocks and pushed the voice away. No point in what-ifs. She couldn't jump back to February to re-do her date and stay home, because the earth's position around the sun limited time travel—she could only jump back to this time of year in the past.

Her ribs squeezed. Such a change could be disastrous—Mr. Pippin, Chad, and all the Society materials she'd read concurred on that. Even if next February she tried to relive that night, she didn't know if she'd be able to say no to Tony.

Especially since by then, the baby would be born. She'd have gotten to hold him, feed him, wake to his cries. Or hers.

A child of her own. Someone to love, who wouldn't care what she'd done years ago, that she couldn't remember. Someone she wouldn't have to hide from. Someone who wouldn't sling accusations for acts she knew nothing about.

She couldn't give that up.

Her steps slowed as she neared Tony's apartment, jittery heaviness filling her belly. Maybe he wasn't home. She'd tried to call several times last night, and again during lunch break. She hadn't wanted to leave a message on his machine.

But his dark blue Buick sat in the carport, the laser damage repaired.

He needs to know. Heavens, she wished she had a cigarette.

No you don't. Straightening, she marched to Tony's door and gave three sharp raps.

Heavy metal music drifted out the open window of the apartment next door. A lawnmower droned in the distance, but otherwise no one was around. She knocked again.

No answer. Had Tony left town? Perhaps the people at the rental office could tell her—if it had been open.

She knocked once more. Dread trickled down her throat. What if Tony had seen her and didn't want to answer?

A door swung open. Not Tony's.

A burly, young man in a Harley-Davidson t-shirt stepped out the next door. "You looking for Tony?" Violet gave one nod. The man cocked his head. "You didn't see the news?"

She wrapped a lock of hair around her finger. "I've been a little under the weather." After the attack, they'd kept her overnight in the hospital. She'd been in no frame of mind to watch television.

The fellow's face took on an odd expression. "Kid who worked in the rental office was killed the other night. Tony did it. No one's seen him since."

The bottom dropped from Violet's stomach. "Wha— It can't be. He would never—"

"Got it on the security cameras." The man shook his head. "Who'd've thought—Tony always seemed like a nice guy."

It had to be the man who attacked her. "It wasn't him. There's someone who looks like him, he came after me too—"

The man shook his head. "Believe what you want, lady, the video was clear as day. Even showed that weird scar on his neck. It was him, all right." He withdrew inside and shut the door.

Violet's shoulders sagged as she returned to her car and dug through her pocketbook for her cell phone. When she'd spoken to the police, she'd simply described her attacker as "about six feet tall, lean and muscular, dark, spiky hair, glasses. And a scar across his neck."

She had to call the police, tell them Tony didn't do it. She pushed aside a packet of prenatal vitamins, lipstick, compact, sunglasses, the *Star Trek* novel she'd been reading at lunch. But no cell phone. She must have forgotten it. *Pregnancy.* Ever since she'd learned of it, her brain had turned to mush. She'd have to ring the police from home.

Then she'd call Mr. Everly. This time, she'd take him up on his offer to stay at the House. She shuddered, and her hand slipped on her car door handle. For her safety—and the baby's—she'd even put up with that horrible Fred fellow.

As soon she got home she dug the policeman's card out of her pocketbook and went straight to the kitchen phone. She dialed half the number before she realized there was no dial tone. "Well, fiddle-sticks." She turned the phone over in her hand. It was old, no surprise that it had died.

She trudged down the hall to her bedroom. Her shoes clicked on the hardwood floor as she made her way around the bed toward the phone on her desk.

Her nose prickled. A barely-there tang hung in the air. She sniffed, but the smell was gone. She grabbed the phone and the odor came back. She sniffed again. Smoke.

Something swished on the floor. Hands shot from beneath the bed and clamped onto her ankles.

Violet screamed. She tried to jump, but the hands yanked her toward the bed. She tumbled onto her fanny, clutching at the desk. DVDs, papers, a flash drive, an empty Diet Coke can, and her pencil can crashed to the floor, raining pencils, pens, and clutter.

She tried to scoot away from the bed, tried to dislodge the hands, but he gripped tighter. She pushed harder, but her heels slipped on the smooth floor. Panic knotted her insides. The man from the office. The one who looked like Tony. He'd come to finish the job. She kicked.

He pulled harder.

Then he let go.

Violet scrambled to her feet, stumbled toward the door, but her foot slid on a CD and she crashed to the ground. The edge of her stapler poked her fanny as the man slipped out from under the bed. She tried to swallow and couldn't, her throat dry.

It was him.

She tried to push herself up, but he leapt at her and pinned her down, the cigar smoke smell so thick it nearly choked her. Straddling her, he reached for her neck and squeezed, a glint in his eyes. Pain blossomed beneath his forceful hands. Unable to draw in enough air to scream, she clawed at his arms. He laughed, quietly, deliberately, as he squeezed tighter. Her demise would be drawn-out and painful.

Violet's gaze darted around the room. Something cast a silver glint in the fading sunlight streaming in the window. Hope soared through her.

She had to be quick. Before he saw.

Before he cut off her air. She lowered her hands.

The scissors from her pencil can. Slowly, she closed her hand around them, and pulled them up to her chest, inch by agonizing inch, her movements small so he wouldn't notice, then mustering all her strength, jammed the scissors into his solar plexus.

With a howl, he released her neck. She leaped on top of him and shoved the scissors into his belly, a hard, downward thrust.

Everything happened as if she were watching a program played in slow motion on a dirty television set with a pillow taped over the speakers. The slow rip of his flesh giving beneath the blades. His shrieks of pain. His flailing hands. The cigar smoke smell, mingling with the metallic scent of blood. Her screams, louder than his, yet oddly muffled. The blood spurting beneath her fingers, warm and wet on her dress. All she could do was jerk the scissors out, and stab him again, and again...

Someone shouted. Not the attacker. A woman.

Rough hands grabbed her arms and jerked her backward. "Miss Sinclair!" Violet couldn't turn around. "Miss Sinclair!" the woman repeated, her voice deep and throaty. "Are you all right?"

Violet couldn't speak. Couldn't do anything but stare at the man who'd tried to kill her as she squeezed the slippery, bloody scissors as hard as she could. Her breath rattled in her ears over the moans of her attacker-turned-victim.

A chill rose in her chest. *So like Tony.* Yet not. She couldn't wrench her eyes off his stomach and the spurting, then bubbling blood.

He made a gurgling sound, then stilled. The scar around his neck gleamed white in the sunlight slanting through the window. Blood bubbled once more from his wounds.

Violet's captor released her. She wobbled, but remained upright, her breath coming in shallow puffs, the scissors clutched in her fist. "He's dead," the woman said.

The body wavered like a mirage, then grew indistinct, as if slowly fading out on television. "What the..." Violet's would-be rescuer muttered.

The attacker's form grew fainter, then transparent, like he was a ghost—

The scissors slid from her hand as dizziness swamped her. The room spun. *No!* She couldn't jump in time! Not now—

But as fast as the dizziness had struck, it dissipated.

Along with the man who'd tried to kill her. Nothing was left but a pool of blood—

Blood. Like when Mr. Pippin's car hit Tony. And like another time that flashed in her mind. Blood, spurting from beneath her hands. She'd seen this before. Sadness overwhelmed her, then the horror sank in.

She'd *done* this before.

Bile rose in her throat. She wasn't sure if it was morning sickness or—

She retched, tossing the remains of her lunch into the blood.

"Miss Sinclair! Violet!" Hands again gripped her forearms. "Are you—"

Shaking, she slowly turned her head. Blood spattered the woman's broad, buxom chest and once-tidy blazer and smart, black dress slacks. A few drops even clung to her short-cropped, curly brown hair. Kindness, concern, and bewilderment filled her caramel-colored face. "What the hell just happened?"

"I- I don't know." *He went back in time* wasn't an explanation the woman was likely to buy.

Violet's shakes slowed, and the other woman relaxed her hold. "Are you okay? Did he hurt you?"

Violet touched a blood-slicked hand to her neck. A little sore, but nothing like the attack two days ago. "I'm all right." It only hurt a little to speak.

She studied the stranger. The phrase *built like a brick shit house* went through her mind. The woman looked familiar, not from *before*, but recently.

"My name's Phoebe Benson." The woman reached into her pocket, dug out a business card, and handed it to her. "I was sent by our mutual employer."

Violet frowned at the card. "Benson Security Services?"

"Personal protection. Keith Lynch uses our services from time to time."

Keith Lynch. That was where Violet had seen Ms. Benson— around the office. A tiny bit of relief slipped over her. Still, why would the CEO of the company send a bodyguard to watch over a computer technician? "But why—"

"Keith was afraid the wacko who came after you last week might try again." Phoebe Benson eyed the bloody scissors. "Though you seem to have managed without me."

Violet's gaze locked on the pool of blood. So much. And all over her. Like the last time. She placed her palm on the floor and pushed herself up, careful not to slip on the slick wood. Her knees trembled, but she managed to stand. Ms. Benson kept her eyes on her. "You sure you're all right? Maybe I should take you to the hospital—"

"No! No hospital." Panic shot through her. They'd call the police. "I- I'm fine, really." With this, the police might connect her with the woman she was six years ago—one who'd been much thinner, with short brown hair, but a woman covered in blood—as she was now.

One who'd killed. And who'd just done so a second time.

Five

Bethany hung back in the funeral parlor's anteroom. So far she'd avoided looking inside Danny's casket.

She'd told Aunt Lisa that the sickeningly sweet flowers were giving her a headache, though it was better than the underlying odor of chemicals. "They made him look real nice," Bethany's grandma said to a friend as she dabbed her eyes.

Bethany's head itched and she faced the windows, hoping Grandma wouldn't make her go look at him. She'd rather remember her cousin playing basketball or whipping her on the Playstation or making eyes at Taylor over Sunday dinner. Not a dead body made up to look *nice*.

Her mom appeared at her side. "Honey, you ought to be in there to see everyone."

"I don't want to." Of course, at seventeen, she was old enough to be expected to stand in the receiving line—or whatever it was called at a funeral—with her mom, Aunt Lisa, Uncle Charlie, and her cousin Mark. But she couldn't deal with any more fake smiles or hugs from people she barely knew. She'd heard enough murmured I'm sorrys and whispers about her dad when people thought she was out of earshot.

"Listen, I know it's hard—you and Danny were close—"

"It isn't that." Bethany glared at her mother.

Dora Solomon's face paled beneath her perfect makeup. "Bethany, he was my husband."

"He didn't do it." Bethany started down the hall.

"Don't you run away," her mom snapped.

Bethany stopped and whirled around. "I'm not the one who wants to move. I'm not changing my name. I'm not the one who decided to have the funeral on his birthday!" Her dad would be thirty-seven that day. She should be sitting at a Mexican restaurant with him, not attending a funeral for the cousin everyone said her dad had murdered. *That stupid video's wrong.*

Her mom's ice-blue eyes melted. "Bethany..."

Bethany flung open the powder room door and fled inside. The scent of oranges made her stop.

Danny's girlfriend Taylor sat at the vanity counter with an orange from the hospitality room, peeling it in tiny pieces with her black-polished fingernails.

Taylor glanced up in the mirror. Mascara smudges rimmed her eyes behind her glasses.

"Um, hi," Bethany mumbled. Red and white striped socks peeked from beneath Taylor's ruffled, black skirt. *Weird. She even dresses the same for a funeral.*

"Hey, Bethany."

Bethany leaned toward the door, but Taylor motioned to a chair beside her.

In no hurry to return to the visitation, Bethany joined her.

"I thought I could handle this." Taylor ripped off a long, narrow strip of orange rind. "I've handled enough other shit in my life. It's been what, five days? I mean, I thought I'd accepted it. That he's really gone." She peeled another strip off the orange, but it broke. "God, this sucks."

"It sucks twice for me." Bethany stared at the orange.

"He didn't do it."

"What?" Bethany's gaze jerked up.

"Your dad." Taylor set the orange down.

"But—" Suddenly, the air in the room seemed lighter. "How do you know? Everyone else—"

"I don't know your dad that well, but I know he'd never...." Taylor sniffled. "Especially Danny. Danny used to talk about him all the time. How he used to take him and Mark to Dragons games with you guys every summer, go camping and stuff. The time Danny screwed up someone's deposit at the apartment, your dad was totally cool about it, even though he should've been pissed."

Bethany's fingers fidgeted. "But you don't have any proof, or—"

Taylor gave her a tight-lipped, half-smile. "No. But... I think he's safe. Laying low until something comes out to prove he didn't do it."

It was like gray clouds parting after weeks of nothing but rain. Bethany had a freakish urge to laugh hysterically like a cartoon character. "You're the first person who's said that. Besides my grandma, I mean." Did Taylor know something no one else did?

"Even your aunt thinks he did it?" Taylor tipped her face down, looking over the top of her glasses.

Bethany pushed her bangs back. "She says that video from the apartment office could've been doctored, but... I don't think she really believes that."

"Chad—my housemate—he saw it on the news. He doesn't think your dad did it either."

Bethany let out a shuddering breath. Someone believed. But why had her dad disappeared? It was that, as much as the security tapes, that condemned him. And how was this Chad guy so sure her dad didn't do it, either? "How does your roommate know my dad?" How did Taylor know him besides from Sunday dinners at Grandma's? Come to think, he'd given Taylor a really weird look the first time he saw her there.

"I met your dad... through work. Same with Chad." Taylor picked the orange back up and peered at it studiously from above her little, square glasses.

Bethany wrinkled her nose. "You work at LCT?" Somehow, she couldn't picture Taylor's retro Goth getup going over too well at the conservative office where both her parents and her uncle worked.

"No, through my work. And Chad's." She started picking at the orange again.

"Where—?"

"A research organization—"

"Bethany?" Her mom pushed the door open and leaned in.

Bethany sighed. "I'd better get going." Thank God the visitation was almost over. She pushed away from the table and forced herself to rise. "You going to dinner with us?"

"Your aunt invited me, but..." Taylor picked up the orange and turned it in her hands. "I don't know. I was thinking about going to a movie. Think Lisa will be upset if I bail?" She put the orange down in a plate of potpourri.

Bethany shook her head. "I just wish I could."

"Why don't you?" Taylor stood, fluffing her skirt. Bethany hesitated. "This sucks more for you than any of them. I mean, it's your dad. You lived with him every weekend."

What the crap. "Okay. Let me go tell my mom." If she bitched at Bethany about running away, Bethany would remind her again who was moving to Atlanta.

And she would find out more about this research organization, and what Taylor and the mysterious Chad knew about her dad.

I've been shot. The burn blasted through Tony's body, radiating from his back outward, as he crashed to the ground. *Dying...* The gun's report still echoing in his ears, he tried to turn his head, look up, and see who'd sneaked up behind him on the trail through the woods...

He blinked as the pain disappeared and the loamy scent of vegetation and the calls of starlings assaulted his senses. Bright sunlight. A glimpse of red-orange brick, and white siding through the trees.

He'd warped back into the present in the woods behind the apartment complex.

Not dying. A dream, or perhaps another hallucination. As he sat up, the mental fog of recovery cleared, and he recalled the last five days. The killer with his face. Twisting out of the guy's grip just long enough to jump into the closet and warp.

The image of his nephew's face hovered in his mind. *I've already taken care of the boy.* The strangler's words were a blow to the gut that stole Tony's breath.

He lowered his head, chin on his chest. Was there any chance Danny had lived and that psycho had been lying?

He got up and tramped through the weeds until he found the familiar path between the apartments and the shopping center on the other side of the wood. Ironically, he'd spent his time in 1972 laboring on a farm that occupied the land he now owned. Thankfully, Pippin hadn't found him, and the Pull had come a week later. He'd gone back to the woods behind the farm, and rolled under a bush upon his return to the present to hide while he spent the day in recovery.

His stomach growled. Hopefully, he'd have some Lean Cuisines in the freezer.

He stopped when he neared the carport.

That white car did not belong in the parking space beside his.

Especially since it was a white Impala with a pudgy guy inside wolfing down a Big Mac. An array of computer and radio equipment barely visible below the dash confirmed Tony's suspicion that it was a cop.

Dread rising through his body, Tony slipped back into the woods, then crept to the other end of the lot. Near the entrance, another guy lurked in an innocuous-looking, silver sedan.

Tony's pulse pounded in his throat. Another cop. The killer's words echoed in his mind. *Guess who'll be blamed...*

Tony raced down the trail, paranoid that the police would hear every snapping twig, each thundering footfall. If Danny was dead, they'd have found the surveillance tapes, seen the murder. Ironically, Tony had bought the system when he suspected his former office manager had been stealing from him—which she had. Now it was him the video footage would condemn.

No one would believe Tony wasn't the killer. Somehow, he had to contact his family and convince them he was innocent. Something that would be tough to do if he wound up in the slammer.

He passed the turnoff trail that led to the shopping center. Too many off-duty cops hung out at the corner bar there, and the shopping center had taken out the payphone.

The other path led to the neighborhood where Bernie lived.

Darting behind bushes and privacy fences, Tony managed to slip inside the open garage of his friend's McMansion without incident.

He knocked, wondering if Bernie was gone, since his car wasn't there. R&B music seeped through the door leading into the house. Tony vaguely remembered Bernie mentioning someone giving him a hit-and-run fender-bender downtown. The car was probably in the body shop. Tony knocked again. Finally, the door opened.

"Tony! What the hell you doin' here?" Bernie wore only a towel around his waist, and water glistened on his dark brown forehead.

"I was—"

Bernie grabbed his wrist and yanked him inside, then slammed the door. "Are you crazy? The shop's been crawlin' with cops!"

"Shit." Tony ate at the bagel shop Bernie owned almost every day. It would be one of the first places anyone looked for him. He met his friend's eyes. "Bernie... I didn't do it." He shuddered as his nephew's face again flashed in his mind. The nephew he'd never see again, thanks to— "The guy looks just like me."

"Yeah, they said on the news they got you on the security tape. Tony, you in a heap o' trouble. Look, man, I'd like ta help you out, but—"

"I swear. I didn't—" Tony swallowed, trying to push away Danny's image.

Bernie grabbed his shoulder and propelled him to the living room. Tony's stomach rumbled as Bernie nudged him onto the L-shaped, leather sofa where the two of them often sat watching sports and drinking beer. "Sit," Bernie said. "Lemme get some clothes on. I got leftover pizza, want some?"

"Sure." Even though he should be starving, Tony's stomach flip-flopped at the mere thought of food. But he figured he'd better eat. Who knew when he'd get to again?

As Bernie disappeared into the kitchen, Tony sank into the couch, elbows on his knees, and rested his forehead on his hands. His eyes stung. His muscles felt about to snap. *I'm wanted for murder. Of my nephew—*

Glass clinked on the coffee table. Tony's head jerked up. A beer sat in front of him, condensation forming on the bottle. "Thanks." He twisted the cap off and took a swig.

Bernie flipped open a cardboard box. "Dig in, man, tell me what the hell's goin' on."

"I came home from the shooting range the other day," Tony said through a bite of pizza. Bernie didn't interrupt as he related the story. "I still don't know how I got away." Tony's mouth twitched at the lie, but Bernie didn't seem to notice. "I swear to God, the guy looked just like me—"

"Look!" Bernie pointed to the TV.

"...Tony Solomon remains at large," the newscaster announced. Tony's face appeared behind her, then the scene switched to a familiar place—his sister's family room.

Lisa sat on the plushy, light green sofa, the one his brother-in-law Charlie described as dog-puke green. The one where Tony sat with Bethany every Sunday after dinner. "Oh God," Tony croaked. He hadn't even spent his usual birthday dinner with his daughter.

On TV, Lisa's voice trembled. "I just want to ask my brother why. I can't think about anything beyond that..." She buried her face in her hands. The picture cut back to the newsroom.

Tony leaned back on Bernie's couch, his eyes closed. Even his family thought he did it. His older sister, who'd laughed at him when he was twelve and refused to ride the roller coasters at Kings Island. Who'd made fun of him for not stepping on a spider. Who'd played slugbug with him in the car. She'd believed him when he told her that his wife Dora was having an affair with her husband. He'd listened while she ranted about Charlie. Lisa'd stood by Tony when he went through a divorce while she struggled to save her marriage. But now his sister believed he killed her son.

Tony forced the last, leaden bite of pizza down his throat. "I have to go." He got up.

Bernie walked him to the door. "Turn yourself in, man. If you're innocent, thing's'll work themselves out."

Tony wasn't so sure, but what else could he do? He slipped out the door and slunk toward the woods.

A sense of doom settled over him as he crept down the path. Birds chirped above, their song a stark contrast to Tony's prospects. The farther he went, the heavier his feet grew, along with his doubts. What if they never caught the guy? He'd spend his life in jail, his family forever convinced he was a murderer.

He stopped when the path forked. To the right would take him home, but something compelled him to go left, toward the shopping center.

He stopped and turned around, but when he willed his feet to move, they wouldn't. *You can't go home*, a little voice in his head said. He took a step toward the apartment complex. *You'll rot in jail.*

He stopped. *Hurry, or she'll die!*

His insides twisted. He tried to swallow, but his mouth had gone dry. He'd heard that voice before. Himself, from the future, occupying his body, along with his present awareness.

Obeying it had once saved his life.

A chill coursed over him like a bucket of water. Snipers, in the woods behind the apartment, shooting at him just like in the dream. Only in reality, they'd missed. He'd lived, because he'd heeded the voice's warning.

Go!

He hurried down the left fork, barely able to feel his feet pounding the path. Soon he emerged behind the strip mall. Everything was closed except Mulroney's Pub. *Must be Sunday.* He started toward the bar, but his feet wanted to go toward the street.

He obeyed, paying little mind to where his future self was leading him until he stopped at the former corner gas station that now housed Trammel's Automotive.

He cast a nervous glance across the parking lot at Mulroney's, then stared up at the plastic sign. Why would his future self direct him to a car repair shop?

Drive south. Now.

Adrenaline raced through Tony's body. It had to be Bethany. She was in danger.

He gazed at the parked cars, and it struck him what his future self wanted him to do.

His future self was out of his fucking mind.

You can't exactly go back for the Buick when every cop in town's looking for you.

But steal a car? His arms and legs went rubbery at the idea.

But Bethany…

Duh, call her! He dug into his pocket for his cell phone before he remembered that he'd left it at home before his jump to 1972. *Idiot.* Even if he had it with him, the battery would be dead.

One thing was for sure, there'd be no going home, not with cops all over the place.

But he had to call her, see if she was all right. He couldn't re-member where—or when—he'd last seen a payphone. Which left one choice.

A frantic dash through the woods brought him back to Bernie's house. But his calls to Bethany went unanswered, while the little voice and feeling of dread grew more and more insistent, and he soon found himself running back to the auto repair shop.

He tamped down his unease as he took a last look at Mulroney's, then surveyed the cars awaiting service or pickup.

For Bethany, he could do this.

He swallowed his scruples and jerked the door handle of the car beside him. Locked. Glancing toward Mulroney's every few seconds, he moved up the row of vehicles. The fifth one, a black Chevy pickup, was unlocked. Though he resisted, the other presence in his mind made him bend down, lift the floor mat, and grab the keys from beneath it. His fingers tingling and numb, he did his best to ignore the Budweiser ball cap on the passenger seat, the tin of Skoal in the cup holder, and the St. Christopher medal hanging from the rearview mirror, all reminders that the truck belonged to someone—someone who wasn't him.

Bethany. He climbed in, hoping the truck had either already been serviced, or wasn't in need of anything major. The part of him that reviled what he was doing retreated to hide and observe from the dark recesses of his mind. His future self heaved a sigh of relief when he started the engine and the gas gauge went to F.

Bethany. For her, he could lie to his best friend. He could steal. He could kill, though pray to God he'd never have to. Clenching his jaw, he put the truck into gear, pulled out of the parking lot, and turned toward I-75.

Violet woke drenched in sweat. "No! No...." Her cries trailed off as she took in the sunlight streaming in through a louvered window above, splashing bright rectangles on the trailer's paneled wall.

She held up her hands, half expecting them to be covered in blood. "Tony..." she whispered.

She'd killed him again, the third time she'd had the nightmare in the two days since the attack in her home. Everything played out the same. The attacker never spoke until she stabbed him, but when he did, it wasn't in the killer's deep, accented voice.

It was Tony's. "No," she whimpered.

"Violet? You okay?" Phoebe called from down the hall. After a hurried cleanup and leaving Stephanie a note, she'd taken Violet away to hide. All Violet knew was the old singlewide trailer belonged to Keith Lynch, and it was somewhere in the hills of northern Tennessee.

"Yes," she answered. They hadn't called the police. What will we tell them, Phoebe had said. She'd waited long enough for Violet to log on to the company network, look up Mr. Lynch's phone number in the personnel database, and contact him to verify that he had, indeed, sent Phoebe. He'd told Violet her life was at risk, and Violet took him at his word, though it was beyond her why the CEO would have such concern for a lowly I.T. worker. Neither Mr. Lynch nor Phoebe had asked why the man who looked like Tony was after her, and for that Violet was thankful.

Her stomach unknotting as the effects of the dream wore off, she made her way to the washroom. As she rubbed soap on her hands, she peered into the mirror, the trailer's weak fluorescent lights emphasizing the dark circles beneath her brown eyes.

Who had she wronged that day six years ago, the day before which she could remember nothing? Who was Tony's mysterious double, and how had he finally found her?

And how long would she and Phoebe be in hiding? She had yet to tell Tony about the baby.

Her stomach lurched, but she had nothing to throw up.

Food. She needed to eat. Phoebe had stocked up on groceries en route. Violet remembered her grabbing a box of crackers, saying her sister had always wanted them when she was pregnant.

Violet quickly found them, relieved when the salt and crunch settled her tummy. "Hungry, huh?" the bodyguard said from behind her.

Violet jumped. "Phoebe! I didn't hear you—"

"You need to pay more attention to your surroundings." Phoebe tossed a couple crackers into her mouth, crunching loudly. "I could've been—"

"I know." Violet's gaze dropped to the countertop, her nausea rolling back at Phoebe's stale coffee breath.

"I'm here to keep you safe. But you need to watch out for yourself, too."

A cracker crumbled in Violet's fist. What if Tony's lookalike found her? The way she'd let her guard down, he'd have little trouble finishing the job.

Phoebe retreated into the living room, switched the television on and plopped onto the couch. The picture was pixelated and the sound had frequent dropouts, but the area was too remote for cable, and Violet suspected there was no satellite dish because service could be easily traced. She ate a few more crackers, glad her queasiness was subsiding.

A sweet scent lingered in the air. She sniffed. No, not sweet, more... chemical. A cleaning product? She sniffed again, but couldn't identify the odor. Whatever it was, it seemed out of place. "Phoebe? Do you smell something odd?"

The other woman sniffed, her eyes looking up to one side. "No."

Violet took another whiff. Faint, but there.

Phoebe joined her in the kitchen and inhaled. "I don't smell anything."

"My nose is pretty sensitive right now."

"I have a pretty good sense of smell myself. I used to be able to tell if a pack of lunchmeat was bad way before my ex. But...." She sniffed again, then shrugged.

Violet popped another cracker into her mouth. "I'm probably imagining it."

Dusk was falling by the time Tony's future self led him off the highway at an exit in the middle of nowhere just south of the Kentucky-Tennessee state line. The compulsion led him down state routes, then county roads that became less well maintained the farther he traveled, until they were more crumbled gravel than pavement. *Where the roads end and the trails begin*, as his grandpa used to say. The fields and pastures that had lined the road had long since given way to uncultivated meadows, then woodlands.

Though it wasn't warm in the truck, his sweaty hands slipped on the wheel as he turned onto a gravel drive that didn't even have a street sign. His sense of urgency grew. The truck bumped and bounced over more ruts than level patches. The setting sun flared in his eyes. He grabbed the Budweiser cap and slapped it on, pulling it low.

Smoke—from a bonfire, maybe—came in through the vents. What the hell was Bethany doing way out here in the middle of nowhere, two states away?

Maybe Dora had taken her on a camping trip to get away from it all, though that was hard to imagine. But things had to be pretty shitty for Bethany at school, with him being accused of murder, on top of losing her cousin.

Hurry! his future self urged. His panic rising, he pushed the truck faster, though his logical self railed against such foolhardy behavior on the curvy, gravel drive in the deepening twilight. His body strummed as if he'd downed a gallon of coffee.

He rounded a curve toward an orange glow. Dread clutched him as his suspicion of a bonfire dwindled. He emerged into a clearing, where an old mobile home sat. *Bethany!*

The trailer was engulfed in flames.

Six

BETHANY DROPPED THE BOX OF SUMMER CLOTHES ON HER AUNT'S PUKE-green sofa, and dashed outside for the next box as a white Jeep Grand Cherokee pulled into her aunt and uncle's driveway behind her yellow Camaro.

The car Bethany's dad had bought for her before—

She pushed the thought away as Taylor climbed out of the Jeep. "Hey," she said in a swirl of black skirts.

"Hey, yourself," Bethany said. *Good, now I'll get some answers.*

"How much more do you got?"

"Uh, my whole back seat." Bethany yanked the Camaro's door open. In a short time, they had the car emptied, and boxes filled Bethany's new bedroom.

Taylor smoothed her skirt as she hopped onto the bed Uncle Charlie had moved over from Bethany's mom's house earlier that week. "What was this room?" Taylor asked. "The door's always been shut every time I've been here."

"My aunt's craft room. We moved her stuff into Danny's old room." Bethany suppressed a cringe. She'd been grateful when Lisa and Charlie had invited her to stay with them when her mom moved, but using Danny's room would've been too creepy. Aunt Lisa hadn't touched that craft junk in years.

Bethany flipped on the TV atop the dresser and joined Taylor on the bed, their backs against the wall. Her cousin Mark walked past, backed up, and leaned around the doorframe. "Hey Taylor, what's happening?"

"Bethany invited me over for Sunday dinner. Pot roast."

That was all the explanation needed. The savory smell of onions and beef had pervaded the house for hours, and every time they had it, Taylor had enthusiastically complimented Aunt Lisa. Bethany gave herself a mental pat on the back for using Taylor's favorite meal as an excuse to invite her over.

They'd had fun at the movies last week, even though Bethany'd had to back off the questions about her dad when Taylor had started to get short and snippy with her.

She pushed away the bummed-out feelings that threatened.

Mark had disappeared, so it was time she worked the conversation around to her dad, and what Taylor knew about him. "How've things been at work?" Hopefully, it sounded like an ordinary, casual question, enough that Taylor wouldn't quickly change the subject like she had before.

"Okay." Taylor shrugged. "Keeps me busy, but it's not super-stressful, so it's cool."

"That's good," Bethany said. *Not stressful, huh?* Interesting. "How are you doing? I mean at school and everything."

"Sucky. People talk, then pretend they don't. People I thought were my friends are blowing me off." Bethany shrugged. "No one believes me that my dad didn't..." Her throat thickened. "Not even Ashley, and she's my best friend—or she was."

Taylor made a sympathetic grunt.

"At least you believe me. You said you knew my dad through your job. Some research organization. What is it, anyway?"

Taylor grabbed the TV remote and turned it over in her hands. "It's called the Saturn Society."

Bethany wrinkled her nose. "What kind of research is that? Astronomy?" She couldn't imagine why LCT would be involved with such a thing. Although, who knew?

Taylor met her gaze and gave her a wide, close-mouthed smile. "Time travel."

Bethany drew back. "Ohhhhh-kaaaaayyyy." What the heck could her dad have to do with that? "But what—"

"I don't know what your dad was doing there." Taylor looked up and away from Bethany. "Maybe his company is one of our donors."

Bethany's brows pressed down as she gazed, unseeing, at the TV, barely noticing that the news had come on. "I can't imagine that being something LCT would get involved in." *Time travel? Puh-lease.*

"Girls?" Aunt Lisa called from the kitchen. "Dinner's ready!"

Bethany hopped off the bed. Taylor followed, gasping as her feet hit the floor.

Bethany's head whipped around.

Taylor stared at the TV, her mouth hanging open. "What—" Bethany began, then followed her friend's gaze. *Please, don't let it be about Daddy, unless they found—*

"...bridge literally disappeared," the anchorwoman said. A banner across the screen's bottom read Breaking News. "Investigators are baffled as they continue to comb the gorge for survivors."

"Whoa," Bethany said. A sense of unreality fell over her as the cameras scanned a wooded valley littered with cars and trucks in two parallel lines. The picture briefly changed to a four-lane bridge hundreds of feet above, then flipped back to the original scene, identical except for the wreckage and lack of a bridge. There were no metal supports, no scrap, no sign the bridge had ever been there.

Bethany wanted to think it was a movie. Her mind numb, she sank back onto the bed.

"'Scuse me, I gotta make a phone call." Taylor bolted from the room.

"Taylor?" Bethany jumped up and followed her to the living room. "You know someone there, or—"

Taylor burst outside, letting the storm door slam behind her.

Bethany hung back in the entryway. Taylor's voice drifted in from the porch. "...you think it's one of those temporal disturbances? Yeah, me, too. What's the Society Coun—" She glanced at the door, her eyes meeting Bethany's through the storm door. "Yeah, I'll be home soon," she said into her cell phone, then hung up. "Hey, you left a box in your car, want me to grab it?" She stepped off the porch in the direction of Bethany's Camaro.

"Yeah, sure." Thunder rumbled. Bethany looked up. Hadn't the sky been clear moments ago?

Weird. Like Taylor's phone call. What was a temporal disturbance, and what did it have to do with the freaky story in the news?

One thing was for sure, as soon as Taylor left, Bethany was going to do some research on that Saturn Society.

Tony threw the truck into park and sprinted for the trailer. Black smoke darkened the sky. Tony coughed as the scent of burning plastic grew stronger the closer he got to the trailer. He was ten yards or so away when dizziness slammed him, and he tumbled to the ground. *No!* He couldn't warp, not now! The dizziness faded, and he pushed himself up.

Someone else had warped. Someone near, judging from the strength of the vertigo. The occupant of the trailer?

The fire had started at the far end, but tendrils ate at the aluminum panels, inching nearer. Tony's mind seemed to shut down, and all he could do was stand and stare.

Hurry! his future self shouted.

He ran to the trailer. "Bethany!" Heat radiated from the fire, bringing sweat to his brow. Anyone in the trailer's far end would be toast. Surely whoever was inside had gotten out.

The sense of urgency from his future self told him otherwise. Flames consumed the trailer's sole exit, and licked the side panels of the green van parked alongside.

His breath coming faster, he raced back to the truck. Seconds ticked by as he scrambled to locate the tire iron. He finally found it beneath the seat and worked it loose. He rushed back to the trailer.

His eyes fixed on the window in the near end, opposite of where the fire was concentrated. A high-pitched ringing in his ears mixed with the fire's roar. *She's in there.* "Bethany!"

She must have been knocked unconscious. He couldn't let himself think otherwise. He'd figure out later why the hell she was there in the first place.

The narrow window loomed just out of reach. The fire crept nearer each second.

No lawn chairs sat nearby. No logs for a campfire, no picnic table–nothing he could stand on to reach that window. Except—

He leaped into the truck and backed it beneath the window. Without turning it off, he hopped out, then climbed into the bed and peered through the window's dusty, louvered panels. Dread nearly choked him, along with the smoke.

Sheer curtains fluttered in the fire's hot draft. Beneath them, a woman in a denim dress lay stretched across a twin bed, her face obscured by long blond hair.

Longer than Bethany's, and wavy.

And she was bigger than Bethany.

Oh, hell. For a second, Tony couldn't move. The other presence in his mind gave him a mental kick so hard it was almost physical, jerking him into action. "Violet!"

She didn't stir.

Tony swung the tire iron at the window. Chunks of glass flew. He barely noticed bright bursts of pain where shards struck his face. Something was very wrong if she could sleep through the roaring fire and breaking glass.

Finally, the window fell apart. Tony clawed at the glass in the flimsy aluminum frame, tore the frame out and flung the misshapen pieces of metal aside.

He wedged himself through the window and landed on the bed inches away from Violet's head. "Viole—" He choked on the smoky air.

Violet's side rose and fell with shallow breaths. Tony's chest shuddered in relief. *Thank God.* He shook her shoulder. "Violet!"

The fire's roar on the other side of the bedroom door muffled his voice. Violet didn't move. Somewhere in the trailer, something made a loud bang, then another. A third small explosion went off as he shook her again. He rolled her over and smacked her face. "Violet!" No response.

He glanced at the door, coughing in the thickening smoke. If anyone else was in the trailer...

Tony slid off the bed and pressed his palm to the fiberboard door, then jerked his hand away, shaking it. The little voice remained quiet. No one was out there.

Grabbing Violet under her arms, he dragged her to the head of the bed, beneath the window, then hefted her from behind to shove her through the opening.

He got her shoulders almost up to the window when a coughing spasm overtook him. She started to slide from his grasp. It was only a few feet to the window, but would Violet fit?

Hell with it. Adrenaline buzzing through his body, he hooked one arm around her belly and the other beneath her ass and latched his hands together at her crotch, then pushed to slide her up the wall. *One, two... three!* A final big push got her over the sill. He stopped to hack up more smoky air, then placed his hands on her butt and shoved. Something ripped as she tumbled through the window and landed in the truck bed with a muted thud.

He pushed himself through, twisting as he dropped so he wouldn't land on top of Violet, then climbed over the side wall, hopped behind the wheel, and pulled away until he was a good hundred feet or so from the burning trailer. He almost forgot to put the truck in park before he leaped out.

Violet sprawled in the truck's bed, her dress flipped up over her waist. He flung the tailgate open and dragged her out.

Sweat poured down his face. He grabbed her beneath her knees and shoulders, and hefted her against his chest. He carried her to the passenger door and yanked it open. When he slid her onto the seat, her eyelids fluttered. "Violet?" She coughed, but her eyes fell closed. He repeated her name, but she remained unconscious.

Tony gazed at the trailer. The flames had reached the bedroom.

A chill fell over him despite the fire's heat. If he'd arrived five minutes later...

He probed the other presence in his mind, and though he sensed no words, a feeling of calm and relief told him again that no one else was in the trailer.

He hopped behind the wheel. Violet slumped against the door but didn't wake.

He pulled her limp form upright enough so he could buckle her seatbelt, hoping the hospital he remembered seeing somewhere between the trailer and I-75 wasn't too far. He threw the pickup into gear and barreled down the gravel drive, mindless of the bumps and scrapes on its underside. Lights appeared around a curve, and he almost sideswiped another truck heading in the opposite direction.

Whoever it was, he hoped they had a cell phone to call in the fire before it spread. He glanced in the rearview mirror, but all he could tell in the falling darkness was that it was a big, black SUV—perhaps a Lincoln Navigator.

Or a Cadillac, like Keith Lynch's. Tony's head whipped around as the vehicle's taillights disappeared around a curve, and he caught one last detail.

The SUV had Ohio plates.

Violet woke as she was being pushed on a gurney. The scent of plastic and antiseptic mingled with smoke. Something rubbery ringed her face around her nose and mouth—an oxygen mask. Prickles skittered down her arms. *Hospital.* What on earth? How— "Excuse— " Coughs racked her, muffled by the oxygen mask. A nurse pushed her into a corner, then dragged a curtain shut around her.

"How are you feeling?" she asked in a soothing tone as she taped some sensors to Violet's finger, then lifted the mask.

Violet's eyes followed the sensor wires to a machine with digital readouts. "I'm—" She coughed violently, a tide of panic rising within her. What was wrong with her? And were the police—

"It's okay, relax," the nurse said.

"I'm— where am I? What's going on?" She coughed again as the nurse replaced the mask and adjusted some settings on the equipment. Smiling, cartoon babies and clouds adorned her yellow-green scrubs.

Baby! Violet's panic grew, pulling her body tight. "Excuse—" she began as a young, Asian woman with a clipboard slipped inside the curtain. "I'm Dr. Perry." Her name badge identified her as a University of Tennessee medical resident, and her understated smile that touched her eyes more than her mouth made Violet think, if only for a moment, that maybe everything would be all right. The doctor pulled a stool to Violet's side. "I understand you had a close call in that fire."

"Fire?" Violet clutched the gurney's rails.

"You were unconscious when you arrived." Concern crossed the doctor's face. "What's the last thing you remember?"

Violet described the funny smell, and the fatigue that had fallen over her. The doctor made notes on a clipboard. "You inhaled quite a bit of smoke, but your blood oxygen looks good. Do you smoke?"

Violet nodded, then shook her head. "I quit."

"Good." The doctor scribbled on her clipboard. A frown flashed across her face. "We should run some more tests since we don't know what the funny smell was, but most likely you'll just have a nasty cough for a few days."

Had the hospital staff called the police? Violet twiddled her fingers, the sheet beneath them suddenly cold. Then another worry resurfaced. "I—you should probably know... I'm pregnant."

"Oh!" The doctor slid the mask down so Violet could speak more easily. "How far along are you?"

"Twelve weeks." Violet bunched the sheet in her fists. Already the baby was so real. "How will this affect the baby?"

The doctor gave her another smile, one of those placating ones they must teach in all medical schools. "Hopefully, very little, if at all. But we'll do an ultrasound just to be sure."

Violet closed her eyes and exhaled, then succumbed to another coughing fit.

The doctor grabbed a tissue from a box on the counter and handed it to her. Violet hacked something into it.

"You'll probably cough up black stuff for a while." The doctor slipped the mask back over Violet's face. "Let's get you more oxygen, and I'll go order that ultrasound." She moved to the curtain. "Are you comfortable for now?"

Violet started to nod, then stopped. "There was a woman. In the trailer, before the fire."

The nurse pursed her lips. "The man who brought you in said you were alone."

"Man?"

"He's out in the waiting room." The nurse left.

Violet twisted a lock of hair around her forefinger. Keith Lynch? Who else would've known about the trailer? And what had happened to Phoebe?

The doctor slipped out as the nurse returned and pulled the curtain aside. "Thanks," a man said.

Violet's breath lodged in her throat at the familiar voice. Similar to Mr. Lynch, but not him. She felt like a boa constrictor had wrapped itself around her and was slowly tightening its coils. *It can't be.* Hope warred within her. She didn't want to let herself believe.

Though a Budweiser ball cap was pulled low over his eyes and he wasn't wearing glasses, she instantly recognized him. Lightness rose within her, though she tried to restrain it. After all this time, he showed up now? Here? Especially after he'd been so angry with her? "Tony?" She squeezed her right hand with her left.

His clothes—an old undershirt and too-big blue jeans—were more soot-smudged than clean. As he released the curtain his hand shook.

"Thank God," he said in a shuddering breath as he moved to her side. He leaned over her and she instinctively reached for him, wrapped her arms around him, buried her face in his chest as he held her close, as if he'd forgotten all his accusations, the weeks they'd spent apart irrelevant. His smoke-laden clothes brought on another burst of coughing.

He jerked away, like he'd just remembered. "What are you doing here? Who are you hiding from?"

"I... I don't know." Violet bit back her own questions. "You didn't hear about...?"

"About what?"

"At the office. I was working late, and..." Her voice caught. "A man attacked me. He- he looked just like you," she whispered.

Tony sucked in a breath. "That was you?"

She described the assault. Tony's face went slack. "Holy shit."

"I- I'm sorry about your nephew." She studied her hands, twiddling her fingers.

"Why didn't you go to the cops, tell them I didn't do it?"

"I was going to, but," she swallowed, "I forgot my cell phone. When I got home. He was there. In my house."

"The guy who looks like me?"

"Yes. Hiding under my bed. I barely escaped. I..." Her voice went flat. "I killed him," she whispered. "Stabbed him with a pair of scissors. Only he didn't die. He disappeared. Like you, when Mr. Pippin's car..." She clenched her jaw, hating the way the quaver crept back into her voice.

"Damn, he's... like us. He came after me, too." Violet's eyes went wide and the air in her lungs went cold. "He goddamn near choked me to death before I jumped into the closet and warped." He reached for his glasses, then grabbed the ball cap instead, lifted it, slid his fingers through his hair.

"Tony..." She gripped the bed rail and tried to steady her voice. "I don't think that fire was an accident." She brought her fingers to her lips. How could she have forgotten about Phoebe? "Oh, good heavens! Was there anyone else at the trailer?" *Oh please let her have gotten out...*

"No."

"Are you sure?" Phoebe wouldn't have left her. Would she?

Tony shook his head, his jaw tight. "The room you were in was the only place the fire hadn't reached. If anyone was in there..."

"Oh, no." The overhead light suddenly harsh, Violet closed her eyes and pressed her fingertips to her forehead.

"Who was with you?"

"Her name was Phoebe Benson. A professional bodyguard. Keith Lynch hired her, I talked to him myself before we left to verify..." Her eyes turned upward. "Oh, mercy. She was a good person. If anything happened—"

"No one else was inside. I'm sure—I had this sense—I guess from my future self. And as I drove up, I felt someone warp."

"How did you know?" Violet asked.

"Know what?"

"About me. Where I was, the fire—" She broke off, coughing.

Tony backed toward the curtain, but as his hand brushed it, a look of terror crossed his face, and he went still, holding his breath.

"Tony?" Violet started to sit, until coughs racked her, slamming her back to the bed.

Tony whirled around. Her coughs subsided. "Tony? What's wrong?" Had he heard her ask the nurse about the baby?

"Besides all this? Nothing." His face relaxed, but not quickly enough. There was something he wasn't telling her.

Fine. "But... how did you know?"

He brushed back the curtain and looked out, glancing from side to side. "I- I just knew. It's hard to explain—"

"Please..."

He lowered himself into the chair beside her bed, then popped up and peered around the curtain again before returning to his seat. "Did Everly—or Pippin—tell you about time-traveling within your own life?"

"Ye-es," she said slowly. "Mr. Pippin said it's dangerous, it's too easy to change something you... shouldn't." A chill coursed through her, just like it had when Mr. Pippin had brought it up. She'd done it. *Before*. It hadn't been good.

Tony's mouth pressed into a tight line. "Sometimes you don't have much choice."

Violet gasped. "Did you-"

"Apparently so. All I knew was I had to come down here, *now*. It was like I was possessed. By me, from the future." He shifted in his chair and his shoulder brushed the curtain. He flinched, as if it burned him, and the terrified expression flashed across his face again.

"Tony... what's—"

His gaze flitted around the room. "It's like a flashback... no, more like a memory, but not quite that either. A memory that never happened... someone tried to suffocate me in a big curtain like that, I couldn't move, couldn't breathe..."

Violet searched his eyes. "A memory that never happened?"

"Yet it did. Like maybe in another timeline, one that got changed, is the only thing I can think of."

Violet lifted three fingers to her lips. "Mercy..." Did she have a part in those other timelines, too? And what of his fugitive run across two state lines to save her? "Was it like... what brought you here, to me?"

He tilted his head from side to side, one corner of his mouth pressed tight. "Sort of. Not as compelling or urgent. Not something that would make me steal a truck."

"Oh my." Violet pressed her fingertips against her mouth. Her thoughts tumbled over each other. Did she and Tony have a future together? "You did that... for me?" Hope struggled to rise within her.

"Well, actually, I thought it was my daughter."

"Oh." Violet's gaze fell on her belly.

Where their baby was growing.

She had to tell him, now. But he'd been so angry, so hateful, when she'd gone to give him his glasses. Now that he knew his daughter wasn't in danger, he'd go home. Surely he'd want nothing to do with her, or the baby. But as she dredged her mind for a way to segue into the Tony-I'm-pregnant discussion, the curtains parted and the nurse with the babies-and-clouds scrubs flounced in. "We're going to take you down the hall for that ultrasound now, Ms. Sinclair."

Tony jerked upright in his seat. "Ultrasound?"

"Well, the doc's sure the baby's fine, but it's always good to check things out."

Violet's eyes connected with Tony's.

He'd gone as white as the clouds on the nurse's scrubs. "Baby?"

After the nurse rolled her away in a wheelchair, Tony remained in the chair, fidgeting. *A baby. After all these years.* Of course, he'd never planned to be father at age 20, but when Dora had wound up pregnant with Bethany their sophomore year in college, it hadn't turned out to be a bad thing at all. Especially after Keith had offered both him and Dora paid internships at LCT, then taken it further when he learned of Bethany's impending arrival. He'd given them a loan, helped them buy a house after their hurried wedding, and had been like a doting uncle to Bethany from the day she was born. Before long, Tony had wanted another child, but Dora always demurred, citing Tony's frequent travel at first. Only later had she admitted one was enough.

He dug his glasses out of his pocket and jammed them on beneath the Budweiser hat. Not much of a disguise, but so far no one had connected him with the news, thankfully.

Damn glasses were smudged. He swiped them off, furiously rubbed the lenses with his shirt, then slid them back on.

He'd made them worse. He grabbed a tissue and tried again.

Better.

It didn't stop the stabbing sensation in his chest.

The irony. The second child he'd always wanted, with the woman who'd betrayed him, who'd tried to give him over to the Society.

The only person who could exonerate him of his nephew's murder.

He meandered around the hospital, one off-white-walled corridor blending into the next. Violet hadn't even suggested to the nurse that he be allowed to see the ultrasound. He supposed he couldn't blame her, considering the way he'd snapped at her when she'd brought him his glasses. Still, he should be pissed off, should have demanded to join them for the ultrasound, but he'd been too shocked to think straight.

His heart twisted at the possibility the smoke had hurt the baby.

It seemed unreal, yet he couldn't distance himself. But more unnerving was how he'd welcomed Violet—*Charlotte*—into his arms in relief at finding her unharmed, forgetting what she'd done.

He stopped at a vending machine and scanned the snacks and candy bars. Not much more appetizing than the bland institutional food he smelled everywhere, but doubted he could eat anyway. He wandered some more, then sat in a dimly lit waiting room— thankfully unoccupied.

Who was his murderous, time-traveling double? Why was he after Tony—and now, Violet? Where did Keith Lynch fit in? That black SUV Tony had passed leaving the trailer was too coincidental. Why would the CEO take such an interest in an I.T. worker, to the point he'd send her away with a company-provided bodyguard?

He glanced at the courtesy phone. He needed to find a payphone and call Bethany. She'd be worried. So would his parents—

A rock lodged in his gut, adding to the heaviness there. He couldn't call home. Not when his sister believed him a murderer. Not unless he wanted to rot in jail.

He gazed up at the TV, hoping he had become old news. When the cable news channel rattled off the same stories for the third time, he traipsed back to the snack machine.

He leaned his forehead on the cool glass, fingering the change he'd pilfered from the pickup's cup holder. Nothing looked good—

"Tony Solomon?"

He whirled around.

A middle-aged woman with short, graying hair sauntered toward him, a huge, quilted tote bag looped over her shoulder. "Are you Tony?"

He hesitated. "No." His mouth twitched at the lie.

A smile touched her face, understated enough to be sincere. "It's all right, Tony." She spoke in a gentle, reassuring tone with a soft Southern accent. "My name is Florence Allen. I'm the Watchkeeper for the Cumberland Gap Society House. Chad Everly called and told me you were stranded."

Tony choked on his breath. "How did he know where I am?" And who else knew? Were the cops on their way to arrest him? What if the person who set the fire—

"I haven't the foggiest. He just told me you needed help." She patted her tote bag. "I brought you some clean clothes—" She leaned aside to look past him. "Oh good, the dress fit."

At the now-familiar cough, Tony whirled around. Violet padded toward them, wearing a short-sleeved, pink flower print dress with her hospital socks. At her relaxed expression and even gait, his tension slipped away, then crept back when he reminded himself who she was, what she'd done—and that he was still a fugitive.

Violet smoothed the cotton dress's skirt. "It's perfect, Mrs. Allen. Thank you again."

The older woman eyed her appraisingly. "It's no trouble, that's what the Kitchen Sink's for."

Tony wrinkled his nose. "Kitchen Sink?"

Florence Allen patted her bag with a toothy grin. "That and shoes are about all that's not in here." She turned to Violet. "How are you, dear?"

"Everything's all right, thank heavens." She stifled another cough as her gaze drifted to Tony.

New relief cascaded over him like a waterfall, though one riddled with rocks. "You know her?"

"We just met," Mrs. Allen said.

"I called Mr. Everly," Violet explained, "and he called Mrs. Allen." Tony's face slipped into a scowl. What was she up to, calling the Society at every turn? Violet's hands twisted around each other. "I had to tell him about the fire. In case it's related. Besides, we have nowhere to go." Her gaze fixed on his. "Tony, Mr. Everly knows you didn't do it."

"The Society'll take care of you," Mrs. Allen said in a gentle voice. She dug into her voluminous tote bag. Two large-size dog biscuits fell on the floor as she pulled out a pair of jeans and a collared, knit shirt. "Oh dear... y'all aren't allergic to dogs, are you?" She bent to scoop the dog treats off the tile.

"No," Violet said. Tony shook his head.

"Good. Rufus loves company, and I hate to have to lock him up." She thrust the clothing at Tony. "Here, go ahead and change if y'want, then we'd best be going."

"I can take care of myself." Tony regarded Violet through narrowed eyes.

Her face hardened. "Do what you want. I'm going with Mrs. Allen."

He wanted to look away. Couldn't. No way in hell was he letting her out of his sight. Not when she was carrying his child. Not when she was all that stood between him and a sure conviction of murder. Not when—baby and her knowledge aside—he still cared, damn it. About *her*. Never mind the Society—

Florence Allen read his mind. "You needn't fear the Society, Tony. Come to the House, at least for tonight."

As much as he hated to admit it, Violet was right. Even if he had money, he couldn't exactly check into a motel.

And there was definitely no going home.

He spit out one word. "Okay." He took the clothes and slipped into the men's room. As he changed, he couldn't quiet the questions in his mind. What were Violet's—*Charlotte's*—ties to the Society in this time? What the hell kind of game was she playing—and why?

"Almos' there," Florie—as she'd insisted they call her—said as her Land Rover bounced onto a steel framed bridge. Moonlight seeped between the mountains and illuminated the valley far below. Tony shut his eyes, suppressing a shudder. "Don't like heights, huh?" Florie guided the truck across and up a road that curved in switchbacks up another forested hillside.

"I can take them or leave them." Preferably leave them, along with the image that flashed through his mind—more like a memory—of someone pushing him off that bridge. He glanced at Violet, who slumped in the back seat, asleep. Beside her, Rufus, Florie's Rottweiler/Shepherd mix, lifted his head.

Tony thought about asking Florie to call Bethany, but discarded the idea. As much as he longed to hear her voice, to tell her he was all right, that he hadn't killed Danny, and he loved her, the risk of giving away his location was too great.

He squeezed his eyes shut until the ache subsided, if only a little.

The truck slowed and rolled to a stop before an L-shaped log cabin. "Welcome to the Cumberland Gap Saturn Society House." Florie hopped out and opened the truck's back door. Rufus bounded out. Tony followed, taking in the sights while Florie roused Violet and helped her out of the truck.

"It's beautiful," Violet murmured before a coughing fit struck.

Tony couldn't argue. Birds sang in anticipation of the coming dawn. Lights glowing in the House's windows set it apart from the shadowed woods and gave it the ethereal quality of a watercolor painting.

The picturesque House could also be a prison. Or a place where it would be easy to make someone disappear—forever—and the gravel driveway was the only way out. The town they'd passed through a few miles back—Hollowville, Tony had read on a sign—hadn't even rated a McDonald's.

Florie led Violet to the front door, in the L's inner corner. A carved, wooden sign hung from a peg beside it, and the carriage lamp mounted on the house illuminated the relief image of the planet Saturn flanked by three stars.

THE SATURN SOCIETY
CUMBERLAND GAP HOUSE
EST. 1752

"Mercy!" Violet touched her chest below her neck. "This house is over two hundred years old!"

"Oldest one outside o' the original colonies," Florie said. "And Florida, of course."

At a lick on his hand, Tony looked down to see Rufus, who looked up at him quizzically as if waiting for Tony to precede him. Tony cast a look back before he followed Florie and Violet inside.

The House was much bigger than it looked. Handmade quilts draped the sofa and two chairs in the living room. Cross-stitch samplers and three oil paintings of woodland scenes adorned the log walls. The flat-screen TV looked out of place, as did the computer sitting on an aged, rough-hewn, wood desk beside it. Florie pointed out the wing with two guest rooms and a bathroom, where she laid out clean towels. "You'uns can clean up while I fix us something to eat." Tony followed her to the kitchen while Violet took a bath. He lingered in the dining area, where he could keep an eye on both Florie and the bathroom.

And the back door. Just in case.

Florie chuckled while she cracked eggs into a skillet. "You needn't worry, Tony. No one knows you're here 'cept me and Mr. Everly."

The familiar panic arose inside Tony. *Chill out!* Everly and Taylor hadn't done anything except take care of him, feed him, and send him on his way. He would stay the hell away from the Society if he went into past again, but maybe they were okay now.

The eggs' fragrance filled the room. Tony's stomach growled. He forced himself to stop shifting his weight from one foot to the other and sat. "What about Violet? What about her hospital bills?" He glanced at the bathroom door, still unsure if he should thank Violet or condemn her.

"All taken care of by the Society." Florie stirred the eggs. "Your lodging, too, o'course. You're welcome to stay here as long as you like. Shoot, I could use help watchin' the House, I'd welcome an assistant—or two."

Breakfast was ready by the time Violet emerged from the bathroom, so Tony ate, then quickly showered, loath to let her out of his sight for even that long.

Despite his misgivings about the Society, his jitters subsided. He found it hard not to like Florie with her easy-going, friendly conversation. Even Violet relaxed when Florie told them about her phone call to the county sheriff. "They managed to put out the fire afore the woods caught. Anonymous tip, Sheriff Winston said. They'd just finished th'investigation when I talked to him. No evidence of a body in that trailer."

Violet coughed into her fist, concern knitting her brows. "Was Phoebe's van still there? A green one, with no windows in the back?"

"Yeah, and that's what bothers me." Tony rubbed his stubbly chin. "Any chance she was... like us?"

"What's the name?" Florie asked. Violet told her. "Let's give the Society Intranet a look-see." She led Tony and Violet to the computer.

Her search turned up nothing. "If she's one of us, she's not known to the Society in this time." Florie pushed back her chair and stood. "Don't necessarily mean anything, but we're at a dead end for now."

"Thank you for checking," Violet mumbled through a yawn. She sank onto the sofa.

"Oh Lordy, you two must be beat. Let me show you to your room."

Room? As in only one? Tony wanted to keep his sights on Violet, but the thought of sharing a bed with her again made his body tense in ways he didn't want to acknowledge. "Uh, I'll just crash here." He eyed Violet. Her face was drawn with fatigue, her expression weary at the mere suggestion she get up. "Or she can."

"Oh dear." Florie wrung her hands. "I just assumed—her bein' in the family way and all..." Muttering apologies, she led him into the far wing then hurried away.

The four-poster bed topped with a homey quilt tempted, but his suspicious side warned him not to fall asleep. Not with Violet *(Charlotte)* in the next room, planning who knew what.

He sat on the bed, fighting sleep until he no longer could.

When he woke, sun streamed through the lace curtains, and the old-fashioned, wind-up alarm clock on the nightstand read twelve-thirty.

Damn! Tossing back the covers, Tony jumped out of bed.

He wandered down the hall, ears prickling at every bird chirp from outside, every distant bark. But a glance out the window revealed only Florie's Land Rover. When he reached the living room, he found Violet at the computer, studying what looked like the Saturn Society Intranet.

His jaw tensed. "Where's Florie?"

Violet whirled around. "She took Rufus and went to Wal-Mart. I... needed a few things, and she said she'd be happy to do some shopping; and it's a special treat having us here, because she can't leave the House unattended for long with no one to help, in case someone jumps in and all..." She trailed off as Tony crossed his arms over his chest.

Baby. Oh, God. Hopefully, she hadn't seen his hands shaking. "How long have you known?" he asked quietly.

"I..." She started coughing, and grabbed a glass of water off the desk, took a swallow, then wiped her mouth on the back of her other hand as she set the glass down. "About two weeks."

"Two weeks? That's—"

"I'm—I have female problems, and I didn't think anything of it when I was late... you know." She wrung her hands. "I tried to tell you." Her speech quickened as she spoke. "I was going to call, and I looked up your number in the HR database even though we're not supposed to, but then I decided I needed to tell you in person, but not at work, and then you went on leave again, so I went to your apartment, and this biker fellow who lives next door to you came out and said you were accused of murder and I was going to call the police but I couldn't find my phone in my pocketbook then I remembered I left it at home so I..." Her words faltered into another coughing spell.

Tony leaned against the wall, arms still crossed over his chest.

Violet shifted in her chair. She spoke softly but firmly. "I want you to know, I don't expect anything. I was only going to tell you because you deserve to know—"

He jerked straight. "You're damn right I deserve to know!"

Violet opened her mouth to say something, then shut it as if she didn't know what to say.

Tony waited, his gaze never leaving her.

She twisted a lock of hair around her index finger. "I imagined you'd offer to help financially, though I wasn't going to ask—"

"You won't have to worry about money." She lapsed into a coughing fit, and he forced himself to relax his jaw. "Don't think you'll get rid of me that easily. I'm going to be a part of this kid's life."

Violet's fingertips kept twisting her hair, a gesture she couldn't stop. "How do you- aren't you even going to ask if I'm sure it's yours?"

"Should I?"

Violet grabbed the computer mouse and wrapped its cord around her finger, unwound it, then wrapped it around again. "Why... why do you say that?"

Tony's voice grated. "Somehow, you don't strike me as a woman who goes home with a different guy every week."

Violet stiffened, and the mouse fell into her lap.

"Are you?"

"No!" She studied the mouse. "No. Of course not. There hasn't been anyone else since..."

She twisted the mouse cord around her index finger, then her thumb, then untwisted it.

"Since?" He made a rolling motion with his hand.

She grabbed the glass of water with both hands, and lifted it to her lips, finishing the last of it. The glass made a bang when she set it down on the desk. "For as long as I can remember."

"What?" His face twisted. Of all the crazy excuses, he'd never expected that.

"I have retrograde amnesia." She grabbed the glass again, glanced inside, then set it down. "I... I can't remember anything before June ninth. Six years ago."

He quirked an eyebrow. What a crock of bullshit. How could she look so convincing?

"I... I don't know what I did... before. I have no idea how I ended up in the back of Stephanie's ex's truck, in her garage. I don't even know my real name." She started to grab the glass, then picked at her skirt instead. "All I know is I did something terrible. Something that... will probably get me in a great deal of trouble." She looked up and met his gaze. "I was hoping you knew. What did I do?"

"Six years ago? I never met you until you started working in the cafeteria at LCT." He took a step sideways, his narrowed eyes still focused on her as he drew his head away. "I told you that, when you asked me if we'd met." And as far as he knew, they hadn't.

She chewed on her lower lip, nodding, then looked back at her skirt, coughing.

Tony glanced back at the computer screen, and did a double-take when he saw the word entered in the search bar on the Society Intranet web site: *Charlotte.*

As good as Florie's breakfast had tasted, Tony's gut roiled. What if she was telling the truth? What if Everly was wrong, and it was possible to warp into the future after all? *People have tried. Most didn't go anywhere. But the ones who did... no one ever heard from them again.* What if that was because once someone warped into the future, they stayed?

She looked back up at him, her honey-brown eyes shining with such innocence, he almost believed her. Still, the idea didn't sit any better than Florie's skillet gravy. His face hardened, and his words came out short, clipped. "What were you doing with Pippin in 1959?"

"I..." Her mouth moved, but no words came out. She looked down, smoothed her skirt again, then met his gaze. "When I found that card from your wallet... I'd seen that symbol before. I thought maybe I could find help."

Tony's jaw stiffened. *Yeah, help turning me into a mindless zombie like that Fred guy.* "Help with what?"

Her hands finally stilled. "Money. A place to stay. I know I'd said something about asking for work at the motel, but... after seeing how little business they had in the restaurant, I wasn't too hopeful. And... all this time travel... I was scared! Weren't you, when you first did it?"

Hell, yeah, he was scared, he'd gotten his head chopped off. But he wasn't going to let her change the subject. "So the Saturn Society logo looked familiar. You've gone back in time before?"

She looked down and shook her head. "Not that I can remember, but...yes, I think I have. Before." Her eyes went round as she flattened her palms over her lap. "Tony... could it be possible, that we have met? That maybe I went back to a time in the past, but you haven't gone back to that time yet?"

"I guess." Interesting. But wrong. And he couldn't let himself forget that Charlotte had been a skilled liar. He recrossed his arms over his chest and leaned against the doorframe. "I still want to know what you were doing with Pippin."

"Looking for you! He would have given us a place to stay..." She made a sweeping motion. "Like Florie. And Mr. Everly." She pressed her lips together tightly, as if something had just occurred to her. "Do you know Mr. Pippin?"

"What did he tell you?"

"About you?"

Tony tipped his head and glared at her over the top of his glasses.

"Nothing! He just... seemed anxious to find you. So he could help you, too."

"And you stayed with him for two weeks?"

"Of course. He told me that was what the Saturn Society was for, and so did Florie. Why wouldn't I have stayed with him?"

"He treated you well? Did he act like he knew you?"

"He was nothing but kind to me. Why..." She trailed off as Tony backed toward the door.

He turned away, fearing his eyes would betray the feeling of a knife digging into his gut, just like in 1933 when she'd stabbed him, killed him, sent him home.

His breath coming in thick gulps, he strode toward the door and jerked it open.

She jumped up. "Tony, wait! What are—"

He didn't want to turn around, but he couldn't stop himself.

"You- you don't believe me." Her voice wobbled.

"About your *amnesia*?" He jerked his head from side to side with each syllable. "Shit like that only happens in books and movies."

He whirled around and out the door, slamming it behind him, his fears confirmed. Pippin being "nothing but kind" to her clinched it. She hadn't meant to kill him, that night in the river.

She'd intended to disable him. Then hand him over to Pippin.

And now she was pregnant with his child. All he had to do was figure out how to keep her around until the baby was born—and in the meantime, keep his wits about him.

Seven

TONY HAD A BAD FEELING WHEN HE RETURNED TO THE HOUSE TO FIND A white Jeep Grand Cherokee with Ohio plates parked beside Florie's Land Rover.

He hesitated at the front door. If Everly had come to take him and Violet back to Dayton, did that mean the Society would post bail when Tony was inevitably arrested? Hopefully, the fact that there wasn't a police cruiser parked beside the Jeep was a good sign.

He took a last glance behind him as he opened the door. Had the dark haze gathering over the mountains thickened? He lingered in the doorway, studying the clouds—no, not clouds. Smoke.

He hurried inside to the living room. "Hey, Flo—whoa!" He barely caught himself before he fell over Rufus—and the woman on the floor beneath the big dog.

Giggles erupted from her, and as Rufus leaned close to get in another lick on her face, her shimmering, blond hair caught the light.

"You!" Tony's mouth fell open but he snapped it shut. *The dog lady!* "I mean, what—how..."

Everly appeared in the doorway to the kitchen. "I was going to call you when you when Alpha woke from recovery, but she couldn't stay." He looked sideways at her, reproach beneath his ever-present smile.

"I had things to do. Like keep an eye on Tony." Her mouth tipped up in a tiny imitation of Everly's as she extricated herself from Rufus and pushed herself up, brushing her legs as she stood.

"Who—why—" Tony started to ask.

"Dinner's on!" Florie leaned through the doorway, making a waving motion. Rufus dashed into the kitchen.

Everly cracked a big smile. "You haven't known Florie for long, but believe me, keeping dinner waiting isn't wise." He, Tony, and Alpha filed into the eat-in kitchen, where Violet already sat at the table. Tony couldn't push aside the niggling idea that he needed to tell Florie something, but damned if he could remember what.

Everyone sat. Tony took the last spot left where a place had been set.

"Dig in, everyone," Florie urged. "Won't be no good cold."

Tony reached for the bowl of green beans in front of him, only to meet the gaze of Violet, seated across from him. He looked away.

He hardly tasted Florie's fried chicken, mashed potatoes and gravy, or the green beans cooked the way his grandma used to make them. Seeing Violet across from him made it hard to force a bite down his throat, so he kept his eyes on his plate and made himself eat. For all he knew, it could be the last good, home-cooked meal he'd get in a long time.

Beside him, the dog lady—*Alpha*—pushed her hair behind her ears, then bent to sneak Rufus a bite of chicken, even that simple motion full of grace. She could have been a model, but stirred nothing in Tony except curiosity and gratitude. "Um, Alpha, I don't mean to sound ungrateful, but... who are you? And why—"

"You're a very important person in the Society—or you will be. As will your descendants." She laughed, a musical chuckle. Rufus, hovering at her side, sneaked a lick on her hand.

"You mean..." Tony glanced at Violet, and his stomach pitched to the floor.

"Yes. That's why your enemies are after her, too."

"But how—what about the man who looks like Tony?" Violet asked. "Do you know him?"

Alpha's expression darkened. "I know of him. An assassin with a strangling fixation. Lucky for you, an incompetent one. Be assured his superiors will deal with him—and send someone else after you. Someone who won't botch the job. You're not safe here. Or anywhere in this time. No matter where you go, they'll find you."

"Then how can we get away from those people?" Violet asked. "If they can find us anywhere we go..."

Alpha gave her a tight-lipped smile. "I said they could find you no matter *where* you go. Did they find you when you went into the past?

Violet and Tony looked at each other. "No," Tony said. "But I wasn't there for long." *Thanks to you.* He kept his gaze on Violet.

She jerked hers back to Alpha. "I was there—ah, *then*, for two and a half weeks. At the Dayton Society House. They never came after me, and I'd think that would be the first place they'd look."

"Exactly. They can find you in a limited span of time—your natural time."

Everly held up a finger. "But when you add in centuries, or even decades, the world becomes that much bigger a place."

"But won't they pursue us into the past?" Violet asked.

"If they figure out when you go to." Alpha gave her a smile that might have come across as patronizing if it had come from someone else, in a less serious situation.

"But what about the baby? Is it safe for me to jump—"

"You jumped home from 1959, didn't you?" Alpha said.

"As far as we know, regular jumps are fine," Everly said. "The biggest risk is death in the past. You'll still return to the present, but you're almost certain to miscarry—more so the further along your pregnancy is. So try not to get killed." His usual smile slipped back into place at his lame attempt to inject levity into the conversation.

"But what about medical care?" Violet pressed.

"You needn't go back far." Alpha's expression remained impassive.

"They didn't find me in 1972." Then Tony's hope crashed down. "But if we only go back forty years, it won't take long for Pull to hit. Not to mention if Theodore Pippin finds me—"

"Humph!" Florie said. "That man's a disgrace to the Society. Tracking people, flinging wild accusations—"

"You know him?" Tony's eyes went wide.

Florie snorted. "Theodore Pippin's no better than the folks who are huntin' you. The Society's supposed to be all about helpin' people, not huntin' 'em down."

A tiny bit of Tony's tension trickled away. Florie's firm expression and sharp tone held a sincerity he couldn't imagine being faked. If she despised Pippin, then she was okay as far as he was concerned. "So what—"

Florie cut him off. "Just who are these people who're after Violet and Tony?" she asked Alpha.

"Yeah," Tony said. "Who are they, and why are they after us?"

"They're with a group called the Order of Titan. A splinter faction of the Society many years in your future. They believe those with our gift should be able to use it however they please—and now they've brought the Society's struggle to this era, seeking to destroy their opponents before they become a threat." She met Tony's gaze. "Your progeny will lead the Society in opposition, so they're trying to eliminate its roots. You."

Queasiness trickled down Tony's throat. The baby. He—or she—was the whole reason behind their pursuit.

Violet frowned. "Aren't they worried that their deliberate changes to the past will create time bubbles?"

"Oh, Lordy," Florie said. "Like that bridge on the news."

Violet's face went blank, and her question echoed Tony's. "Bridge?"

"Last week," Everly said. "In West Virginia. Huge bridge, disappeared, just like that." He snapped his fingers. "Killed dozens of people in cars that were traveling over it at the time."

"Holy shit," Tony said.

"Mercy!" Violet squeezed her hands together. "That doesn't concern them?"

"Not these people." Alpha set her silverware on her plate and pushed back her chair, though she'd eaten little. "They consider it a small price to pay for supremacy."

"Heavens to Betsy," Florie murmured.

Tony chewed on his lower lip. One thing didn't add up.

He studied Alpha's face. His guardian angel from the future. "The times you've come back to help me—weren't you breaking Society law as much as these people are?"

"It was a matter of committing small wrongs to right larger ones. As is my offer of future technology to make your trip to the past safer."

Everly's smile folded in on itself. "I'm still not sure that's a good idea."

"You agreed that we need to do all we can to even the battlefield."

Violet sat up straight. "What future technology?"

"An injection that will provide immunity against many more illnesses than possible today. Especially considering your condition and the fact that you'll miss your next few doctors' visits."

"Good heavens, I will, won't I?"

"The injection will also reduce your recovery time. If you don't go back far, an ordinary night's sleep may be all you need. And you'll be able to stay in the past a lot longer before the Pull brings you back. You should be able to stay in the sixties for two or three months." She pushed back her chair and stood. "Which should give me time to neutralize our enemies in this time."

Everly's obnoxious smile dimmed as he looked from Violet to Tony. "Did Florie give you the paperwork?"

"Yes," Violet said.

Tony's jaw tensed. The paperwork Everly had tried to get him to sign a dozen times since his first trip to the past. Paperwork that gave the Society control of his assets, "for when you're gone long enough that you need help taking care of business on this end," Everly had said.

"My parents have power of attorney over all my stuff," Tony grumbled. He'd signed those papers before the second time he went back to see Charlotte in 1933, in case anything happened to him.

But of course, Violet would have signed her life over to the Society. She had in the early 20th century, why would today be any different? Not to mention that she didn't even own property. Signing the papers meant the Society would take care of her car payment and student loans.

His insides twisted. How the hell could he live with her for three months? But if Alpha spoke the truth, did he have a choice?

He had to. Had to stick with Violet, had to protect her, had to keep the baby safe. It didn't matter who she was.

He trusted Alpha. After all, she was his guardian angel. "So what's our plan? Where do we make the jump? And when to?"

Alpha gave him that almost-patronizing smile again. "We'll have to go back to Dayton. I didn't bring the universal immunizations here with me. But as far as when, that's up to you. Within your limitations, of course."

Great. He cast a narrowed glance at Everly. "So is the Society going to bail me out of jail first? Or do I jump from there and make a nice target for Pippin?"

Everly at least had the decency to wipe that annoying, ever-present grin off his face. "The Society will take care of you. I've already contacted headquarters to get legal counsel lined up. But you're right, it would probably be better to go back in another location."

Alpha looked from Everly to Tony, then back. "But they really need the universal—"

Tony broke in. "So we go back to Dayton. Fortunately, it will be dark by the time we get there. Then we'll go... I don't know, somewhere Pippin's not."

"Pippin?" Alpha asked. "What's the problem with—"

"He's in the Black Book," Everly explained.

Alpha's mouth formed an O as she met Tony's gaze. "What did you do?"

Tony drew back. "Nothing!" At least nothing that was for his own gain. "It's probably the guy who looks like me."

"Then we can just tell Mr. Pippin," Violet said. "I've seen your double, I'll vouch—"

"Yeah, like Pippin would believe that." Tony snorted. "He wasn't exactly interested in talking the last time he saw me."

"It was an accident!" Violet's hands gripped wads of her skirt.

Florie humphed.

Everly started to say something when the phone rang from the entryway.

Florie's eyebrows shot up. "I better get that." She hurried off, muttering about not getting many phone calls. Rufus tore himself away from Alpha's petting hand to follow.

Violet picked at the seam of her dress, avoiding Tony's gaze. "You know, you don't have to go with me. It's the baby those horrible people are after, and—"

"No way in hell are you going alone. Not when they could figure out where—or when—we've gone, and follow." He crossed his arms over his chest. "You're not going without me." Not when his son or daughter was growing inside her.

Florie returned, wringing her hands, Rufus at her side. "That was Sheriff Winston."

Tony's scalp prickled. They'd found him.

"Wildfires, a little ways south o' here." Florie grabbed her Kitchen Sink bag off a stand. "County's ordered an evacuation."

"The smoke!" Tony's heart slowed back to normal. "I saw it when I was out running."

"Well, that's it." Alpha drew herself straight and leaned toward the door. "We'd best be leaving anyway."

"What about you?" Violet asked Florie.

The other woman waved her off. "Don't you worry about me, honey, I'll go visit with Jim O'Donnell in Lexington fer a spell."

Alpha gripped the doorknob. "Anyone need anything else before we go?"

Tony's hand flexed in his pocket. Both of his choices sucked, but he'd do what he could to reduce the risks. He turned to Everly. "Do you have any weapons at your place that I could..." He tried to ignore Violet's wide-eyed stare. "...take with me when we go back?" He let his gaze rest on her. "I don't want to go more than a hundred years. And we can't travel far in this time, or I might be recognized, so..."

"Pippin," Florie finished.

"I've got firearms." Everly held out his hands, palms up. "But I doubt eighteenth-century flintlocks are what you had in mind."

"Here." Florie reached into her bag and pulled out a black handgun and pressed it into Tony's hands.

A Sig Sauer 40mm. "Just like mine." He double-checked that the safety was on, then popped the magazine out. Six rounds filled it.

Before he could close the magazine, Florie dropped a box of ammo into his hands on top of the weapon. "Hope y'never have to use it, but..."

"Me, too." Thanking her, he dropped the ammo into the pocket of the khaki slacks she'd given him the night before.

Violet fought to contain her coughing as they walked out the door and headed for Everly's Jeep. Smoke blanketed the valley, but wasn't thick enough to conceal the pond far below. It was heavier in the valley where the bridge crossed, making the structure look like it floated on gray clouds. Tony shuddered at a sensation of falling, of rough hands pushing him over the rail...

Violet glanced up sharply, and he knew that she knew he'd had another alternate-timeline memory episode.

Alpha crouched to wrap her arms around Rufus' neck, murmuring baby talk to the big dog as she let him lick her face. Florie gave Violet a hug. "Be careful." She grasped Tony's hand. "Take care of her." As he assured her he would, she reached into the Kitchen Sink looped over her shoulder. "Oh! Here, take these for later, in case y'all get hungry." She grabbed something from her bag, dropping two dog biscuits, which Rufus snapped up, before she thrust a few packages of peanut butter crackers into Violet's shaking hands.

Violet thanked her, then dropped the crackers into her windbreaker's pockets, two on each side. She grabbed the Jeep's back door handle, but didn't open it. A cool breeze lifted her hair.

Something sank inside Tony. As hurt and angry as he was, her fear tore at him. "You okay?" he asked softly.

Her nod was barely visible in the smoke-obscured sunlight. In the distance, thunder rolled. Her hand dropped to her lap. "I- I just have a bad feeling."

Bethany punched the lock button when she pulled up to an intersection where three skinheads loitered beneath a streetlight, giving her leering stares. *They're just checking out the car,* she told herself. The bright yellow Camaro wasn't exactly inconspicuous. But still, it was no wonder Aunt Lisa had argued about her going out so late. Good thing Bethany hadn't mentioned to her aunt exactly where Taylor lived. The city and the university had cleaned up the student housing neighborhood known as the Ghetto, enough that the name no longer fit, but Taylor's house was beyond the area of new development. Besides, Bethany couldn't say no to Taylor. Not when her friend said it was urgent, and couldn't tell her anything over the phone because it was too important.

The light changed to green and Bethany's grip on the wheel relaxed as she drove past the far end of campus and spied the Harrison Street sign.

Her tummy tingled with excitement and dread as she scanned the house numbers. *Still a ways away.* Maybe Taylor had won the lottery. Or gotten asked out by that cute guy in her history class at Sinclair, and she needed advice on something to wear. That Goth stuff had to get old sometimes.

A horn blared as she crossed a side street. Crap, she'd run a stop sign. *Stupid Mark.*

He'd told Bethany she ought to stop hanging out with Taylor; that it upset his mom. But Aunt Lisa had never seemed to mind Taylor coming over. Mark was full of B.S., and Bethany told him so. Then Mark accused her of only liking Taylor because she was the only one who thought her dad didn't kill Danny.

Bethany had wanted to claw his face off, even though she knew he'd retaliate and beat the crap out of her. So she left. Probably a good thing, although she'd wasted a good couple gallons of gas driving around aimlessly. Finally, eleven rolled around, and she went to meet Taylor.

Bethany squinted at the house numbers. They were getting lower, so she slowed down. The residences grew more run-down the farther she got from U.D., but Taylor said hers was the one kept up nice.

A porch light cast a welcoming glow at a stately, red brick Victorian. Bethany slowed to read the wall plaque. *143, that's it.* She parked and walked up the sidewalk, casting nervous glances aside, keys in her fist.

She tried to talk herself out of feeling jumpy. *Chill out. Taylor's probably just being a drama queen.* But she'd never invited Bethany over before, and every time Bethany had hinted at it, Taylor always had some excuse.

As she walked up the three steps to the porch, Bethany scanned the plaque. Beneath a logo of the planet Saturn and three stars—the same symbol she'd seen on Taylor's MasterCard and her car decal—Bethany read:

THE SATURN SOCIETY

DAYTON HOUSE

EST. 1914

Oh, yeah. She'd looked up the Saturn Society on the Internet, after Taylor left that time she made the weird phone call. As Taylor had told her, the organization's web site said they researched time travel. *Yeah, right,* her dad would say. No way would he involve himself in something that whacked.

Shivering in a cool breeze that smelled of coming rain, Bethany gazed at the sky. Reflected, city light bathed the clouds in an orange-tinted haze. Did Taylor's phone call have something to do with her dad?

Bethany lifted her hand, but as she reached for the doorbell, the door swung open and a man burst out. She barely saw his black ski mask before he barreled into her, forcing the breath from her lungs. The next thing she knew, her butt hit the porch with a muffled thud. "Sorry, B," he muttered, then picked himself up and ran off.

What the crap? Bethany rubbed her butt as Taylor flew out the door and crouched beside her. "Oh, God, are you okay?" Her voice was even louder than usual.

Bethany pushed herself up. "Yeah, he just knocked the wind out of me." She patted the gray-painted, wood planks. "Glad your porch isn't concrete."

Taylor waited while she stood, then led her inside, through an ornate foyer with a roll-top desk, and into an elegant dining room where expensive-looking wallpaper and paintings decorated the walls. She pulled out a chair from a polished, dark wood dining table that had to be an antique. "Man, is Chad going to be pissed."

"Did he get something valuable?"

"No, but I'm not supposed to leave while he's gone. But I was dying for a Mountain Dew, and we were out. I figured, what could a five minute trip to the carryout hurt, y'know?" She grabbed a cordless phone and waved at the table. "I gotta call the cops. Help yourself."

Condensation glistened on a six-pack of Mountain Dew. "You got any diet?"

"Oh crap, I forgot you're diabetic. There might be some Diet Coke in the fridge."

Bethany found it and sat at the table. Her fingers twitched on the pop can and the jumpy feeling came back. Taylor described the incident to the police, then called Chad and did the same. "No, it was just an ordinary burglar. Far as I can tell, he didn't get anything. All I saw was the TV in the parlor pulled out, like he was about to take it. Probably wanting cash to buy his next rock, y'know?" A pause. "Fred's upstairs watching TV. Never even came out."

Bethany took a swig of her Diet Coke. Who was Fred?

The doorbell rang. "I gotta go, the cops are here." Taylor hurried to the door. "Yeah, she's here now. You're in northern Kentucky? Okay, see you in about an hour."

Bethany waited in the kitchen while Taylor talked to the policemen. Thanks to Taylor's loud voice, she had little trouble hearing. As Taylor described the burglar's flight, Bethany wondered if she should mention that the man apologized to her. Would an ordinary thief have done that? And she wasn't sure, but it'd sounded like he said *Sorry, B.*

B as in Bethany.

A shudder coursed through her. Did the guy know her?

Nuh-uh. She just imagined it. Or maybe he mistook her for someone else.

But his voice had sounded familiar.

She traced circles in the moisture on Taylor's pop. Who had the burglar's voice reminded her of? Not someone she knew well, but someone she liked. Not someone who'd break into a house and steal. She racked her brain while she paged through a history textbook lying on the table, but nothing more came to her.

Bored, she wandered to an antique bookshelf where a hardback novel in a bright, orange jacket caught her attention. *The Boone Conspiracy*, by Charles Everly. She tilted her head. Taylor's roommate was a writer?

She grabbed the book and skimmed the reviews. According to them, Mr. Everly was the up-and-coming author to watch in historical fiction, and the twenty-first century's answer to James Fenimore Cooper. Taylor's discussion with the cops faded as Bethany took the book to the table. It quickly pulled her in.

She didn't stop reading until she started to feel lightheaded.

She glanced at the wall clock. She hadn't eaten in... she counted off on her fingers. Five hours since dinner. No wonder she felt like crap. As she rose to ask Taylor for a bite to eat, a low groan came from the foyer.

"Hhuuuuuuuunnnnggggghhhh!"

Bethany's insides curdled. What the heck was that?

She crept toward the doorway, then the moan came again. From upstairs.

Taylor emerged from the parlor, holding up a hand as Bethany approached. "Hang on, I gotta go take care of something..."

Bethany leaned toward the steps as her friend pounded up them. "Taylor? I gotta get something to eat. My blood sugar—"

Taylor stopped and waved toward the dining room. "Get whatever you want from the fridge or the cabinets." She rushed up the stairs, disappearing around the landing in a froth of black skirts.

Bethany rummaged through the cabinets and fridge until she found cheese and crackers—enough to tide her over—then returned to the dining room and the book.

Ten minutes later, Taylor came downstairs and finished talking to the cops. As she showed them to the door, Bethany dug into her purse.

Crap, crap, crap. Her insulin pen wasn't there. She'd been so pissed at Mark, she'd rushed out the door without one. First time she'd done that in years. She jammed her hand to the bottom of her purse to double check. No insulin pen. But as she withdrew her hand, her fingers grazed a smooth, irregularly shaped object.

She pulled out a finger-sized, blown glass cat figurine. *Huh?* Her lip curled.

Taylor. She'd admired the little cat in a gift shop the other day at the mall.

Bethany's chest felt crackly. Taylor had ripped the cat off. But why had she stuck it in Bethany's purse? What if the cops saw it?

Taylor lingered in the doorway, assuring the cops she'd call if she remembered anything else. Bethany laid the cat beside the textbook. "Taylor?"

The other girl returned to the kitchen. "Ugh, that took about forever." She frowned. "You sure you're okay? That guy didn't hurt—"

"I have to go, I forgot my insulin. What'd you need me for, anyway?"

"Chad... uh..." Taylor chewed on her lip. "It has to do with your dad."

Bethany gasped. "Oh. My. God. Is he okay? Where's he been? What's he have to do with Chad? And how—"

"I don't know, they'll be here in about twenty minutes—"

"They'll? You mean my dad—"

"Umm... if you can just hang on another twenty minutes or so..."

"Oh crap, no—"

"Go get your stuff. And hurry back."

Violet followed Tony closely as Mr. Everly led them into the Dayton House's back door. "Thank heavens Florie's all right." Florie had called just before they reached Dayton to let them know the wildfire had been contained, the cause determined to be a campfire.

Alpha closed the door behind her. "It just goes to show, we need to get you two out of here and now as soon as possible."

Tony stopped, and Violet almost ran into him. "You don't think those fires were accidental?"

"We can't discount the possibility," Alpha said.

"I want to see my daughter," Tony grumbled. Violet's lips tightened. Would he be as caring a parent to their child?

Mr. Everly started to answer him as Taylor appeared in a mass of swirling, black skirts. "Bethany had to go home for her insulin."

Tony's shoulders slumped, and Violet could almost feel his happiness drain away. "When did she leave?" he asked.

Taylor shrugged. "About ten minutes ago."

Mr. Everly led them to the parlor. "Sit down, make yourself comfortable." He motioned to a Victorian-styled, upholstered sofa—the same one that Mr. Pippin had owned in 1959. It had given her a squeamish feeling whenever she sat in it.

As if something bad had happened there *before.*

Tony plopped onto the couch. Alpha slid into the overstuffed chair where Mr. Pippin had always sat, leaving Violet no choice but to sit beside Tony. She lowered herself onto the sofa, taking care to leave plenty of space between them.

"I'll be back," Mr. Everly muttered as he disappeared into the kitchen. Violet had no trouble hearing him. "What *ever* possessed you to leave the House? What if we got a visitor? What about Fred?"

"*Law and Order* was on, you know he never moves—"

"He does during commercials! Let me guess, you didn't think."

Taylor blubbered incoherently. Violet wanted to squirm. She tuned her out by turning her attention to Alpha. "What about that immunization you're going to give us?"

Alpha jerked straight. "Oh! Let me go get them." She jumped up and dashed out of the room.

Violet let her gaze drift to Tony. Her skin tingled, as if her body was suddenly aware they were alone. He didn't look at her, his gaze fixed on the doorway into the kitchen, where Mr. Everly and Taylor now spoke in hushed tones.

Alpha returned, gripping a stainless steel cylinder the size of a thick marker. "We might as well get this taken care of. Who's first?"

Tony shuddered. "What's that?"

"It's like a syringe. But unlike the ones in use today, you'll barely feel it."

Tony gave a sharp nod and stood, holding his arm out to Alpha. The tube made a *pffft* as she pressed its end to the back of his hand.

He pressed his thumb to the injection site. "There's something in here. Like a splinter."

Alpha nodded. "It's a time-release delivery mechanism that enables the immunity to mutate and combat new strains of disease as they develop."

Violet rose slowly. Her belly twitched, and she gripped her left wrist with her other hand. "You're sure this is safe for the baby?"

"In my time, everyone gets it," Alpha said. "The baby's much better off with the immunization."

Violet gave a shaky nod, then held out her hand. Alpha pressed the tube to Violet's hand. After the *pffft*—it felt like someone poked her hand with a finger, more pressure than pain—Alpha slipped the tube into her jeans pocket and sat in Mr. Pippin's chair. She grabbed the remote from the end table beside her and turned on the flat screen TV that looked out of place on the doily-topped, antique radio cabinet in the corner.

Violet ran her fingers over the back of her hand. Like Tony said, the thin, raised bump felt like a splinter just beneath her skin, but wasn't painful. "How does it work?" she asked. "What diseases does it prevent that we can't today, and how does it speed recovery time?"

Alpha gave her a patronizing smile, like insincere customer service reps gave to people whose problems they couldn't—or didn't want to—solve. "You know I can't answer that."

"You mean you're not allowed, or you don't know—"

"Hhhnnnnnnggggg!"

Violet's head whirled around at the groan in the doorway. "Oh, no." *Not him.*

"Haaaarrrrr!" Mr. Everly's brain-damaged ward tumbled though the entryway and lurched toward her. "Shaaaaarrrrr!" Violet recoiled as he drew near, but the old man grabbed her shoulders and pulled her toward him, fixing her with a wild-eyed stare.

Violet smacked his hand. "Get away!" He jerked his hand away, but gripped harder with the other.

"Fred! No!" Alpha jumped up and pulled him off of Violet. "Let's go back to your room. Your show's back on." She dragged him away.

Violet shuddered. Why was he so interested in her? She'd tried to be nice to him during her prior stay at the House, but the fellow had literally thrown himself at her—no, more like tried to attack her. Mr. Everly said he'd never seen Fred behave like that.

Tony just sat there, chin propped on his hand. "Doesn't like you very much, does he?" He stared straight ahead, refusing to look at her. As he'd done the rest of the ride home, after Violet had asked Mr. Everly about the baby.

The Watchkeeper had confirmed her fear that the child would almost certainly be time travel gifted—not genetically, but from her, through the trauma of birth. He'd also explained that when young children born with the ability started to jump—usually no sooner than age five or six—the mother was often pulled along, due to the emotional bond. But the only time Mr. Everly had heard of it happening with a father was in one case where the child's mother had died.

At that, Tony had given her an almost-imperceptible glare.

As if it was all Violet's fault.

The rest of the ride home was no better, and gave Violet too much time to think about him. Did he resent her because of the baby? Even though he insisted he wanted the child? Or was it her willingness to rely on the Society when he held them in such distrust?

The hardest part was the wanting, the longing to touch him, the yearning to sink into his arms. *A mistake,* he'd said of her pregnancy. Violet couldn't disagree, but his words cut.

She picked at the parlor sofa's floral print upholstery. Though

Tony sat but inches away, it might as well have been a mile. Violet ached to scoot over, close the distance between them, and fold herself into his side.

Instead, she pretended to watch television. On the news, a reporter droned on about unrest in the Middle East. Some things never changed.

The picture grew blurry and wavered. Violet blinked. It worsened, and the newscaster's face contorted in pixelated blocks. The sounds jumbled, then faded. "What's wrong with the television?"

"Probably the cable." Tony grabbed the remote control and pointed it at the television, but before he touched a button, the picture cleared.

A moonlit, woodland scene appeared. Green undergrowth adorned the forest floor. Silver shafts of moonlight streamed in horizontal bands through budding trees that stretched to the sky. An unseen brook danced over rocks or perhaps a waterfall. Every few seconds, a tree frog croaked.

Violet frowned. A commercial for a cleaning product? Or perhaps an environmental message? That forest was probably what the world had been like before people had polluted the air and water. Untouched. Pristine. No highway noise or aircraft. Just the sounds of nature. That air would smell as clean as—

Her vision went black as dizziness knocked her to the side. "Tony!" She groped for him and found his trousers and held on tight. His arms wrapped around her, then all sensation slipped away but the reeling, twisting, whirling...

Violet's head stopped spinning to leave her with a prickly, scratchy sensation beneath her hands and her fanny. She opened her eyes and looked down.

Weeds and brush, bathed in ghostly white moonlight.

Everything was deathly still. No traffic buzzing by outside. No TV.

No sirens blaring from the nearby hospital.

From a few feet away, a cricket chirped. Not one hundred percent quiet, then.

The hospital wasn't there. Nor was the House. No street or traffic. The Society House's parlor had disappeared, replaced by forestland and budding trees stretching up in the moonlight.

As if to confirm her conclusion, a tree frog croaked.

Like on television. A chill rushed down her throat.

A breeze ruffled her sleeve, her arm cold when Tony withdrew his hand. Her chills turned to quivers at the realization he'd been touching her. An ache swelled beneath her breast. She longed to lean into him, soak in his warmth, but she didn't dare.

He gazed around with a wide-eyed, open-mouthed stare.

"Where on earth are we?" Violet asked. The crisp tang of recent rain hung in the air. In the distance, the frog croaked again.

"Hell if I know," Tony said. Something rustled in the underbrush. Probably a squirrel or some other woodland creature.

"We jumped, didn't we?" As the ground's coldness seeped into her skin, Violet pushed herself up. Undergrowth crackled beneath her. She took a few tentative steps, her legs and arms growing heavier with each motion. "Only we must have jumped in space, too."

"I've never heard of it working that way." Tony rose beside her. "All I know is, recovery's already hitting me. We need to find somewhere to crash, fast."

Heavens, he was right. She needed to lie down. Now. "Yes, but where?"

They surveyed their surroundings again, as if wishing would make a Paradise Motel magically appear.

Tony took another wobbly step. "Doesn't look like we have much choice, I'm..." He yawned.

Violet's eyes fell closed. Her knees buckled, and she started to collapse, but Tony caught her.

He helped her to a pile of undergrowth at the base of a gigantic tree, one that had to have been over eight feet in diameter, with a little hollow formed by the roots. As soon as he released her, she sank into it. A breeze lifted a few dry leaves, and she shivered. Underbrush crackled as Tony lowered himself to the ground and squeezed in beside her. "We'll need to keep warm, okay?" She mumbled an assent as he wrapped his arm over her and pressed against her back. *He's only being practical.*

She wouldn't think about how good he felt, or the heat rising inside her that had nothing to do with physical warmth. *Necessity. Nothing more.* Her worries about the baby, the killers, and what Tony thought of her slipped away. There was only now, cold, and recovery.

A shiver drove down her. Not from the wind, but something she remembered Mr. Pippin saying: *You jump in time, never in space.*

They'd gone back indeed, much further than intended.

Not decades. Centuries.

Eight

BETHANY SPED ALL THE WAY BACK TO TAYLOR'S HOUSE, AND WAS OUT OF breath by the time she ran up the steps and rang the doorbell. Luckily, that cop she'd seen when she crossed Stewart Street hadn't come after her. In Dayton, surely they had bigger things to worry about.

She punched the doorbell again, then pressed herself close to the door as the cop car rolled past. *Pay no attention to that yellow Camaro parked on Harrison Street.* After the cruiser turned the corner, she peeled herself away from the wall and rang the doorbell again before she noticed the door was open a crack. She nudged it open farther.

"...gone back much farther than we planned," a woman said. Light spilled through the doorway into the room to the left where Taylor had talked to the cops. Bethany crept inside, banging her shin on the roll top desk. "Hello?"

A short Hispanic guy with a black goatee and ponytail held up something that looked like a computer chip, about the size of a disposable lighter. "Some kind of hypnotic—" He looked up at Bethany, along with Taylor and the tall blonde he'd been talking to. "You must be Bethany." A big smile spread across his face.

"Ye-es," Bethany said slowly.

"Oh! I'm sorry." Taylor leaped to her side and made the introductions.

Bethany scanned the room, a living room—no, a parlor, filled with antique furniture—as she mumbled a hello to Chad and Alpha. "Um, Taylor? What about..." Where was her dad? "You told me they had information..."

"Um, well…" Taylor looked at Chad.

"I'm really sorry, Bethany." The man's smile faded, but not completely. "Taylor was a bit… *premature* in calling you. We thought we had a lead on your dad, but…" He turned up his hands. "Turned out to be bogus. I'm sorry you drove all the way out here for nothing. If we hear anything from your dad, you'll be the first to know."

Bethany cocked her head. "But… didn't you call the police?"

"Do you want your dad to go to jail?"

"No! But…" Her mind tumbled over the possibilities. "How do you know… he didn't do it?"

The blond woman—she looked a little familiar, but Bethany couldn't place her—spoke up. "Your father has a double, Bethany."

A double? "You mean someone who looks like him?"

"Exactly," Alpha said with a decisive nod.

"We believe that's the guilty party," Chad said. "But until we find him, there's not much we can do. Nor is it safe for your dad to return from wherever he went."

This was getting weirder and weirder. Bethany searched the room, but found no clues in the doily-draped, overstuffed chair or the old-fashioned radio cabinet, or the flat-screen TV on the floor beside it.

Her gaze landed on the computer chip thing that Chad held in a fist. Only a black corner of it showed beneath his thumb. "So what do you guys have to do with all this? What's this Saturn Society, anyway?"

He flashed her that smile again—jeez, did the guy ever stop smiling?—and spoke in a patient voice, like her mom used to when she was explaining something she didn't think Bethany was quite old enough to understand. "We're a research organization. Your dad… we'd been talking to him about a funding grant from his company."

Bethany wrinkled her nose. "Why would LCT fund… whatever kind of research you're doing?"

"Well, um…" Taylor looked at Chad again, and when he met her gaze, filled in. "We research time travel. Which, okay, it's a long shot, but if there's something to it… well, it would give any company an advantage, you know?"

"I guess." Bethany's gaze slid over Chad, the other woman—the one she couldn't figure out where she'd seen before—and back to her friend. "So, you don't know anything about my dad?"

Chad pressed his lips together tightly as he shook his head once. "Afraid not. Other than that he's alive and okay..." He turned up his hands again, his smile fainter, but still there.

Alive and okay. Well, that was something, at least. Bethany exhaled a thick breath and realized she was really tired. What had Alpha meant—who'd gone back farther than planned? Her dad? And gone back where?

"Wow, it's late." Taylor laid a hand on her shoulder. "I'll call you tomorrow. Maybe we can go check out that new shoe store at the mall you were telling me about?"

Bethany searched her friend's face.

Taylor's left eye twitched.

"Yeah, sure, sounds good."

Taylor walked her through the foyer and stood in the doorway until Bethany got into her car and drove away.

Sure, they'd go shoe shopping tomorrow. But before she and Taylor met up, Bethany might do some shopping of her own.

Listening devices and hidden cameras weren't that expensive—Danny had done his senior research paper on spy technology last year in school. Bethany had read it.

She could buy something like that, hide it in Taylor's car, or better yet, her house.

Taylor and Chad and that Alpha chick were lying to her. They might not know where her dad was, but they knew something.

And she would find out.

Tony woke to a musty scent of earth and vegetation, and his arms wrapped around something warm and soft, like a pillow, but bigger—

Violet! The fogginess of recovery slipped away. He pulled his arm off of her, but it was stiff, hard to move—no, the fabric of his jacket sleeve was crusted with something. *What the...* He rolled aside, and his sleeve crackled. Couldn't see worth shit, his glasses were a mess, but at least he still had them. Unable to see anything but murky haze, he patted his arm. *Dried mud?*

Dirt flaked off as he pulled off the windbreaker Florie had given him, grateful to find his shirt beneath clean and dry. He swiped his glasses off and spit on them enough to clean them with the shirttail, then looked up.

Leaves filled the branches, blocking out most of a sunny, blue sky. A lush, green undergrowth surrounded him and Violet. Unease grew like a balloon in his chest, swelling, choking, cutting off his air. *Centuries.* Before the Society House. Before Dayton. Nothing but forestland. How long had they slept?

A warm breeze lifted a few strands of Violet's hair. As she stirred, dried mud flecked off her clothing. She made a startled noise and her eyes went round.

Tony brushed the dirt off her. "How're you feeling?" Breathing in all that dust and mold couldn't be good for her or the baby.

She drew in a big breath, then exhaled as she pushed herself up. "All right. I think."

No coughing. Recovery must have cured the effects of the smoke inhalation.

His heart jumped when he glimpsed movement in the underbrush. He scanned the area, didn't see anything else. *An animal.* No shooters from the future. No one chasing them.

Violet's lower lip trembled.

A hollowness swelled beneath Tony's ribs, one he didn't want to dwell on. "I think we're safe, at least for now." His words and logic didn't quell the pull toward her. He gathered her into his arms. She sank into his embrace and tipped her face up, and it seemed the most natural thing in the world to brush his lips across hers.

He stroked her hair and she met his kiss. The hollowness grew, then became fullness, in the soft sensation of her mouth on his. She left her eyes open. Like Charlotte had—

He jerked away. *Charlotte.*

"Tony? What's wrong?"

"Nothing. It's just..." He searched her eyes. No sign of subterfuge. No veiled threat hidden beneath her desire. Nothing but fierce need, an emptiness only he could fill. The same as it had been at the motel in 1959.

Want and anxiety shrank into leaden resolve. This time, he wouldn't fall for her schemes. He got up, brushing dirt off himself. "We need to find food. And water."

Violet stood and took off her jacket. "Mercy, it's warm. How long do you suppose we slept?"

Tony peered at the greenery. "Well, considering that the trees were just beginning to get leaves when we warped, I'd say at least a week."

Violet followed his gaze. "It looks more like mid-May to me. And all this dried mud..." She tried to thread her fingers through her hair but they caught on tangles. "We got rained on more than once, too." She cocked her head, studying his face. "Yet if we'd been in recovery that long, wouldn't you have a beard?"

Tony rubbed his chin. "Everly told me it's sort of like hibernation, so maybe hair growth also slows down."

She tied the arms of her jacket around her waist, frowning when something else crackled. She stuck a hand into the pocket and withdrew two plastic-wrapped snacks.

"What's that?" Tony asked.

She held them out. "From Florie. Crushed, I'm afraid, but it's food." She grimaced. The crackers were mostly crumbs pressed into flat squares of peanut butter.

"You eat them. I'll be okay." His stomach grumbled.

"I have more." She thrust them at him while she pulled two more from her other pocket.

It wasn't much, but Tony was grateful for Florie's foresight. He opened the plastic carefully so he wouldn't drop a single crumb, ate the big chunks first, then tipped the wrapper back to pour the rest into his mouth.

Violet did the same, then turned the plastic over and licked off the last traces of peanut butter. Tony looked away as he shoved his trash into his pocket. Her tongue swirling over the plastic reminded him of things he shouldn't be thinking of. Like her pink tongue swirling over him instead...

Tightness built below his waist, but he was able to stop it. *Don't think about it.* He unclenched fists he hadn't realized he'd made. "I figure our best bet to find water is to go that way." He pointed.

Violet looked in that direction. "Why?"

"Because if this is where the Society House will eventually be built, the river's just west of here." He looked up at the sun. It had been a little lower behind them when they'd first awoke, which meant west was ahead.

She swallowed. "Hopefully, we'll find a little stream or creek before then."

"Maybe. Let's go." He started to walk, but she remained. "Unless you'd rather just stand here?" He plowed through the undergrowth, heading west. When he turned around again, she finally followed.

They trudged through the forest, the sun warm on Tony's back as they passed through larger gaps between trees. The air tasted crisp, fresh, almost like the air from the oxygen tank at the hospital, but without the sterile smell. Just fresh. No pollution. The only sounds were the steady whir of locusts, and twigs and underbrush snapping beneath their feet.

Holding Violet upon waking from recovery had felt too good, so good he'd forgotten her trickery and lies. There had to be a reason she was hiding her identity. Until he found it, he had to earn and keep her trust. Once they returned home and the baby was born, Tony would make sure he got custody.

Little air moved, even when the trees thinned. The hike was mostly uphill, making Tony hot and sweaty and wishing he'd worn shorts. He pulled his shirt off and slung it over his arm with the jacket. Hopefully, the river would be deep enough for a swim.

Though it seemed longer, it was probably only a half hour later when the ground sloped down sharply. "Tony... do you have any idea where we are?"

"I'm thinking the bluffs over near Carillon Park and Calvary Cemetery." After a few more steps, they emerged from the woods and topped a rise to behold the Great Miami.

It wound in a serene S-curve, a ribbon of blue reflecting a cloudless sky. Violet drew up beside him, her steps hesitant and her gaze fixed on the ground. The drop-off, though a good thirty or forty feet, was gradual enough that Tony didn't get his usual height-induced jitters. "So weird." Violet looked up questioningly. "I-75 would be down there in our time," he explained.

She followed his gaze, taking a step backward. "And now nothing." Not even a dirt trail, just more woodlands.

Slowly they made their way down. Tony went first, picking out the least steep spots, though sometimes they had to grip trees and protruding rocks. He kept an eye on Violet, his heart jumping into his throat every time her foot slipped or a sapling bent in her grip. Finally, they reached the river basin.

Tony pushed his way through the weeds to where the water lapped the mud and gravel bank. He kicked off his socks and shoes, then stripped. "What are you doing?" Violet's voice was higher-pitched than usual.

He pushed his underwear down, then kicked it into a pile with the rest of his clothes. "I'm filthy, thirsty, and it's hotter than hell." He waded to the middle of the river, where the depth maxed at his waist. He scooped water into his hands and slurped. "Oh, man, this is awesome!" It was the cleanest, clearest water he'd ever drunk. Even though the river had been cleaned up considerably in their time, Tony wouldn't want to drink directly from it. But this was not the Great Miami he knew. He sucked down another handful.

Violet sat on the bank facing away, her knees drawn up to her chin. "It looks cold."

"It's not bad once you get in." He couldn't suppress a grin at her discomfort. "Come on, the baby needs a drink. And you're dirty, too."

Shivering, Violet stole a quick glance, but turned away again.

"Violet? You've got to get something—"

"I can't swim."

"You don't need—" *Oh shit, that's right.* Charlotte had been terrified of water.

Violet crept to the water's edge, then crouched at a gravelly spot and bent over to lap like an animal. Her hair streamed in the water, and after a few slurps, she rose up, spitting out hair. She splashed water on her arms, then her face. "You'll never get clean that way."

Her round eyes and trembling hands stole the jibe on the tip of his tongue.

As a child, she'd almost drowned in a flood.

As an adult, she'd conquered her fear with his help.

He spoke gently. "If you come in, I'll hold onto you." Not the way he wanted to hold her. Not like he had with her as Charlotte. He was doing this purely to regain her trust, after being an asshole during the ride home yesterday. There would not be a reenactment of the time in the Clearwater River, when they'd—

He barely heard her reply as she stood and slipped her shoes off, then turned her back to him and unbuttoned her dress. When she pushed it down over her hips, Tony's gut did a flip-flop.

She was wearing thigh-high stockings. And low-cut, lacy undies. Florie must've gotten them for Violet when she'd gone shopping— probably at Violet's request.

He couldn't tear his eyes off her as she peeled off one stocking, then the other.

Maybe this wasn't such a good idea.

She turned and saw him staring. "Do you mind?"

"Oh. Sorry."

He faced away until he heard the gentle splash of her walking in. "T- Tony?"

He whirled around, and his mouth fell open. All he could see were her pink, lace-trimmed panties. Her matching bra barely restrained her round, beautiful breasts.

A lot bigger than he remembered. Pregnancy agreed with her. "Uh..." His brain turned to mush.

"Tony?" Her brows pressed in.

Her trembling jarred him from his stupor. "Uh, yeah?" Jerking his gaze off her breasts, he reached for her hand. She took it and moved close, turning her back to him. She bent to dip her hair in the river, then scooped water in her hands to dump it over her head.

Tony helped, bracing a hand against her forehead so water wouldn't get in her eyes. "Thank you," she murmured.

He dropped his hand to her upper arm and scooped water onto her shoulders, fascinated by the play of sunlight on the water droplets sparkling on her smooth back. She backed into him, forcing him to twist to the side so his dick wouldn't poke her in the hip.

Bathing together was a very bad idea. He hadn't been laid since the 1959 motel. *She could be any attractive woman*, he told himself, but that was a lie.

She rubbed water over herself, and he ached to do it for her like he had in the shower. Like in the Clearwater River in 1933. He forced himself to be content to watch.

When she bent to rub her leg, she lost her balance. He caught her, and her round, brown, frightened eyes met his. He pulled her against him and wrapped her in a tight embrace, her water-slicked skin cool against his chest. She tipped her head up and slid her arms around him, pressing close.

His heart pounded. Time stopped. There was nothing except the rise and fall of her chest, the crush of her breasts against him, the tip of her tongue tracing her lips.

Hell. Tony leaned in to kiss her.

She captured his mouth, and her lips moved with his. She tasted of sunshine, of fresh water, of possibilities.

He ran his hands up and down her silken back.

She froze.

He pulled back. "I'm sorry. I swear, this wasn't my intent—"

"Tony?" Her voice squeaked. "We have an audience."

The two strange men on the riverbank with broad foreheads, dark skin, and black eyes wore nothing but loincloths. They also clutched fearsome-looking spears. Violet thought her heart had stopped until she became aware of it thudding in her throat.

She barely got her legs beneath her before Tony dropped her.

Water, all around. She was drowning—

She screamed.

The men fled into the trees.

Silly goose! Her scream had run off their best chance of finding food and shelter, never mind the men's appearance.

Water lapped at her waist, and tremors racked her. *Drowning...* "Tony?" she called in a quavering voice. *Water, everywhere...*

She spied him on the shore, grabbing his slacks, his gaze focused on where the men had disappeared.

She crept to the shore, trying not to think about the water. Heat rose in her cheeks at the image that had stolen her breath when Tony kissed her.

He held her in the river with her legs wrapped around his waist, her naked body pressed against his, the cool water lightly smacking her bare bottom as he lifted her up and down on his—

She bit her lip. It was from *before*. It had to be, it was so real. She'd heard the light splashing as he lifted her up and down, seen the sunlight glinting off the water droplets on his body, heard her own sighs of pleasure, felt the rush of rapture chasing away her fear—

Enough. Think about what you're doing. Woolgathering like that could get her killed.

She stepped onto the shore, glad Tony was occupied. He didn't need to see her absurd fear of the sluggish, three-foot-deep river.

A cloud had drifted over the sun, and the breeze chilled her wet skin. She hurried to dress, glancing at the trees every few seconds to make sure the watchers hadn't returned.

Her stockings lay on the ground, laddered with runs. Leaving them would violate Society code, and for good reason. What if the indigenous people found them? She scooped them up, then straightened to meet several pairs of dark eyes.

The men were back. With three friends. With lowered spears, pointed at her. She bit back a shriek..

A line from an old sci-fi television show sprang to mind: *We come in peace.* "Friends." She slowly raised her hands, palms outward.

One of them—barely more than a boy—shifted nervously.

"Please. We won't hurt you." Something dark flecked one of the stone spearheads. She gulped. "We just need food. We'll work, whatever you want..." The words lodged in her mouth. Of course, these people wouldn't speak English.

The men hesitated. Three lowered their spears.

A gunshot split the air.

The people scattered, but the boy-man lunged forward and hurled his spear at her before he, too, dashed into the woods.

Violet gasped at the flare of pain in her calf. Her leg buckled, and she crashed to the ground. Tony leaped to her side, clutching his gun. "Violet! Did they—"

"Lovely," Violet snapped. "You've run off our best chance for food and shelter."

"They were about to skewer you!"

Violet slumped, closing her eyes. "I know." He was only trying to protect her.

He crouched beside her as she sat up to assess her injury.

Blood gathered in a thin line, but the boy hadn't thrown the spear with enough force to do real damage. She pressed her fingers to the skin along the burning cut. "It's just a scratch." As minor as it was, the darn thing hurt like the dickens. She prayed the spearhead was clean and pushed herself up, ignoring the pain. "I'll just have to keep an eye out for infection."

With no antibiotics, that could mean death. Returning to the twenty-first century too soon would land her right back in the path of the Order of Titan.

And cost her the baby's life.

"Those injections Alpha gave us should prevent that." Tony extended a hand, the other still gripping the gun.

She ignored his offer of help. "I don't want to count on that." She brushed the leaves off her skirt, but as she rose something caught her eye.

The young man's spear. She grasped the smooth, wooden shaft. "This could come in handy." Her own blood glistened on its fluted, stone tip, and the sore streak on her calf stung at the reminder.

Tony shrank away from the bloodied spear as if it gave him the willies. "Let's go wash that cut." He walked her back to the river, where he helped her splash water on the wound. "We still need to find people. Those guys must have a camp around here somewhere. Maybe the women will be friendlier." He shoved the gun into his pocket. "Thank God they didn't find this. You still okay to walk?"

"Of course." The cut stung, but she followed when he trekked northward along the river, averting her eyes from the water.

It seemed they walked for hours, though Violet figured it was much less when thunder rumbled. She looked skyward. She'd been so intent on not looking at the river, she hadn't noticed the dark clouds gathering.

As if spurred by her thoughts, lightning flickered. A fat drop of water splashed Violet's hand. Then one struck her face. Tony glanced up. "Shit, just what we need."

Rain pinged the river in a continuous barrage, and soon it plastered Violet's dress and jacket to her skin. Every breeze chilled. Lightning flashed and thunder boomed through the woods. What she wouldn't give to be safe and dry at home. Only home wasn't safe. That horrible man who'd tried to choke her had seen to that.

The rain intensified. They moved on, until a rock outcropping maybe twice Tony's height rose before them. As they neared, some of the heaviness that clung to Violet like her sodden clothes lifted.

A wide, horizontal fissure in the rock's side created a gap along the ground, high enough to sit beneath, and deep enough that the straw, grass and leaves inside were dry. Violet thanked whatever animal had vacated the shelter as she crawled in, tucking the spear deep into the crevice.

Grass rustled and a twig snapped as Tony scooted in behind her.

"How's your leg?"

"I'd forgotten all about it." Now that they'd escaped the rain, she could see it had started bleeding again. "It's clean, at least."

Tony swiped a finger over his glasses and shoved them back on. "We need something to bandage that with."

The pink, flowered dress Florie had given Violet was long enough she could tear off some and still be decent. She grabbed the spear and lifted the sharp-edged tip to her hem when Tony's hand clamped around her wrist. "You'll need that later for warmth. Let's use my shirt." He held out his hand for the spear. She gave it to him. He sliced off about three inches, leaving it barely long enough to reach his waist.

Violet reached for the strip of cloth, but he took her ankle and dabbed the wound, then wrapped the fabric around her calf, tight enough to stay put, but not bind. He knotted the cloth slowly, as if he was tying off a surgical incision and she was the most important patient in the world, a prize to be treated like the finest china.

He did care. And not just for the baby. He'd tightened a thread that bound them together, and the feelings she kept trying to suppress welled up inside her like the air in an over-inflated balloon.

He settled into the straw in the back of the crevice. "Damn, it's chilly, even in here."

"Yes, it is." The straw scratched her bare legs, but Violet burrowed in, hoping it would trap her body heat.

A clap of thunder made her stop mid-dig as a memory assaulted her, so strong she could smell dry lumber.

She'd been wet and cold like this before. Miserable, waiting out a storm. With Tony.

She closed her eyes, willing the rumbling thunder and the pattering rain to take her back to that place and time, but the memory hung out of reach. She opened her eyes, forced herself to relax and let her gaze drift over him. Even soaked and dirty, he was beautiful, with his hair sticking up in dark clumps and moisture clinging to his eyelashes. She longed to touch him, to nuzzle close like they had upon awakening, to kiss him like they had in the river.

"Come here." He patted the straw beside him.

Violet hesitated, her heart wound like a compressed spring. He was only offering to keep her warm.

He'd pushed her away so many times, she didn't want to move close, didn't want to touch him, didn't want to lose control like she had in the river. Yet she longed to, and she hated that.

But he was right. There was no point in being cold when they could share their warmth. The straw rustled as she scooted to his side.

He wrapped his arm around her, and she settled against him.

He stared out at the rain, his eyes unfocused. "Are you... all right?" she asked. "I mean, as all right as we can be, under the circumstances."

He kept his gaze straight ahead. "I never got to see my daughter. Never got to tell her goodbye." Violet heard what he didn't say. *Might never see her again.* She ached for him.

Too soon, the rain stopped. Tony slipped his arm from around her, crawled out, and lurched to his feet. "Might as well move on, try to find something to eat."

"I'm famished." She took his proffered hand and pulled herself up, grabbing the spear. Though it was futile, she brushed off her skirt.

Sunlight gleamed in bright bands through holes in the lightening clouds. Raindrops on the leaves glistened like diamonds, and the fresh rain scent pervaded everything, stronger than she'd ever noticed in her own time. As they neared the river, the undergrowth gave out to a beaten path they hadn't noticed earlier. "Hopefully the way to humanity," Tony said.

"Are you any good at hunting?"

"My uncle took me a couple of times when I was a kid. Haven't been since then. But I'm pretty good on the shooting range." He pulled out his gun, and they scanned the forest as they walked. Rabbits and squirrels bounded through the treetops and undergrowth, drawn out by the rain. Violet didn't know much about guns, but she guessed Tony's would blow a small animal to bits.

The sun was sinking in the west when she spotted movement—something big. "Tony!" She grabbed his hand, and he stopped. "Look!"

Less than a dozen yards away, a young deer, scarcely bigger than Florie's dog, bent to graze on some greenery.

Tony lifted his gun. The click of him disengaging the safety cracked in Violet's ears. The doe foraged, oblivious to the danger. Tony squeezed the trigger.

Violet clapped her hands over her ears at the deafening report. The animal bolted down the path, marking its passage with a trail of blood. Tony raced after it, and Violet rushed to catch up.

"Knew that... wouldn't kill it," Tony panted.

The deer faltered, its gait degrading to a stagger. It wove erratically, slowed to a stumbling walk, then crashed into a pile of brush.

Violet and Tony hurried to its side.

The deer thrashed a couple of times, then lay motionless. Blood poured from a hole in its side. It stared up at Violet with big, brown eyes. What if the deer had a fawn? A pang struck Violet.

Too late. *We're hungry! I'm sorry—*

Tony raised his gun, aiming at the animal's head.

Violet stayed his hand. "Don't waste your ammo." She lifted the spear. "This'll put the poor thing out of its misery." She closed her eyes and visualized the horrible man who'd tried to strangle her, the man who stank of cigars and taunted her in a deep, accented voice.

The man who looked like Tony.

She opened her eyes enough to aim, then slammed the spear into the deer's side, yanked it out, and drove it in again. And again. As if through earmuffs, she heard the deer's piteous bleats. Warm liquid splattered her dress. She jerked the spear out a third time, and drew it back once more—

"Violet!" Tony grabbed her arm. "Violet! It's dead!"

She met his wild-eyed stare and realized it wasn't because of the deer, it was because of her frenzy. Her arms went rubbery. The spear slid out of her hand. "I'm... it's just... I'm so hungry." Her expression sagged. "I'm sorry," she whispered, though she wasn't sure why she was apologizing to Tony. She hadn't done anything to him. Had she?

Tony regarded her trembling frame as he picked up the spear. What kind of monster was she? The look in her eyes when she attacked the hapless animal had been one of pure bloodlust. Not desperation for food, but anger.

Her gaze softened. Her lower lip trembled, her big brown eyes reminiscent of the deer's.

The man who tried to kill her. *Who looks like me.* Tony's heart twisted. He laid down the gun and spear, and reached for her.

She sagged into his arms. He wrapped her in his embrace, speaking softly. "It's okay. No wonder you're freaked out. Hell, I am." She clung to him like she was adrift at sea and he was her last hope of survival.

He stroked her hair, his hand skimming over the tangled mess. If he'd had some self-control at the motel in 1959, he wouldn't have to drag her into his problems. Wouldn't have to worry about a baby on the way, much less making sure that baby lived to influence the course of humanity decades in the future.

After a long moment, he slid his arms away. She straightened and regarded the deer, a shaft of sunlight illuminating her pale face. "All we have to do now is figure out how on earth we'll cook it. I doubt rubbing two sticks together will work, with everything wet."

"If worst comes to worst, we could hack off some meat and eat it raw. We shouldn't have to worry about food poisoning, with the injections from Alpha."

Shuddering, Violet made a face. "I'd prefer not to depend on that." Her gaze lingered on the deer, then she drew up straight. "I have an idea. Come on." She hurried up the trail, her feet pounding the drying mud.

At the rock crevice, she knelt and pulled out an armload of dry brush. She piled it into a mound, then sat back on her heels and pointed. "Your gun. Shoot it into the straw."

He arched an eyebrow, but pointed the firearm at the straw. "No," she said. "Down close. Stick it right in there, so the fire that comes out—"

He crouched beside her and pulled the trigger. The gunshot roared in his ears.

A few pieces of straw glowed in the center. Violet bent down and puffed on them, but the fire went out. "Fudge!"

"Get back." Tony lifted the gun for another shot. Flinching, Violet covered her ears. They stared into the straw.

Again, strands near where Tony had stuck the gun glowed. "Come on!" Violet fanned the straw with her hand. The smoldering tinder burned brighter.

"Awesome," Tony said. "I'll go find some firewood."

By the time he dragged a broken bough back to their makeshift camp, flames licked at Violet's pile of straw and some twigs she'd added. She had cleared the fallen leaves and weeds from around the fire and encircled it in rocks.

Tony's stomach growled with renewed intensity. "We're in luck." He dropped the branch and began breaking it into pieces. "This was under some thick pines, so it didn't get real wet."

"Hopefully, it'll be dry enough." She gripped the spearhead and helped him strip the branch. The activity helped them focus on something besides their discomfort, and by the time twilight fell, they had a decent fire going.

"We should have moved the straw to the deer," Tony said.

Violet's shoulders sagged. "Why didn't I think of that? Between worrying about the baby and being so hungry, my mind's not working."

"It didn't occur to me either." She was messing with his head. First at the motel, then his crazy trek to Tennessee in a stolen truck, now this. It was all so not him. Being with her—*Charlotte*—had stolen his common sense.

While Violet tended the fire, he gripped the spear and went back to the deer. Forcing back images of the Mayan priests and their blood-encrusted, stone axe, he sawed off a hunk of its back, next to the spine. The blood and slippery meat turned his stomach, and he was sure he'd have puked if he'd eaten anything.

When he returned to their camp, Violet skewered the meat on two sticks. She handed one to Tony and held hers over the flame like a huge, bloody marshmallow. Eventually, the blood dried and the meat took on a delectable fragrance.

Tony pulled his shank away from the fire, waited for it to cool, then chewed off a hunk. It felt barbaric, but he didn't care. "Mmm..." He took another bite as soon as the first was chewed enough to swallow.

"Good, huh?" Violet pulled hers from the fire.

"It's a bit rare, but who cares."

By the time they finished, dark had fallen, bringing with it a damp chill. Tony unwrapped the bandage on Violet's leg and examined the cut in the firelight. "Looks okay far as I can tell." He wrapped it back up, then crawled toward the crevice in the rock outcropping. "Don't know about you, but I'm beat."

She set her skewer down. "All that walking took it out of me, too." She huddled by the fire, her arms drawn over her knees. Though the fire popped and burned brightly, the cotton dress Florie had given her couldn't have been very warm.

After they banked the fire, they crawled into the crevice. Tony patted the ground beside him. "Come here." Violet hesitated. "To keep warm," he said. Even to him, it sounded like a lame pickup line.

"Very well." She scooted over to him. His side warmed where she leaned against him, and the heaviness in his chest lightened at her nearness. It felt too good, too right, to huddle close with her, the mother of his child. Almost enough to make him forget who she was—and what she'd done. He'd screwed up in the river that afternoon, let himself get caught up in holding her, let himself worry about her feelings. Let himself care.

He'd made that mistake with Dora. He'd made it once with Charlotte. He sure as hell wouldn't make the same mistake again. He had to keep up appearances, but it would stop there. He rubbed up and down Violet's back. "Thought about baby names yet?" Keep it about the baby. Get his mind off her nearness.

"With all that's gone on... I have to admit I haven't. Perhaps Timothy."

"Someone you know?" An old boyfriend? Tony's stomach curdled at the thought. *It doesn't. Matter.* He didn't like the idea, but he liked the fact that it bothered him even less.

"A dear friend. Timmy's the fellow who found me when... after I couldn't remember anything. He and his sister Stephanie, they took me in and helped me make a new life."

Oh, so we're back to that story again. Maybe he could trip her up, get her to admit to her true identity. "So, what exactly happened that day?"

She leaned back against the rock wall and closed her eyes. "I woke up in the back of a pickup truck. In someone's garage. I had no idea where I was, how I got there, or what I'd—" Her eyes opened, and she swallowed. "Why I'd gone to sleep there. The garage door was opening—that's what woke me—and Timmy found me there."

Tony studied her face. She'd started to say something, then stopped herself. As if she'd almost slipped up. It all could be a carefully crafted lie. Just like the way she'd played him in 1933, as Charlotte. "Didn't you go to the police, see if anyone had filed a missing person report?"

She shrank toward the wall. "I was afraid. I knew I was in trouble. Big trouble. I couldn't remember from whom, I just knew I couldn't go to the police. And now, with those people after me—after us..."

It made sense if she'd just committed murder. And if she'd come forward in time, knowing she should have died decades before, she'd know that no one would be looking for her. "How did you get a job, a driver's license, stuff like that?"

She fingered a seam in her jacket. "When I woke up in the truck, I was wearing a necklace. A beautiful, antique, gold chain, inlaid with tiny diamonds. Stephanie's husband Vince had some shady friends, and one of them was able to get me a birth certificate and social security card in exchange for my necklace. Vince might have been a poor excuse for a man in many ways, but for getting me an identity, I'll always be grateful."

Tony's hands squeezed into fists. He knew that necklace. The one she'd always fiddled with in 1933. It held the Ohio quarter he'd dropped in the attic the day they met. The day he'd saved her life.

He couldn't think about that. Not now. She couldn't know he'd figured it out. He unclenched his fists. "What did you do then?"

"I got a job as a waitress, at a little greasy spoon place over by U.D. And I helped take care of Stephanie's invalid grandmother. Eventually, I saved up enough money to buy a car, and applied for aid at Sinclair. Since I couldn't produce a high school diploma, they had me take placement tests. All on computers. I found them fascinating."

"The computers, not the placement tests."

"Yes. The tests were easy, and my scores were good. Since I liked using the computers, that's what I decided to get my degree in. I graduated last year."

Tony could do nothing but stare at the ground. Charlotte had a degree in physics, and had worked as a researcher before her job had been lost to the Depression. Computers would have been new to her, as would much of the sciences. Still, it was a lot of effort if all she wanted to do was insinuate herself into twenty-first century life to capture him for the Society.

And why had she waited for years? Something was fishy with her story. Either that, or...

What if she was telling the truth? Even if the kind of memory loss she described happened only in books and movies, who could know that for sure? Especially when time travel to the future was thrown into the mix? *Never heard from again* was a far cry from dead forever.

The memory of her sitting in Pippin's car with that psycho flashed through Tony's mind. Yet—what if it really was nothing more than the fact that the Saturn Society logo looked familiar?

Her brown eyes shone liquid in the firelight. Before he knew what he was doing, he lowered his face to hers and kissed her, gently at first, then as she responded, more deeply. Her lips moist and soft, she met each thrust of his tongue with equal strength, delving in and exploring as if she were seeking the same answers he was.

He shifted so that they were face to face, heart to heart, her breasts pressed into his chest, and something fierce like rage overcame him. He had to have her, Charlotte be damned. It didn't matter what she'd done. His body moved without direction from his mind, and he found himself unbuttoning her dress. A sigh escaped her, fueling his desire.

Just sex. He wouldn't get attached. He'd pleasure her, expose her vulnerability, get to her. With animal urgency, he leaned close, pressing his mouth to hers. He captured her lips hungrily, pushing her down on the straw.

He moved lower, mouthing her chin, then down her neck. She bucked beneath him, grinding her breasts against his chest. He moved lower, layering kisses all over the smooth skin above her breasts, then back up to her neck, eliciting a soft moan.

Satisfaction surged through him. Charlotte or not, that wasn't faked. As fine an actress as the woman could be, he'd challenge her, make her submit to her desires, put an end to the charade. He drew a finger down her cleavage and flicked open her bra.

The cups fell away and he greedily clasped her breasts, lightly massaging, then drawing his fingers up until his thumbs encircled her taut nipples. He twisted lightly. She tipped her head back. "Tony..." she moaned.

He couldn't take any more. If he waited a second longer, his dick would bust through his pants. He fumbled at his belt, but she grabbed his hands. "Let me."

As she unbuckled his belt and pushed his slacks down, something fell to the straw with a thud. She looked up. "The gun," he said.

She brought her face back to his, grasping the back of his neck to pull him to her. She unbuttoned his shirt and slid her fingers through his chest hair, skimming around his scars. He wasn't sure who did the rest, he only knew that in a minute, her panties lay on the straw and her dress and slip were bunched up around her waist.

Her mouth devoured his, and he crushed her to him and attacked her mouth until she again lay on her back. He lowered himself over her, his mouth never leaving hers.

He needed her, needed to touch, needed to be inside her. He'd win her trust, make her believe he cared for *her*, Violet Sinclair, as if he had no clue who she really was.

Her lips moved with his. Poetic justice had never tasted so good. He raised up, trailing kisses down her throat, her chest, down to the puckered tip of one breast then the other, then down her belly.

He pressed against her, taking care not to put his weight on her. His dick nestled between her legs, and he couldn't stop himself from moving up and down, the feel of her soft skin above and below her wadded-up dress almost driving him to the edge. God, he'd missed that sensation, the closeness, being against her smooth body. Their state of partial undress fueled his urgency, and when her hips rose to meet him, he pressed harder with his. "Oh, yes!" she breathed.

She spread her legs, and he accepted the invitation. As he met her hot wetness, her hand clamped around him and guided him inside. In one swift thrust, her warmth enveloped him.

This was what he'd been missing for the past four months.

Her hips tipped up and they moved in harmony, a perfect merging of bodies and souls. Past, present, and future slipped into oblivion. Nothing existed but this moment. Nothing else mattered. There was nothing but him and this woman.

He tensed, and knew it would be over too soon if he wasn't careful. Though it pained him, he sat up, pulling her onto his lap.

He crushed her against him and brought his lips to hers. While they kissed he drew his hands down and up her back, then pulled them away until only his fingertips brushed her skin. She gasped, then pressed her chest into him harder, pushing with her hips at the same time.

He leaned backward until he lay on his back, then twisted to straighten his legs so she straddled him. He gripped her hips and guided her up and down, meeting the movements with an opposite motion.

He drew his hands up and down her back again, then brought them around to her front. When his thumbs reached her nipples and flicked lightly, she tipped her head back. She moaned softly, then louder as she tightened around him. She rocked her hips, making his body react. He gripped her ass, pulling himself into and out of her with greater force, until she began to squeeze him. Her rhythmic contractions threw him over the edge and he exploded into her, pulling her to him with one last thrust.

For a long moment, she sat still, stunned, then rolled off him.

He pulled her into his arms. She lay beside him, her head nestled in the hollow beneath his shoulder. Where, and when, they were didn't matter. Everything was good and right with the world, and contentment filled him. He brushed aside her hair and kissed her forehead.

"Tony?"

"Hmm?" He stroked her hair, long and soft.

"I love you."

"I lo—" Reality slammed him, and the words lodged in this throat. She *loved* him? *Charlotte?* After what she'd done?

Straw bit into his ass, and a chilly breeze blew over his bare stomach. He pushed her away. His breath came in big gulps. He wanted to smash something. He should have known better. He'd gotten caught up in the moment, caught up in feelings, in what he'd been missing. He'd made a big mistake. "Look, I..." He couldn't look at her.

Charlotte. Liar and deceiver.

He got up and yanked up his pants. "Violet... this isn't going to work. You're holding back from me. Something important, and as long as you're keeping things from me..." he grabbed his jacket "we have to be..." he reached for the gun "just friends." Afraid to look at her but unable to stop himself, he turned as he buttoned his shirt.

Her lips parted, her wary eyes focused on his. "Wh- what are you talking about?"

His throat swelled. He couldn't force out another word. He slipped out of the crevice and walked away.

The next morning, Tony checked Violet's wound before they resumed their search for humanity. Unable to sleep between the guilt gnawing at him and freezing his ass off, he'd returned to the crevice just before dawn. He didn't want to think of her elaborate story or how convincing she'd been. He had to remember how quickly she'd gone to Pippin in 1959, ready to turn him in.

Neither spoke of the night before.

He picked apart the bandage's knot and peeled the fabric away. The edges of the scratch were puffy and red, and the skin around it was swollen. "That doesn't look good."

"It is a little sore." She met his gaze. "I hope it's not getting infected."

"Could just be swollen from all the walking we did yesterday." He retied the wrap.

They returned to the river, the rising sun at their backs filtering through the trees. While they walked, they gnawed on leftover deer meat. Tony hardly tasted it. He prayed Alpha's injection would protect them from food poisoning.

When they reached the riverbank, he yanked off his shirt, shoes and socks and waded in. Violet lingered in the grassy area above the bank, twirling her hair.

When Tony looked back, she kicked off her shoes and hurried to untie the wrapping on her leg, as if she were a child caught dawdling. Though the day was already getting warm, she waded in just deep enough to get an un-muddied drink, splashed water on her leg with shaking hands, then quickly waded out.

As she slipped her shoes back on, she met his gaze. "Tony... what happened last night... it was a mistake."

He felt his gaze harden. "Yeah. It was."

"I didn't..." She looked down, waving at the ground. "Just forget about what I said. Everything."

He jerked hard on his jacket sleeves as he tied them around his waist and tossed his shirt over his shoulder.

As if he could. As much as he wanted to, her words echoed in his mind. *Tony... I love you.* Something inside him curled in on itself.

They plodded through the woods in silence. The day grew hot. The sun was nearly overhead when the trail rounded a curve to reveal a long, grass-covered ridge maybe ten feet high.

Too smooth and uniform to be natural. "Tony! Look!"

He stopped. "Do you think it's..." He pulled off his glasses and polished them with his shirt.

Tidy lines of thatch rose above the ridge's rim. Roofs. "A village!"

Nine

Tony hung back. Those guys at the river hadn't exactly given them a warm reception. *Better observe first.* He dropped to the ground and crawled up the ridge, watching for movement. Grass and weeds scratched his belly. To his relief, Violet did the same without question.

The ridge formed a ring, and inside it, a stockade fence of lashed sticks formed a fortification around a compound of about three dozen thatched huts of straw. Each had a sloped roof with triangle-shaped holes in the gable ends—to let smoke escape, most likely. Animal skins hung over the doors. The people working around the buildings reminded Tony of his dad's old *National Geographic* magazines. Between the ridge and the fence, dark-skinned women and children poked the earth with sharp sticks and wood-handled, stone hoes. None wore more than short, coarse-woven skirts or loincloths. One woman scraped a deerskin stretched across a wooden frame. Others worked clay into bowls and jars, or scooped mud onto the wood-and-grass framework of another hut. Some tended fires or ground corn or carried baskets and pottery bowls among the buildings.

Shouts and conversation, the barking of dogs, the faint pounding and scrapes of tools rang in Tony's ears. A few loincloth-clad men used stone implements to scoop the smoking center of a long, thick, split log. One guy banged at rocks beneath a shade fashioned of grasses laid across a frame attached to one of the huts. A toolmaker, Tony guessed. Most of the men were probably out hunting. With the exception of children chasing each other and playing fetch with dogs, everyone worked.

A chill fell over Tony as the reality sank in of how far back they'd warped. He shook it off. *Survival*. That was all that mattered.

The sun was high overhead, and it was already hot. Violet slipped off her jacket and wiped the sheen of sweat on her forehead. "How should we approach them?" Her gaze darted to the far side of the compound, where women and children were laying fish—some as big as Tony's arm—across a wooden lattice. Coals smoldered beneath it, and even at a distance, the smoked fish smell made Tony's mouth water.

Anger gnawed at his stomach along with hunger. Violet—and the baby—were also hungry. Because he'd failed to provide for her. "Somehow, we have to convince them to give us food and shelter," he said. "And let them know that we're willing to work. Which is going to be hard when we don't speak their language. I don't know how to make dugout canoes or smoke fish. Hell, I don't know what half of them are doing."

Violet picked at some tall grasses. "We could learn."

Tony shook his head. "That won't help us now."

She wrapped a grass stem around her finger. "What about that deer we killed? Didn't the early settlers trade in furs?"

"You know how to prepare a deerskin?"

"I'm afraid I don't." She picked another piece of grass and twisted it around the first. "Perhaps we could pretend to be traders. Then it would make sense that we look strange and don't speak their language—"

"What do we have to trade?"

Violet pulled the grasses between her fingers and thumb. "Our clothing. Especially our shoes... except that would violate Society Code—"

"Fuck Society Code. Remember what Alpha said. Small wrongs to right a much larger—"

"All right. But... oh dear, we really need to look like them as much as possible..."

"Uh-huh." She leaned against a tree to slip her shoes and stockings off, and shoved them beneath some brush. The thought of her going topless, wearing nothing but a skimpy, woven twine skirt made his insides smolder. But she was right, the fewer the differences between them and the natives, the better their chances of acceptance.

Survival. The baby.

Given his lack of self-control in the rock crevice last night, he would just have to stay away from her.

She pointed at the hut nearest the opening in the fence. "That big hut... not a soul's gone in or out since we've been here. Maybe there's some clothing inside we could... ah, *borrow*."

Tony's mouth tightened. He hated the idea of stealing, but saw no better alternative. He rose to his knees and dug the gun out of his pocket. "Okay. Take this and keep watch while I—"

She pulled back. "I don't know how to shoot! You keep watch, I'll go in."

Tony squeezed the gun. He didn't like letting her go into danger. But she was right, he could better protect her if he kept watch. Using the fence for concealment, they crawled up the rise, then scooted down the other side, then crept around to the opening and sneaked through.

Tony tiptoed toward the hut's back entrance, but before he got there, Violet held up a hand. She put her ear against the hut's straw side. Tony did the same.

No sounds came from within. Violet edged toward the entry.

Tony raised his gun and crept behind her, his heart turning somersaults in his throat. Violet slowly leaned into the entrance. She turned back, gave him a sharp nod, then disappeared through the portal.

The scent of smoke assaulted Tony as he sidled past and glanced inside. Furs covered built-in bunks made by branches lashed to the walls. A ring of stones marked a fire pit in the center, and smooth rocks the size of a man's head encircled it. Leather pouches, bundles of herbs, and bones hung from the rafters. Sunlight slanted through another entry opposite.

Violet appeared in the doorway and thrust a pile of buckskins at him. "Here," she whispered. "I'm going to try to find something like the women wear." Before he could respond, she disappeared back inside.

He moved on and leaned around the corner enough to see if anyone approached. What kind of man had he become? First stealing cars, now stealing someone's clothes, for Pete's sake?

A man who'd do whatever was necessary to protect his family.

The thought gave him little comfort.

No one was near, so he ducked behind the building and held up the buckskins. A loop of twine fell from a rectangle of skin that was about a foot wide by three long.

Time to look like the locals. He shimmied out of his clothes and shoes. After tying the twine around his waist, he threaded the rectangle of buckskin under the rope at his back, pulled it under his groin, then draped it over the rope at his waist.

He gazed down at himself. The wind caressed his bare hips, and he grimaced. He looked like a fucking male stripper.

Men's voices drifted on the breeze.

Panic shot down his throat and the air in his lungs froze. He couldn't move. Then he forced himself to be calm, and leaned around the corner of the hut.

Two men approached. Tony jerked behind the building. "Violet!" he whispered.

No response. "Violet!"

He peered around the doorway as the one opposite darkened.

Violet screamed.

"Ossessoo!" The outraged shout sent Tony ducking out of view as the native babbled, the threat in his voice unmistakable.

Tony frantically dug into the pile of his clothes until he felt the gun's cool, smooth metal. From inside the hut came the sounds of a scuffle, along with mutters and shouts. "Friends!" Violet pleaded. "We mean no harm!"

The man barked something that sounded like an order.

Tony burst through the hut's back door as the men dragged Violet out the front. "Hey! Stop!" His words were lost in shouts and exclamations from outside.

Tony dashed for the exit, tripping over the fire pit. Luckily, only ashes remained. He got up and ran outside to find himself at the back of a gathering crowd.

He understood none of the people's words, but their sharp chants, raised fists, and angry shouts bore a disturbing resemblance to an angry mob.

He tried to tamp down his alarm. He wouldn't help Violet if he angered the people by rushing out waving his gun.

He was a good six inches taller than any of the villagers, and peered over the crowd, squeezing the gun. If one of those men hurt Violet, he'd shoot, hell with the Society Code.

A pole at least two stories high rose from the village's center, and at its base, a man wearing necklaces of animal claws and bone beads climbed onto an upended log.

A breath lodged in Tony's throat. *Just like the guy in ancient Mayan times.* The one who'd had him beheaded.

The chief—or so Tony assumed—shouted, and the people backed away. Tony caught a flash of pink at the man's feet.

The chief bent down, gripped Violet's dress at the base of her neck and hauled her upright. She staggered. Her fists at her sides trembled. The blood from the deer they'd killed probably didn't help. The man jabbered in an angry voice, then yanked at her collar. It tore, sending buttons flying. Then he grabbed a wad of her blond hair and jerked her closer. Tony almost leapt out from behind the building, his gun drawn, but hesitated when the man addressed the people.

He'd barely gotten three sentences in when the crowd parted, and an old woman stepped forward. Three tiny, bright red cardinal feathers fluttered in her graying hair as she approached the chief on his stump.

Her words sharp, she shook her fist at the man. Leather pouches tied to the rope belted around her waist quivered. Her pottery chip necklace rattled.

The chief's face fell slack, and he released Violet's hair. The two men who'd found her raised their voices in argument.

No one had seen Tony, so he lifted the buckskin flap at his waist and jammed the gun under the rope. He stole behind the hut and scooped up his clothes. A bullet plopped onto the dirt. Florie's extra ammo. He dug the rest out of his pants pocket and stashed the ammo beneath a clump of weeds, then wadded his clothing into a ball. Hopefully an odd-looking trader would be an adequate diversion—and not land him in the same fix as Violet.

He crept to the crowd's edge. The men with the chief and the old woman were still arguing. Others craned their necks to see.

Violet bent down, then straightened, lifting her shoes high. Tony couldn't hear what she said, but the men quieted. She pointed at the shoes, then at the men's feet. One of the men smacked her face.

Tony flung down the clothes and pushed through the crowd, shoving people aside. *"Ossessok!"* A man pointed at him. Others picked up the cry. Tony ignored the angry shouts.

The man in the animal claw necklace snatched Violet's shoes and smacked her again. Tony lunged at him and grabbed the necklaces. The man's head snapped forward and Tony swung, his fist connecting squarely with the native's jaw.

The man staggered backward, but recovered and launched himself at Tony. Tony sidestepped the smaller man's punch, digging for his gun. Two other men rushed at Tony. He raised the gun, thumb poised to fire into the air, when a third man tackled him and knocked him to the ground.

Tony drove his fist into the man's ribs. The native slugged Tony's face, sending pain bursting from his cheek. *"Ossessok!"*

Tony brought the gun up, turning aside in time to avoid another punch, then clocked the man in the jaw.

The man slumped and rolled aside, howling in pain. Tony sprang to his feet. "Violet! Run!" The other two men lurched toward him, and he couldn't see if she got away. He raised his gun, not sure what he'd do with it. The men stopped.

Everything slowed, as if he were watching a slow-motion video, the sounds drawn out and muffled.

He glimpsed pink off to one side. The man he'd pistol-whipped got up on his hands and knees, his forehead dripping blood. Chants rose from the crowd.

Tony looked around. They were yelling at him. Pointing at the fallen man. Shouting with raised fists.

They wanted him to continue the fight.

The man collapsed with a groan. The others watched Tony with narrowed eyes.

Clenching his jaw, Tony jammed the gun back under his loincloth.

He would not kick the fallen villager like an animal. The metallic taste of blood trickled into his awareness, and he realized he'd bit his mouth when the guy punched him. Tony spat on the ground and scooped up his clothes. Straightening his glasses, he strode toward Violet.

The crowd parted, the people giving him wide-eyed stares and jabbering excitedly. One woman pointed at his face, and a small child ducked between her legs. An older boy pointed at him, yelling.

Shit. His glasses.

Movement flashed in the corner of his view. "Let me go!" *Violet!* He ran for her.

The other two men he'd fought held her wrists. They'd bound her ankles with twine, loose enough she could walk but couldn't kick. The man with the animal claw necklace stroked her hair, cocking his head while he squinted and leaned close to study it.

They'd never seen blond hair. Or glasses. Or woven, cotton cloth, Tony realized. He marched to the tall pole and climbed onto the stump that claw-necklace had vacated when the fight broke out. As a pair of women led the injured man away, Tony lifted his bundle of clothes. "Twenty-first century clothing and shoes!" He felt silly, knowing they couldn't understand him, but his shout got the natives' attention.

Those still in the plaza crept closer, chattering in sharp, punctuated tones. Tony felt their curious gazes as he held up his slacks. "Wrangler Easy Care, wrinkle resistant pants, size thirty-four! Free the woman and they're yours." He eyed the man with the animal claw necklace.

The guy grunted. Tony lifted his shirt. "Faded Glory golf shirt, navy blue, large. A steal at this price!"

The man cocked his head, frowning, and said something in a questioning tone. The other man holding Violet craned his neck to see.

Tony held up his belt. "You'll find the finest top grain cowhide in this belt—"

Bear-claw-necklace-guy lunged at Tony and snatched the belt as he snarled another word.

"Let her go!" Tony pointed to Violet, then to himself. "She's mine." He dumped his shoes and underwear at the man's feet. "You take this," he pointed at the man, "and give me her." He indicated Violet.

The man pointed at the L-shaped scar on Tony's chest, then to the pile of clothing, then turned up his palms, then said something in a derisive voice. He curled his lip.

Tony clenched his jaw. If only he knew what the hell the guy was saying.

"Aldi b'nak!" Bear-claw-necklace jabbed at the pile of Tony's clothes, at Violet, at the clothing again, then made a slashing motion.

The deer. He had to go back for it, bring it to the village, show the people he could contribute. Violet strained against the men holding her, her eyes pleading. *The sooner the better.*

Tony ran for the fortification. As he climbed the slope, he looked back to see the old woman leading her away.

Violet stood straight, trying to look confident and unafraid. Dust rose beneath her feet as the old woman pulled her toward the huts circling the village. The other villagers stepped aside, opening a path through the dispersing crowd. A younger woman with two little children followed from a few feet away, then a preteen girl joined them. They spoke in hushed tones and pointed at Violet's hair, her dress, her belly, the top of her head.

They must think her a freak. Dressed in clothes like they'd never seen, paler than the youngest babe, taller than the tallest man.

And none of the villagers' lean, fit bodies carried a spare ounce of fat.

She pushed the last thought away. She was just different. A curiosity she might use to her advantage while trying her best to blend in.

But where had Tony gone? Even with his comical attempt to barter his clothing, had the natives simply let him leave?

And if so, would he return?

Sidestepping two patches of earth the size of a man, bordered by stones—graves, Violet guessed—the women led her to a hut near the stockade fence.

The old woman lifted a buckskin flap over the door and slipped inside. She motioned to Violet to follow. Violet obeyed. The other woman and the children crept in behind her.

The old woman spread her arms in a sweeping gesture and said something that sounded like a welcome.

Violet nodded. "Thank you."

The old woman gave her a gap-toothed smile, and the other woman and the children did the same. Violet felt some of her tenseness dissipate.

Though the fire pit lay dormant, the smell of smoke pervaded the hut's interior. Violet stifled a cough. Like the building she'd sneaked into, it also boasted built-in bunks, and bundles of skins, herbs, and gourds hanging from the rafters. Curtains of woven grasses hung over bunks that were covered with straw, skins, and furs.

The old woman pointed at her and motioned to one of several woven grass mats on the ground. The other woman sat, so Violet followed her example. No one protested.

"Ald ba'ayar?" the old woman said.

Violet twiddled her fingers in her dress. What if she responded in the wrong way?

The woman repeated the question. At Violet's continued blank stare, she pointed at the wrap on Violet's leg.

Little light came in through the door-hole and the gaps in each end of the roof, but it was enough that she could see the line of blood seeping through the blue strip of Tony's shirt. "Ah, yes." Was the woman curious about the cloth, asking if she was hurt, or was she inquiring about Tony?

"Ald ba'aper." The old woman pointed at Violet, then turned to the preteen girl and gave her an order.

The girl crawled under one of the lashed-wood bunks, then scooted out with a clay jar, with a buckskin lid tied around its lip with twine. The other woman asked the old one something, but the latter shook her head as she took the jar. Muttering, she pointed to Violet's leg again, then slipped off the jar's covering.

Pushing her doubts aside, Violet stuck her leg out and untied the wrap as the children and the younger woman watched in fascination.

Muttering to herself, the old woman studied the scratch, then barked an order at the other woman, who handed her a strip of buckskin. The old woman spoke in a singsong voice as she held the jar over Violet's leg and touched her forehead to the jar. Still murmuring a chant, she dribbled a vinegary-smelling liquid over the cut. It burned, but Violet managed not to flinch. The woman rewrapped Violet's leg in the clean, buckskin strips, then carefully tied the covering back over the jar. She offered Violet a gentle smile and dipped her head in a shallow bow.

It seemed like the thing to do, so Violet mimicked her action. "Thank you." She hoped the woman heard the appreciation in her voice.

The women and children watched Violet with expectant expressions. Violet's gaze darted from one to the other, seeking a clue as to what to do. What did they want? She pointed at her chest. "Violet." She pointed at the old woman, tilting her head and lifting her brows in an exaggerated, questioning expression. The woman cocked her head and frowned. "Violet," Violet repeated, jabbing herself in the chest.

Comprehension dawned on the old woman. "Ga-noo." She tapped

herself in the chest, then pointed at the other woman. "Bood-way."

Bood-way gave Violet a smile, displaying several missing teeth as she pointed at the oldest girl. "Ach-sayay."

The younger boy, who looked maybe five or six, was Kay-dan, and the girl, a year or two younger, was Durch-eye. The woman ended by pointing at Violet. "Via-led."

"Yes!" Violet nodded emphatically.

"Vi-led," Ga-noo said. The older girl repeated her.

"Yes!" the little girl said, pointing at Violet.

Violet pointed at herself. "Violet."

"Vi-yed, yes," Durch-eye repeated.

Footsteps approached from outside, and a queasy feeling rose in Violet's stomach. Her relief when the footsteps passed was short-lived as she remembered her first objective upon entering the village.

She had little doubt that much of her harsh treatment at the men's hands was due to her strange appearance, and the differences she needed to minimize. She faced Ga-noo. "I want to look like you." It felt silly knowing they couldn't understand, but it felt sillier to say nothing. She pulled her dress away from her belly, then pointed at Ga-noo's wrap-around skirt. "Trade?"

Ga-noo barked an order at Ach-sayay, who jumped up to retrieve something from behind one of the hanging grass drapes. The girl returned with a long rectangle of coarse, woven cloth, which she handed to Violet. Ga-noo pointed to the native cloth, then to Violet. Speaking in choppy, mysterious syllables, she waved over Violet's dress, then indicated herself.

A chill coursed down Violet's body. The old woman had accepted her offer. Now Violet had to fulfill her part of the bargain.

Which meant she had to undress before five pairs of curious eyes.

She would not be afraid.

She would not be modest.

She would be strong. *Whatever it takes.* She needed these people's acceptance. For the baby, if not herself. Slowly, she unbuttoned her dress.

"Riz-or?" Ach-sayay pointed to Violet's lacy, pink bra. Bood-way

cocked her head, one eyebrow pressed down. The two younger children leaned close.

Violet wanted to shrink into the grass mat. *It's the bra,* she told herself. She refused to allow herself to squirm. Instead, she stood, crossed her arms, and pulled the bloodstained dress over her head.

Durch-eye leapt for the fabric. With a shout, Kay-dan yanked it from her hands to a reprimand from Bood-way. Durch-eye whined until Violet reached for her bra clasp.

She shriveled under their scrutiny.

She could never be an exotic dancer, even if she had a perfect figure. All those eyes on her while she disrobed. The vulnerability. The immodesty, the impropriety of it all.

It's not improper to them. This was not her culture, these were not her people. But for the baby, she had to make them so. Closing her eyes and gritting her teeth, she forced her fingers to unhook the bra. It slid to the ground and her breasts fell free to a cacophony of chatter.

Bood-way reached for the bra, but Ga-noo grabbed it first. Kay-dan tried to snag it, but she held it out of reach. Durch-eye beheld Violet's breasts with an open-mouthed stare, highlighting another difference.

Not only was she taller and heavier than the native women, she was much bigger in the chest, especially with the pregnancy.

She tried to put herself in the child's place. The girl was only curious.

And Violet had a reason for her girth. Drawing strength from that reason, she pointed to her belly—"Baby"—then put her arms together over it, swinging them in a cradling motion.

A smile lit the girl's face. *"Alga newk!"* She tugged at Bood-way's elbow.

The woman flashed a gap-toothed grin like Ga-noo's.

"Ald b'awai?" Ga-noo asked.

Violet had no idea if they understood, but she nodded and handed Ga-noo the dress.

The old woman took it, holding the fabric up to the light that came in through the hole in the eave of the roof. The children rushed to her side, Bood-way behind them.

Violet grabbed the woven twine skirt they'd given her and tied it around her waist. It didn't quite meet at her hip, leaving a gap.

It would have to do. As hot as it was outside, the skirt would be more comfortable than the clinging, cotton dress. Thankful she'd switched to bikini panties soon after moving in with Stephanie, she pushed them high on her hips. She shifted the skirt to conceal as much of the lacy waistband as possible, when shouts came from outside.

Bood-way scurried to the door, chattering excitedly. She burst outside, followed by the children and Ga-noo.

Violet hung back, cringing at the feel of air on her bare hip.

She couldn't go out. Couldn't face the villagers' stares and reprobation. Couldn't leave the hut, practically naked. Her chest felt as if a forceful hand pressed down on it, and her body wanted to fold in on itself like an origami sculpture.

The old woman turned as she lifted the door-flap. *"Ald ba'aper?"*

You're no more naked than they are, Violet chided herself.

But everyone would see how fat she was.

You're pregnant, you're allowed to be fat. Pushing back her qualms, Violet followed the old woman out the door.

Across the compound, people gathered at the gap in the stockade fence. Shouts and chatter rose from the crowd. When Violet saw the figure in the middle, the breath rushed out of her mouth.

Tony stood above the crowd, the deer slung across his shoulders. He'd taken off his glasses and like the village men, wore nothing but a loincloth. Violet's knees buckled, and longing rose within her. *Heavens, the natives' style suits him.* She gripped the hut's wall to steady herself. She'd had little opportunity to notice while in fear for her life at the hands of the man with the claw necklace, but now Tony was a vision from heaven. Tall and strong, with a sheen of sweat emphasizing the gleaming, white scars on the lean planes of his chest, he staggered toward the village center.

At the big stump, Tony bent, and the deer slid to the ground at the leader-men's feet.

Bood-way ran toward Tony, shouting and motioning for the children to follow. They scrambled to catch up, and Ga-noo shuffled after them.

"Tony!" Violet broke into a run.

He straightened, looking up. Violet wended her way through the crowd. When Tony saw her, his mouth slid open.

She wanted to sink into the dirt. Compared to the villagers, she was a whale.

He didn't seem to mind in the river, her sensible side pointed out. *Or last night.*

She forced herself to look relaxed. If the villagers saw her insecurity, it could mean the difference between their acceptance—or not. She stood straighter, pressing her shoulders back.

Tony's mouth moved before he spoke. "Are- are you okay? Have they done—"

Violet's mouth went dry. "I'm fine," she managed. "The old woman..." Her gaze trailed down his body. Scrapes and newly-formed bruises marred his legs and arms from his tussle with the men. His words while he bargained with them echoed in her mind. *She's mine.* She wet her lips and met his eyes. "These people have been kind. Ga-noo—the old woman—put something on my cut. Perhaps she can treat you—"

"It's nothing." He looked at something behind her.

Violet turned to see Ga-noo and Bood-way, flanked by the children. She tapped Tony's arm. "Tony," she said to the family.

"Doh-nee," the old woman repeated. She pointed to herself. "Ga-noo."

Tony bent down and pushed the deer toward the old woman's feet. A grin split her face, and she chattered to the villagers nearby. A boy pushed his way to Ga-noo's side.

A gasp caught in Violet's throat. The boy who'd thrown the spear at her. "Rod-orak!" the old woman yelled at him. She spoke sternly to him as she pointed at the deer.

The boy muttered under his breath, then snarled something at Tony. Ga-noo repeated her command. Grumbling, he shot Tony a venomous look, then grabbed the deer's forelegs and dragged it through the dust toward the women's hut.

Tony bent to help. *"Nak!"* the boy barked.

Ga-noo and her family led Violet and Tony behind their hut, where woven grass mats circled a smoky fire. Fish lay across a wooden rack over the coals, and Violet's mouth watered at the delectable fragrance. Using a pair of woven grass potholders, Bood-way removed a flat, clay pot from the fire and motioned Violet and Tony to sit. Rod-orak dumped the deer carcass a few feet away, still grumbling.

The meal of cornbread, fish, and broth was surprisingly tasty, flavored with wild onions and savory herbs Violet couldn't name. While they ate, other villagers stopped by to gawk at the newcomers. Violet tried not to feel like she was an exhibitionist—*you're wearing no less than they are!*—ignored the curious stares, and smiled when spoken to kindly. Besides, the villagers were more intrigued by her blond hair and Tony's glasses—which he'd slid back on—than with her size or state of undress. Durch-eye kept touching her hair, and Kay-dan tried to grab Tony's glasses as Ga-noo introduced the rest of the family to him.

As they ate, Violet tried not to look at Tony. A scruffy dog hovered at her back, and three more sat a few feet away. One whined sharply, but since no one else fed them, she pretended not to see the mutt's begging, brown eyes. Rod-orak sat across from Tony, scowling.

After everyone had eaten, Ach-sayay threw scraps to the dogs, and Ga-noo did the same, so Violet tossed them the two bites she couldn't hold. The animals flocked to her side, their tongues lolling. Violet held up her hands. "All gone." Durch-eye giggled, and Bood-way smiled. Violet watched the children collect the leavings, taking care to note which bones they collected in a pile, and which they dropped into a hole beneath a grass mat. Bood-way had moved to the deer, and cut into it with a stone knife, barking orders at Rod-orak, who grudgingly helped. A cloud of flies rose from the carcass as entrails spilled out.

Violet's stomach heaved, and she turned away—only to meet Tony's gaze.

Her belly roiled again, differently.

All morning while they'd walked, she'd mentally relived his leaving her in the rock crevice. She heard constant echoes of his accusations. *You're keeping things from me.* Fear wrapped her in an icy grip.

He knew who she was, what she'd done.

And she still had no idea.

"Tony?" She tossed out her question before she could chicken out. "About last night—"

"You said forget it. I have."

Her heart tumbled over, and the tears she'd cried herself to sleep with threatened to return.

She'd told him she loved him. *Fool.*

She glanced at Bood-way and Rod-orak cutting the deer's skin away from its flesh, and the guts and gore helped her to suck up her feelings. "Last night... you said I'm not being honest. What..." She swallowed. "What on earth were you talking about? What am I keeping from you?"

"I think you know."

"I don't!" The lump lodged in her throat might as well have been a boulder. She'd told him about her memory loss. He hadn't believed her.

Yet, he knew something.

The only way to learn was to convince him to tell her. "I have no idea what you're talking about." She wanted to flinch from his glare, but stood firm. "Have I done something to offend you? Because if I have, I have no idea what. Please, tell me—"

"If you can't admit to it, there's no point. I can't tell you what it is. When you figure it out, we can talk. Until then...." He walked away.

What they'd shared in the rock crevice meant nothing to him.

She couldn't move. Couldn't breathe. Couldn't do anything but stare at the corner of the hut where he'd disappeared. *Damn him.*

She tried to put herself in her worldly roommate Stephanie's mindset. It was just sex. Great sex, yes, but nothing more.

Get over it. Right now, she needed to find some work to do, fit in, and repay Ga-noo for her hospitality. Violet took a deep breath, then emerged from behind the hut to the scrutiny of a thousand eyes.

She stopped and looked around. In truth, there were maybe a dozen eyes on her. A pair of old men ate in the shade beside a nearby hut, and one had stopped chewing, though his mouth was full. He stared at her in unabashed curiosity, while the other man eyed her askance, the tilt of his head showing his intrigue.

Ga-noo sat with a group of women across the compound beneath a wooden lattice covered with dried grasses. They were chopping up something with wide, stone knives and dipping it into urns. Some kind of food preparation, Violet deduced. Perhaps she could help.

Standing straight, she ignored the stares and faced ahead as she walked toward the awning. She refused to look for Tony.

She didn't see him until she almost reached the women and caught a glimpse of pale skin among the men scraping at the dugout canoe.

As she passed, she felt his heated gaze and wanted to cringe. But she managed to reach the women without succumbing, relieved that the nearest hut cut off his view.

"Ulero Via-led." Ga-noo patted the ground between her and a water urn. Fish bones and skins littered flat stones in front of the women. Violet allowed a smile to creep onto her face and sat. A fishy smell laced the smoke, and she was thankful she hadn't been afflicted by morning sickness since waking from recovery.

Ga-noo grabbed a sharp stick and speared something in a pottery jar beside her, then pulled the stick out, revealing a silvery bluegill as big as Violet's foot. The old woman murmured some words to the sky, then held out the stick and a stone knife to Violet. The six other women watched, some with suspicion, some with curiosity, others with doubt. *"Ossessoo,"* a woman wearing a necklace of brown feathers muttered under her breath.

Whatever that word meant, it must be some kind of insult. Violet's soft shape and callous-less hands no doubt made the women think she was a spoiled princess who never worked.

Swallowing her doubts, she took the stick and the knife. She gave Ga-noo a respectful—she hoped—tip of her head, then knelt by one of the stone slabs. She laid the fish on its side, then gripped its head in her left hand, fighting the squeamishness that threatened to rise within her. *It's less gross than the deer!* Gripping the knife firmly in hand, she sliced the fish's head off in a neat angle just behind the gills. The two women opposite her watched silently, their faces indecipherable masks as she pondered where to make the next cut.

Along the guts, vertically...

Excitement jumped inside her. She'd done this before! No pictures came to mind, but the slippery feel of the fish and the way she'd instinctively known where to make the cut told her that she knew how to clean it. She sliced up its underside, then scooped the entrails into a shallow pit beside the fire.

A woman who wore a necklace of drilled shells—smaller than Ga-noo's pottery chips—pointed to a shallow bowl of water. Violet rinsed the fish, then sawed up its body to get two even fillets.

The women's faces held everything from surprise to scowls. Ga-noo beamed. She pointed at Violet's fish, then at the wooden lattice over the fire.

Violet laid the fillets on the rack, then speared another fish from the jar. The others resumed their work.

She had passed her first test.

She looked at the woman with the shell necklace, then pointed to herself. "Violet." She pointed at the woman, then turned up her hand, brows lifted.

Shell-necklace frowned and tilted her head. Ga-noo pointed to her, as Violet had done. "Eard-nay."

"Eard-nay," Violet repeated with a nod.

Ga-noo pointed to the woman on her other side, whose belly bore the distinct roundness of late pregnancy. "O-yo," she said. The woman nodded as Violet pronounced her name.

The one beside her pointed to herself and gave her name. The next woman followed, then the others.

Violet tried to remember the names, noting something about each woman's features, like the moon-shaped scar on Eard-nay's chin and another woman's long earlobes. O-yo was easy—an O like her round belly.

An ache rose in Violet as she thought of her friends, so far away. Stephanie, her housemate. Deshawna and the fellows from the smoking area at work. Their talk seldom went deeper than idle chatter, but now, unable to even tell the village women hello or thank you, Violet suspected the dull ache that had settled beneath her ribs was from loneliness, made worse by Tony's rejection. She cursed the language barrier that prevented her from making conversation. She glanced at O-yo, longing to compare notes on their pregnancies, or if nothing else, ask when her baby was due.

Thank heavens she and Tony would return home before their child was born.

The other women gradually started to chit-chat again, so Violet cut into her second fish. The sooner she showed them she could contribute, the more quickly she'd gain their acceptance.

The sun was sinking in the west by the time all the fish lay on the smoking racks. Violet set the knife down with a sigh. Her hand was blistered and her ankle had begun to hurt again, but she felt she'd proven her worth.

Ga-noo pointed at the dressing on Violet's ankle. *"Ald ba'qyar?"* Though Violet had no idea what that meant, she nodded. The woman pointed at her ankle again.

"Oh!" Violet stretched out her leg. Ga-noo untied the wrap. Violet peered at the wound.

Tony and the work had taken her mind off the soreness, but now that Ga-noo had brought Violet's attention back to it, it hurt like the devil, and was red and puffy. *So much for Alpha's anti-infective injection.* When Ga-noo re-tied the strip of leather, Violet winced.

Ga-noo stood and motioned for Violet to follow.

When they walked around the nearest hut, Violet's gaze darted to the grassy area where she'd last seen Tony. Thankfully, no one lingered near the partially dug-out canoes.

They walked toward Ga-noo's hut. Just outside the front door-flap, Ach-sayay scraped a stretched hide from the deer Violet and Tony had killed. Bood-way sawed at the remains of the carcass, cutting off strips of meat.

In front of the hut where Violet had stolen Tony's loincloth, three men sat beneath a woven grass canopy, stirring jars of black, ochre and red liquids, and mixing powders and roots. Six others sat in a circle, chanting in low, sing-song voices. They stopped and crouched, bowing so low their heads nearly touched the ground.

In the center of the circle sat Tony.

What on earth was going on?

Violet stopped. Tony didn't move. Sunlight glinted off the gold frames of his glasses, sweat glistened on his forehead.

She couldn't take her eyes off him. He was ethereally beautiful, serene, and—

His fingertips twitched on his knee and betrayed his discomfort, which gave Violet an odd surge of satisfaction.

When she passed, he didn't turn his head, but his eyes tracked her movement, his expression frozen and impassive. The men around him raised up, obscuring Violet's view, but not quickly enough to hide his one movement.

He turned away. As if he didn't know her at all. And didn't want to.

Violet hurried to Ga-noo's hut and ducked under the door-flap. Her eyes stung. *Darned smoke.* Though the fire pit in the hut's center didn't look like it had been used in weeks, the scent still pervaded the air. Ga-noo motioned for Violet to sit on a bunk. Violet unwrapped her ankle and tried to stop thinking about Tony. The old woman dug into her herbs and concoctions and dabbed more vinegary-smelling liquid on the wound. She tied the wrap back on, then stood and reached for a bundle of herbs hanging from the hut's rafters, the effort clearly straining her age-weary back.

The old woman couldn't be five feet tall. Violet leaped up, soreness shooting up her leg, and touched the bundle. She looked at the old woman questioningly.

Ga-noo nodded. Violet untied the bundle of herbs and handed it to her.

The woman said something with a gentle face, then spoke sternly as she pointed at the grass mats on the floor, an obvious admonishment to stay off her feet. Violet obeyed.

Ga-noo puttered in her stores, then set a couple of jars on the ground, along with a bundle of dried weeds. She murmured to the weeds in a sing-song voice Violet assumed was a prayer or incantation, then motioned Violet to help her break the stems. They filled the first jar, then started on a second.

Violet couldn't stop thinking of Tony. Who did he think she was, and why did he think she was lying to him? What had she done to him

(killed someone)

in her previous life that was so terrible? Was it someone dear to him?

The thought made her throat clench. Tears burned in her eyes. Her hands stilled on the herbs, and she took a deep breath, trying to regain enough composure to continue working.

Somehow, she'd managed to break up most of the herbs when she heard voices outside. The doorway darkened, and Ach-sayay entered with two women and Rod-orak.

The first woman smiled and said something that sounded friendly.

Rod-orak sat before Violet, holding out a leather pouch. His words held a questioning tone. Violet simply smiled and nodded. The boy opened the pouch so Violet could see the contents.

Leather thongs—like the one Eard-nay's shells were threaded on—and a variety of stones and pottery trinkets with holes in them. *"Kelzoo,"* Rod-orak repeated, and pushed the pouch toward Violet. Ach-sayay and the two women nodded.

The boy lowered his gaze, looking at her through his long, dark lashes. Was he making a peace offering? Hesitantly, she touched a smooth, round, silver-gray pottery chip resembling a coin with a hole in it—

Like the quarter she'd worn on a sparkling, gold chain with inlaid diamond chips, beneath her blood-covered dress on the day Timmy had found her. The first day she could remember.

"Vi-led?" Ach-sayay thrust a leather thong at her. Ga-noo had chosen a trinket, and was threading it onto a leather thong, so Violet did the same. When she finished, Ach-sayay took it and tied the leather behind Violet's neck.

Violet fingered the charm. When she dropped it, it lay cool between her breasts, just as the Ohio quarter had until the day she'd sold the chain five years ago to buy her identity. Or would, many years in the future.

Rod-orak looked at her expectantly, so she gave him another smile, a real one this time. "Thank you." It seemed the thing to say, even though she knew he wouldn't understand.

A sense of peace settled over her like a warm cloak. The coin charm felt right, more than anything had in this forsaken time.

Ten

Tony sat on a rock in the middle of the ceremony, wanting to fidget, wishing he dared to scratch off the war paint—or whatever it was—the native men had applied in rings around his arms, his chest, and his neck. Smoke filled the night air and made him cough, but at least it kept the mosquitoes at bay. The paint helped, too, though Tony would have preferred to dab mud on himself like the villagers—it would probably be less itchy.

Men beat drums, banged sticks and shook rattles made of brightly painted gourds. Women danced in a circle around him, painted with swooshes, circles, and spirals, their breasts bobbing with their movements while others sang. Funny—Bernie, or Tony's brother-in-law Charlie, or any of the guys at Mulroney's would eat this up, but all Tony wanted to do was go to bed. On the hard, lashed-wood bunks. Or on the ground, it didn't matter. After he washed off that damn paint. It had felt good at first, cool on his heated skin. No doubt he was red as a lobster after working in the sun all day. But the coolness had faded as the paint dried, and every time he moved, one of the men hissed a command that he interpreted as an order to stay put, so he figured he'd better obey.

Earlier, they'd taken him inside the sauna hut—the building where Violet had stolen his clothing. He'd carefully mimicked their actions, sitting amidst the heated rocks until sweat trickled down his forehead. Some kind of ritual, he'd realized when the man with the animal claw necklaces had begun a weird, rambling chant. The other men gawked and pointed at Tony's scars. They probably thought he was a great hunter or warrior. He'd sat still and hoped he looked appropriately respectful. The hardest part had been keeping a straight face when another leader-type had walked in wearing Tony's underpants on his head. He wished Violet could've seen it, but the women steered clear of the place—apparently a prehistoric old boys' club. And anyway, Violet was pissed at him, not that he could blame her.

It felt weird, being the center of attention, like a bug on display. Tony hadn't liked it in the sweat hut, and he liked it even less at the ceremony, party, or whatever it was, with the entire village looking on. Some of the villagers' faces bore kindness and respect, but others held haughtiness and judgment. They looked down on him, muttering *ossessok* and other probable insults.

His chest tightened when he glimpsed a long, blond braid. *Violet. Charlotte.*

Beneath the rock crevice, she'd said she loved him.

Like hell. It was a trick. Had to be. Unless...

What if she was telling the truth?

The gnawing, hollowness of guilt swelled in his gut. He'd dismissed her claim out of hand. If she didn't remember, she'd have no idea why—and he'd treated her like dirt for no reason. He'd—

The beat slowed. A woman with painted rings around her arms, neck, and breasts approached, her shell necklaces clinking as she glided toward him. Smiling seductively at him, she reached for his hand.

He let her take it, but didn't clasp hers. She leaned away from him, as if trying to get him to come with her.

He glanced around. Everyone watched. What was this, some kind of mating ritual? Did they think his larger build equaled greater strength—and made him a desirable partner, good for breeding? Whatever the case, he wasn't interested. The woman dropped his hand and slipped away, her disappointment clear in her painted face.

The drummers resumed their fast tempo, and the rhythmic chants and dancing continued.

A few minutes later, a girl who couldn't have been older than Bethany approached. Tony had no more interest in her than the first woman. He was relieved when she, too, gave up and returned to the circle.

They were all too skinny. Too dark. Too... not Violet.

He gaze roved around the assemblage and found her among a group of women laying food out on woven grass mats beyond the fires.

Like before, she wore nothing but a skirt of woven grasses. His muscles tensed, and he fought the urge to run to her and enact the scene in the crevice all over again. Given the modest blouses and below-the-knee skirts she always wore to work, she had to be uncomfortable in that skimpy getup, but she walked through the village like she'd lived there and held those social conventions all her life. It was that inner pride more than anything that made Tony unable to do anything but stare like an idiot.

The leader—Tony thought he'd heard some of the men call him Sesh-wah—approached and stood at Tony's side. He now wore feather-embellished buckskins and a necklace of shells and animal claws. He lifted a clay horn to his lips and blew, and the dancing, drumming and singing stopped. He shouted a command, and the dancers and drummers melted away toward the food-laden mats. Three of the women gestured to Tony to accompany them, so he hopped off the stone and followed.

Carved wooden bowls, pottery, and stiffened skins held all sorts of fragrant delicacies. The village men sat while the women served them. Tony followed their example. A woman placed a wooden platter on the mat before him, and at the flash of her pink dress, his heart leaped.

Not Violet. Bood-way, wearing Violet's dress. He let out his breath. "Uh, thanks." Bood-way smiled at his acknowledgement.

He scanned the gathering. The old woman Ga-noo wore Violet's jacket, and another woman wore Violet's slip over her native garb. Tony caught a glimpse of his jacket on one of the men, then he saw Violet. She moved among the women at the far end of the grass mats, watching the other women, then mimicking their actions as they served the men. As she handed a bowl of soup to Rod-orak, she met

Tony's gaze.

He let himself look, but she whirled around and returned to the stacked wooden platters at the far end of the feast.

Tony turned his attention to his food. Bean soup, turkey broth, deer, rabbit, squirrel, and wild fowl, lightly flavored with onions and herbs. Cornbread was plentiful, and the small pots in the mats' middle held honey. Tony barely tasted anything. All he could think of was Violet, sitting several yards down and across from him. Every time he tried to meet her eyes, she looked away.

His stomach went sour. He'd been a major ass. He needed to apologize, needed to have her again—

The image of her in Pippin's car flashed through his mind, reminding him of where her loyalties lay.

He owed her nothing, after the way she'd played him, the lies she'd told. She might be the mother of his child, be she was also Pippin's puppet. *Fuck her.*

A hush fell over the diners when three couples entered the open area beneath the big pole and performed a play. Though they spoke, it was like watching mimes, since Tony could understand none of the dialogue. All he could figure out was that it had something to do with planting and harvest.

Someone passed him a skin pouch of liquid. He'd seen others drink, so he tipped the skin to his lips. Alcohol burned his throat. "Arrgh!" He shut his mouth, glancing from side to side. The skinny, beak-nosed guy beside him regarded him with a raised eyebrow as he pointed at the wineskin and asked Tony a question.

"Uh…" Unsure what else to do, Tony passed the wineskin back to him.

The guy shook his head and pointed to the man on Tony's other side. As Tony passed the drink to him, the first guy asked him another question.

Tony held up his hands and shook his head. How the hell was he supposed to get on here, when he hadn't a clue what these people were saying?

The beak-nosed man leaned close, squinting at Tony's chest, then straightened, speaking questioningly.

Tony again turned up his palms. The guy might be asking about his scar, but what? And what could Tony tell him, anyway?

The man jabbed a thumb at his own chest. "Aye-sack." He pointed at Tony, his head cocked.

The tension slipped from Tony's shoulders. Finally, something he could understand. He tapped himself in the chest, being careful to avoid the scar

(Charlotte)

where she'd stabbed him. "Tony," he said.

"Doh-nee," the man repeated.

"Aye-sack." Tony pointed at the man.

One of the elders across the mat pointed at the ground in front of Tony and made a tipping motion. The wineskin had made the rounds back to him. *Great.* Tony raised it for another sip. He managed a swallow, then passed the skin to Aye-sack.

When the food was gone, the women collected the dishes. A man wearing three necklaces loaded with shells, feathers, and bones lit a clay pipe, and its earthy fragrance filled the air. Squinting—this time at Tony's glasses—Aye-sack passed the pipe to him. Tony took a cautious toke. Just enough to be polite. Tobacco, combined with something else. He passed it on, and soon another booze-skin came his way.

A sharp voice made him whirl around. It was Ga-noo, speaking to Violet, who was carrying a jug of water. The old woman motioned for Violet to give the jug to another woman, then pointed at one of the logs that the elderly villagers used as seats.

Violet sat, then the woman rolled another log to her, and pointed at Violet's injured ankle, indicating she should prop it up.

Tony couldn't take his eyes off her. The old woman spoke and gestured animatedly. Violet's hand went up to her chest, where a little charm—a small, round piece of pottery, like a coin—hung on a thin, leather strap between her breasts. She rubbed it between her thumb and forefinger like a worry stone.

Tony felt as if his body had frozen from the inside out. It was

Charlotte all over, with the quarter from the future he'd given her.

She'd rubbed the quarter just like that.

If he'd harbored any doubts who Violet really was, they were gone now.

"Doh-nee?" Aye-sack held out another skin of fermented liquid.

Tony didn't want to drink any more, and the last thing he needed was to get shitfaced, but he feared he'd offend his hosts, so he accepted the skin and took a tiny sip before he passed it to the man on his other side.

The men continued to pass the pipes and drink until night fell, bringing with it a chill.

Women carried furs and buckskin capes to the men. The drumming and singing resumed. Across the mats, Ach-sayay draped a deer fur over Rod-orak's shoulders.

"Doh-nee?" a feminine voice said from behind him.

Bood-way crouched behind him, holding a feather in her outstretched hand. A deerskin draped her shoulders, but covered little. "Doh-nee *bunna rild*?" She thrust the feather at him.

"Uh..." Damn. He didn't want to offend her, but who knew what it meant if he accepted the feather? He held up his hands, helplessly shaking his head.

She pointed to the fires, where villagers danced around—mostly young couples, their hands joined. She pointed to one of the women he'd seen with Violet that afternoon, and tried to explain, repeating the words *bunna rild*.

Beside him, a woman tapped his neighbor's shoulder, and offered him a feather. "Tin-darel *bunna rild?*" The man took the feather and allowed her to lead him to the dancing.

Bood-way regarded Tony expectantly.

Holy shit, she was hitting on him. "Uh... no thanks." He wasn't much of a dancer, preferring to sit and drink beer and watch the ladies dance when Mulroney's had music.

Bood-way's expression fell. She touched his elbow, her gaze imploring.

What the hell. They needed to blend in, didn't they? He stood, a

slight dizziness falling over him. Not a jump coming on, unfortunate-
ly, but from the spirits and whatever the hell he'd been smoking.
Unwilling to offend his hostess, he let Bood-way press the feather
into his hand. She tapped his hip at the twine holding his loincloth.
Tony scanned the dancers, and when one crossed behind the fire, he
saw a feather stuck in the man's loincloth like a G-string. With a
sigh, Tony stuck his in *(like a fucking stripper)* and let Bood-way take
his hand and lead him to the dancing.

Tony woke to sunlight streaming in the hut's vent-holes, a sore
back, and a headache from hell. He vaguely remembered Violet coming in with Ga-noo, Bood-way and the children, and taking an empty
bunk across the hut from him. With a groan, he pushed himself up.

Thankfully, the hut was now empty. All he'd done the night before was fall into bed. Although with the dagger-eyed stare he'd
gotten from Violet as he'd left with Bood-way, both women had
undoubtedly expected something more. But hell, as wasted as he'd
been, Tony doubted he'd have been capable of doing anything besides
passing out. He hoped Bood-way wasn't offended that he didn't
return her flirtations beyond dancing.

A male voice spoke sharply from the doorway. Sunlight silhouetted
the speaker, and although Tony couldn't understand the words, they
held an unmistakable tone of "about time you decided to get up."

Rod-orak.

"Good, uh..." *Never mind.* Tony swung his legs over the side of
the bunk and stood.

Ugh, his head hurt. His arms and face itched from those damned
pigments.

With another snide-sounding comment, Rod-orak slipped outside,
letting the door-skin fall before Tony caught it.

He squinted in the harsh light. Though the sun was still in the
east, the day was already growing warm.

After a brief stop at the latrine area, he followed Rod-orak behind the hut, where Bood-way sat on a cluster of woven grass mats with Ga-noo, the kids, and Violet. A breeze carried the fragrance of cornbread, layered beneath the campfire's smoke.

Violet saw him, but turned away, concentrating on her corn cake.

He'd seen her at the ceremony, watching him dancing with Bood-way, her gaze narrow. As if she was angry with him.

Ga-noo chattered in greeting as she pointed to a bowl of what looked like grits or a coarse corn meal cereal.

The whole time he ate, Tony felt Violet's gaze on him. He wanted to ask her how she was feeling. He wanted to ask her if she was mad at him for dancing with Bood-way. He wanted to tell her he was sorry for everything.

No, I don't. Not after all her lies, her betrayal of him to Pippin, her pretending to care—all to help her mentor catch a time criminal. Him.

He scarfed down the cereal. As he finished, Rod-orak spoke with a sneer. *"Ald ba vork."* The boy rubbed his chin.

Tony repeated the motion, and realized what the boy was talking about when his hand brushed his stubbly, three-day beard.

In the early twentieth century, they'd had safety razors, so he'd managed to skirt the facial hair issue then, but there was no getting around it now. None of the village men had beards, and wore their hair past their shoulders. Tony couldn't do anything about his close-cropped hairstyle, but his beard was a difference he could minimize. He drew his finger up the underside of his chin, then held up his hands.

"B'aper." Rod-orak disappeared into the hut, then returned, holding out a thin, flint knife.

(The Mayan priest held the dagger, high above Tony's chest...)

He would not let the punk see his fear. He would do this. Pushing the images away, he forced himself to breathe and grabbed the knife.

It's just chipped stone. And it was gray flint, not black like the one the Mayan priest had plunged into his ribs. Yet he couldn't stop himself from shivering as he dragged his finger along the sharp edge, couldn't stop himself from seeing it in the priest's hand, coming toward his—

With a rude-sounding exclamation, Rod-orak stomped away.

Tony squeezed the knife's smooth handle. He could do this. Ignoring the women's stares, he strode through the opening in the fence and to the river.

He crouched at the bank and scanned the area. Everyone else was still eating the morning meal, so he had the riverbank to himself. *Good.* He laid the knife on the ground and leaned over to splash water over his face, but stopped as he caught a glimpse of his reflection in the water. Damn, the kid was right, he was looking rather scruffy. He splashed his face. With a shaking hand, he reached for the knife, but as he grabbed it, his hand slipped. *For God's sake, get a grip!* Gritting his teeth, he snatched the knife and lifted it to his chin.

Don't-think-about-it-don't-think-about-it. He slowly drew the knife upward, then let out a big breath as he curved it over his chin without the telltale sting of a cut. Somehow he managed to finish without slicing his neck. He got a few nicks for his trouble, but hopefully appeared less of an outsider.

As he neared the entrance through the fence, Rod-orak burst out shouting in an annoyed tone of voice. He motioned Tony forward with one arm, the other full of a half-dozen or so spears, which he thrust at Tony when he reached him. The boy chattered on as he urged Tony through the gate, where the village men were gathering. Most carried spears or bows, and pouches of arrows slung over their shoulders.

A hunting party. Tony glanced back at Ga-noo's hut as he joined the group.

Ga-noo sat in the sun in front of the hut, weaving grasses into mats and talking to Durch-eye and Kay-dan in an animated, storyteller's voice. Bood-way, Ach-sayay, and Violet worked in the garden a few feet away, poking holes in the ground with sharpened branches and pushing the dirt into mounds with hoes made of flat stones tied to sticks. Sweat glistened on their backs, emphasizing Violet's pale skin. Bood-way and Ach-sayay worked steadily, dropping seeds and mounding the dirt, then moving on. Violet paused to catch her breath after covering her seeds. She moved slowly, bending to poke three holes in the ground. As she straightened and reached into the pouch tied at her waist, she listed to one side. She righted herself, grabbed some seeds, placed them into the holes, and bent to reach for her hoe. Swayed. Then crumpled to the ground.

Tony returned from the hunt with heavy steps. His feet were killing him, not only sore from all of the walking, but scratched and bruised. He couldn't remember the last time he'd gone barefoot outdoors. Clutching two rabbits by their ears, Rod-orak smirked at him. Of all the hunters, only Tony was coming back empty-handed. The group had departed as soon as Ga-noo and Bood-way got Violet inside the hut and cooled down. "It's just the heat," she'd said, bristling at Tony's concern when he'd rushed to her side.

All day he'd endured the men's stares. As the afternoon wore on, expectant expressions turned to scorn and derision when Tony claimed no spoils, the men's words a mystery but their tone unmistakable. *Loser.*

With sharp words, Rod-orak wandered behind the hut. Tony followed to find Violet with Bood-way and Ach-sayay, seated before an animal skin stretched over a wooden frame.

The two village women watched while Violet scraped the hide with a wide, flat piece of bone, occasionally commenting and pointing to the skin. Violet nodded and continued scraping.

Life in the village seemed to agree with her much better than it did with him.

Bood-way looked up as they approached. "Rod-orak *ulero.*" The boy handed her his rabbits. She praised his take—or so it sounded—then questioned Tony.

Rod-orak looked sideways at him and responded to his mother, his tone of voice dismissive. Disappointment flashed across Bood-way's face, then she rose. "Vi-led?" She stood and made a come-with-me gesture. Violet got up and followed without looking back.

Tony stared at the packed-dirt ground. He was a failure. Not only that, but Violet wouldn't even look at him. He supposed he deserved that, lousy hunting day or not. His stomach leaden, he wanted to do nothing but sink into the ground. Anything to escape Rod-orak's judging gaze, and those of Ach-sayay and Ga-noo, who sat nearby whittling some bone and rock.

"Etonok," Rod-orak said. *Loser.* A boy shouted from the next hut. Rod-orak spat on the ground near Tony's feet and dashed off.

Anger rose in Tony's belly. Not at Rod-orak, but at himself. He'd fucked up. He'd failed to provide for his hosts—and Violet. Next time, he wouldn't come home empty-handed. Gripping the spears in his fist, he grabbed a bow and Rod-orak's arrows from inside the hut and set off to practice shooting.

By the time Ach-sayay found him, Tony could consistently hit the center of the grass mat he'd staked to the stockade fence from twenty paces. Not a moving target, but a start. At the girl's urging, he followed her behind the hut.

The family sat around the fire. Bood-way was lifting the two spitted rabbits from the coals. "Don-nee *ulero.*" Ga-noo and the children echoed her greeting. Rod-orak scowled. Violet took a sudden interest in the mud she'd dabbed on a bug-bite on her leg. Tony wanted to sink into the ground. *Failure.*

Everyone took a wooden bowl. Bood-way cut meat off the rabbits and dropped some onto each dish.

Small servings when divided eight ways, even with the ever-present cornbread. When Kay-dan tugged at Bood-way's skirt with an unmistakable I'm-still-hungry whine, Tony wanted to curl into himself and disappear.

He tore his meat in two and scraped part onto Kay-dan's plate. As he got up to give the other half to Violet, someone called out from around the hut. "Ga-noo!"

Two women approached around the corner, bearing a wooden platter full of meat. One chattered at Ga-noo and Bood-way as the other laid the platter beside the fire. The woman shot Tony a glance as she spoke questioningly. Rod-orak hid his face in his hands.

Bood-way tipped her head in a slight bow and palmed her chest as she responded to the women. Ach-sayay echoed her action. Ga-noo murmured a prayer over the meat, then tore off a hunk and passed the platter to Rod-orak. *"Etonok,"* he muttered, glaring at Tony. Bood-way shot him a sharp look.

The neighbors chatted with Ga-noo, and she accompanied them around the front of the hut. Bood-way followed, Ach-sayay on her heels.

Tony's stomach growled, so he reached for the meat the neighbors had brought, feeling Rod-orak's gaze. His hand touched a shank the same time as a smaller, pale hand. He looked up to meet Violet's eyes and snatched his hand away to grab a different piece.

She looked warily at him as she tore off a bite of venison. Dark circled her eyes, and her motions were slow and jerky and labored. Yet her skin gleamed in the setting sun, soft and clean. She must have mustered up the courage to go to the river and bathe.

"How... how are you doing?" Tony asked.

She gave a shrug that he could tell was supposed to come across as indifferent. "As well as can be expected."

"What happened out there this morning?"

"I told you. It was the heat. I'm not used to it, working in an air conditioned office, and..." Her gaze drifted down to her belly.

Guilt twinged in Tony. "You look exhausted."

"Of course I'm exhausted!" She heaved a sigh, then pulled something from under her skirt. The gun. "It was lying in your bed. You really should keep it with you."

He snatched it away and gave her a curt nod as he shoved it into the rope holding up his loincloth. Between thinking about her and dealing with Rod-orak's attitude that morning, he'd let the situation get the better of him, made him not pay attention.

Made him forget something important. Something that could get someone killed.

He didn't want to think about that. "So what did you do today?"

She glared. "Tony, if you're trying to make polite conversation, why don't you go find Bood-way? Because I'm not in the mood."

Ouch. He wished he was somewhere else. Anywhere else. Any*time* else. Unable to bear her scrutiny, he looked away—right into the attentive eyes of Rod-orak.

He doesn't know what we're saying. Tony finished off his deer meat, watching Violet eat. Even without cutlery, she managed to look well-mannered, polite and tidy, picking small bites off the venison hank before she put it in her mouth.

He couldn't stand any more of her silent treatment, never mind who she was. He needed to regain her trust. "Look, Violet... I was an asshole yesterday..."

"To put it mildly." She picked off another bite of meat without looking up.

He deserved that. "For what it's worth, what happened the other night... it was a mistake."

"I believe I said that." She took another bite of venison, her gaze fixed on the wooden plate in her lap.

"Well... yeah." He swallowed what felt like a boulder in his throat. If he'd been wearing a shirt, he'd need to loosen his collar.

She sniffed and scrubbed at her eyes with a fist. "Pollen," she muttered.

"Look, uh..." He couldn't bear it, seeing her looking like she was trying to keep from crying and knowing the whole fucking mess was his fault. "I'm sorry. About everything." Even if she was Charlotte. "I guess I'm just an asshole."

She looked off to the side, her eyes unfocused. "You did say we should just be friends."

"Yeah. Believe me, you don't want anything to do with me, and I don't blame you, but... we need to stick together."

She thumbed the coin-like pottery chip between her breasts. "For the baby."

Anger boiled up inside him, burning away his self-loathing. "No, not just for the baby. You're the only other person in this godforsaken time I can talk to."

She studied the grass mat at her feet. "I can't be friends with you. Not after... all this. But you're right, we do need each other." She met his gaze. "Tell me if you feel the Pull coming on, and... I'll keep you informed about the baby. Otherwise, I think it's best if you just... stay away." She let go of the pottery chip and scraped the scraps off her plate.

All Tony could manage was a single nod. He tossed a piece of fat to one of the dogs, then headed for the gap in the stockade fence. He felt dirty. A bath would feel good.

He couldn't chase her image from his mind as he neared the gate. How afraid she'd been. How she'd trembled in his arms, and how he'd calmed her. Just like when he and Charlotte—

Not going there. He looked around the village. Engrossed in campfire chats, the men smoked or whittled or worked stone. The women and children were all busy tending fires and dealing with food preparation or cleanup. No one looked up as he walked out the gate and over the fortification mound to the river. Gritting his teeth, he yanked the gun from under the rope and untied his loincloth. He placed the gun on the ground, then draped the buckskin over it, though he doubted anyone would happen along.

He waded into the river, the cool, moving water a blessing on his skin.

Had Violet conquered her phobia to come in and wash? Or had she sponge-bathed herself like she had as Charlotte, before he'd driven away her fear?

He splashed water on his arms, and his heart twisted. Served him right for getting mixed up with her again, when he knew damn well who she was. His only concern should be for the baby, and gaining her trust so the baby would be his. He had no business making love to her again. No business getting caught up—

On the riverbank, something clicked. Tony's head jerked up, and all he saw was the barrel of his gun. In Rod-orak's hands. Pointing at him.

Eleven

Bethany wove her way through the Riverscape crowd, keeping herself between Mark, Aunt Lisa, and Uncle Charlie. With so many people filling the blocked-off streets for the Fourth of July festival, they were bound to run into someone she knew. Hopefully, between the darkness and the crowds, no one would see her.

Aunt Lisa stopped at a curb. "This should be a good place to see fireworks." Mark and Uncle Charlie mumbled an agreement. Bethany would have rather watched fireworks on TV. Then she wouldn't have to deal with the sidewise glances of pity and scorn, the whispered comments like "Isn't that the family where the uncle strangled that kid..." Even the scent of cotton candy mingled with hotdogs from a nearby cart lacked appeal.

Her aunt sat, and Bethany dropped beside her, untucking her new T-shirt. If anyone said anything, the snarky cartoon bunny on the shirt would speak for her: *Hi. Cram it.*

Lisa wrinkled her nose. "Is that what came in the mail today?"

"Yeah." Bethany folded her arms across her lap.

Mark laughed. Though he was lucky enough to have a different last name, kids at school knew she was his cousin, and he'd gotten his share of whispered, rude comments amidst the expressions of sympathy. He nudged Bethany with his elbow. "Isn't that Mrs. Michaelson? The Civics teacher?"

"Uh huh." *Crap.* Bethany wanted to shrink and hide. She looked away, but too late. The woman turned to her husband. "Poor thing, that's the girl whose dad..." Bethany could hear her even over the nearby vendor hawking overpriced, bottled water.

He didn't do it! Bethany wanted to yell. She cradled her face in her hands and looked into the gutter. In the dim light, a wad of gum lay there like a big, gray blob.

Lisa squeezed her arm. They'd all dealt with it, especially Uncle Charlie, who like Bethany's mom, had worked with her dad.

At least Charlie didn't leave town. Bethany hadn't spoken to her mom in three weeks.

She watched the night sky. The sooner the fireworks started, the sooner they'd be over and the sooner Bethany could go back to hiding in her aunt's house. She chewed on her lip, unable to stop the thoughts that sneaked into her mind at times like this.

What if her dad really had killed Danny?

He didn't!

But then why did he disappear? It looked pretty bad. She felt like she was riding in a runaway truck, barreling over a hilly road and leaving her stomach behind.

There had been no evidence of a struggle. But even if her dad had killed Danny, he wouldn't have run. Not her dad. He was always honest, sometimes more than he should be. He'd own up to what happened, no matter how far-fetched—

Mark elbowed her ribs, making her unclench fists she didn't realize she'd made. "Hey Beth, isn't that—"

"Taylor!" Bethany called to the girl in the halter top and ruffled, black skirt over red-and-white-striped stockings and army boots.

"Hey, Bethany," Taylor greeted her. "Hi Mark."

"Glad Chad finally let you out of the house," Bethany said. It had been six weeks since the night she'd run to Taylor's house for the information on her dad that turned out to be nothing.

She'd spent over a hundred bucks on a miniature listening device that she hid in the corner of a window so she could hear them talking. But after three days of sitting in her car, one street over, the most interesting thing she learned was that Alpha had left—and taken a dog from the Humane Society with her, which wasn't allowed, wherever she was going. Bethany had talked to Taylor several times since then, but every time she suggested getting together, Taylor had some lame-sounding excuse.

Bethany scooted over to make room on the curb between her and Mark. Taylor accepted the unspoken invitation and sat.

"So, uh," Bethany said, "you heard from anyone interesting lately?"

Taylor's mouth tightened. "You know I'd call if I did."

"Keith!" Bethany's Uncle Charlie stood, waving. Bethany stood and stretched up to see.

Keith Lynch, Charlie's boss. And her mom's. Until a couple months ago, her dad's, too.

Bethany had known Keith as long as she could remember. When she was little he'd come over for dinner every now and then, and he'd always brought her a toy or special treat. He'd talked to her like she was an adult—usually about movies or sports, and when he asked her a question, he listened to the answer, no matter how long she blathered.

Just like her dad always had. The CEO waved and wended his way through the crowd. He hadn't stayed long at Danny's funeral, but after giving the requisite "I'm sorrys" about Danny, he'd taken Bethany aside, and told her he was sure her dad was innocent. Since then, he'd called her once a week or so, just to see how she—and Charlie's family—were doing.

He emerged from the crowd beside Charlie and greeted everyone. "Bethany. How are you doing?" He squeezed her hand.

"Okay, I guess." Bethany looked into his warm, brown eyes and all of a sudden she wanted to throw herself at the older man and cry.

Keith patted her on the back and the teary feeling went away. She pointed to her left. "Keith, this is Taylor. She was... Danny's girl-friend." Taylor looked down, her posture tense. "And my friend," Bethany quickly added.

Keith gave her a nod. "Good to meet you." He started to say something else when a derisive, female voice broke through the noise of the crowd.

"Look, it's Bethany Solomon, the murderer's daughter." Girls cackled.

Tammy Kitchener and her clique from school, clad in baby-doll tops and super-short shorts Bethany's dad would have never let her wear. "Bite me," Bethany snarled.

The girls walked away, tittering.

"That's sad about your classmates, Bethany," Aunt Lisa said in a voice just loud enough for the snooty bitches to hear. "Their lives must be so boring, if they don't have anything better to talk about."

Taylor leaned close. "You know, if I was a big girl like her, I'd have figured out that I don't look good in something that skimpy."

Bethany couldn't suppress a giggle.

"We know he didn't do it, and we'll find the truth," Keith said. Lisa gave him a strange look. He pulled out a smartphone, glanced at it, wiped the screen with his thumb, and shoved it back into his pocket. "Hey Charlie, did you see on the news where that fisherman in Indiana found a trilobite?"

Mark wrinkled his nose. "Why would a fossil be on the news? Those things are everywhere."

"Not live ones," Charlie said.

Bethany jerked her chin down. "A live trilobite?"

"Got scientists stumped," Keith said. "I'm surprised you didn't see—"

"Um, we don't watch the news much." Bethany jammed her hands into her pockets. Taylor fingered her cell phone, making Bethany think of the call she'd made after the disappearing bridge incident. The same kind of weird happening.

Bethany studied Keith as the men chatted about sports. He'd sounded pretty sure about her dad. Did he know about the alleged double?

Keith stood and told everyone goodbye. He turned to Bethany. "Hey, stop by the office sometime. You ever decide you want a job, I'll hook you up."

If Keith knew something, what better way to find out? "Thanks, Mr. Lynch."

He cocked his head. "Hey, what's with the Mr. Lynch stuff? It's been Keith ever since you could talk."

She gave him a tight-mouthed smile, and the squinched-up feeling like she was about to cry returned. God, he reminded her so much of her dad.

He touched her arm. "Hey, B, keep your chin up, 'kay?"

She swallowed and gave a sharp nod. "I will." As she watched him disappear into the crowd, something hung in the back of her mind. Something he reminded her of.

A few minutes later the fireworks started, and it came to her. The burglar at Taylor's house. His voice had reminded her of someone—and he'd called her "B."

Like Keith.

When Tony and the hunters emerged from the sweat lodge, he sneaked off behind the hut to wipe his gun on his loincloth. His sweat-dampened clothing couldn't be good for it, especially on top of the typical, summer humidity. But since the close call with Rod-orak, Tony kept the firearm close at hand. Next time, he might not be so lucky to be able to wrest it away before someone got hurt.

He wrapped the weapon back up in the scrap of leather he'd found, then jammed it back under the rope around his waist, where the buckskin flap of his loincloth hid it. He always felt gross after sitting in the sweat lodge, and that morning, they'd stayed in there a good couple of hours—longer than usual. Did he have time for a bath?

The village was a flurry of activity as men collected bedrolls, women packed their knapsacks full of jerky, corn cakes and other provisions, and children gathered up tools and weapons. He hadn't seen any deer near the village in several weeks. That and the extra-long preparatory ritual in the sweat hut told him the men were going on an extended hunting trip.

He started to sneak off to the river, but a shout made him stop. "Doh-nee!" Tin-darel thrust a handful of arrows and spearheads into

Tony's hands. He pointed at Aye-sack's hut, where the toolmaker sat beneath a grass awning in front, chipping at something on a flat stone.

The spears and arrowheads were chipped and broken. Tony nodded.

On his way across the plaza, he passed groups of men chatting, laughing, sharing pipes, or playing a game where they tossed pebbles into a circle drawn in the dirt. *"Etonok,"* muttered one of the men as Tony walked past. *Loser.* Vin-gah was one of those who'd argued when Tony and Violet first arrived, and never regarded Tony without a sneer, even though he hadn't returned empty-handed from a hunt since that first day.

Aye-sack was engrossed in conversation with Sesh-wah, the leader who'd donned the feather cape for the ceremony on Tony and Violet's first night in the village. Tony slid to the ground in the shade to wait.

Half-chiseled arrowheads and pieces of flint lay in a pile beside him. He picked one up and turned it over, examining the neatly chipped stone.

Other than the silence between him and Violet, things hadn't been so bad once his stomach had grown used to the diet. Not seeing Bethany was the worst.

He laid down the arrowhead and grabbed another, fingering its smooth-chiseled side. He'd missed her eighteenth birthday. He hadn't been there for her graduation. And it wrenched his heart to think she'd spent the Fourth of July without him. They always went to see fireworks together—it was a special night each summer. He set the arrowhead next to the first and grabbed a third.

Bethany at least got to see fireworks—Lisa and Charlie surely would have taken her. But Danny would never see fireworks again, thanks to the killer with Tony's face.

His jaw tightened. No doubt his disappearance had already confirmed his guilt in the court of public opinion. On top of the loss of her cousin, did Bethany have to put up with gossip about her dad being a murderer?

He put the arrowhead down beside the first. The villagers seldom stared or whispered anymore, though Tony's glasses still made a few nervous. He'd finally gotten so he could shave without images swimming in his head of the ancient Mayans about to sacrifice him.

He gazed across the compound as he picked up a half-chiseled rock. At Ga-noo's hut, a round, pale form with a blond braid bustled around a deerskin stretched on a wooden frame, scraping it with a wide, flat bone. Her movements were sure and confident as she went about the task with no more difficulty than she'd have typing on her computer at work.

The first time she'd skinned a rabbit, she'd retched and run behind the hut to puke. When he'd field-dressed the deer, Tony had to admit it he'd found it pretty gross, too, even though he'd done it that one time, years ago with his uncle. Now, he barely noticed.

But keeping his mind off Violet was one thing that hadn't grown easier with time.

She rubbed the pottery chip hanging between her breasts while she examined the buckskin with an appraising look, then dropped the bone scraper and moved to a pile of wood stacked alongside the hut. She pulled out a thin, split log. Tony's stomach twisted. That was where he'd stashed his extra ammo. *Just don't dig too far.* He fingered the leather pouch at his hip that concealed his gun. He'd counted on the wood to last a while before he'd have to move the ammo. He hadn't thought to mention it to Violet.

She positioned the split piece of wood over a smaller, whole limb, then grabbed a piece of twine and bound the wood together with a tidy X. After that, she lashed several more pieces of wood to the first. What the heck was she building?

Want smoldered in his gut. He longed to touch her smooth skin, brush the loose strands of hair from her face, rub his hands over her round belly. Had she felt the baby move yet?

"Doh-nee?" Aye-sack called as Sesh-wah departed. Tony gathered his weapons.

Aye-sack gave Tony a questioning look as he pointed at Tony's tidy row of arrowheads and flint. Biggest to smallest, with the finished ones first.

Tony hadn't even realized he'd done it.

He laid the dull and broken arrows, spears, and tools out before the craftsman. Although all of the men knew how to make tools and often gathered in the sweat hut in the evenings to work the stone, they tended to expect extra from Aye-sack. He was physically hale, and Tony guessed he was no older than twenty-five, yet the man never hunted.

Aye-sack picked up a spearhead and held it inches from his face to examine it, then placed the spearhead on an upended stump, leaning close as he struck the edges with the stone.

Tony drew back. Was the guy crazy? If a piece of flint chipped off and hit him in the eye, he'd be blinded—

That's why he doesn't hunt. "Aye-sack?" Tony slid his glasses off.

The toolmaker looked up, his hand poised and about to strike. *"Orp?"*

Tony held out his glasses, then thrust them at the toolmaker's face, trying to indicate that he should put them on.

The man recoiled, pointing at the shining, gold frames. *"Nak!"* Chattering in sharp, high-pitched words, he shook his head emphatically.

"They won't hurt you," Tony said in a calm voice. "Just try it... look." Tony bent close to the toolmaker's stump, squinting at the spearhead while he picked up the stone Aye-sack had dropped and pretended to work. Then he slid his glasses on, picked up the rock and repeated the motions, but without leaning so close. Aye-sack regarded Tony with curiosity. Tony took off his glasses and motioned the man to come near.

Hesitantly, Aye-sack leaned forward and let Tony slide the glasses on him.

The toolmaker blinked. Then as he gazed around the compound, a huge grin spread across his face. Jabbering excitedly, he pointed at a hawk circling overhead. *"Rayboo!"* He gazed at the river. *"Blikok!"* He prattled on, and pointed out other objects Tony guessed he'd never seen clearly from such a distance.

Tony had made a friend.

The sun was high in the sky by the time the men were ready to leave. Tony counted thirty-three at the fence gate, including himself and Rod-orak. He suspected this was the boy's first such trip, judging from his attitude, which alternated between diffidence and haughtiness.

When Tony saw Violet he stopped short.

She'd built a chair. A comfortable-looking, Adirondack-style chair. Ga-noo hobbled toward it, grasping Violet's hand. Violet motioned for her to sit. Ga-noo gave Violet a doubtful look. Violet repeated the gesture. The old woman lowered herself into the chair, and when Violet gently pushed her against the backrest, Ga-noo's face lit up like a bonfire.

As Charlotte, Violet had worked in R&D, so her cleverness was no surprise. Before he met her in 1933, she'd often repaired electronics and mechanical things for neighbors, taking pleasure in performing simple acts of kindness. It didn't matter that few of the recipients were able to pay her cash, instead offering canned vegetables or even tinfoil, which she'd graciously accepted.

Tony's throat swelled and he rejoined the men before his mind wandered to places it shouldn't.

He wished he could speak the villagers' language. Days filled with hunting, tool making and re-thatching the huts left him exhausted at the end of each day, and all he wanted to do after supper was collapse onto his bunk, leaving little time to learn more than a few words. Like *deasok* was corn, and *hyok* meant hunt. *Nak* meant no, and *orp* was an affirmative. A *newk* was a house, and *brugoo* meant "deer" but *ba brug* meant "to hunt deer." He'd figured out that *etonok* was an insult when Bood-way had smacked Rod-orak on the head for saying it to Tony.

Thankfully, he had little time to gaze at Violet's round form in her bunk across the hut and wonder and want.

The hunters shouldered their packs, slings, and quivers of arrows, then lined up by the gap in the fence. Tony slid into the middle of the line beside Tin-darel. Two men behind him muttered amongst themselves as Sesh-wah surveyed the group.

The chief stopped and scowled at Tony, his downturned eyebrows matching the quillwork on his vest. He pointed toward the village and barked an order at Tony.

Tony fingered his gun in its pouch. What the hell?

Vin-gah jabbed Tony in the ribs, repeating the leader's words in a sharp voice. Sesh-wah's glare deepened. He pointed to the hunter who brought up the rear. Tony realized the leader wanted him to go last, and scurried to the end of the line amidst derisive-sounding mutters and quiet catcalls.

Sesh-wah gave a smug, satisfied nod, and the group filed out of the village.

They walked upriver all day, stopping only occasionally to rest or snag some small game. When they stopped for lunch in a clearing, Tony rubbed his aching feet and glanced at Rod-orak. The kid had grumbled and whined for the last couple hours, unmistakably reminiscent of "are-we-there-yet." Tin-darel spoke harshly to the boy as he thrust a corn cake at him.

The night was uneventful, though the sentries posted at the edge of the camp made Tony expect otherwise. He tried to sleep, but did nothing but toss and turn. He wanted to think it was because of the bumpy ground, but when he was honest with himself, he had to admit it was because he couldn't stop thinking of Violet. He wanted to see her, to be beside her, to talk to her, even though she rarely spoke to him, even though by all rights, he shouldn't want her to, unless it was about the baby.

When the sun rose, they packed up and continued walking. Throughout the morning, the group cut away from the river and made its way up a ravine that looked vaguely familiar. As they walked along the trail that ran along the bluffs, Tony realized it was the Community Golf Course in his time. On the ridge above would be Hills and Dales Park, where he'd taken Bethany, Mark, and Danny hiking when they were little. He tried not to think about the last time he'd played golf at Community—with Danny.

His throat thick, he forced himself to move forward, staring at the ground.

At shouts from above, the party stopped. Men pointed, chattering wildly. In his daydreaming, Tony had fallen behind. He craned his neck, trying to see what they were looking at atop the sloped, gorge wall.

Then he saw it. A huge, black bear.

And Rod-orak, climbing the bluff, trying to get closer.

"Rod-orak! *Nak!*" Tony shouted, but the boy continued upward, gripping a root to pull himself up.

The animal roared and reared on its hind legs. Tony's grip tightened on his spear. Something crashed through the underbrush near the bear, then two cubs appeared. Rod-orak lunged at one with his spear.

The big bear howled.

Tony glanced down the trail. The others were running toward him, but they were too far to be of any help to Rod-orak.

The mother bear closed the distance between herself and her cub, and took a swipe at the boy.

Rod-orak leapt away. "Hyah!" He hefted his spear and jumped at her again.

Idiot! Gripping his spear, Tony climbed up the rocky slope, barely conscious of pounding footfalls below.

As he pulled himself over the top, the mother bear roared and loomed closer to Rod-orak. Tony's hand slipped. When he grabbed for a sapling with his other hand, his spear clattered down the hill. The bear reared up again and growled. Rod-orak's eyes went round and he bolted for the bluff's edge, as if he'd suddenly realized his stupidity. "Rod-orak!" Tony reached for him, but the bear got there first, swiping at him with huge, sharp claws.

The flesh on Rod-orak's leg tore away in bloody tatters. The boy screamed as the bear rushed him again. Tony groped for his spear, then remembered he'd dropped it.

He jammed his hand into the leather pouch and whipped out the Sig. He sighted the gun and fired.

The report echoed through the forest. The bear fell to all fours, howling. The metallic scent of blood mingled with the damp, earthy fragrance of the forest and the tang of gunpowder.

Rod-orak's wails reached through the haze in Tony's mind. The bear stumbled away, red oozing down its flank. Tony rushed to Rod-orak's side as three men crested the hill.

Tin-darel surveyed the teen's leg, then barked orders at the others. *"Llirdi b'athas,"* he said to Tony with a slight bow.

It might have been an expression of gratitude. But Tony couldn't mistake the suspicion and fear in the men's eyes as they wrapped the boy in a deerskin blanket and carried him down the bluff.

Tin-darel and Tony bound Rod-orak's leg in scraps of leather, but blood soon soaked through. They fashioned a litter by stretching the blanket between two sticks, and carried Rod-orak. The boy whined and moaned, then fell silent, which worried Tony more. Had he passed out from the pain, gone into shock, or worse?

The group stopped at the next clearing. As the men broke out the corn cakes and jerky, Vin-gah and Sesh-wah appeared, dragging the bear. The gunshot must've wounded it, slowed it down enough for them to close in for a kill.

Tin-darel mixed up a concoction of herbs and applied it to the boy's injured leg. When the hunter sang a song over him, Rod-orak stirred and moaned. Tin-darel lifted a hollowed-out gourd of herb tea to the boy's lips, but most of it dribbled out the corner of his mouth. Tony grabbed his knife and slipped away to help the others field dress the bear.

He'd gotten over his fear. Gotten so he didn't see the Mayan priest and his stone dagger every time he picked up a stone knife. Only about every other time. Gritting his teeth, he cut into the bear. Though the men didn't refuse his help, none met his gaze.

He swiped off his glasses to wipe them on his loincloth. Even after saving a boy's life, they regarded him with wariness and suspicion.

The herbs and tea helped Rod-orak, for when Tony returned, he sat up and ate.

"Doh-nee!" he called as the men cleaned up from the meal. "Doh-nee!" He pointed at himself and gave Tony an order. Tony hurried to the boy's side.

Rod-orak repeated the request, reaching for the bump at Tony's waist.

Tony scooted away. *"Nak!"* Rod-orak grabbed at him again, but Tony jumped to his feet, and Rod-orak's hand flopped on the ground.

Tin-darel approached, said something in an apologetic tone to Tony, then crouched beside Rod-orak, speaking sternly.

Unease stirred in Tony's gut as he collected his spears and arrows. Rod-orak was the sort to experiment first, and ask questions later—if at all.

Across the clearing, Tin-darel clutched something in his fist, shaking it at Sesh-wah. "Doh-nee *bin drok!*"

"Doh-nee *ba'osessok!*" The leader snarled.

They were arguing. Tony scooted aside, so that a tree blocked him from their view. Tin-darel shouted something about Rod-orak, then Tony heard his name again.

Tin-darel walked away from Sesh-wah with a snort, then strode across the clearing toward Tony.

Tony remained seated and forced his body not to tense. Tin-darel crouched in front of him, and held out the subject of his and Sesh-wah's argument, speaking in a soft, respectful tone. *"Doekoo kelz."*

Ten bear claws with holes punched through them hung on a leather thong, a smaller, simpler version of the necklace Sesh-wah wore. "Doh-nee, *ba-byll."* Tin-darel thrust the necklace at him.

He was giving Tony a gift for saving his nephew's life. Tony took it. Tin-darel traced around his neck, indicating that he should put it on.

Tony reached behind his neck and tied the leather thong, grateful that the hunter had left it long enough not to hit the scar. His neck never hurt, but wearing anything tight gave him the creeps.

The man nodded and spoke emphatically, tipping his head down and palming his chest. Tony mimicked the action, and it apparently satisfied Tin-darel, for he smiled, then returned to his post beside Rod-orak.

Tony chewed his jerky, facing the injured teen, who whined,

pointing to his leg. Tin-darel gave him more tea. But as the men collected their weapons to return to the village, Tony crept over to Rod-orak's side.

The boy lay silent, his skin ashen. Blood soaked the wraps on his legs and pooled beneath them. There'd been a lot of blood as the men had carried him away, too.

He might not have to worry about his gun after all.

After the men brought Rod-orak home, Violet stayed inside the hut with the feverish teenager while the other women worked in the gardens. Although she wasn't happy about the reason, it was a relief to stay inside, out of the relentless sun.

She held a waterskin to Rod-orak's parched lips. His skin burned beneath her hand, and he mumbled incoherently. Tony had told her he was concerned about blood loss, but by the time they'd reached the village, infection had set in, as well.

"Poor fellow," Violet murmured. "I wish there was more I could do." She dabbed his forehead with a soft, moistened rabbit skin, then peeled the wrappings off his leg and dabbed more of Ga-noo's herbal concoction on his crusty wounds.

Futile. She looked down and saw that in her frustration, she'd torn the rabbit skin wipe in two. What they needed were antibiotics. Without them, the boy's chances of recovery weren't good.

As she slid the jar back under Ga-noo's bunk, an idea struck her. Penicillin was grown from mold. And hadn't she seen on one of those history documentaries that the ancient Greeks had used mold to treat infection?

She patted Rod-orak's arm. "I'll be back," she said, even though the boy wouldn't hear her in his delirium.

She dashed out to the garbage pit and dug through bones, cartilage and gristle left from lunch, scraps of leather too small or worn to be of use, and broken chips of pottery, until she found the moldy corncobs she'd seen a couple days earlier. She moved the offal away, careful not to lose any of the mold. It had spread since she'd first seen it. Good.

She returned to the feverish boy and picked some mold off the corncobs. Then she dropped the small pieces onto the nasty welts, crumbling the larger globs. Rod-orak turned his head from side to side, but didn't otherwise react. She rewrapped his leg. A small groan escaped his lips, but his eyes remained shut.

The door flap lifted, and Sesh-wah burst in, flanked by Ga-noo and Tin-darel, who Violet had figured out was the older woman's son and Bood-way's brother. Sesh-wah pointed at Rod-orak, barking orders. Violet rolled back on her heels and twiddled her pottery chip necklace.

Ga-noo protested. Sesh-wah held up a hand, silencing her, then turned to Violet, his admonishment clear, even though she didn't understand his words.

If Rod-orak didn't make it, he'd hold her responsible.

Violet woke to the sound of thunder, and rain pelting the hut's roof. It had been three days since the hunting party had returned. She'd managed to explain to Ga-noo, Bood-way, and Ach-sayay what she wanted, and the villagers had brought her more mold, though they regarded her with wary expressions. Tony'd told her about firing the gun, and she noticed that the villagers kept an even wider distance than they had before.

She applied mold to Rod-orak's leg three times a day, along with Ga-noo's herbal tincture. Ga-noo had placed fist-sized, leather pouches beside the boy's leg, his head, and his arms, and she and Bood-way sang and prayed over him several times a day. Violet took care not to disturb the bundles. She pressed the back of her hand to his forehead. Was his skin cooler than it had been that afternoon? She hoped it wasn't wishful thinking.

Lightning flickered in the triangle-shaped ventilation holes, illuminating the almost-empty hut. Bood-way and Ach-sayay had left Violet with Rod-orak and the young children. They were spending their *ingengoo* in the big hut that only women entered, as Violet had realized was customary—a monthly inconvenience her pregnancy spared her.

Ga-noo was with O-yo and her family, participating in a funeral ritual. Violet could hear the wails and chants from O-yo's hut between thunderclaps. She wanted to cover her ears, bury herself under the furs on her bunk, slide close to the sleeping Rod-orak or little Durch-eye, anything to wipe away the image of O-yo's premature, stillborn baby. Violet twiddled her pottery chip. Usually, the trinket's similarity to her quarter brought her comfort, but that night, it didn't help.

O-yo's was the second delivery Ga-noo, who was apparently the village midwife, had indicated she wanted Violet to assist with. Not bad training for someone soon to give birth herself. But Violet couldn't stop thinking about O-yo and the tiny baby, couldn't stop the tears from springing to her eyes, couldn't stop wanting to go to Tony and cling to him, tell him about the horrible event, share her fears.

Fortunately, she had no idea where he was. And thank heavens her baby wouldn't be born until after the Pull took them home.

Another flash of lightning illuminated Kay-dan, sleeping on the bunk below Tony's. The little boy's chest slowly expanded and contracted with his breathing. Thunder rumbled again, reverberating through the village. How lucky Rod-orak and the little ones were to sleep through it.

"Vi-led?"

She jumped at the sound of her name from the bunk beside hers. "Rod-orak?" His voice sounded stronger, less wavering. She leapt to his side and touched his forehead.

The heaviness in her chest lightened. *Thank heavens.* His skin had definitely cooled. She pressed the back of her hand to her own forehead. It was the same temperature as Rod-orak's. Had his fever finally broken?

"Kalchoo," the boy said.

Water. She groped for the gourd dipper, but it wasn't in its usual place between the door and the water urn. When lightning flared again, she saw what had happened.

Rod-orak and Tony's tools and weapons hung in a tidy row, biggest to smallest, spears first, then arrows, then knives. Then other tools, including the gourd dipper.

Tony. Ordering things again. Trying not to laugh—she didn't want Rod-orak to think she was amused at him—she grabbed the gourd and helped him sit up to drink. A crack of thunder almost made her drop the gourd, but Rod-orak lifted it from her hands. After he finished, they sat and watched the lightning in the vent-holes.

"Izznok," Rod-orak said.

"Izznok?" Violet's tongue tripped over the awkward syllables.

He remained silent. When lightning flashed again, he repeated the word.

Lightning! At least that's what Violet thought he was saying. *"Izznok,"* she said, and this time her pronunciation came closer to his. As lightning flashed again, he repeated the word, his tone one of confirmation.

By the time the storm abated, Violet had learned *honzoo* was dirt (or maybe floor), *zharroo* meant bed, and *vroldok* was thunder. Rod-orak taught her words for other things around the hut until he tired and drifted back to sleep.

Violet huddled on her bunk, wishing she could do the same. Rod-orak's language lessons had occupied her mind, but now she couldn't stop worrying about her child. Couldn't exorcise the image of O-yo's silent, still baby and his ashy, blue skin. Between that and the bubbly, gassy feeling in her tummy, it would be a miracle if she slept at all.

The door flap lifted. "Violet?"

The quivering in Violet's belly stilled. "Tony?" Silhouetted amidst the lightning, a tall form ducked inside. "Where were you?"

"I ate dinner with Aye-sack and his family. Eard-nay about went nuts. They're used to having to take whatever everyone else gives them, but Aye-sack was actually able to hunt when I let him wear my glasses." She heard the shaking of cloth, spraying water droplets near the door. "I figured I might as well stick around with them when the storm came up."

She waited for him to climb into his bunk above Kay-dan's.

She didn't want him to.

O-yo's baby... if he'd been born in the twenty-first century, he'd probably have lived.

She squeezed her eyes shut against the threatening tears. She wanted Tony to sit with her, comfort her, hold her, like he had in the rock crevice their first night after recovery. Sometimes it was almost more than she could bear, sharing meals and sleeping in the same room yet hardly speaking to him, never touching him.

In the silence, she heard no swish of leathers, could barely hear his breathing. "Tony?"

"I was just wondering how you were doing," he finally said from beside her bunk. "I... I saw O-yo's baby... the funeral ceremony."

Violet wrapped her arms around her belly, tried to control her breathing, tried to will away the tears. *Blasted hormones.* "It... It was horrible. He was so little. So still. So cold. All I could think of was my- our baby..."

Footsteps padded toward her, then her lashed-wood bunk creaked as he sat beside her.

Fireworks shot up her body, and the air in the hut's interior went stale with danger. Warmth circled her along with Tony's arm. He drew her close and pulled her against him, the dampness on his skin burning through her blanket like it was scalding water and not just drying rain. "Everything'll be okay," he said softly.

Alarm choked her, warring with a sense of rightness and comfort. She wanted to pull away, yet she didn't. She wanted to believe him. Wanted to drink in the closeness, the tenderness of his voice, the caring in his words. Wanted to lift her face to his and kiss him sense-less. "Tony, I don't think—"

A crack of thunder broke her thoughts, and his embrace tight-ened. "Tony," she began again, "this isn't a good idea."

"What isn't?" His hand shifted on her shoulder.

"You... and me. This..."

He moved his hand up and down her back, sending tingles through her, even though his hand was over the blanket. "I'm just... that baby. It kinda freaked me out, too."

She bit down on her tongue. The urge to press herself to him, to feel him against the length of her body almost overwhelmed her.

She wanted him there. And wanted much more. *It's the pregnancy.* Her hormones going wild. This time, she wouldn't give in to her impulses.

She reached for his neck, fingering the bear claw necklace she'd glimpsed when he'd returned from the hunt. "Where did you get this?"

"Tin-darel gave it to me. For saving Rod-orak's life, I think."

She traced the claws, and her chest swelled with pride and want.

Tony had saved a life. He was a hero, deserving of honor. And the necklace had looked incredibly sexy on him, made him look animalistic, wild and strong. She swallowed before she said something she shouldn't. "That... must be a great honor."

"I guess so. Shooting that bear..." She felt him shrug. "I just did what any decent person would've."

"Maybe. Maybe not—" Her stomach bubbled again, and she jumped.

"What?" Tony's arm on her back stilled.

"I'm just... my stomach's been a little upset these past few days."

His arm stiffened. "You're not sick like when we first got here—"

"No, nothing like that, thank heavens." A couple of days after they'd arrived in the village, she must've run to the toilet area behind the gardens every twenty minutes, until her constitution grew used to the diet. "Just... sort of bubbly in my tummy. Otherwise, I feel fine—"

He drew away a little. "Have you felt the baby move?"

"Have I—" It dawned on her. When her coworker Deshawna was pregnant, that was how she described it. "I— I'm not sure." Violet pressed her palm to her belly.

Something beneath it fluttered.

Violet went breathless. "It *is* the baby!" She grabbed Tony's hand and placed it on her abdomen where she'd felt the fluttering.

Her belly bubbled again. She sensed Tony smiling in the darkness. "I think you're right." His hand on her belly and his closeness pushed away her unease. For this short time, she could pretend they were the family she longed to be. A normal, happy, twenty-first century couple expecting their first child.

She snuggled closer to him. If holding her was all he wanted, she would let him.

The rain slacked off. Tony drew back. Violet sensed him lowering his head toward hers. When his lips met hers, thrills rushed through her.

Along with fear. She forced herself to push him away. "Tony, I think you'd better go to your own bed."

"I'm not sleepy." But he got up, the bunk creaking. Though she couldn't see him in the darkness, she tracked him crossing the packed-dirt floor, lifting the door flap and walking away.

This time, she couldn't stop the tears or the ache the swelled inside her. *It's for the best.*

Twelve

Bethany wanted to hide behind the brick planter and the fake trees that made up the pizza joint's Italian piazza décor—but their former neighbor had already seen her and her mom. She plastered on a smile.

A look of horror flashed across her mom's face before she did the same. "Sue! How nice to see you," she said in what Bethany recognized as her fake-friendly voice.

"Dora! How've you been? And Bethany. You graduated this year, didn't you? What've you been up to, Dora?" The woman flashed a too-big smile that was as fake as the one Bethany's mom gave in return.

"Getting settled down south."

The women chatted about the weather and how hot Atlanta was in August. Finally, a cashier called out a number over the P.A. "Oh! That's my order," Mrs. Parker said. "Take care, okay?"

Bethany didn't look up when she left. Better to concentrate on her food. Going out for pizza was a lot more fun with Taylor. It had become a habit with the girls—a movie every Saturday afternoon, then Marion's afterward.

And later, the occasional fork, salt shaker, or handful of straws in Bethany's purse.

As much as Bethany liked Taylor, she guessed there were a lot worse things her friend could be into than the occasional petty theft, so she never mentioned it.

"Bethany? Hello-oooo?" her mom said. Bethany looked up. "I

said, I'm getting married."

Bethany almost choked on her pizza. "Uh, that's nice." She tried to ignore the *ugh* feeling in her stomach.

Her parents weren't getting back together. She knew that, had known it since way before the divorce, and when the divorce had finally happened, it was a relief. No more icy silences, no more arguments over what she got to do or what they bought for her. Still, her mom getting married... Dave was a nice guy, she guessed, but kind of a dork.

Her mom peered across the table, her smile slowly fading. "Um, congratulations," Bethany said. *I guess.* "When?"

Her mom's toothpaste commercial smile came back. "Second Saturday in December. It was the soonest the chapel had an opening—"

"Chapel? You mean you're like, having a wedding?"

Her mom let out a huff. "Is there something wrong with that?"

"No, but... didn't you already do the big wedding thing once?"

"I'd like to think of it as starting over." She tilted her head, her expression pleading, like a child begging for candy. "Bethany... try to understand. Your father and I—"

"I know. Were never right for each other." Bethany twisted her napkin into a thin roll. "So is this happening here or in Atlanta?"

"The wedding's in Gatlinburg. Nothing major, just family and a few friends." Which meant there'd be a hundred guests instead of three hundred. "I'd like you to be my maid of honor."

Bethany shoved pizza into her mouth before she said something she regretted. From the corner of her eye, she saw the Parkers walk out. Mrs. Parker shook her head and leaned close to speak to her husband as she cast a sideways glance at Bethany and her mom, then quickly looked away.

Bethany's mom sighed. "Isn't your father old news by now?"

"Welcome to my world."

"Is it always this bad? People still talk—"

"Uh huh." Bethany picked at the sausage crumbles on the cardboard pizza square.

"You know you can move in with Dave and me any time you

want."

"I can deal." Bethany popped a stray mushroom into her mouth. She had her job in the mailroom at LCT, and Aunt Lisa was ready to help her look at colleges whenever Bethany figured out what she wanted to do.

Her mom gathered her purse and stood. "I've picked out a gorgeous bridesmaid dress, and the lady at Josephine's said they could do your fitting at their Cincinnati store. They should be in by next month—end of October at the latest. Plenty of time for a December wedding—"

"Uh, Mom, I don't know about this." Bethany pushed away from the table and stood facing her mom.

Her mother's expression turned to ice. "What do you mean, you don't know? I picked that dress out with you in mind—"

"Not the dress. It... being a bridesmaid... it just feels kinda weird."

Her mom shoved in her chair and whirled toward the exit. "I'll tell you what weird is, Bethany," she snapped. They walked out the door into the sauna-like, August heat and humidity, Bethany dashing to keep up with her mom's lengthy stride. "Weird is holding out this irrational hope that your father did not..." she jerked open the door of her rental car "...is innocent, and that everything will be hunky dory once he decides to show up again. Me getting married has nothing to do with him. Nothing. It wouldn't make one bit of difference if your dad was around, and that... ugliness never happened."

"I know." Bethany got in and stared at her hands on her seatbelt.

"Do you have a problem with Dave?"

"No." *He's a dork, but...* It wasn't a problem. She sighed. "Mom, I'll do it."

"Don't put yourself out on my account," her mom snapped. "I'm only your mother."

Bethany leaned on the armrest and stared out the window. They were halfway back to Aunt Lisa's before she thought of a safe topic to breach the silence. "Hey, Mom, you see Keith while you were in town?"

"Briefly. Why?"

Bethany shrugged. "I don't know. He calls every now and then. Wants to make sure I'm dealing okay with all the crap."

"Keith's always liked you." Her mom's brows dipped. "Never saw him take that much of an interest in Danny and Mark, or anyone else's kids. But it's nice that he cares."

Bethany didn't push the topic. Obviously, her mom's mind was on the wedding. When she pulled into Lisa and Charlie's driveway, she declined Bethany's offer to come in.

Taylor showed up fifteen minutes later, Mountain Dew in hand, as Bethany was watching some mind-numbing reality show on TV. "Hey, what's happening?" She plopped down beside Bethany on the bed.

"Not much." Bethany studied the wall. How had she never noticed the lighter square in the paint where a picture of Danny had hung when this was her aunt's spare room?

Or more importantly, how could she work the conversation around to her dad? Last time she'd asked, Taylor had gotten snippy. Maybe she really didn't know anything.

Bethany's slouch deepened. That was just too depressing. Surely there was something...

"How was dinner with your mom?" Taylor asked.

"Okay." Bethany decided the Blue team was going to win, because two girls on the Red team couldn't stop arguing.

"You register for classes yet?"

"No." Unsure of what she wanted to study, Bethany had enrolled at Sinclair Community College, where Taylor was also taking classes.

"Jeez, Beth, it's halfway through August. If you don't do it soon, all the good stuff will fill up."

"What the crap?" Bethany pointed at the TV.

On a news commercial, a reporter described massive footprints found in Minnesota, that looked like those of a wooly mammoth. Not in an unpopulated forest, but on the shore of Lake Superior, bordering a campground. They hadn't been there the day before.

Taylor snorted. "It has to be a hoax."

Her friend's skeptical face looked faked. Bethany scowled. "Whatever."

The commercial ended. "Who shit in your Cheerios?" Taylor asked.

"What do you mean?"

"You're pissed off about something."

Bethany picked at the bedspread, a fussy, flowery thing her aunt had chosen. "My mom's getting married."

"Is the guy a jerk?"

"He's okay. It's just... it feels weird. Especially since she's having a big wedding—in Gatlinburg—and she wants me to be her maid of honor."

Taylor's lip curled. "Ugh." She looked to her left, her brows lowered. "When is it?"

"December. After classes let out for the holidays."

"You allowed to bring a guest?"

Bethany shrugged. "I'm sure she'd be okay with it, but I don't know who—"

"Chad says I need to get out more, that I deserve a vacation."

Bethany cocked one eyebrow. "Wanna go?"

"Hell yeah. A girls' road trip. You and me—"

"Like *Thelma and Louise*." Bethany bounced on the bed. That was one of her aunt's favorite old movies.

"Exactly. Only without the bar fight and driving over a cliff."

"Cool. Let's do it."

She'd be in the car with Taylor for five hours each way, plus hang out with her all weekend. If there was anything to learn about her dad and this Saturn Society, she'd hopefully find out before then, but if not, during the trip for sure.

Tony put down the stone axe and leaned it against his stack of wood, giving in to his urge to draw his finger inside his bear-claw necklace. The leather thong suddenly felt tight, though it hung an inch below his collarbone. Even after three months, wielding stone tools gave him the heebie-jeebies sometimes.

Firewood had taken over the village, piled against huts, stashed under bunks, stacked along the walls in the big meeting house. Across the compound, Violet sat beside Ga-noo's hut, sewing Tony a pair of fur-lined boots. She'd measured him that morning for winter clothes. When she'd pawed his arms, his legs, and his chest with long strips of notched leather, only the sobering thought of impeding winter had kept him from embarrassing himself.

It was hard to think about winter in the sweltering heat and humidity of mid-August, but according to the stick Violet made a scratch on every day, it wouldn't be long before the arrival of cold and snow. And neither of them had seen or felt any hint of the Pull.

Violet put down the boots and moved to the fire, where she was baking three clay mugs. She examined the pottery, thumbing her coin-like charm. Her hair had grown out, enough that it was almost all brown on top. (Like Charlotte's.) Her belly had burgeoned, but she'd lost weight elsewhere, the strength in her lean arms obvious as she leaned over to loop a stick through a cup handle and pull it off the fire.

He forced himself to look away before his desire grew evident.

He had to sleep facing the wall when moonlight slanted in through the hut's roof vents. The more he saw of her, the more he wanted. He grabbed the axe and resumed chopping—

A shout came from across the village. Tony's head snapped up as Rod-orak burst out of their hut, gripping a squat, black object. Ga-noo hobbled after him, yelling.

The breath in Tony's lungs froze. *The gun.* He'd taken to stashing it in his bunk again, thinking Rod-orak had developed a healthy respect for the weapon after the bear incident. He dropped his axe and rushed for the boy.

Violet tossed down her cup, and it shattered. "Rod-orak! *Nak!*" She ran after him, but he evaded her.

A couple men sharpening arrows by the sweat lodge shouted.

Rod-orak stopped, yelled, then pointed the gun skyward and fired.

Villagers fled for their homes or dropped to the ground. Tony ran toward the boy. *"Nak!"* Sesh-wah shouted.

"No!" Violet caught up with Rod-orak and grabbed his arm, but he jerked the gun away and bolted across the compound.

Rod-orak yelled. Violet ran after him. Time came to a standstill, as if Tony were watching a slow-motion replay on TV, and wading through mud.

Sesh-wah reached Rod-orak first.

The boy lowered the weapon. Steadied it. Squeezed the trigger.

Violet's shout sounded distant, muffled. "Rod-orak! No!" She flew into him, knocking him to the ground, and wrested the firearm from his hand. As she grabbed for it, the gun went off.

The report echoed across the compound, reverberating in Tony's ears. "NO!"

Sesh-wah staggered, clutching at his gut. He wobbled, then crumpled to the ground.

Violet crouched at Sesh-wah's side. Tony reached him seconds later. Dark red blossomed from a hole in the leader's belly. The gun slipped from Rod-orak's shaking hand and landed with a thud, raising a cloud of dust. Tony snatched it off the packed-dirt plaza.

Villagers gathered around. Murmurs and angry-sounding words filled the air. Violet met Tony's gaze, her eyes wide. Her lower lip trembled. "He's dead."

Tin-darel pushed his way through the crowd and bent beside Sesh-wah. He pressed his palm to the chief's bloodied, motionless chest, his wrist, his throat.

Tin-darel stood. The feathers in his necklace stirred in the breeze. Someone coughed. "Sesh-wah *bin derak.*"

Derak. Dead. Tony's scalp tingled, and blood roared in his ears. The villagers remained still and eerily silent.

Vin-gah pushed through the crowd and pointed at Violet, shouting.

Murmurings and angry shouts rose from the crowd. *"Osessoo!"* someone yelled. Others took up the chant.

Violet backed away, but two men surged forward and grabbed her arms. "No!" She squirmed in their grasp. Tony pushed people aside to reach her, but strong hands grabbed him and pulled him back. Other villagers moved in, blocking his view of Violet. Vin-gah grabbed at the gun.

"Nak!" Tony struggled to hold it out of his reach, but he was no match for his four captors. Vin-gah pried it from his grip. Someone brought ropes, and the men bound Tony's wrists behind his back and tethered his ankles, leaving barely enough slack for him to walk.

A horn sounded. Vin-gah held his arms up, and all speech ceased as the new leader—so it appeared—made an announcement.

Shouts rose from the crowd. A metallic taste filled Tony's dry mouth. *Osessoo* meant outsider—Violet. Vin-gah barked an order and lifted the gun. He wrapped it in a square of buckskin, then laid it on a boulder at his feet, with a dire-sounding declaration.

In the silence, Tony heard shuffling in the dirt behind him. *"Aldishi Vi-led!"* Rod-orak shouted. *"Vi-led ba byll!"* A hand smacked flesh, and the boy fell silent. Mutterings and catcalls rose from the crowd, then two men dragged Violet to the big pole to face Vin-gah.

Ropes bound her wrists and ankles. Vin-gah grabbed her necklace and jerked it toward him. Violet cried out as the leather thong snapped, and her head jerked back as the pottery coin went flying. *"Osessoo obel!"* Vin-gah roared. Violet cringed.

Tony's gut burned. He bucked in his bonds, slamming his weight against his captors, but they held steady. One snarled something at him.

Guilt enveloped Tony, more inescapable than his restraints. He was the one who'd brought the gun into this time. He hadn't shot Sesh-wah, but he'd let his guard down, let his vigilance over the firearm slack off, left it under Violet's watch—without warning her. It was his fault the weapon was loaded and left where Rod-orak could find it. It was his fault the man had been killed. His fault that Violet would pay the price.

Vin-gah shouted an order. Four men in ceremonial paint picked up the corpse and carried it away, presumably to be prepared for burial. Vin-gah addressed Tony's captors. *"Ba'osessok!"* He pointed to the men's sweat hut. Tony couldn't see Rod-orak, but he heard the boy blubbering. Someone snapped a response, then a slap met with a wail.

They dragged Tony across the compound. He dug his heels into the dirt, then when that failed to stop the hunters, he went slack, but the men simply picked him up and carried him. In the sweat lodge, they left his wrists and ankles bound and tied him to a support pole. Then they disappeared, dropping the door flap to leave him in near darkness.

He strained against his bonds, then picked at them, but couldn't reach the knots the way his wrists were bound. The rope's strength amazed him, considering it was nothing more than twisted grass twines.

He couldn't even take off his glasses to clean them. Defeated, he slumped to the floor. *Think, Solomon!* There had to be some way to get out—

Across the hut, someone sobbed. Tony squinted in the dim light, trying to make out the slim form tied to the opposite corner support. "Rod-orak?"

"Doh-nee?" The boy sniffled. *"Vi-led ba derak."*

The boy's juxtaposition of *Violet* and *dead* sent a chill down Tony's body. If she died, she'd return to their present, but she'd lose the baby. Tony's hands curled into fists. "Violet *derak nak.*" He hoped the boy understood him.

The door flap lifted to admit Tin-darel. He tied the flap up, then carried a tall pitcher to Tony. *"Ba kalch."* He set the pitcher down, then took a second jar to Rod-orak.

The boy grumbled, turning away.

Tin-darel paused at the door-flap and inclined his head toward Rod-orak. He held out his hands, palms up, and said something that sounded regretful as he slipped out. He left the door flap tied open, giving Tony a view of the central plaza and the pole in its center.

Rod-orak's whining and the village's hustle and bustle faded, and Tony's ears, his hands, and his heart went numb.

Lashed to the pole, her body painted in slashes of red and black, was Violet.

Tony tried to pace, but it wasn't very stress-relieving or idea-producing when he could only take three steps. He wanted to clean his glasses, but with his hands tied, that was impossible. As he slid to the ground in resignation, the sun slanting in through the vent hole caught the edge of his glasses and cast a blindingly bright spot through the lens.

Tony jerked straight. If his glasses could focus the sun just right, maybe...

He twisted around until the lens caught the sunlight again, and focused the bright spot on the rope tied to the support pole.

He stared at the brilliant spot of light until the sun's movement caused the beam to slant away and dim.

His hope dimmed with it.

Across the hut, Rod-orak had backed up to the support pole and rubbed his wrists up and down the wood, trying to wear through his bonds.

But the ropes held fast. Both he and Tony remained restrained when the sky grew dark. Firelight flickered on the sweat lodge's wall beside the entry. Someone beat a drum, then another joined in. Singing and chants filled the air.

A trial. Or maybe they didn't do that and were going straight for an execution ceremony.

The memories that weren't quite memories flashed through Tony's mind. Being pushed over the ledge near Florie's house. Being shot at in the woods behind his apartment. Being nearly smothered in his bed. And then, the guy who looked like him had tried to kill him—and had killed Danny.

Tony drew upon his anger. He struggled against the ropes, but with no more effect than before.

Footsteps approached the sweat lodge. Outside, someone uttered a sharp command. Tony recognized the voice of the guy who'd been ordered to guard the hut, along with Tin-darel.

Tony caught the words *kalchoo* and *kelzoo* as he recognized the voice. Aye-sack, with water and food. *"Orp,"* the guard grunted.

The door hole darkened, and Aye-sack slipped in with two wooden bowls. He crept to Tony's side and set them down. Whispering, he drew a knife from beneath his loincloth and sawed the twine around Tony's ankles until the bonds fell away, then cut the ties on Tony's wrists.

Tony stood, rubbing his wrists as Aye-sack slipped over to Rod-orak and repeated the instruction while he cut the boy's bonds. *"Vi-led cheald."* Urgency filled the toolmaker's whisper. Rod-orak rubbed his ankles and got up.

Aye-sack held up his hand, palm out, indicating they needed to be quiet. He crept to the door, lifted the skin, and peered out. He held up a hand. *"Nak,"* he whispered.

The back entrance was guarded, too. Hadn't Aye-sack thought through how Tony and Rod-orak would get past them?

The chanting and drums stopped. Vin-gah raised his voice and gave an intonation. Chills trickled down Tony like a line of ants down his back. *"Osessoo bunna derak,"* Tin-darel muttered from his post at the front door.

Tony couldn't move, couldn't breathe. His fingers twitched.

He peered into the rafters and an idea struck. If he could lure the guards in, take them by surprise... "Aye-sack," he whispered.

"Doh-nee, *nak*," his friend whispered back.

Tony pointed to the rafters, then climbed up the pole, using knots and sawed-off branches as footholds. Aye-sack and Rod-orak watched Tony crawl onto a rafter. He pointed to himself, then to the door, then to himself again, making an arcing motion toward the floor.

In the dim firelight, he saw a smile stretch across the boy's face, but Aye-sack's remained blank. Rod-orak crept to the man's side and whispered an explanation. Aye-sack nodded.

Rod-orak climbed up the next pole over, then inched along the rafter, sure-footed as a monkey. Casting a doubtful glance at the door, Aye-sack followed until the three of them lay in wait above the door.

Outside, the drums and chanting resumed.

"Brard," Rod-orak said.

Aye-sack held up a hand with the twisted fingers that signaled agreement.

"Dina-sok!" Rod-orak called. Tony echoed him.

"Tin-darel!" Aye-sack shouted.

As the man burst through the back door, Tony launched himself off the rafter and landed on the man's back, knocking him to the ground face-first. "Arrgh!" Tin-darel yelped. Forcing away his revulsion at what he was doing, Tony grabbed him by the hair and slammed his face into the ground. He thought of Violet, tied to the tall pole, and slammed again with renewed strength. Behind him, scuffling and Dina-sok's outraged shouts told him Rod-orak and Aye-sack had also succeeded in surprising their quarry.

"Sorry, buddy," Tony choked as he grabbed the rope he'd been tethered him with, then bound Tin-darel's wrists.

Tin-darel shouted. Thankful for all the noise outside, Tony wound rope around the man's ankles, then slammed his head into the ground once more. Tin-darel lay still.

Rod-orak tied Dina-sok to a bunk support, then stuffed a wad of leather into his mouth and tied it behind his head. Aye-sack held a knife to the man's throat to ensure he didn't try to escape. Rod-orak dashed for the door, but Aye-sack held up a hand. *"B'aper-nak,"* he whispered. *Wait.*

Tony peered out the door. The drumming and chanting continued. *"B'aper!"* Aye-sack motioned Tony to follow, then slipped out, Rod-orak close behind.

Tony grabbed a knife hanging on the wall and followed. Aye-sack motioned for them to keep near the sweat lodge's walls, beyond the firelight.

All eyes faced the bonfire at the village center. Violet was still tied to the center pole, her chin resting on her chest. They'd shorn her hair, and what was left fell in dark, damp ringlets around her face.

The wind rushed out of Tony as if someone had punched him in the chest. *Charlotte.*

One of the men poked her breast. She hung limply in her bonds, and barely twitched.

A burn rose inside Tony, searing him from the inside out, radiating out to his hands and feet. He squeezed his knife and leaped forward. Aye-sack grabbed his arm. *"B'aper-nak,"* he whispered through clenched teeth.

Tony swallowed, his anger like nails, but let the man yank him back into the darkness beneath the sweat lodge's overhanging thatch. He needed a plan. He set aside his anger, pushing it into a dark corner of his mind.

A murmur rose from the crowd, and the drums and chanting stopped. Vin-gah moved to the pole, and cut Violet's bonds. As she fell forward, the four painted men grabbed her, two on each side.

Vin-gah held up his hands and issued a command. One of the men holding Violet whipped out a knife and sliced her skirt ties. The cloth fluttered to the ground, leaving her naked.

Tony lunged forward, but Aye-sack and Rod-orak held him back. *"B'aper-nak,"* the boy warned. *"Bunna derak!"*

Tony retreated into the shadows. The boy was right, if he went after Violet now, they'd grab him and kill him, too.

Vin-gah held up Violet's skirt and made a pronouncement over it, then tossed it onto the fire. Sparks flew up, and a log popped like a tiny explosion.

Tony jerked straight. *Explosion!* The extra ammo was still hidden beneath Ga-noo's wood pile. If he could get to it...

He lifted his hand and pointed up. Aye-sack gave a single nod. Tony sidled along the sweat lodge wall, then dashed to the next hut. Aye-sack watched behind them as Tony kept moving until he reached Ga-noo's hut, Aye-sack and Rod-orak on his heels.

Casting a nervous glance at the assemblage every few seconds, he jammed his hand into the space between two big logs at the bottom and groped for the ammo.

Damn! Nothing there. He jerked his hand out, his breath coming in short bursts.

In the plaza, Vin-gah held up handfuls of something—dirt, maybe—and shouted a chant. The crowd dipped in a bow, and he tossed whatever he held into the fire.

It fluttered and fell slowly, shimmering in the firelight.

Not dirt. Violet's hair. Vin-gah chanted over something on the ground as the audience straightened. They'd cut her down from the pole, and he couldn't see her over the crowd.

He crouched and shoved his hand into another gap. As his fingers lit on the cool, metal cylinders, Violet shrieked.

Panic seized Tony. Violet screamed again, and he lunged toward the gathering, but Aye-sack and Rod-orak grabbed his elbows, restraining him. Aye-sack hissed another warning.

Violet's screams went on and on as he scooped up the ammo and hurried back to the sweat lodge. Footsteps followed him as he burst inside. *"Ba ruskoo?"* Aye-sack asked.

Tony snatched a feathered mask off the lodge's wall, then grabbed a bearskin cloak. Aye-sack's eyes went wide as he made a horrified exclamation. Tony was probably committing some religious faux pas.

Rod-orak made a choked gasp as Tony donned the mask and cloak.

As Tony strode to the door, Dina-sok burst in, having escaped. With an outraged shout, he lunged at Tony. Tony leaped aside, but the other man caught his necklace, pulling Tony to the ground with him. Tony clawed the man's hands off the leather thong, fighting conflicting images of the ancient Mayans and the killer with his face. He jerked the man's wrist backward, and freed, he rolled over. As Dina-sok lunged for him again, Tony yanked the knife from under his cloak and jammed it into the villager's gut. As he withdrew the weapon, warm liquid gushed over his hands. Dina-sok went limp with a choked gurgle.

Rod-orak and Aye-sack stared in round-eyed horror. Tony pushed them aside. "Get out of my way."

He crept out and slipped into the crowd, wiping the bear fur with his blood-slicked hands. As he sneaked past one of the outlying fires, he swiped a burning stick and hurled it onto a nearby hut.

He disappeared into the throng, walking in a crouch in hopes that the villagers wouldn't realize who was beneath the cloak before he reached Violet. A backward glance told him the fire had taken, the dry thatch already starting to burn. Someone shouted, and the crowd shifted as villagers ran for water jugs. He wove through the crowd toward Violet. No one moved to stop him, their attention snared by the fire.

Violet's screams had died down to wails as he neared the plaza. When he pushed through the villagers still ringing the big pole, chills speared his heart and radiated out to his toes, his fingertips, the ends of his hair.

At the pole's base, Violet lay on the ground, her arms and legs stretched in an X. The gun lay on her round belly, and a thick stick staked her left hand to the hard-packed earth. Two of Vin-gah's flunkies, held her feet to the ground while Vin-gah held another stake to her right hand and lifted a stone mallet. As Tony sprang forward, the hunter slammed the hammer down.

Tony barely noticed Violet's screams as he leaped for Vin-gah's throat. The man stumbled and swayed. Approaching footsteps pounded the dust.

Tony threw Vin-gah at one of the helpers, then spun and chucked his bullets into the ceremonial fire as three more men tackled him.

He elbowed their guts and clawed at their faces and tried to extricate himself. Someone shoved a knee into his face, pushing the mask off, then another pounced on the pileup—

A bullet exploded, louder than a firecracker. The men jumped and ran as a second bullet went off, then a third and fourth. Vin-gah bolted for the nearest hut. The villagers scattered, knocking each other over in their haste to get away as the rest of the ammo went off in ear-shattering explosions.

Tony dropped to Violet's side and pried up her hand, still impaled by the stake. Where her hand had lain, blood seeped into the earth. She blubbered and flopped like a fish while he worked to free her other hand. The sight of her in so much pain gripped his chest like a vise. He tugged at her hand, and her wails died to whimpers. As the stake loosened, another pair of hands reached in and helped pull her free.

As Tony gathered Violet to his chest, the gun thudded to the ground. Tony looked up into Aye-sack's face. "Doh-nee!" Aye-sack pointed to the opening in the fence, then lifted Violet's feet. Tony grabbed the gun and jammed it into his waist rope, then hefted her shoulders. The two men scrambled for the gate. Shouts came from the villagers emerging from their huts.

Tony and Aye-sack scuttled out the opening, Tony's fur cloak slipping off as he ran. Aye-sack veered toward the river. Rod-orak called out in the darkness. Shouts from the village grew nearer as they reached the riverbank. "Doh-nee!" Rod-orak yelled as something splashed in the water. The half-moon lit the river just enough for Tony to see him dragging a dugout canoe to the shore.

Violet let out a whimper as Tony and Aye-sack lowered her into the craft. Tony turned to get in when a man leaped out from behind a tree and hurled a spear at him. It missed.

Tony whipped out the gun and fired. The man fell with a howl. "*Ba-rod!*" Rod-orak shoved a flattened stick into Tony's hand and pushed him into the boat. Angry shouts, rustling, and pounding footsteps rose from the village. Tony barely sat before Rod-orak and Aye-sack launched the boat into the current. *"Sliero, Doh-nee,"* Aye-sack called. It sounded like a grieved farewell.

"Sliero, Vi-led..." Rod-orak choked. As the boat floated around a bend, Tony took a last glance at their friends. The boy's cheeks shone in the moonlight with trails of tears.

The shouts faded as the boat drifted downriver, but Tony knew it wouldn't be long before the villagers climbed into the other boats and followed. He grabbed the stick and gouged the river bottom, propelling the boat faster, but the villagers' yelps and exclamations grew louder. When the boat drifted into a clearing, Tony poled it ashore.

Violet lay huddled in a half-fetal curl. Tony touched her arm, and horror washed over him anew at all the blood.

He glanced up the river. The natives weren't yet in sight, though their angry shouts still drifted from the direction of the village. He lifted Violet as gently as possible, but as he wedged his hands beneath her knees and back, she cried out. He climbed out of the boat, clutching her to his chest, and stumbled up the gravelly bank. Something looked familiar about the area...

He staggered a few more steps before it came to him. The rock crevice where they'd sheltered that first night. His muscles rigid, his heart slamming in his chest, he hurried on. He had to reach the rock crevice before she went into shock...

The shouting from upriver grew nearer.

Biting back his fear, Tony stumbled into the trees as fast as he could without dropping her. Finally, he reached the moonlit rock wedge and laid her on the straw inside.

"Baby," she whispered. "Die..."

"The baby's not going to die."

"I'm..." She trailed off in a choked sob.

"Listen to me." Tony gripped her right hand in one of his and the stake in the other. "I'm going to pull these out, then we're going to warp—"

"Baby..." she wailed. "The... Pull?"

"I wish. But no." Tony untied his loincloth. The stone knife and his gun fell to the straw with a muted thud. More shouting came from the river. Louder. He gripped the knife and snatched the leather breechclout from the ground, then sliced off a strip. "We're going to go farther back." He ripped another strip of buckskin, then grabbed the stake through Violet's hand. "To before these people were here." Gritting his teeth, he yanked out the stake.

Violet screamed. He wrapped the leather around her hand and tied it in a loose knot, then tore out the other stake. She wailed again, not as loudly.

Her head lolled to one side as he bandaged her other hand. Her face shone ghostly pale in the moonlight seeping through the trees.

He crawled into the crevice behind her. "Stay with me, Violet. Think of the baby..."

"Ummm," she whimpered.

Snapping twigs and barked orders grew nearer.

"Think of this woods, like it is now, but with no people. Ten years ago. Maybe fifteen." Gripping the knife and gun, he scooped her into his arms and pictured the woods, unchanged. *Ten years ago, ten years ago...*

The dizziness didn't come. "Violet! Think, dammit!"

She moaned.

Then the dizziness hit. *Thank God.*

The vertigo faded, along with the incessant whir of crickets.

His first awareness was straw biting into his bare ass and a muffled, pattering sound. Rain.

His ears pricked as he listened for pursuit, for the villagers' angry cries.

Nothing but rain. He exhaled, and his muscles relaxed. "Violet?"

No answer. Recovery hit faster when one was injured. He pressed a hand to her throat. Her pulse beat steadily, the healing process already begun.

He took her left hand in his and pressed the wrapping. Bones shifted, then snapped into place. He repeated the effort with her other hand. Hopefully, they wouldn't be too fucked up.

He scooted her to the back of the crevice, then spooned against her. As sleep fell over him, one disturbing thought lingered.

She'd worried about the baby. He'd only worried about her.

Thirteen

Violet woke to the scent of campfire and cooking meat. Her mouth watered. Baked chicken—or more likely turkey.

She was in a small room, with walls of dirt and stone... no, a shallow cave, open on one side. She frowned. Then her confusion eased as she realized where she was. The rock crevice where she and Tony had sheltered their first night in prehistoric times. She lifted a hand to rub her nose, but her arm seemed made of stone. She was so tired. Finally, she managed to get her arm to cooperate. Her breath caught. What on earth?

Someone had wrapped her hands in soft buckskin strips. But why? What hap—

Memories flashed through her mind. Rod-orak and the gun. Her capture. Being tied to the pole. Vin-gah driving stakes through her hands, the blinding pain, her own screams.

But she felt no pain now. Only the hot, humid air, sunlight, and the smell of smoke. She looked toward the crevice's opening. A few yards away, a campfire burned in a pit, where a turkey hung over it on a makeshift spit. Tony stoked the fire, making the smoke rise in billowy clouds. Sunlight speared through the trees from directly overhead, casting dappled shadows over his back, his shoulders, his—

Her belly jumped. He wore nothing but his glasses and the bear claw necklace. Over the past few months, his hair had grown several inches. A far cry from the short, spiked style he'd worn before. His longer hair, along with the shadow of a beard, created a tantalizing contrast with the civility lent by his glasses. A memory flashed through her mind. She'd awoken one day *before*, to find Tony shirtless, cooking for her over a campfire. She reached for the fleeting image, clutched at it, tried to make it solidify, but all she could grasp was that instead of a night of horror, the night she'd woken from that morning had been one of making love.

The muscles in his legs and his tight rear flexed as he crouched beside the fire, eying the turkey. The man had no right to look that good, especially considering what they'd run from...

She swallowed. He'd saved her. He'd carried her away, kept her alive and conscious until they jumped.

She pushed herself up, the straw crackling and prickly beneath her bare fanny.

Tony turned around. "Finally awake, huh?" He laid down his stick and knelt beside her. "How are you feeling?"

She had to think about it. "Tired. A little stiff, but..." She tried to curl her hands, and though the buckskins wrapped around them were too tight for her to make a fist, she felt little soreness. "Nothing like before." Healed. By recovery, just like he'd told her. Her amazement was trumped only by hunger. "What are you cooking? It smells wonderful."

"Turkey. I woke up a couple hours ago."

"Where— when are we?"

He half-shrugged, his mouth set in a grim line. "We warped."

"The Pull?" Hope surged through her.

He shook his head, looking down and to the side. "We warped back farther. It was the only way we could escape, the only way your hands would heal—"

"You saved me." Memories surged though Violet's mind. The explosions. Tony carrying her. Pulling the stakes from her hands.

He shuddered, staring at the ground. "I killed a man. God, I killed someone." He shook his head, his eyes glassy, unseeing. "I can't believe..."

She reached for him, touched his arm. "You did what any caring parent would do to protect his child."

"His—oh, God. How is—"

"The baby's fine. Stretching and squirming like crazy. That was what woke me up."

"Thank God." He reached for her hand. "How are your hands?"

She held them out, and he untied the leather strips. "Amazing," she breathed. Her hands were whole beneath the crusted blood.

He took her right hand in his, gently rubbing the tough, scarred knot in the center. It looked like she'd been injured years ago, not days, or even weeks. When he turned her hand over and stroked her palm with his thumb, she ached to reach for him, draw him to her, wrap herself in his arms.

But she was nothing more than a vessel for his child. "Tony... thank you." It was the least she could say.

With a sharp nod, he rose, returning to the distant, uncommunicative man she'd known for the past four months. The airy ache inside her plummeted.

He walked to the fire and speared a chunk of meat, then returned to her side. He held out a skewered turkey leg. She took the stick, trying to avoid looking at his nakedness, trying to ignore the heat pooling between her legs.

He scooted out of the crevice. "I'm going to the river."

Thank heavens. She needed to eat. And take care of other things. Yet the sight of him in the altogether stole her concentration, not to mention her hunger.

Once he was out of sight, she crept far enough out of the crevice to relieve herself, than huddled inside while she ate, trying to banish the image of his fine backside from her mind.

Vin-gah had taken her skirt in preparation for her execution, but why—

Her gaze lit on the leather strips Tony had removed from her hands, and the realization struck her like a blow to the chest.

He'd sacrificed his clothing—all he had—for her.

Something glinted in the sunlight. A tiny sliver of silver. She frowned and picked it up, rolling it between her thumb and index finger.

A shadow fell over her. "The injection. From Alpha." She looked up to meet Tony's gaze. "It must've come out when I pulled out the stakes."

She tilted it in the light, studying it. "Fascinating." The metal shard bent across the middle, fractured almost in two like a wooden splinter.

Tony crouched beside her "Do you think we can put it back in?"

She handed it to him. "I doubt it. It's broken."

He studied it. "Hope to God the Pull comes soon." He laid the tiny piece of metal against the crevice's back wall. "Now I'm going to be paranoid about every little scratch on you, every time you sniffle or sneeze."

"There's nothing we can do. Besides, we should have good resistance to a lot of the germs in this time anyway. We've grown up taking antibiotics, had immunizations none of the people in this time have. That could be why we've stayed healthy so far."

"I hope so." He scooted closer. She saw that he gripped a pouch formed by tying the edges of a square of leather. The rest of his breechclout. His gaze traveled over her body, and she wanted to curl into a ball and throw herself on him at the same time, self-consciousness warring with desire. He poured a trickle of water into his hand and rubbed her belly, the water's coolness refreshing in the summer heat. Desire won out as he ran his moistened hand down her leg, and her hips clenched. "What are you doing?" she asked.

"Best way to stay healthy is to keep clean." He poured more water into his hands and gently massaged her left foot, rubbing off the black marks Vin-gah's lackeys had painted on her. The bubbly ache rose within her again. She wanted him to rub her like that all over, and not just because—

"That okay?" he asked.

"Of course, but..." She was capable of going to the river to wash. Not a task she relished, but... "Why are you doing this?"

He rubbed out a painted, red slash on her belly. "I told you. To prevent infection."

"No, I mean... why are you..."

He stopped. "What?"

"Why are you being so... so kind? I thought..."

That he loathed her. That he only stayed with her because of the baby.

He picked up her other foot, but didn't rub it. Instead, he looked into her eyes. "Violet... I never stopped caring."

Her heart pounded in her throat. "Wh- what?" She drew back, and saw something else that hadn't changed.

He still wanted her. Obvious evidence rose from where his loincloth would have covered.

Tony returned his attention to her right foot, slowly, deliberately rubbing off every speck of red pigment. When he finished, she pushed herself up, her back against the wall, drawing her feet under herself. "Lord, I'd dearly love a cigarette right now. One of the things I truly miss..." Tony shot her a hard stare. "If I wasn't pregnant, of course."

Tony's face relaxed. She looked outside, up at the crevice wall, at the bloodied leather strips beside her. Anywhere but at him, at his—

She tried to get her mind off his obvious desire and her own wanting, longing for him in her—

Enough. "I wish I had some coffee. Just one cup."

"Yeah, hazelnut, with extra cream." He leaned against the crevice's stone wall, angling his knees so they blocked his erection from her view. He gazed upward. "Hell, even the vending machine crap from the cafeteria would be a godsend."

Violet tipped her head up, eyes closed. "Television. A night with nothing to do but relax and watch hours of mindless sitcoms, with a Coke and a cig— No, some healthy snacks. Fresh fruit."

"A john that's more than a hole in the ground. And the Sunday *Dayton Daily News*."

"Toilet paper. Microwave ovens. *Any* oven."

"Giving Bethany a hug before she goes to bed at night. Hearing her TV turned down low, so she thinks I don't hear, and she's getting away with staying up on a school night. Sunday night dinners at my mom and dad's, with my sister and her family."

Violet's heart twinged. She'd never be part of that family, but at least the baby would. She wouldn't think about that now, focusing on things she missed, simple things. "Watching World War II documentaries with Stephanie and Timmy. Or a wrestling pay-per-view."

Tony's eyebrow lifted. "Wrestling?"

Violet shrugged. "Lots of women like soap operas. Stephanie and I just like action and comedy with the lying, cheating, and scheming."

"She's probably like your family, huh?" The warmth in his eyes mingled with suspicion.

"Steph and her brother Timmy are all I have." She looked down, her lips tight. He was treading too close, too near to revealing her secret. Bad enough that she'd told him about her amnesia—which he didn't believe. He didn't need to know that she'd killed someone. She picked up a buckskin bandage and fiddled with it, hoping he'd think her nervousness was due to painful memories. "I- I can only assume—hope—that my parents are gone. Because no one ever came looking for me."

"I'm sorry." His face took on an odd twist, so slight that someone who didn't know him well might not notice.

"No siblings. No friends... no significant other has ever sought me out. That I know of, at least." Which was fine by her. Whoever she'd been *before,* she wouldn't have wanted to endanger a loved one.

He regarded her with his head tilted up, looking down at her through the corner of his eyes. She wanted to shrink into the straw, hide from his probing gaze that laid raw what she wanted—no, *needed*—to cover up. Instead, he'd stripped it as bare as they were physically.

She wouldn't let herself flinch beneath his stare. Bracing herself for his accusation, she tipped her chin up and fully met his gaze.

His hand brushed hers. She looked at it with a start. He'd moved nearer. The next thing she knew, he pulled her close, and she tumbled into his arms. Her belly pressed into his, the roundness more obvious against his flat stomach. Fire blazed between her thighs. Unable to stop herself, she tipped her face to his. Their mouths met, the press of his lips on hers pure heaven—

You're keeping things from me. She jerked away, the sting of his accusation as sharp as it had been when he'd voiced it aloud months ago.

"I'm sorry." He withdrew his arms.

"Stress," she rationalized, as much for herself as him.

The sun was setting and she hadn't even noticed. Firelight flickered in his gaze, drawing out its intensity, the shadows around them chilling her despite the warm, humid night. As if he'd read her mind, he slid an arm over her back. The light touch of his calloused hand sent shivers through her. *I never stopped caring, either.* She wouldn't say it out loud. But she couldn't hide it from herself any longer. *I never stopped loving you.*

He slid his arm the rest of the way around her, pulling her against him. "I never stopped wanting you," he said into her hair, and it was nearly her undoing. She'd longed for this, yearned to hear those things. It wasn't the same as saying he loved her, but maybe that was all right. She'd take his caring, and his wanting, if that was all she could get. She lifted her face, her lips parted, and when his met hers in a gentle yet strong kiss, the heavens opened.

Her mouth moved with his, the stubble of his beard an intoxicating mix of soft and rough. His hand trailed over her shoulder, sending sparks tingling through her. He slid his hand down her arm and brushed her breast—

Charlotte...

Violet froze. *You're hiding things from me...* "I can't," she whispered.

He withdrew his hand. "Can't what?"

She tried to bring her knees up to her chin, but her belly got in the way. "I can't... you know. What's going to happen if we don't stop now."

He ran his arm down her back, then up again. Mercy, did he know what that was doing to her? How hard it was to say no with tingles skittering over her whole body? "Tell me you don't want this," he said softly. "Tell me you don't want me."

"I can't." *Blast him!* His gentle voice was making it even harder to resist. Harder not to hope that maybe this time, he wouldn't say something horrid afterward.

"Then why?" That same gentle voice. The same one that said in tone as well as words that he did care.

She rubbed her eye—she would *not* cry—and her gaze settled on the perfect excuse. She spread her hands over her belly, round as a beach ball. "How can I, like this?"

His voice grew stern. "Have you had problems you haven't told me about?"

"No."

"It won't hurt the baby. You know I'd never touch you if it would."

"I know." She'd devoured every pregnancy book the library had before the attack at the office, the night everything changed.

"Are you self-conscious?" he asked. That hadn't even occurred to her. "Because you shouldn't be." He drew her close again, and the warmth of his skin against hers made her tingle. "You're beautiful. Always have been, but especially now..." He ran his hand over her belly.

Fireworks burst inside her. Beautiful? Her? "I still don't—" His hand moved up her side, curving around to her front. Her breath caught. "...think it's a good idea." She tried to ignore his roving hands. "I mean, just the mechanics..."

"We'll have to be creative."

The idea intrigued her, made her even more anxious to jump into his arms.

He slid his arm from behind her, leaving her bereft without his touch. His eyes asked the question he didn't voice.

As much as she hated giving him power over her by saying it out loud, she owed him an answer. "When it happened before, it was wonderful..." Wonderful beyond words. Beyond heaven. "But you did say we should just be friends."

He gazed toward the fire. "You're right." There was too much between them. Too little trust. Too many secrets.

He spoke so softly she had to strain to hear. "Violet Sinclair... what's your real name?"

She couldn't stop herself from lowering her head, burying her face in her hands. It would have been easier if he hurled accusations the way he had in 1959.

"Violet?" His voice was gentle. Not accusing, but kind.

She couldn't look at him. She'd done something terrible in the past, something that hurt him deeply, something as shuttered away from her as it ever had been. But now, she needed him. She couldn't survive alone. Couldn't give birth without his help if it came to that. *Oh Lord, please no.* But the possibility grew with each day that passed without the slightest hint of the Pull.

If she couldn't trust Tony, then who? "I don't know," she whispered. "I swear, I have no idea."

Something about her downcast face, and the quaver beneath her whispers, chipped away at Tony's resolve like the hard stones Aye-sack used to beat flint into spearheads. What if she was telling the truth? And for whatever reason, Pippin hadn't filled her in? Why would she have been searching for Charlotte, that day at Florie's house?

Tony had called her that, in the motel in 1959. Had Pippin, as well? But why would she search, if she knew who she was, and what she'd done?

She rubbed at the palm of her right hand. "I swear, I can't remember a thing before the day Timmy found me in his garage, six years ago. Nothing. Not even my name."

Tony gathered his wits and snapped his mouth shut. As much as he wanted to believe her, this whole amnesia thing was too convenient. He carefully framed his response. "You mean, you can't remember any personal details, yet you still understood social conventions, knew how to read and write... other stuff you would've learned in school?"

"I know it's far-fetched."

"And what about computers? Did you know that, too?" If she'd really jumped into the twenty-first century from 1933, she wouldn't have.

"No. In fact, I was certain I'd never seen one before. Everything I know about computers, I've learned in the past five years. There were other holes in my knowledge. Like World War II. And odd things like... I could've sworn I'd never seen soda pop in a can. I thought someone who was gay was just cheerful, and politically-correct terms? I'd never heard of most of them. But otherwise, my knowledge was reasonably complete."

All of which made sense—if she'd come forward from the 1930s.

"I know that kind of amnesia only happens in books and movies. But it's the truth. My therapist says this type of memory loss often occurs as a result of a traumatic event."

Well, killing him would certainly constitute a traumatic event. Even if she'd planned to turn him over to the Society, Charlotte was not a killer. Knifing him was more of a knee-jerk reaction, a last-ditch effort to salvage her worth to Pippin.

Like him stabbing Dina-sok. A shudder coursed through Tony, and his stomach turned, even though he'd only killed in Violet's defense.

He supposed it was possible. "So what happened after that guy found you in his garage?"

"Timmy let me in to use the washroom and get a drink. He's a simp- slow, but he's kindhearted. He was trying to fix a leaky pipe in the kitchen... mercy, what a mess he'd have made if I hadn't helped. Steph's husband Vince would have thrown a fit. Stephanie was so grateful, she invited me to stay when she found out I had no place to go." She looked sideways at Tony. "Vince was not a nice fellow. He drank too much, and did... other things, then took any little frustration out on Stephanie or Timmy."

"You mean he was abusive."

"Yes. Even when he wasn't on a toot, he was ill-tempered and prone to have a fit over the slightest thing. Stephanie would have never worked up the nerve to leave him if I hadn't been there. She's told me that a thousand times. She's the only one who knows about my memory loss. Besides my therapist." She stared off toward the fire. "I wonder how she's doing now. I mean, in our time."

Tony wondered how Bethany was doing. And Lisa and Mark, hell, even Dora. Had anyone ever found his double who'd killed Danny? Had Alpha been able to neutralize the rogue Saturn Society people who were after him, Violet, and their child? Or was Violet a part of a trap? Tony's stomach wrenched. What if she was telling the truth?

He'd held happiness in his arms and thrown it aside. Everything he wanted. Everything he hoped for. Trying to ignore the quivering in his gut, he pushed for more answers. "The first time I saw you, in the cafeteria at work, you asked if I knew you. Why'd you think that?"

"I saw your photo in the paper. When you were promoted to Vice President at LCT." She twiddled her fingers.

Tony's gaze never left her. She was about to slip up. "I was sure I knew you," she said. "I'd never felt such a strong sense of familiarity, that sometime in the past, we'd..." She swallowed and studied her hands.

Tony knew what she'd been about to say. That their acquaintance had been far more than casual. "What about the guy who looks like me, who tried to attack you?"

She shook her head. "The only other person who's ever sparked that kind of familiarity was Mr. Pippin. But with him, I got the sense that he was more of a friend—no, not quite, more like someone in authority that I'd had a mentor relationship with, like a minister or professor."

Tony ached to hold her. So convincing. All she'd had to do was wrap a bit of truth around the lie, and she almost had him. God, he wanted to believe her.

"After I saw your picture in the paper, I kept an eye on the classified ads, and when LCT advertised for a cafeteria worker, I jumped at the chance. Then worked my way into tech support." Her gaze slowly lifted to meet Tony's. "I'd hoped you'd give me some clue as to who I'd been before."

"But I'd never seen you before that day at the office."

"So you said."

What did she mean by that? Was she aware of their relationship in 1933? He asked one more question, a final test. "So... do you think you lived in the area before, or did you come from somewhere else?"

"I think I did live in Dayton, because some things looked familiar, like the old courthouse... Memorial Hall, the statue at Main and Monument."

"But not everything."

"No. I'm sure I'd never seen Sinclair Community College. Or Carillon Park, or the Kettering Tower, or the Schuster Center—none of the newer, bigger buildings, or the sculpture at Fifth and Main, or Riverscape."

Logical for someone who'd been suddenly transplanted from 1933 to... the twenty-first century?

It had to have been the Ohio quarter. He'd told her exactly what the place where her house looked like in his time. She could have visualized it and jumped to the future.

Could it be that simple?

She'd stabbed him on the seventh of June. If she'd come forward... tack on a couple of days for recovery, it added up. He'd never told her the exact year he'd come from, only that it was in the twenty-first century.

Something swelled within him, like a balloon trying to burst from his chest. Maybe they had a chance. It was only when he went back to 1933 and met Charlotte, to learn how he could prevent Bethany's death, that he found out how unhappy—how goddamn lonely—he'd been for years.

Only to learn Charlotte's affection was all a lie. Or was it?

She looked at him sideways, her words hesitant. "Do you... believe me now?"

He wanted to. Wanted to hold her, and make up for the shitty way he'd acted the past few months.

He decided to take his chances. "Yes." He edged close, sliding his arm over her back and threaded his fingers through her short, blond-tipped curls. *Totally Charlotte.* He kissed her soft cheek. "Does your therapist think you'll ever regain your memory?"

Her hands fidgeted on her belly. "She says never say never, but after all this time, it's unlikely. We even tried hypnotherapy, until I tired of it. I decided I'd rather make the most of this life."

He pulled her against him. Why couldn't he have seen it before? He could've saved himself—and her—so much grief. All those days of watching her, wanting her. It would've stopped those cutting words from coming out of his mouth.

But fear had made him suspicious, unwilling to believe.

When he was ten, in swimming lessons, he was the only kid who wouldn't jump off the high dive. The whole class waited in line at the ladder, while he stood on the edge of the diving board, staring down at the water. In reality, he knew it was only about twelve feet, but at the time, it might as well have been a hundred.

He'd turned back and climbed down, defeated by his phobia. He'd choked, given up. Let fear steal his victory.

He trailed his fingers over her curves, her full breasts, her belly. He'd come too close to losing her, twice now, to let her go. He wrapped his arms around her. "I believe you now."

She pressed into him, and he pulled her against him as tightly as he could. She tipped her face up and his mouth met hers, soft, silky and sweet beyond his imaginings. God, he needed this. Now, most of all, when all they had was each other. She melted into him, and a tiny sigh escaped her as she broke their kiss, then met his mouth again.

He wouldn't tell her about her past. She didn't need to know who she'd been to Pippin... hell, Pippin himself hadn't told her when she'd gone to him in 1959, so maybe her actions in '33 hadn't kept her in his good graces after all.

Tony didn't want to think about 1933. All he wanted was here and now. Her name didn't matter. Her past didn't matter. What she'd done in 1933 didn't matter.

She pressed her breasts into his chest. Still kissing her, the bristle of his beard meshing with her soft lips, he drew his hand around her, trailing his fingertips over her silken skin, around the curve of her breast. She gasped and tipped her head up. He brought his lips down the smooth column of her neck, trickling kisses as he went. He nipped lightly at her throat, eliciting a quiet moan. "Tony..."

"Mmm," was his only response. He moved his hand lower on her back, with the lightest touch, feeling her skin prickle. Her back arched.

He pulled away and gently lowered her onto the straw. He lay beside her and marveled over her perfect, naked body. How lean her arms and legs had grown with a summer of hard work, how round her belly with their child growing inside. He ran his hand over the tightly-drawn skin, feeling the contour. A bump rose beneath his hand. He looked questioningly at her.

"He's usually the most active when I'm sitting still," she said. "Or she."

"And settles down when you're moving?"

She nodded. "It's like rocking him to sleep."

"Or her." Tony drew his hand up her side, across her belly again, over the curve of her hip. She closed her eyes, her face relaxed in contentment. He could rub her all over. All day... no. He'd go crazy.

He brought his hand over her belly again, then around her breast. Her breath caught. He circled the base, then moved higher, in a gradual rise until he ringed the darkness around her nipple, then thumbed the distended tip. "Ohhh!" She arched up and reached for him, but he only leaned over her for a quick kiss. Still hovering above her, he dragged his hand up her other side, taking the same slow course until he reached the base of her other breast.

She grabbed his wrist and yanked him down until their mouths again came together.

No more light kisses. Her mouth open wide and moving with his, she devoured him like she had the food he cooked earlier.

He slid his arm around her back. "Sit up."

With his help, she obeyed. He gathered her into his arms and kissed her, starting out gentle, then letting need take over. He wanted to press into her, touch her body in every place, every way.

He lowered his head and rained kisses over her cheek, down her neck, along her arm, down to her elbow, then suckled her fingers, one by one. She inhaled thickly, then relaxed as he released her hand and lay down beside her. He grasped her hips, hoping she'd realize what he wanted her to do.

She rose up and lifted a leg over him until she sat astride him. He grasped her hips, lifting, his body straining with the need for release—

She tensed. "I can't."

He wanted to scream. "What's wrong?" He forced calm into his voice. "I thought you wanted—"

"I do. But... it's always ended badly. I don't know if I can bear it again, after..." Her eyes downcast, she shuddered as if suppressing a sob.

She was afraid he'd say something hurtful again. "It won't be like that, I promise."

Her bottom lip quivered. "I know, but..."

"How about I don't speak, until you tell me I can. Make a game of it." The firelight sparkled in her eyes. "I'll do whatever you tell me. And I'll say nothing." He dragged his fingertips down her arm. "What do you think?"

A smile stole across her lips. "All right."

He grabbed her hips again and eased her forward. "Now where were we?"

She lay a finger over her lips, silencing him.

The game had begun.

He gripped her hips and she relaxed, letting him guide her. He pulled with his right hand and pushed with his left, indicating that she should turn around. Her eyes went round, but she did what he wanted. The fire cast a warm glow over her, bathing her supple curves in orange and shadow. He wanted to tell her how beautiful she was, but that could wait.

Wrapping his arms around her belly, he rose into a kneel behind her and lifted her to her knees. Her head whipped around. "Mercy! Are we going to... like animals?"

He smiled.

"You can answer me."

"Do you have a problem with that?"

"Ah, no..." He rocked against her and slid inside. "Heavens, no!"

The sensation amazed him. Small moans escaped her with each thrust until she tensed, crying out as she squeezed him in rhythmic pulses. It swept him over the edge, and he went rigid and spilled into her. They sighed in unison, then he slowly backed away, lay down, and pulled her into his arms.

Her face burrowed into his chest, then she rolled onto her side so that her back curled into his stomach. He held her close. Warmth flooded him. This was what he wanted. The way it should be. Everything felt right.

Even if she was the woman who'd seduced him only to betray him.

But if her memory was gone, she was no longer that woman. He'd just have to hope that if she ever warped back to the Saturn Society during Pippin's reign, the Watchkeeper would keep her identity to himself as he had in 1959, for whatever reason.

She never needed to know she'd loved Tony, killed him, and nearly given him over to the Society for a fate worse than death.

It would be his secret to keep.

By the time they finished making love (like animals again! Violet had no idea something so naughty could be so wonderful), the sun was rising. Tony rolled out of her arms with reluctance. "I could lie here all day, but we need to eat." He grabbed his glasses and gun.

"Of course." She pushed herself up and followed him out of the crevice, trying to ignore the blaze between her thighs at the sight of his naked backside.

He fingered his gun. "I'm going to see what I can scare up for dinner. Then we'll get started making some tools. This thing's only got a few more rounds."

Violet poked the campfire, where thankfully, a few embers still glowed. "How did you get the fire going?"

He tapped his glasses. "Good thing yesterday was sunny."

She smiled at his cleverness. "I'll see if I can get some logs started so we can begin building a home."

Tony squeezed the gun. "You're in no condition to do heavy labor. I want you to rest."

"But there's so much we need—"

"Stay. Here." His gaze drifted over her and her skin burned in desire. His hand curled and uncurled, and she knew the same thoughts were going through his mind. She jerked her gaze to his face as he leaned his hand on a tree. "Maybe you could weave something for us to sit on. It's so damn hot I wouldn't wear much if I had anything, but rocks and weeds don't exactly feel good on your bare ass, do they?"

"All right."

He grabbed some of last night's turkey and walked away. After she'd eaten the rest of the leftovers, she wandered through the trees near the crevice, picking long grasses when she happened upon them and scouring the woods for rocks that would make good tools. She forgot her quest for grasses when she spotted a sharp-edged stone that would make a perfect axe.

Once she had the fire built back up, she grabbed a burning stick, then went to work on the first log for their home. She singed a ring around a tree, then worked on the grass mats while it burned. Every so often, she chipped away the burnt ring, putting out of her mind how quickly she was tiring and Tony's admonishment to rest. There was too much to do. The women in the village were usually back in the gardens and at the cook fires the day after giving birth, sometimes within hours.

The sun was starting to arc toward the west and she'd almost cut through the log, when leaves crackled behind her.

Tony scowled. "I told you to rest. Weren't you going to make us something to sit on?"

Violet flinched at his harsh tone, then squeezed her stone. "I did." She jerked a thumb toward the crevice, where two mats lay. "I thought it prudent that we not let the fire go out, considering that neither of us has flint and pyrite. As for that," she pointed at the tree she'd started to work on, "we need all the time we can get to build a home. Neither of us have felt the Pull, and I'm not willing to count on getting it before winter." As if her anger had sapped the last of her energy, the sharp stone slipped from her hands and fell to the ground.

His face went slack. "I'm sorry. I— I just worry." He dropped the deer he'd dragged back to the camp and slipped his arms around her. He led her to the mats, then gently pressed her into a seated position. "Let's eat, then you can tell me what to do with the deerskin. We'll need all of that we can get, too."

As they skinned and prepared the deer, Violet couldn't believe how right it felt to work side by side with him, nor could she shake the sense of déjà vu that had settled over her like a heavy fog. They'd done this before, prepared a meal, sharing the labor as equals. As lovers.

Afterward, Violet set the skin aside to be cleaned and cured. The entrails would make useful bags and herb pouches. The bones were for scrapers, needles, and other tools. They'd use the brain to cure the leather. Almost everything was usable.

She avoided looking below Tony's waist. He, too, kept his gaze focused on her face. If they didn't, they'd never get anything accomplished. As they worked, she couldn't get her mind off the one question that had gnawed at her since the motel in 1959, worse now that Tony believed her about her memory loss.

"Tony?" Her gaze followed his hand, scraping the inside of the deerskin with its hip bone, as she'd shown him. "Who's Charlotte?"

He froze. She opened her mouth to repeat her question, but he recovered. "An old girlfriend." His words were sharp and clipped. He concentrated on the skin, scraping so hard Violet feared he'd wear a hole through it. With each scrape, her dread grew.

What if *she* was this Charlotte? "What's she li—"

"She was deceptive, and manipulative, and interested only in furthering Theodore Pippin's agenda." Tony scowled at the skin as he scraped the same spot over and over.

Violet fought to keep her voice even, and her tone curious. "Was? You mean she was from the past? Your past?" Mr. Pippin had started to call her something else when he'd picked her up at the motel in 1959.

Tony frowned at the deerskin and stopped scraping. "I saved her life in the 1913 Flood. She was just a kid. I went back to see her about twenty years later—to her, it was only about six weeks later for me. I wanted to see how she'd turned out, see if she could answer some questions for me that Everly wouldn't..."

"And one thing led to another," Violet finished. Dear heavens, could it be?

He lowered his face, peering at her through his lashes. "Yeah." His voice dropped to almost a whisper. "And then she gave me over to the Society."

She gripped the deer shank and her knife more tightly, trying not to recoil. "What's so terrible about that? Mr. Pippin was nothing but kind—"

"You weren't on his shit list. I was."

"Mercy, that's right." Mr. Everly had told them, when he and Ms. Warren had come to pick them up at Florie's.

"Yeah. And she tried to give me over to Pippin, so he could make me like that Fred guy Everly takes care of—"

"Good heavens!" She slowly lowered her fingers and reached for a short lock of hair below her ear. "Mr. Everly told me he was brain damaged. What- what happened to him? Is he—"

"He was in the Black Book. Somehow, the Society found out he'd been making trips to the past to buy stock, based on his knowledge of the future. When Pippin caught up with him—with Charlotte's help— he gave him the Treatment. Sort of like a lobotomy."

"My word!" she breathed. "I had no idea that was what Mr. Pippin was talking about when he mentioned... consequences. I can't imagine—" Her words cut off, choked. If she was Charlotte...

"Believe it. That's how Pippin made sure his enemies never traveled in time again."

Had Fred recognized her when he'd seen her at Mr. Everly's House, and that was why he'd grown so agitated? She fingered the base of her neck, tracing up and down her collarbone. "It had to have been that horrid man who looks like you. Unless..."

"Maybe. Maybe not." Tony sighed and turned the bone scraper over in his hand. "I'm pretty sure I went back three years and prevented my daughter's death. I- the memories are vague, but they're there. She went to a party. Something made me go after her, and I found her and her best friend drinking—she's diabetic, so that could kill her—and those guys.... They were a lot older. I made her leave. But one of her friends left with them, and they turned out to be," he swallowed, "into young girls. And beating them up. And... they would've killed her, if I hadn't made Bethany suspicious, and she called the cops. But in that other timeline, I think... it was Bethany who left with them. And they killed her. Brutally."

"For that, Mr. Pippin wanted to make you into a drooling idiot?"

"Yeah." He snorted, with a shake of his head. "And Charlotte helped. Or tried. But she fucked up and killed me instead."

Violet sucked in air, a drawn-out, inhaled gasp, as she reached for her non-existent pottery chip. *She'd* killed him. After all those years, it was Tony's blood all over her. But it hadn't yet happened for him when he first met her, hadn't even happened in the same century. That was why no one had come looking for her. "So you- you returned to the present, right?"

One corner of his mouth tipped up. "They found me lying in the middle of the river. You came to visit me in the hospital, remember?"

She swallowed and took a deep breath. "Yes." He'd looked at her with that same need, that same yearning as he had in the 1959 motel. He'd asked about her family. About her past. Probing. Trying to get her to admit to something, just like now.

She had to be this Charlotte, and if she'd done the horrible things he said she had, it was no wonder he despised her. But if he knew, why didn't he say so? "Why did you call me by her name? Why—"

"You look like her." He shrugged, but it was forced. "And she was a time traveler, too, thanks to me."

"When you saved her life." A shiver ran through Violet. If Charlotte had nearly drowned, she was probably afraid of water, too. Too many coincidences. But why wouldn't he tell her?

The stone knife slipped from her hands.

Maybe she wasn't this Charlotte after all. Maybe she really just looked like her. Violet wouldn't have hurt Tony like that. Not for anything. She loved him, always had, as long as she'd known—

He tossed down the deerskin. "You're bleeding!" He took her hand. A rivulet of red flowed across her palm.

She hadn't even noticed.

He grasped her other hand. "Come on, let's wash that before it gets infec—"

"It's not a big deal," she protested, but let him pull her up.

As she followed him down the path to the water, her mind tumbled with his revelations.

She reminded him of a woman who'd tried to kill him—or, worse, she *was* the woman who'd killed him.

Though the evening was stiflingly warm, she couldn't repress a shudder. She couldn't be this Charlotte. But perhaps the woman was a relative. Even so, could Violet's fear of water be merely a coincidence?

Tony glanced back as he led her to the river, and barely noticed when a tree branch slapped him. She'd handled that well. Perfectly caught each curveball he tossed her, convincingly displayed surprise and dismay in all the right places.

"Tony?" He caught her hand as she stumbled over a root. "What happened to this woman?"

One last chance. He'd see if she slipped up, if she betrayed her emotions. If she didn't...

Then he'd believe her. For real.

"Supposedly she died after she killed me. At least that's what's in her family's records." He watched her face. "But I think she ran. Pippin wouldn't have been too happy with her for letting me get away. Charlotte was an incredibly smart woman, she could've easily made herself disappear."

"You never tried to find out what happened to her? In our time, it should be doable."

They reached the sandy riverbank, and he made up his mind. "Enough about her. Let's get that cut cleaned up." He took her hand,

and she followed him into the river without hesitation.

He filled his cupped hands with water and poured it over her, rinsing off the deer blood from earlier that day, along with her own. The cut had already stopped bleeding, and he realized his concern over it was secondary. What he really wanted was to reenact the time in 1933 when he and Charlotte had made love in the river, when he'd chased away her fears. The time he wanted to remember, before she betrayed him.

He rubbed his hands over her silken skin, down her shoulders, over her breasts. Her nipples beaded at his touch, and the bad memories fled. There was only here, only now, only Violet. His hand glided over her round belly, the knowledge that it was their baby inside stoking his desire—

Her stomach bulged beneath his hand. Violet giggled. "Evidently, the baby likes baths, too. Perhaps that can be your job once he—or she—arrives."

"I'd like that." Tony ran his hand back over the moving lump, marveling at the wonder within. "You thought any more about names?"

She hesitated. "I would like to name our baby after our friends who helped us. Ga-noo if it's a girl, Rod-orak if it's a boy."

Tony's rubbing slowed. "I agree with you about our friends, but I'd hate to stick a kid with either of those names."

"Maybe not Ga-noo, but Rod-orak could be Roderick. And it sounds good with Sinclair."

Tony slid his hand away. "Sinclair?"

"Shouldn't his name should be the same as his mother's?" Her words were short, defensive.

His desire shrunk into a hot coal in the pit of his stomach. No son—or daughter—of his was going to have a different last name than him. "It doesn't matter now. It's not like there'll be a birth certificate until we get home." Tony knew she was thinking the same thing he was. *If* the baby went with them.

Violet stepped away and turned her back to him, pretending to scrub her elbow. "It matters to me."

It mattered to Tony, too. Especially since he'd take the child if she regained her memory and realigned herself with those in the Society who considered him an enemy.

She stood an arm's length away, trembling. Compassion welled up in him. She was not that woman now. "Violet?" He gripped her elbow just hard enough to direct her to turn around.

Beneath brows drawn tight in anger, her eyes glistened with tears.

She may as well have driven a spear down his throat. He pulled her against him. "What's wrong, baby?"

She touched the base of her neck, and failing to find her pottery chip necklace, drew her fingers along her collarbone. Sympathy pulled at him like a hand reaching into his chest. He wanted to do something, anything, to ease her tension. He lifted the bear claw necklace over his head. "You can have it if you want."

She rolled her lips in, then took the necklace, and dropped it back over his head. "Thank you, but no." She settled it around his neck, staying clear of his scars. "I like it too much on you. It's incredibly," she wet her lips, "sexy. Especially when you're wearing nothing else."

Warmth burst through him, settling in his groin. He wanted to take her right then. But not until he found out what was troubling her. "What's wrong, then? And don't say 'Nothing,' even if it's just something silly." That was what Dora had always done, and it was irritating as hell.

"It *is* silly."

"What?" He moved his hand slowly up and down her back.

"I don't... I— talking about names. It's just really hitting me that I'm about to become an unwed mother." He opened his mouth to protest, but she went on. "I hate it. I know millions of unmarried women have babies every year and few think the worse of them, but I can't shake the feeling it's something... shameful." She drew back, her expression stern, but not angry, then her face relaxed a fraction. "Perhaps I grew up in a very strict home. I know it's nonsense, yet..."

For someone who'd grown up in the early twentieth century, having a child out of wedlock would be scandalous. Her neighbors would have shunned her. Her family might have disowned her. But in the twenty-first century, it didn't matter, and it mattered even less in a time before there were even any written records.

They moved onto the riverbank. He stroked her hair, and let his gaze travel down her beautiful, rounded body. At that moment, standing naked in the woods with her, there was nowhere else he'd rather be. No *when* else he'd rather be. No one else he'd rather be with. "We could get married," he mused.

She jerked straight. "What?"

What the hell are you doing? his rational side asked. *Are you out of your mind?* He ignored the voice. "Violet... I love you. Marry me." His heart was right. This time, he'd listen.

"When we get home?"

"No. Now."

"But how? There's no one to marry us. Not even the village's holy man."

He wanted to do this. Now.

A whisper of a thought skittered through the back of his mind that if she turned on him, it would be that much easier for him to legally claim the child.

He pushed the idea from his mind. "I say we make our vows right here, now. Before each other and God. When we get home, we can make it legal."

She blinked rapidly. "Are you sure?"

"More sure than I've ever been of anything." At least the not-logical side of him was, despite the shakiness in his arms and legs. He took both her hands in his. Refusing to consider the possibility she'd say no, he dropped to his knee. "Violet Sinclair, will you marry me?"

She stood stiffly, holding her breath, unmoving except for her hands trembling in his grasp. "Yes," she whispered. "Of course!" He stood but didn't release her hands. "I'm afraid it's been a long time since I've been to a wedding. I don't even know what to say."

"Say whatever you want. This is our ceremony, just for us." The more he talked about it, the more nervousness and excitement surged in his heart. She took a step back, and he let her go. "You need some time to think about it?"

"No." She smiled, a quiet, Mona Lisa smile that shook him to his toes. "But I have nothing to wear—"

"You look perfect." His breath came in choked bursts, his words strangled. "More beautiful than if you were wearing a ten thousand dollar wedding gown."

He took both her hands in his. All he could do was stand there and drink her in.

The river babbled more loudly, and birds chirped in counterpoint, music no organ could do justice. Above the treetops, cottony clouds traced a leisurely path across a brilliant blue sky. A cathedral more majestic than any humanity could create.

Her voice was barely more than a whisper. "Are we ready?"

Swallowing the lump in his throat, he nodded. He wasn't sure what he'd say, he simply let the words come out. "We stand here in the presence of God and each other, to make a vow of marriage. For guests we have the creatures of the woods. For flowers, we have the greenery and beauty of nature. We don't need wedding rings, we need only each other."

"We have all we need," Violet said. "The incredible gift of time travel to find sanctuary from our enemies. Friends to give us aid. Nature's bounty to fill our bellies and give us shelter. Fire to warm our bodies, and love to fill our hearts."

Tony looked into her eyes, their golden-honey depths teeming with emotion. She wouldn't betray him again. Not after this.

It was a chance he'd take.

He squeezed her hands. "I, Anton Joseph Solomon, take you—"

He bit back his words. He'd almost said Charlotte Henderson. He swallowed. "I take you, Violet Sinclair, to be my wedded wife. I promise to love and honor you, for better or worse, for richer or for poorer, in good times and bad times, to have and to hold for as long as we both live, for present, past, and future."

She sniffed and blinked, her eyes never leaving his. She twisted her hands, then gripped his firmly. Though she spoke softly, her words were clear and without hesitation. "I, Violet Sinclair, take you, Anton Solomon, to be my wedded husband, to have and to hold, to love and honor, in sickness and in health, for richer or poorer, I give you my heart, my trust, and my life."

Tony thought his legs were going to give out on him, but he gripped her hands and pulled her close. Drawing his strength from her nearness, he folded her into his arms, willing himself not to shake.

When he'd married Dora, he'd been nervous. But the vows themselves were just words. Part of the spectacle Dora and her mom had put on, with their twelve attendants, twin flower girls and live band.

Violet trembled in his arms, and he swayed back and forth, holding her. Despite the lack of guests, a minister, or any of the trappings, this was much more real than the vows he'd spoken with Dora. The vows she'd later broken.

Stronger than any intuition he'd ever had, was the knowledge that whatever else she did, Violet would never cheat on him.

He slipped a finger under her chin and tipped her face up. "I think this is the part where I get to kiss the bride."

He pulled her to him, as closely as he could while being mindful of her belly. She surged upward to meet his kiss, lips moving with his, softness against his hard planes, his firm mouth. He kissed her forcefully, hungrily, could never get enough. His hands roved over her back, down her hips, up her sides, around her belly and breasts.

She drew in a sharp breath, then tipped her head back. Tony brushed away her short, dark curls and leaned over to nuzzle at her neck, then drew his tongue down the sleek column, over her collarbone. He bent to continue down the satiny slope of her breast until he reached her nipple.

She gasped as he flicked it with his tongue, then drew it into his mouth, swirling his tongue over the hardened tip. He had to remind himself to be gentle, though she gave no indication her pregnancy had made it tender.

He gave equal time to the other, then moved lower, his tongue drawing a wet trail over her belly. The sensation of her skin on his

tongue made him tingle, and he wanted to lick her all over, everywhere, wanted to see her squirm with desire. She kneaded his
shoulders as he knelt before her. "Are we going to consummate our
marriage?"

Tony rolled back on his ankles, need surging though him. "I think
we should."

She slipped away and turned her back to him, then knelt and
bent over.

Stunned, Tony regarded her smooth, pale ass, aching to grab it in
both his hands and drive into her. He knelt behind her, but something
made him stop.

She turned around. "Tony?"

He reached for her, encircled her belly, and pulled her upright. "I
want to see your face."

He gave her a lingering kiss, pulled away reluctantly, then
grabbed her hand and led her to a flat boulder the size of a small bed,
jutting over the river. He lifted her onto it. "This way," he directed.
She scooted forward until she sat on the edge of the rock, her legs
dangling over the edge.

He ached to plunge into her, he was so hard he was sure he'd
have ripped through the thickest buckskin, had he been wearing any.

But first he wanted to pleasure her. He stood between her knees
and lay another kiss on her lips. When he drew his mouth down her
neck, she closed her eyes with a sigh. He moved down her chest and
skimmed the top of her breasts. Then he crouched and moved lower,
licking in short swipes down her belly.

When he reached the curls between her legs he climbed off the
rock and bent before her. He licked the underside of her knee, then
swiped his tongue up her leg, but stopped short when he reached the
top. He moved to the other leg and did the same. "Tony... you're
killing me," she murmured.

He leaned into her thighs and swiped his tongue between her
legs. She gasped. "Do you want me to stop?" he asked.

"Heavens, no!"

He knelt and took her in his mouth, swirling his tongue around, flicking it back and forth where it would give her the most pleasure. Small sighs escaped her, one after another. She threaded her hands through his hair, oblivious that she was pulling. He didn't care. He went on, and she tightened beneath his tongue until her bottom clenched and lifted. "Tony... Oh, my word!" Her exclamation made him almost explode, but he held back, then licked her once more. She shivered.

He stood. Placing his hands on her thighs, he eased her legs apart, then lowered himself until he was the right height to enter her.

She was tight, and he eased in, tipping his head back. "Ahh..." Slowly, he began to rock back and forth on his knees, in and out, savoring her expression of contentment and joy, delighting in the surprise that washed over her as she tightened around him, then throbbed in another orgasm. She called his name, gripping his thighs.

He spilled into her, the release pure ecstasy.

He backed away. She sat up, and he climbed onto the boulder and lay beside her. She rolled onto her side and rested her head in the hollow beneath his shoulder. At Charlotte's home in 1933, he'd gone down on her, and from her reaction, it was the first time she'd experienced it. They'd made love on her living room floor for the last time, made bittersweet by the Pull trying to take him.

Then the Saturn Society had arrived, and Tony had run into the bedroom, barely escaping with his life as he overheard her telling the man she'd only lured Tony there to trap him.

He gazed over the woman in his arms, the one he'd just made love to again. The woman who'd once betrayed him. The woman he'd made his wife—in heart and soul, if not legally.

The chill started high in his gut, skittered down his spine, and spread to his fingers, his toes, the top of his skull. *What the hell have I done?*

Fourteen

Rain beat on the hut's thatched roof as Violet scraped at the rabbit skins on the stretching racks she'd built. When the skins dried, she'd make them into diapers, wraps and hoods for the baby.

Once she and Tony had made tools and spearheads, making clothing had been easy. Finding clay and making pottery, storing food, and collecting firewood had been more difficult. Building their home had been their greatest challenge, and even though no one but she and Tony had seen it—they hadn't encountered a single human since their warp—it was her proudest accomplishment. They'd gone many days with sleep caught in snatches while they waited for trees to burn enough to fell. Two months of grueling, physical labor, especially when all Violet wanted to do was lie down, but it was worth it, for their home was completed by the time the weather grew cold.

Compared to the huts in the village, it was more like a half-house, built against the rock crevice in a lean-to fashion. That had been Tony's idea, and a good one, for not only had it saved them time and effort, but the crevice was the warmest spot in the house, and made a perfect bed once they added straw, pine boughs, deerskins, and a black bear fur.

Wind pounded the hut, shaking the bundled herbs, dried plants, and jerky hanging from the rafters. The main support pole creaked, and the clay bowls and pots rattled, jarring a mug out of the tidy row where Tony had lined them up. But the hut held strong.

Sympathy plucked at Violet's heart as she thought of him out there hunting, but he'd refused to stay in. They needed to store up as much game as possible if they were to have food and clothing to last through the winter.

Her belly cramped, making her double over. She rubbed low, where the baby had settled a few days ago. After a minute, the cramp went away. She'd been having them all day. It had to be false labor. According to the scratches she made each day on the hut's support pole, it was only early November. The baby shouldn't arrive for another two weeks.

Tightness gathered in her chest as if she wore a too-small bra. They'd been in the past for six months, and neither she nor Tony had felt the slightest stirring of the Pull.

She pushed aside her worries over the impending birth and moved to the fire in the hut's center—no easy undertaking, as big as she'd grown. The roomy buckskin shift she'd made a month ago was now snug across the middle. She hoped she wouldn't outgrow it before the baby was born.

Rabbit stew cooked in their biggest pot, and she scooped up a bit with a gourd spoon and sniffed. Not the burrito she craved, but the savory, meaty fragrance made her mouth water. It should be done by the time Tony returned from hunting.

A gust of wind blew rain into one of the triangular-shaped holes at the top of the roof, carrying the smoke from her fire out the other. But their sleeping area in the rock crevice remained dry. Violet scooted onto the fur-covered straw and busied herself by fashioning some cured skins into tiny leggings and a hood, lacing the pieces together with thin leather sinews. Thankfully, Ga-noo had taught her to sew before the horrible incident with the gun.

The rain had stopped, and feeble rays of sun slanted through the vent hole in the west end of the cabin when another cramp hit her, worse than before. She lay down and waited for it to pass. The tight-achy-pressure beneath her breasts hammered harder. What if this time it was real?

She rubbed her belly, praying for relief. Her gaze fell on the dugout log she and Tony had made into a cradle. It had been his idea, but she'd come up with the half-circle shaped log cross sections wedged onto the ends that allowed the cradle to rock. A lining of soft buckskins atop a layer of straw was all it needed to be ready for its occupant.

The cradle was ready, but was she?

"Hello," Tony called. The door-skin lifted. "Oh, no, what's wrong?" He dropped the pair of rabbits in his hand and rushed to Violet's side.

The pain faded. She sat up. "Just... false labor." She scooted away from the puddle that was forming beneath his dripping clothes.

"You sure?" Tony retreated and untied his sodden, buckskin cloak and hung it on a peg beside the row of skins Violet had set aside for the baby. Blankets first, Violet noted with detached amusement, then wraps, then diapers. He'd been organizing again. As he slipped off his boots and turned to her, his expression bore doubt. "The baby's not due for—" she began.

"I know. But it could be early." He sat on the furs beside her. Deep in thought, he stroked his beard. He'd planned to continue shaving, but Violet had pointed out that there was no need, since they no longer had to fit in with others. He'd come across as ragged and unkempt in their own time, but here, his beard lent a wild, rugged quality to his otherwise smooth face, hinting at the hidden strength beneath. She found it appealing.

She brought her knees up and lay on her side. "How was hunting?"

The tension drained from his shoulders. "Two rabbits. Almost got a deer, but my spear just nicked it in the hip."

"The rabbit furs will make nice baby clothes."

"Yeah, but deer would've tasted good." He rubbed her belly, and the warmth from his hand banished the remnants of the ache. "You getting these pains often?"

She shook her head. "One while I was working the rabbit skins, maybe an hour ago."

"Hopefully we won't need them."

Lightness rose inside Violet. "Have you started to get the Pull?"

"No." His mouth pressed into a tight line.

She squeezed his hand, but couldn't stop shaking. "Tony, women have been having babies since the dawn of humanity. We'll be fine. The people of the village manage without a hospital. Even in our time, women have babies in taxicabs, elevators and busses. And they end up fi—"

Wetness seeped from her. "Oh dear."

Tony stiffened. "What?"

She looked down. The wetness had soaked through to the front of her shift, and she was sitting in a puddle. "I think my water's broken."

Violet lay on the sweat-dampened furs, shaking as the contraction faded. Silhouetted in firelight, Tony brushed a wet rabbit skin across her forehead. "You're doing fine," he murmured.

The pains had come and gone for hours. They'd bundled up in furs and strolled around the forest until the wind and rain picked up again, snuffing out Tony's torch. By the time they picked their way back to the hut in the dark, she hurt so much she could barely walk.

Another cramp came, more powerful. Rain and wind battered the hut, hard enough to rattle the pottery and rock the cradle. The slight motion cast eerie shadows in the flickering firelight, and she jerked her mind off the frightening thoughts that threatened. What if something went wrong? What if her baby was born deformed, or worse, stillborn? She focused on how glad she was to be inside and warm, while she blew out sharp puffs like she'd seen the village women do. She gripped Tony's hand like she was hanging on for her life as the rain pounded and the wind howled in time to her contractions.

The cramp subsided. "Go check the rabbits," she said.

Tony moved to the fire and stirred the pot beside the smoking racks, where the skins dried. "Dinner's fine. So are the skins. Don't worry about them."

She couldn't help it. Not only because they couldn't afford to waste a thing, but it took her mind off the pain, which no longer completely went away.

Another cramp wracked her. Worse. She couldn't help letting out a whimper.

Tony returned to her side and took her hand. He asked her about mindless things, and what she'd done when she'd first arrived in the twenty-first century, after the initial shock wore off.

She pushed aside her fear that the delivery was taking too long. "When Stephanie got home and found me with Timmy, she said we should call the police, but I... I couldn't. Something told me I didn't dare."

"Understandable." Tony stroked the back of her hand with his thumb.

Yes, but not for the reason he thought. Tony did not need to know she'd killed someone—*him*.

Don't think about it. "I wasn't quite sure of how to convince her not to call them, then her husband came home, and... oh, he was in a horrid mood that nigh—" Another contraction came, cutting off her breath.

It went on for hours. The rain came and went, then came again. Just as she'd start to worry that the baby was breech, or that the head would be too large to fit, Tony would ask her a question, or talk about his daughter or someone they knew from the office. His soothing voice and the diversion helped her work through the ordeal and focus on the result. The time between cramps grew shorter until her world narrowed to nothing but the pain, Tony's quiet attempts to comfort her, and the urge to push.

She pushed. She was vaguely aware of Tony moving to her bottom, then back to her side. "You're doing fine." He took the rabbit skin off her forehead, dipped it in the water pot, and wiped her brow. "Everything's okay."

But even through the haze of her pain, Violet saw how his hand shook as he lifted the rag to her forehead, caught the tremor in his voice when he scooted to her feet.

"Something's... wrong," she managed between pushes.

He looked up, his mouth pressed tightly closed. "Just keep breathing."

Panic rose in her. "What is it?" Wind pummeled the hut, emphasizing her fears.

"Just me being nervous." He crouched so low she couldn't see him over the swell of her belly, but his strained voice told her he was lying.

Her panic swelled. "Tell me what's wrong!" She lifted her head, straining to see him.

"It's—"

The pressure grew down below. Fire ripped through her crotch, and she had to push again— "Stop!" he yelled.

She couldn't keep from screaming. "What—"

"The cord's around the baby's neck!"

Her head flopped to the furs. "Heavens, no," she whimpered. *Don't let me have gone through all this, lived in this wretched time, for nothing!* Tears sprang to her eyes, she wasn't sure because of the biting, burning pain, or the possibility her baby might die.

More pressure. Tony jerked something around down there. She bit back another scream. She couldn't lose the baby! Not now! Not—

A tingle shot from her bottom up her body, briefly masking the pain. *What on earth—* "Okay!" he said.

She pushed.

"Once more," he urged.

She did, then the pressure was gone.

The cramping lessened. She leaned up, trying to see, straining to hear a cry. Tony frantically rubbed at something. She couldn't take in a breath, her body felt as if something was compressing her with a great weight. Even the air felt heavy. "Is it—"

Tony let out a big breath. "It's a boy!" She tried to push herself up on her elbows, but couldn't see anything. He grabbed a knife and sawed at something, then finally held up his hands.

The baby was a bloody mess, but his arms and legs wiggled.

He's alive! Shaking, Violet reached for him. "Is he... all right?"

Tony wiped the infant with a soft rabbit skin. "I think so, just let me wipe his nose... there." He moved to her side and laid the now-clean baby on her chest. She wrapped her arms around the tiny infant. Awe and amazement washed through her as she ran a finger over his fine, dark hair, stroked the satiny soft skin of his arm, his belly, his leg, barely conscious of Tony hovering beside her. *He's mine. Alive. Mine. And Tony's.*

The baby kicked and flexed his fingers. When she put hers in his palm, he turned his head toward her.

His round, murky, blue eyes met hers. She'd read that newborns couldn't focus, but she swore he did. In that instant, love poured through her more fiercely than anything she'd felt before. A certainty that she'd give anything, do anything, endure anything, for this child. "Oh my word," she breathed. "He's beautiful."

"Yes, he is." Tony sat beside her, beaming at their son. Her love swelled and encompassed him. There was nothing they couldn't conquer. No challenge they couldn't overcome. As long as they were together—

A cramp stung her belly. "Tony?" Mercy, could there be a twin?

No, the ultrasound she'd had after the fire had shown only one fetus. But why—

"The placenta." Tony hurried to her feet.

She was barely aware of Tony as she marveled at her child's dewy, soft skin, his beautiful face, his perfect fingers and toes, five on each limb—she counted.

Tony stood, making a face at the ground.

"Take it away and bury it," she said.

"Huh?"

"That's what Ga-noo always did. I imagine so animals didn't find it and come into the village. Or maybe some spiritual reason we'd have no clue of. But just to be sure..."

He did as she asked.

By the time he returned, she'd gotten the baby to nurse. It didn't feel like he was getting anything, but she remembered from her reading that he wouldn't eat much for the first day or so.

Tony shrugged off his cloak and hung it up, but missed the lashed-wood hook, his gaze fixed on the baby. "Did he... make any noise while I was gone?"

"Not a thing." Violet stroked the baby's downy hair. He'd been so alert when Tony had handed him to her—surely there couldn't be anything wrong—

"Should I have spanked him?" Tony picked his cloak off the floor and found the hook.

Violet couldn't decide if he was serious. "They don't do that any—in our time. But it is strange, that he's so quiet.

"O-yo's baby didn't cry when I was at Aye-sack's—"

The baby released Violet's breast and made a loud cry. She pulled the furs around him more snugly. "I think he's telling us that's his name."

"What?"

"Aye-sack. Isaac."

The infant gurgled, then quieted.

Tony gave a single nod. "I like it."

Violet frowned down at Isaac, who'd fallen to sleep.

"What's wrong?" Tony asked.

She shook her head. "I don't know... it's the strangest thing, but when he was born, right after you told me about the cord... I felt a- a tingle, sort of like electricity, only..."

"The time travel thing." Tony knelt beside her, studying the sleeping baby. "Everly did say it's passed through the trauma of birth. And when the cord was wrapped around his neck..."

"Oh, mercy." The baby shifted in her arms but didn't wake. "He's like us, isn't he?" Her stomach grew heavy, as if she'd eaten too many honey-soaked corn cakes.

Tony's mouth set into a firm line before he spoke. "Yeah. A time traveler."

The next two weeks went by in a blur. Tony settled into a routine of helping to care for Isaac. Though he couldn't feed the baby, Tony changed him, burped him, and bathed him, amazed. *My son.* The one

Alpha claimed would prevent chaos, centuries in the future.

While Violet sewed a pair of buckskin boots, Tony rocked the baby, weary after an unusual, long crying spell, in his cradle. Isaac's puffy, reddened eyes were shaped just like Bethany's, with deep lines curving beneath them. Tony's rocking slowed as his heart swelled with joy and sadness at the same time. Would his son ever get to meet his sister?

"Fiddlesticks," Violet muttered. She slid the leather thong from the bone needle she'd just snapped, and tossed the latter into the fire. Tony kept rocking—*please sleep*—as Violet crossed the hut to grab another needle. As she reached the stone and bone implements lined up against the wall, she stumbled, at the same time dizziness burst through Tony.

She gasped. Was it...?

The dizzy spell passed. Tony looked up at her round, brown eyes. "The Pull?" she whispered.

Could it be? Tony scanned the cabin, searching for glimpses of home fading through, then shook his head slowly. "I don't think so. Must be... someone else."

Violet sucked in a breath. "Who?"

"Hopefully, friends." He frowned at the fire. "Maybe I should go look for them..."

The bone needle slipped in Violet's fingers. "What if they're... not?"

"Whoever it is, they'll be in recovery for a good while."

Violet went back to her sewing, fed Isaac when he woke up for lunch, and held him while Tony ate a bit of venison stew. The baby fussed all afternoon it seemed, and by the time Tony rocked him to sleep for his afternoon nap, the sun had started to peek through the smoke outlet hole on the hut's west side.

Too soon, Isaac stirred and woke. His lip trembled. Tony started rocking again, but the baby's thin, plaintive cry quickly crescendoed to a screech.

Tony lifted him to his shoulder, but patting the baby's back didn't soothe the child. Violet reached for him. "He might be hungry." Tony handed him to her. She settled in to nurse, and Isaac quieted.

Tony felt at odds, suddenly useless, still not used to the fact that the two of them were now three.

Violet looked up. "You're... you're not having one of those memories, are you?"

Tony jerked straight. "No... I haven't had one since we came to this time." *Weird.* But he wasn't about to complain. He reached for his bow. "I'm going to see if I can find some game."

Violet looked up, an eyebrow cocked. "There are still two squirrels from this morning."

"More won't hurt. We can always smoke the leftovers." He voiced the fear that dogged them harder with each passing day. His face went slack. "I still haven't gotten even a hint of the Pull." Neither of them voiced his worry that he was sure she shared—would they *ever* get the Pull?

Violet's brows pressed down. "What about... those jumps? What if..."

"Recovery, remember? But good point, that's another reason we should stock up on meat. Who knows, maybe I'll run across them."

Violet nodded, her attention on Isaac. Tony pulled on his fur tunic, leggings, and cloak, then grabbed his spears and gun off the hooks near the door. He kissed Violet goodbye.

She frowned at the gun. "Why do you always take it?"

"We've gone over this before. After what happened to Rod-orak with that bear, I'm not taking any chances, especially with those dizzy spells." He grabbed a stone knife from the weapons rack. "Keep this handy."

Her lips tightened, and she gave a single nod as she took the knife and laid it on the straw beside her. Isaac pulled away from her as if sensing her tension.

Tony emerged from the hut to a brittle, sharp cold. Dried weeds and vegetation crackled with frost beneath his fur boots, and the leaden gray sky above the bare trees hinted of snow.

He crept down a slope toward the still spot in the river where deer sometimes came to drink. They had enough rabbit skins to keep Isaac in diapers for a good two or three days even if they didn't wash them right away. But the baby would soon need more clothing, as would Tony and Violet. A deer would be good.

He lay on his belly beside some underbrush, eyes on the watering spot. Chances were, something would come along sooner or later.

He didn't realize he'd drifted off to sleep until something woke him. A noise. Not a deer's light step through the wood or a squirrel's chattering. Something that didn't belong.

He scanned the river below. Nothing moved. He listened. Nothing but the wind, rattling a few dead leaves clinging to branches.

No animals, that was what was weird. No squirrels dashing through the treetops, no birds twittering above.

Unease filtered through him like sand through a sieve. He rolled halfway to his side and shook his hand that had fallen asleep, when the wind carried a distant, human voice to his ears.

He froze.

"Dion!"

What the—

Who the hell? Was it someone from Tony's time? Unless it was a native word. Maybe a hunting team from a distant village—

"Dion! Over here!" a man called. Louder.

The breath in Tony's lungs solidified. His head whipping around, he searched the wood.

"Janus?" Another guy answered.

From the direction of the hut! Tony jerked himself upright and tiptoed down the slope, trying not to step on any twigs that might snap or dry leaves that would crunch, and cringing each time one did.

Because if these people spoke his language, he had exactly one theory who they were.

As the door skin fell closed behind Tony, Violet settled back in with Isaac, but the baby turned his head away. "Just wanted a snack, did you?" She hiked her buckskin wrap back over her shoulder and lay the baby against it, lightly rubbing his back. She rocked back and forth, murmuring as she patted his back. "One of these days, we'll go home. You'll have a proper bed to sleep in, with a soft, cotton sheet instead of straw and deerskin, and nice warm jammies and shirts and diapers, and a mother and father who have time just to hold you, and not work ourselves to the bone, day in and day out." She rocked sideways, rubbing more than patting. "When you get a little older, you'll have fresh fruit to eat, and cereal, and vegetables… oh, what I wouldn't give for a nice, green salad right now. Maybe we'll get you a swing, and toys that are made of plastic instead of deerskin scraps and straw. And—"

Something crackled in the leaves outside the door. "Tony?" Had he caught something so soon? She'd expected him to be gone until the sun slanted low in the ventilation hole in the cabin's west end.

"Helloooo," a male voice answered. Not Tony. Violet's arms went rigid around Isaac.

"Who's there?" Was the man a friend… or with the Order?

The deer skin door lifted, and a camouflage-clad man who could've been a movie star walked in, followed by a bald fellow who reminded Violet of one of the wrestlers she and Stephanie used to watch on television. As the two men straightened, the second one spoke, in a gentle tone that contrasted oddly with his gruff voice. "We're with the Society. My name's Dion, and that's Janus." He indicated the other man with his thumb. "We've come to take you home."

Excitement bubbled up inside Violet. Could it be…? Then she tamped it down. Something didn't make sense. "How? I haven't felt an inkling of the Pull."

"We have the technology back at our base camp," Dion said. "Wrap the kid up, and let's go."

"But my husband… he's out hunting."

"Then we'll wait."

She searched their faces, studied their stance. Rigid, with a military bearing. And they carried weapons, or so she assumed the matte-black, flute-sized tubes hanging from their belts were. Black, metal tubes that their hands never strayed far from. Futuristic weapons, like the laser-guns the men in the woods had used, that had driven her and Tony to jump into 1959.

These men were not Society—at least not mainstream Society. The Code would have prohibited them carrying these futuristic weapons so openly.

Which meant they must be with the Order.

They'd want to kill Isaac in this time, then send her and Tony back to their own time, where other members of the Order undoubtedly awaited, ready to kill her and Tony—for good.

She lowered Isaac to her lap with one hand and made a pretense of leaning on the other, inching her hand over until her fingertips brushed the stone knife.

A lot of good it would do against two men armed with lasers.

When Tony returned, he'd be walking into a trap.

Unless she could somehow alert him to the Order's presence.

Three months with the native villagers had made him a skilled hunter—and that included the ability to move with stealth. Thank heavens he'd taken the gun! It would have been useless in her hands, but if Tony knew the men were there and took them unawares from behind, maybe he could get them both.

She leaned more heavily on her hand, trying to look relaxed. "Why don't you two sit down, make yourselves comfortable? Well, as much as you can. He'll probably be a while." She gave a laugh hoping she sounded more amicable than nervous.

With a grunted thanks, Dion lowered himself onto the straw mat closest to the smoldering fire. Movie-star-looks Janus lifted the canteen hooked to his belt, swished it around, and sidled to the water pitcher.

Faking a yawn, Violet slid down the rest of the way until she lay on the straw, clutching Isaac in front of her with one arm. Her other hand closed around the knife at her back. Janus filled his canteen and moved to Dion's side as Violet slowly pushed the knife's tip through the buckskin wrap near her waist. She couldn't imagine them letting her leave the hut alone, but if she dropped the knife without being observed, Tony might see. She had to do something to the knife that would indicate to him that she hadn't dropped it out of carelessness.

The men talked about something called rayball, and their chatter—critique peppered with expressions of disgust, amazement, and argument over who was at fault—sounded remarkably like the fellows in the smoking area at work, discussing football. She worked at the rip until she finally tore off a strip of buckskin.

Now comes the hard part. Feigning a sigh, she heaved herself upright, sliding the knife and the leather strip around her bottom until it was beneath Isaac. She shifted the baby on her lap, and tied the leather strip around the knife. "Excuse me, sirs? I, ah, need to use the privy."

The men looked at each other. "Where is it?" Dion asked.

Violet jerked her head to the left. "Just up above this rock ledge. I won't be long." She stood, picking the knife up beneath his bottom. The baby fussed as she settled him into the carrying pouch she'd built into her wrap.

As she moved toward the door, the men stood, blocking her. "I'll hold the baby, if you want." Dion held out his hands.

Violet leaned away. "No, I'll be fine. But thank you."

Janus loomed behind her. "I need to go, too."

No surprise there. If nothing else, it confirmed her suspicions. If the men's intentions were truly benign, her stepping out to relieve herself wouldn't concern them. She doubted Janus needed to go; instead, he was most likely ensuring she didn't try to escape. With a sharp nod, she lifted the door skin and walked up the path toward the enclosure she and Tony had built by lashing woven grass walls around three small trees.

Janus remained near the leeward side with the opening, his back to Violet, as she hitched up her wrap and sat on the raised frame she and Tony had attached to the trees to form a seat over the depression they'd dug. She didn't really have to go, but she managed a trickle, hopefully enough that Janus wouldn't suspect.

She slipped out behind him. "Your turn."

He glanced down at the seat frame. "Uh... I guess I don't really have to go after all."

"Very well." She moved to the trail, waiting for him. She'd hoped to drop the knife while he was otherwise engaged, but she'd have to make do now. As she walked down the hill and back around to the hut with the Order soldier at her side, she waited until they reached a barren spot in the trail, then let go of the knife.

It landed with a crackle. Damn! She'd miscalculated.

"What's that?" Janus grabbed her arm and looked down, then picked up the knife. "You dropped something." Violet reached for it, but he held it out of her reach as he hauled her to the hut's door and pushed her inside ahead of him.

Violet stumbled in, barely avoiding the fire. Isaac fussed as she sidestepped it, jarring him.

Janus held up the knife. "Looks like someone's trying to warn Solomon away."

"No! I dropped it! An accident."

Dion gave her a steely glare and crossed his arms over his chest.

Violet swallowed. She had to come up with an explanation. Fast. "I had to warn Tony away, it's true. But not for the reason you think. It's for your protection, not his. He's a skilled hunter, trained by the people of this time. He can move through the woods without a sound. If he came home and found the two of you here..." She looked at their laser guns. "He'd shoot you before you could even draw your weapons." She wet her lips.

"And that would concern you because?" Dion prompted.

She tipped her head at his laser. "I know who you are. Tony would know, too. But he'd shoot first, and ask questions later."

"Which you're not exactly equipped to do," Janus said with a sneer.

"That much is true. But I have no need." She swallowed, then drew herself up straight as she met Janus's gaze, then Dion's. "Because I'm with you."

Tony crept faster through the forest, hand on his gun. If the Order got to Violet and Isaac first—

He'd never forgive himself. He shouldn't have left them alone. Shouldn't have strayed so far from the hut. They had food to last a month, why had he had such a need to get out?

He scuttled down the trail until something tripped him and he crashed to the ground. He turned around as he pulled himself up. Damned root. He moved on at a fast walk. Every tree limb impeded him, slapping his face and leaving cuts on his hands. Roots appeared where he could have sworn the path was clear. Finally, he crested the ridge above their home.

His throat turned into a block of ice.

Tracks in the soft mud at the hut's doorway. Human. Made by men wearing large boots. Entering the hut.

He started to surge forward, but restrained himself. It wouldn't do anyone any good for him to rush in and get captured or killed.

He moved slowly, carefully, as he'd learned to do from watching the village men on the hunt. When he neared the hut, he avoided the side with the entrance and instead took the path that led up the rock ledge over the hut, near the latrine. With painstaking movements, he lowered himself to the ground near the overhang and peered over.

All was still. A bird chirped in the distance, but the animals nearby had fled, no doubt due to his presence. Nothing moved outside the hut.

He leaned over farther. The tracks went in, but none exited. At the sound of voices, his ears pricked. "…should have no trouble telling us where your companion went," a man said in a gravelly voice.

Violet's voice rose from the cabin, smaller, but loud enough to carry. "I told you, he went hunting." Another man mumbled something. "Of course he does," Violet said. "There's a spot along the river, where the deer stop to drink. A gravelly shoal that juts into a long, shallow strip right before it curves."

Tony's chest squeezed. What the hell?

"Good," the first man said. "Where else?"

"There's a spot just a short distance that way... where the deer bed down. And over there..."

A high-pitched roar rose in Tony's ears. Who were these men? The bend in the river was just as she'd described, as was the deer's nesting spot.

The second man grumbled again.

"I told you, I dropped it!" Violet said. "Why on earth would I believe that idealistic fool? Those of us who have this gift? We're different. I see no reason to bow to all that nonsense, but Tony believes it lock, stock, and barrel. I've just been biding my time. Do you think it was my idea to come here?"

The guy muttered a negative, then something else.

Violet laughed. "Of course I stayed with him; he was my best chance of survival. Not to mention, I'm aware that the Order needs to be rid of him; I've known it all along. I realized if I kept him with me, it would make it that much easier for you fellows to take care of him."

Tony backed away from the ledge, blood pulsing in his ears.

She'd sold him out again. For real this time.

He stood and crept toward the latrine. He had to get away, but where would he go? Those guys were waiting for him in the hut. Night would soon fall, bringing colder temperatures with it.

He moved around the windbreak behind the toilet. Those guys couldn't stay in the hut with Violet indefinitely. Chances were, they had a camp nearby. They'd have had to recover *(though how had they done it so quickly?)* and they'd have to wait out the Pull somewhere.

He slid to the ground against the latrine wall, carefully so that the dry, woven grasses didn't crackle. His breath came in short, sharp puffs, yet he couldn't seem to draw in air. *Betrayed again.* He'd trusted her. Let down his guard, let himself believe her crazy amnesia story, despite everything that didn't add up.

He'd loved her, treasured her. Good God, he'd *married* her. But one thing was certain. She would *not* take his son from him.

He'd take Isaac away from her and her lying, conniving ways—

Something solid slammed into his side, and Tony crashed to the ground. Rough hands clamped around his neck and squeezed. Tony clawed at his assailant's arm, fighting the paralyzing memories of being beheaded. His fingers couldn't get a hold on the man's camouflage jumpsuit. Whatever it was made of was no ordinary cloth, more like flexible steel.

As he struggled, the man's grip loosened enough for Tony to twist around and see his attacker's face.

His own. His own face, had he been clean shaven, and without his glasses. "You... bastard!" Tony whispered through his compressed throat.

The man gave a low laugh and squeezed harder. Tony gasped for breath as he clawed at the iron hands. His lookalike squeezed tighter. Tony's vision swam, and he was afraid he'd pass out, then on impulse, he jammed two fingers beneath the guy's hands at his throat.

Gasped. Sucked in a breath.

Not enough to dislodge the guy's hands, but...

"Why?" Tony managed to croak. *Go ahead, kill me. Send me back.*

But not until he got Isaac.

He had to stall the guy, and hope someone else—anyone—came along before he passed out, or got sent back to his own time— without his son.

His lookalike quirked an eyebrow, and his grip relaxed a miniscule amount. "Why?" the guy cocked his head. "Because you're in the Order's way, ye lackwit."

"No," Tony grunted. "I mean why... are you doing this? It'll just send me back... to my time."

The guy chortled, but his grip remained firm. "Ah, that's rich. O' course I ain't gonna be killin' ye today, as much as I'd enjoy that. No, we'll be takin' ye back to the camp fer a spell, then it's the Void for ye." He started to squeeze harder.

"Wait! What's... the Void?" The man let up again, holding just tightly enough Tony couldn't struggle free. "Is it like... the Treatment?" That Fred guy at the Society house was certainly void of rational thought. Tony tried to calm his wildly beating heart and focus his thoughts. Whatever this Void was, he needed to know about it, and for that, he needed to keep his wits.

"The Treat—ah, you mean the lobotomies. No, the Void is something much better. Or worse, if yer in it. It's a place between time, where there's no light. No sound. No touchin'. No nothing. I'd gander it'd be but a short while afore it drives a man mad."

"What about... Violet? What'll they do to her?" Especially now that she'd all but joined the Order. "And the baby?"

"It'll be the Void fer them as well. The little fellow's grown up to muck up more'n enough already. And the lady," a wide smirk drew across his face, "p'raps I'll take my pleasures with her while we wait for the containment module to set up."

Tony wanted to puke. "Set up? What's—"

"It ain't programmed to take 'em in until sunset. Gives me plenty o' time to have some fun." His grin reappeared, constant, like Everly's, but with a maniacal undertone. "Startin' with ye."

Tony kicked and bucked as pain swelled around his neck, but he couldn't dislodge the freakishly-strong lookalike. His vision again started to blur, and everything grew lighter...

Then he remembered.

The gun. He pushed his arm under his furs—everything moved in slow motion—and dug for it. His fingers twitched on the grip. His sight blurred, though he still wore his glasses. *Just a little farther...* His hand clamped around the gun and he pulled it out, flicked off the safety.

He whipped the weapon around before his assailant could figure out what he was doing, jammed it into the guy's chest and fired.

The man let go of Tony's neck and fell backward.

Tony lurched to his feet, searching for a bloom of red in the center of the guy's jumpsuit, but there was none. *Bulletproof fabric.* Gasping, the man recovered and launched himself onto Tony, grabbing his neck again. The gun flew out of Tony's hands, landing on the dirt path with a thud.

Tony clawed at his assailant's eyes (his own face, how weird, a detached part of him thought). The man jerked away and grabbed at Tony with one hand, releasing Tony's neck just long enough for Tony to wrench himself free.

The guy recovered and grabbed Tony's cloak, yanking him to the ground. The attacker raised his foot. Tony rolled aside, narrowly avoiding a crushing stomp in the ribs.

The other man stumbled, then lunged for Tony. Tony jumped to his feet and lowered his head. In a move he hoped the guy wouldn't anticipate, he head-butted the guy's chest, slamming him against a tree.

The man sagged to the ground. Tony leaped for the gun and clutched it to his chest as the guy recovered and tackled him. In the second it took Tony to catch his breath, the guy had him in a choke-hold again.

Tony tried to collect his thoughts. Still clutching the gun, sand-wiched between his body and his would-be killer's, Tony shifted his right hand. Brought it up. Slowly, until the barrel pointed under the man's unprotected chin.

Tony fired.

The hands on his neck loosened, and his double made a choked gasp. "Ya... bloody... bastard!" he wheezed. "Don't think... ye'll get..." His body fell limp.

Tony pulled himself from beneath his dying lookalike. In the time he'd spent fighting that dirtbag, the men in the cabin with Violet could have taken Isaac—or killed him.

Which for him, in this time, would be permanent.

Tony scrambled down and around the rock ledge to the hut's door, gun drawn. When the dizziness of a warp struck him, he stumbled and fell.

Picking himself off the ground, he glanced up at the ledge.

His attacker shimmered like a mirage, growing fainter until he disappeared.

Tony reached for the door skin, then hesitated. Those men and Violet would have heard the gunshot. Were they lying in wait for him now?

No sounds came from within. His muscles stretched as tightly as a skin stretched on a frame, he pushed the door flap in.

Coals smoldered in the fire pit. An indentation remained on the fur-covered straw of their bed where Violet had sat. Their home looked as if he'd imagined those men, dreamed he'd heard Violet telling them she was with them. As if she'd simply stepped out to use the latrine, Isaac safe in her sling.

Tony dropped the door flap. Through the cloudy puffs of his breath, he saw the tracks in the mud. More of them than before, including a smaller pair. Leaving the hut in the direction the first two sets had come from, down the trail toward the river, heading south.

He shoved the gun back into its pouch. *One round left.* He hurtled down the trail, pushing himself until his lungs and muscles burned. *Idealistic fool, huh?*

He couldn't let himself think. Couldn't let himself feel. Couldn't let the thought of Isaac and Violet subjected to—

The path forked, and he barely stopped before he plowed into a tree. He'd come this way hunting once or twice since his and Violet's flight from the village, but couldn't remember what lay either way.

He crouched and studied the ground. The dirt gave no clues. Neither did the weeds and dry brush—

A cracked branch hung over the trail.

Could've been an animal. Tony tried not to get his hopes up, but as he searched farther down the right fork of the path, more snapped twigs and small branches told him something big—like a party of humans—had come that way.

He moved on, watching for signs of people, scanning ahead to ensure he didn't walk into a trap.

Angry voices ahead made Tony slow. "What do you mean, Solomon wasn't there?" A man. Though Tony couldn't place it, the voice was vaguely familiar. Someone else mumbled a response. "Hype's going to be furious!" a woman said.

"At least they got the baby!" another man retorted.

Tony crept forward, crouched behind the brush, until he glimpsed two men and a woman walking. Straining to hear, he moved closer, keeping several yards behind them.

The trio emerged into a clearing. Tony hid behind a tree, then slowly peered around it.

Three tents flanked a bonfire—big, boxy tents that looked like they could withstand a hurricane. People wearing camouflage suits milled around, cooking or unrolling sheets of canvas, setting up a fourth tent. They spoke little, until a man—the guy Tony had followed— approached the largest tent.

"Ganny?" someone called from inside. "Ganymede?"

The man mumbled an assent as he reached for the tent flap.

A tall, athletic, black woman—no, biracial, Tony decided— emerged from the tent—the other Order member he'd followed. "There's a party out looking for him around the deer thicket she described. And Quimby's out looking for him, too." She brushed ashes from the campfire from her short, curly, dark hair.

"Fucking psycho," the man grumbled. "That idiot will want to choke him to death as soon as he finds him, and send him back to the wrong place."

"If he hasn't already. Those gunshots—"

The guy mumbled an assent.

Tony crawled behind some brush until he reached another tree he could hide behind. He tried to glean further information, but the conversation turned to gossipy chit-chat.

Tony could barely gulp in enough air as he sneaked from tree to rocky outcropping, to brush for cover. Violet had been in cahoots with them all along, and had betrayed him again. Hadn't Alpha told him that not only the baby's survival, but his own, was paramount to preserving the time stream for the future? Violet—Charlotte—could have been with those who disagreed. For all he knew, she'd set him up from the very start.

He ignored the burning in his chest and pushed onward. She'd gone to Pippin in '59. It added up. Except that she should know there was no way in hell he'd let her take Isaac.

By the time he reached the far side of the campsite, dusk was falling. The forest was growing colder.

He crept behind the tent the woman had exited, hoping it was where they'd sequestered Violet and the baby.

Light glowed through the back of the canvas, but it was too diffused for him to detect shadows or movement within. He touched the canvas—and found that it wasn't. The slippery texture was like vinyl, yet it didn't give beneath his finger. Almost like hard plastic. Some fantastic, futuristic material. Not something he'd be able to slash with his knife.

He knelt down and examined the bottom of the structure. The tent material had looked flexible when the people had been assembling one, but now it lay rigid against the ground.

There'd be no getting in through the back.

He paused in the shadows, fingering his gun. There were a good eighteen or twenty of them. His chances of getting in, getting Isaac, and getting out alive were close to zero.

But if he didn't....

He'd seen firsthand what something left in the wrong time could do to alter the time stream. Something as small as a pocket calculator. If time took a wrong turn, it would not be for his lack of trying to prevent it.

And *if* Violet was one of them, hell if he'd let her put this one over on him.

Gripping the gun, he sidled around the side of the tent.

"...wants to know when we're going to send her home," said the gravelly-voiced guy he'd heard at the hut.

"The containment device won't be ready until sunset," another man said.

"Can't we at least offer her dinner?" gravelly-voice said. "It's so... inhumane. The least we could do is feed her before we send 'em into the Void—"

"You want inhumane?" Skin slapped skin, followed by a thud.

"Oof!" the gravel-voiced guy grumbled something under his breath.

"Perhaps we should wait until we find Solomon," a third man

said—the other guy from the hut. "After all, the containment device only stays enabled for about ten minutes."

The guy who hadn't been at the hut snorted. "Rhea's orders were to contain the woman and the baby, no matter what. She has the other device. We'll have to leave Solomon to her." He grumbled something Tony couldn't hear, as if talking to himself. "Go on, feed her. Then when sunset comes, you can do the honor of containing her."

"But—" gravelly-voice began.

"Get out!"

Something scraped on a rough surface—a chair?—then heavy footsteps clomped toward the entrance. Tony flattened himself against the tent's rigid side, then slowly eased back to the corner and peered around.

A tall, bald guy who looked like he'd taken more than a few doses of steroids tromped across the camp toward the tent on the far side of the bonfire, where two nondescript guys sat on sawed-off logs, hunkered over bowls of something. Between them sat the black woman Tony had seen earlier.

He crept back behind the tent, then slipped farther into the surrounding brush and made his way behind another tent, keeping an eye on the activity near the fire. He drew up behind a dense clump of undergrowth between two tents and studied the scene through a gap in the bushes.

The steroid freak was leading Violet to the campfire.

Tony recalled the man's words inside the tent: *Feed her before we send her into the Void.*

The air in his chest thickened. Hadn't she said she was with them?

Or is she lying? Had she lied to the Order? Or him?

It didn't matter. He fingered the gun, his hand damp with sweat despite the chill air. Never mind what she'd done, he couldn't let them send her to that hellish place of nothingness his lookalike had described.

His nose itched. He rubbed it, pushing aside his dread and fear while he tried to formulate a plan. Maybe he could rush around the other side of the fire where there weren't any Order flunkies, and get her before they figured out what was happening—

He sneezed.

And looked up to see the startled faces of the two men, Violet, and the tough-looking black woman. The men leaped up and rushed toward him. "It's him!"

"Tony! It's okay!" the black woman yelled.

A trick! Tony darted to the side, weighing the option of running into the thick wood, then discarding it. He ran in a circle toward steroid-dude and Violet, pulling his gun from beneath his cloak. There was only one way to get out of this. Only one way to save Isaac, and it might not work. But he had to try.

Violet stopped and held out a hand. "Tony, what are you doing!"

"They're going to send my son into the Void!" He flipped the safety off the gun. If he couldn't keep his son, damned if he'd let them send Isaac—an innocent child!—into that prison of emptiness.

In a flash, he sighted the gun on her. Squeezed the trigger. *One round left.* Fired.

Violet screamed as she crashed to the ground, baby clasped to her chest. Her shrieks died to a strangled cry, then she fell silent. Rough hands grabbed Tony and jerked him away, snatching his gun. He thrashed in his captors' grasp, groping for the stone knife at his waist. He gouged at two of the men, wounding one, before the bald guy took his knife and held him down as another man rushed from the tent he'd hid behind.

From the corner of his eye, Tony saw Violet fade, flicker, then disappear like his lookalike attacker in the woods. The man from the tent—the leader, he guessed—shoved his way through the others as steroid-guy pressed a silver, pencil-like device to Tony's neck.

Fog descended over Tony's mind. Everything he'd fought for, lost. All his running from Pippin—for nothing. Would they send *him* to the Void? Especially now that he'd facilitated Violet's escape?

Despair washed over him as whatever they'd shot into him rendered his arms and legs like gelatin. He couldn't move. Couldn't scream. Couldn't mourn the fact he'd never see his daughter again, never again tell her he loved her. Never be able to prove to his sister that he hadn't killed Danny. Never see Isaac grow up.

And Violet. Or Charlotte. What if she'd been telling the truth about Pippin in 1959? And had been lying to the gravel-voiced 'roid-boy and his sidekick?

Sweat trickled down Tony's neck. At least he'd saved her. He strained to see the spot where she'd fallen, and before the world went away, confirmed one thing.

The baby, too, had disappeared.

Fifteen

Tony woke in a dimly lit room—no, a tent, with a high, sloped ceiling and shadows from outside moving across the wall.

Something whirred from below his line of sight—a heater, he assumed. Someone had removed his cloak and boots, and he was warm. He lay on a soft surface, not cold, hard ground. As consciousness returned, soreness and spots of pain flared in his arms, legs, and in his ribs where steroid-guy had slammed into him.

Everything was blurred—either he'd lost his glasses, or someone had taken them—but he could make out the edge of a cot. He started to lift his arm to check one, but something restrained him.

He tried his other arm, but couldn't lift it either, or his legs. He'd been tied to— He twisted his head. Judging from the hard coolness around his wrists when he lifted them, the silver-gray blurs clamped around his wrists and ankles were metal restraints.

He struggled. His bindings flexed, but didn't give enough for him to slip out.

He lay limply, his energy sapped. Not recovery—God, he wished it was—just the aftereffects of whatever they'd drugged him with. Of course, if he'd regained enough energy to jump, he and Violet and Isaac would have—

Violet and Isaac. Grief settled over him like being buried alive. He wouldn't think about Violet's cooperation with her captors, or what that meant, never mind that she obviously had no clue they'd planned to send her and Isaac into the Void. He wouldn't consider the likelihood that Alpha had been unsuccessful in neutralizing their enemies—otherwise, would they have found them in this time? All he would think about was getting out, getting home, getting Isaac—*if* Violet's—Charlotte's—death had taken her to her natural time, and the baby had gone with her.

The tent flap opened and someone walked in—a woman, holding an electric lantern. The black woman he'd followed from the woods. Built like a black bear, she was at least Tony's height, with a firm, muscular figure that told him she could probably whip his ass. "You're awake." Her voice was warm and smooth like honey, a strange contrast to her appearance.

"No shit," Tony said. "Who the hell—"

"We feared you'd do yourself harm before we could explain—"

Tony bucked against his bonds. "You took my wife and son!"

"We are not the ones who took them. But thanks to you, they're probably safe."

"Who the hell are you?"

She sat on another cot a few feet away. "My name is Phoebe. I'm Society—part of a special task force that polices our own—"

"The ones who want to reinstate the Black Book."

"Our organization employs more humane ways of dealing with those who break our law, but... yes, somewhat similar. And no, we're not after you. Our efforts are focused on stopping those whose disruptions of time are far more egregious than yours."

"So you say." Tony struggled against his bonds, but to no more effect than before.

The woman shifted. "I apologize for restraining you. But truly, you're in no danger from us. Hy—our leader—is familiar with your history, and feared you'd suicide—"

"My history?"

Though she was little more than a dark blur in the lantern's dim light, he sensed her smile in the relaxing of her posture. "What's history to us, hasn't happened for you yet." Her voice sounded familiar, but before Tony could place it, the light from the tent flap dimmed as someone entered. A big man, built like a bodybuilder. "I think you can release him, Phoebe." The gravel-voiced guy. Tony looked from one to the other. "I wouldn't advise running," the man said.

There was something familiar about Phoebe—her stance, her walk, her voice. Tony still couldn't place her. "I won't run," he said. As if it would do him any good. "But I want some answers. And my glasses."

The man nodded at Phoebe. "Let him loose, or Hype'll be pissed."

He disappeared through the tent flap. Phoebe pressed on each restraint in three different spots. "The people who took your wife and son are with the same group as those who tried to kill you back in February. They're our enemies, too. Like us, they're from your future—"

"You were with them! I followed you." Tony sat up and rubbed his wrists. "So was he."

"Yes, Dion and I are with them. But we're also against them." She gave him a barely-there smile. "Double agents, you might say. They want to use their gift for unethical purposes—political gains, for one—and are willing to exploit anyone in any time to achieve their ends. We've managed to infiltrate the Order, convinced them we're on their side. So we then can learn their plans in time to stop their disruptions of the time stream." She released his last restraint.

Her calm voice and the logic in her words chased away some of Tony's misgivings. "The Order of Titan?" He sat up.

"Yes. They insist that the ends are worth the risk, even if it results in paradoxes, time distortions, and ultimately, chaos."

Tony had done the same when he's jumped into the past to save Bethany. But surely a large group of people making changes—big changes—would wreak far more damage than one man saving a loved one. Tony's purpose had been honorable and unselfish, to him, if not the Saturn Society. "Small wrongs. To right much larger ones," he said.

"Exactly," Phoebe agreed. Dion reentered the tent, and handed Tony his glasses. "That's why we oppose this faction." As Tony slipped his glasses on, he got a better look at her.

Splotchy scars marred her skin, like she'd been burned. Rough-edged patches over her cheeks and around her eyes told Tony she'd undergone surgery, but it wasn't yet complete.

"Our purpose is to stop these people," she said. "And you, your wife, and your son will play a pivotal role in furthering our cause."

"But..." Tony frowned. Where had he seen her before? "This place looks exactly like their camp—"

"It *was* their camp," Dion answered. "Now it's ours. We've been tracking them, trying to overcome their defenses since we warped into this time. You running in shooting, foolhardy as that was, gave us the perfect diversion and enabled us to breach their defenses and eliminate them—well, send them back to their ti—"

Dizziness burst through Tony. Phoebe lurched forward, almost falling on top of him. The other man stumbled sideways, but caught himself on the tent wall.

He and Phoebe looked at each other. "Hype," she said.

Dion dashed outside. Phoebe lifted the flap to peer out behind him.

Commotion ensued outside. People shouted greetings, and animated discussions rang through the camp. Tony stood, but Phoebe shot him a dark look so he hung back.

The tent flap darkened, and Phoebe stepped back to allow a man to enter, along with Dion.

The light behind them blocked out the first man's features, but when Phoebe leaned out to yell at someone outside, Tony realized where he'd seen her before.

At the office. With Keith Lynch.

The bodyguard! It was Phoebe who'd been in the fire with Violet. Tony's chin nearly hit his chest.

The man who'd newly warped in allowed Dion to help him to the cot, Phoebe following. When he looked up, Tony staggered in disbelief. "Keith?"

"Hello, Tony."

He could have knocked Tony over with a flick of his finger. Mumbling incoherently, even to himself, Tony stumbled backward and fell onto his cot. Of all people, his cool-minded, always logical boss—a time traveler? "How.... how long have you been—"

"All my life." Keith rested his hands on his knees. "Is the camp secured?" he asked Dion.

"Yes."

"Good. Phoebe, go check over the meal details. If we're short on supplies, organize a hunting party."

"Yes, sir." The two slipped out.

"You knew," Tony said. Keith's lack of questions after all of Tony's disappearances. The leaves of absence. Keith's understanding and compassion, when most bosses would have simply fired him. Then there were Keith's own frequent, extended leaves.

"Yeah. I knew." Keith breathed heavily. Recovery was setting in.

"Why didn't you tell me?"

"Would you have believed me?"

"Not until it happened to me, but then—"

"Tony... I don't have much time. We have... technology to speed recovery. But it also makes it set in faster, within minutes." Tony started to protest, but Keith held up a hand so he shut his mouth. "We need you on our side. There's a woman from two hundred years in your future. Her goal is to gain political and economic power, no matter the price."

"Phoebe told me."

"Then you understand it's imperative that we stop this woman."

Tony only had to think for a second. If Keith were with this group... Keith Lynch, his boss of nearly twenty years. Someone who'd always shown faith in him. Someone Tony had always told the truth, even when it wasn't what Keith wanted to hear, yet for that Keith had always respected him. If Tony couldn't trust him... "I can't argue that."

"You have questions. I'll answer what I can before—"

"Who... you were the one who found me out off North Dixie, near that burned out motel, weren't you? And took me to the Society House?"

"Yes."

"And Violet Sinclair. Did you know she's... like us?"

"Not at first." Keith winced. "Of all people, I should have known, but she threw us by jumping into the future—"

"Oh, God..." Tony felt the color drain from his face. It was true. *Charlotte.* "But everyone says that's impossible!"

"Not if you have the knowledge to visualize it."

A chill fell over Tony despite the tent's heater. *He'd* done that. He'd told Charlotte enough about Dayton in his time and what the area around her home looked like that she'd been able to envision it.

"The price is steep," Keith said. "I was pulled into the future as an infant, so I gained the benefits of jumping into the future without—"

"Benefits?"

"I'm not limited by the Pull. I never get it. Like my— like Violet, I can stay in the past as long as I want. Since I was only a baby, the long-term memory loss was a non-issue for me."

"Memory loss?" Holy shit, she had been telling the truth. And he'd shot her. To save her, yes, but sending her to who knew when? Her own natural time?

"Tony?" Keith broke into his thoughts. "We need your help. The woman who leads this group—the Order of Titan, they call themselves—is someone you know—"

"Violet?"

Keith laughed, looking down at the ground. "Hell no." The seriousness returned to his face. "Her name—in her own time—is Jennifer Warren 8736Alpha. You probably know her as simply Jenny, or Alpha—"

Tony went rigid. "She's saved my life at least three times that I know of! Why—"

"Because she needed you alive so that Bethany could be born, and later so you could save Bethany."

"Why couldn't Alpha save her?"

"I imagine she tried." Keith's words slurred. "Prob'ly... would've created a paradox, which... can't, you know."

His words faded as the implications hit Tony, along with Chad Everly's warning. *Something you think is inconsequential could have far-reaching ramifications...* "Oh my God." A high-pitched roar rose in Tony's ears. *All my fault.* "What have I done?" He sagged forward and braced his elbows on his knees, his face in his hands.

"You did... what any decent parent would. Yeah, by saving Bethany, you've... enabled Alpha... But Bethany... serves us. Beth... saved my life. Many times... Hasn't happened for her yet." Keith's eyes took on a faraway look. "She'd do anything for me..." He met Tony's eyes. "I tried... to save her myself. Couldn't."

"You mean the time she almost died?" Tony could hardly remember that other time stream, the one those creeps who almost killed one of her friends, had instead murdered Bethany. The one he'd negated when he jumped back three years and made her leave that drunken party early.

"Yeah. I couldn't... make her leave—why would she go home with her dad's boss, y'know? Tried setting up a roadblock... guys took off in another direction. And Beth... still died. You were the only one... who could save her."

"So now I've outlived my usefulness to Alpha."

"Yeah, and... you're now... a liability."

"You mean I'm going to be part of this thing, too?"

"Already are. Soon... rest of your family, too." Keith swayed, then lay down.

His eyes closed. Tony tossed out one more question. "Keith?"

His former boss answered slowly, his speech breathy and fatigued. "Yeah?" His eyelids slid open, and Tony studied their golden, honey-brown depths.

"Who the hell are you, anyway?"

A smile touched Keith's lips. "In the Order... Hyperion. To you, Keith Lynch. But the name I was born with... is Isaac Roderick Solomon."

Tony sipped at a soup ration as he half-listened to the others' idle chatter. Beside him sat Phoebe, who he'd learned was from Alpha's time. A blazing campfire kept the cold at bay, but the air bore a sharp crispness, hinting that the next day would be colder. Beneath the laughter, gossip and stories ran an undercurrent of tension, for many in the group had felt others jumping in earlier that day—most likely, more of Alpha's followers.

A shiver raced through him, despite the bonfire's warmth. *Good God, I shot her.* He'd done the right thing, but he couldn't stop thinking about it, as the sight of her crashing to the ground, the sound of her scream, replayed in his mind over and over. And Isaac—Keith, who'd have believed it?—Tony could have killed him, too.

Wherever—whenever—Violet and Isaac had warped to, they had a long recovery in store. They most likely went to Violet's natural time—1939, by Tony's estimation, since six years had passed since Violet had jumped into the twenty-first century.

Pippin would be the Watchkeeper in the Saturn Society House in Dayton. Hopefully, he'd care for them in recovery.

Tony turned and gazed at the tent behind him. Firelight danced over the lowered tent flap, beyond which Keith lay in recovery. Phoebe said the wristbands Keith wore would speed the process, but it would be another hour or so before he woke.

Tony still couldn't believe Keith was his son. Isaac, as an adult. Weirder still, Keith was chronologically older than him by several years.

People had often guessed Tony and Keith were brothers. Tony had always thought it a coincidence, but now that he knew, it was easy to see the resemblance. Keith's eyes were shaped like his, though their color was honey brown, like Violet's. He and Tony were about the same build and size. Like Tony, Keith liked everything in order and in its place, always hung his coat in the same spot, and always ate chili on Tuesday in the company cafeteria.

Tony stared at the ground, shaking his head. Too weird. Yet it all fit. Even the way Keith had always been especially friendly to Bethany, more so than toward other employees' kids.

Crackling underbrush in the woods made him jump.

Probably an animal. He turned back to the fire, where a boisterous bar owner from the twenty-second century was telling a no-doubt highly embellished tale of gaining the time travel gift when he'd nearly died in an air shuttle accident—

Behind him, a twig snapped. Tony jerked around as one of the perimeter guards burst into the camp. "They're coming! More of 'em— they've already sent Campbell back!"

The group leaped to their feet, grabbing weapons at their hips or from the ground. Laser fire slashed from the woods, converging on the fire circle. Tony's group fired back. "Guard Hype!" Phoebe shouted. "He's still recovering!"

Tony dove behind a log. Scarlet laser lines whipped through the trees in all directions like surreal, life-size string-art. "Tony! Here!" Phoebe threw a thick, pen-like object at him. "The button on the side!" she yelled.

As he caught the weapon, someone's laser fire slashed the air right where his head had been. *Holy shit!*

Laser fire sizzled above him again, punctuated by the shouts of his comrades and their assailants.

He crouched lower behind the log, hoping Keith's teammates would run the dirtbags off. Firelight glinted off the smooth, metallic-plastic surface of the laser gun. Squinting, he turned the device over and studied the ridged area molded to fit the user's hand until he located the trigger, then pointed it toward an unfamiliar man rummaging through a supply crate a few yards away. The guy glanced up. His eyes met Tony's, and he reached for his hip holster. Biting back revulsion, Tony lifted his weapon and fired.

The laser sizzled as it struck the man, and he fell forward, his clothes burning along the edges of a neat hole spreading from the center of his chest. Howling, he dropped to a roll, but the laser had cut too deeply, and his cries abated to a gurgling moan. Tony's stomach turned, and he shrank away, not daring to take his eyes off the guy in case he wasn't really dead.

But as he watched, the man's body rippled and faded, the same way Tony's lookalike's had. Dizziness ripped through Tony, and when it passed, the intruder was gone.

He scanned the campsite, expecting a scene of blood and carnage. All he saw were upended camp seats, haphazardly tossed-aside meal rations, and two remaining teammates flanking Keith's tent, firing on two unfamiliar men and a woman. Tony braced himself for the dizziness as the three intruders faded and disappeared.

The rest of the team had withdrawn into the woods, but their shouts and laser fire rang in Tony's ears. He whirled around at a yelp from Keith's tent.

One guard crumpled to the ground, and the acrid, chemical scent of singed combat wear stung Tony's nose. The remaining man—Dion—whipped his weapon around and fired. Judging the location of the new attackers by direction of the laser fire, Tony ran in a crouch toward the tent. As he joined Dion at the entrance, the man grunted in acknowledgement, picking off another intruder who slipped from behind the log where Tony had been hiding. As the attacker went down, faded, and disappeared, five more sprang into the camp. In seconds, they had Tony and Dion surrounded. "Drop your weapons!" one of the attackers ordered.

Another sprang forward and shot, and a singed spot on Dion's bald head spread in a circle as he howled and crumpled to the ground. The man's eyes went glassy, he shimmered and disappeared.

Silver glinted in the firelight. Tony fired at the shooter. Missed. He fired again, but the intruder dove behind a bush.

Tony crept to the side, keeping his laser aimed at the bush, when a red beam shot from behind it, narrowly missing his side.

"Not him, you idiot!" a woman yelled. "Rhea'll be furious if he shows up someplace unexpected and gets away—"

Tony bolted into the tent. Outside, a sizzle and a scorching smell told him someone else had been hit. As the dizziness struck, he almost fell on top of Keith. The other man stirred as the attackers burst in.

"Give it up, Solomon!" one yelled as he reached into his pocket and drew out something that looked like a silver flip phone.

"No!" someone yelled from behind Tony. A fiery pinprick flared in the middle of his back, burning, singeing through his skin. With a shriek, he crashed to the ground, barely aware of laser fire spearing from behind him to strike the two attackers.

Tony twitched on the ground, screaming.

"Tony! Don't fight it!" the man behind him shouted. His words faded as Tony's world narrowed to his burning back, then the pain dimmed into a dull spot of warmth.

Arms grasped him from behind, though he could barely feel them. *Bethany.* All his fault. If he hadn't saved her, Alpha wouldn't come to power, in that distant future. Maybe wouldn't even exist. There would be no order of Titan. There would be no war among time travelers.

Everything went white. *Dying. I'm dying.* "Tony..." The man's voice reached through the haze, choked and high-pitched with emotion. Keith—*Isaac.* "Forgive me..."

Bethany had pretty much given up on getting information from Taylor by the time her mom's December wedding rolled around. She'd hung out with her a lot over the past three months, and nothing.

But now, she had three whole days to make Taylor slip up. If Taylor knew anything, surely it would come out sometime over the weekend, or during the hours in the car while Bethany drove.

But Taylor spent most of the ride talking about guys and movies and music and clothes and the trashy stuff some of the popular kids were wearing, until they stopped in northern Tennessee at a carryout/truck stop/fireworks store called Mad Murphy's.

Bethany paid for gas along with the lunch they'd just eaten, grabbing a couple of plastic-wrapped cookies from the display beside the cash register at the last minute. Wedding rehearsals could take forever, and it was always a good idea to have a snack handy. "Taylor?" she called after the cashier handed her the change.

"Over here."

Bethany walked around an aisle of magazines to find her friend at a countertop display of stuff for truck drivers, studying what looked like a small Roman candle. "You ready to take off?"

"Yeah, after I use the bathroom. I'll meet you at the door, okay?" Bethany slipped into the ladies room to check her blood sugar, then dug into her purse for her insulin pen. Her fingers touched it right away. *Weird.* Hadn't she shoved it down the side like she usually did? She pulled it out and grimaced. *Fifteen Minute Red Emergency Flare* read the long, red tube. Not a Roman candle. And definitely not her insulin.

Just freakin' great. Taylor must've dropped it into Bethany's purse when it sat on the floor while they ate. At the sound of footsteps outside the door, she shoved the flare back into her purse and yanked out her insulin pen. She could go back to Mad Murphy's to return the flare, but it would be just her luck they'd bust her for shoplifting. It was time she said something to Taylor.

Taylor was waiting outside when Bethany emerged from the bathroom. She took a swig of her Mountain Dew. "Hey," she said in a quiet, conspiratorial voice. "That cute guy over there who just walked in? Was checking out your car."

Bethany stole a discreet glance. The guy was in his early twenties, and a Mad Murphy's patch adorned his jacket. Bethany listened to him order food, noting the play of the light on his thick, black hair, and his flexed muscles as he took out his wallet to pay. "We should've gotten full serve," Taylor said. "That would've been worth an extra nickel a gallon."

"Yeah, too bad we have to get going." Bethany gave the guy a long look as she followed Taylor out the door.

They'd been back on the road for a half hour when Taylor pointed at the dashboard. "What's up with that?"

The Check Engine light glared red in the deepening twilight. "I don't know. Hopefully, it's not a big deal."

Taylor gave an agreeing shrug and grabbed Bethany's CD case off the floor. "Got anything good in here?" She opened it and flipped through the disks. "Rob Zombie?" She looked up, eyebrows raised. "Old stuff. Not what I'd expected from you."

"What did you expect?"

"I don't know. Want to play it?"

"Go ahead. Radio reception sucks around here, and the satellite subscription expired a couple months after Daddy..." She couldn't finish the sentence.

Rob Zombie screeched about witches and monsters as the freeway wended its way into the mountains. But within ten minutes, brake lights started to blink on cars and trucks ahead, then traffic slowed to a crawl. "What the crap," Bethany muttered.

"Road construction?"

"In December?"

"Accident, then."

"Just freakin' great." Bethany's mom was going to flip if she was late to the rehearsal.

Traffic snaked along the highway as far as Bethany could see. As the darkness deepened, a full moon came out, a fuzzy, white circle behind the clouds, giving them an eerie look.

A car sped past on the shoulder to the right. "What the crap's he doing?" Bethany said.

"There's an exit." Taylor pointed forward.

"I'm going for it. This is bullshit." Bethany swung the car onto the berm and pressed the accelerator, following the other impatient driver's lead.

She turned off the ramp to the east. Before long, they were the only car on the road. "You know where you're going?" Taylor asked.

"If we keep going this way, we're bound to hit a state route or something that'll take us back to the interstate." Bethany hoped.

"Don't you have OnStar?"

"I did, but it was in Daddy's name, and it ran out in July."

Fifteen minutes later, the only cross-street they'd encountered that even had a name was Old Marshy Creek Road, and the Check Engine light came back on. "Oh shit." Bethany squeezed the steering wheel.

"What?" Taylor looked over. "Oh." She rummaged in her purse and pulled out a cell phone.

"I've got Triple-A," Bethany said. "The card's in my wallet, if you want to dig it out for me—"

"Got it." Taylor started to punch a number, then stopped. "Oh, man."

"What?" Bethany thought the car was laboring harder, though she wasn't going any faster.

"No service."

"Shit. Try mine."

Taylor pulled Bethany's cell phone out of her purse. "Nope, you have the same carrier I do. Guess we'd better hope we come to a gas station or something soon."

Bethany pressed the accelerator harder, but their speed continued to drop. "Come on," she urged the car, panic rising in her belly. Taylor watched the instrument panel and the deserted road in silence until the engine died and the car rolled to a stop.

"Shit! Shit! Shit!" Bethany pounded the steering wheel as tears threatened to choke her.

Taylor slipped her cell phone out of her purse again. A glimmer of hope flared within Bethany, then died as Taylor dropped it back in. "Still no fucking service."

For a long moment, Bethany sat in the driver's seat, staring at the nasty red lights. Rob Zombie was still shrieking about demons and monsters. Bethany snapped off the stereo.

"Well, what now?" Taylor asked.

Bethany laid her forehead on the steering wheel and choked back a sob. "I don't know."

"I think I saw some lights up ahead, before we went around that last curve. Maybe a carryout or something. You wanna get out and walk?"

"It's cold," Bethany whined.

"The heater won't work without the car running. If we keep moving, we'll stay warm. Those lights weren't that far."

They climbed out of the car. Woods bordered the side of the road near them; empty fields lined the other side. Bethany stared at the car. Her lip quivered. "Maybe we should push it off the road."

Taylor agreed. Even through the clouds, the moon was bright enough Bethany could see her breath, but the physical activity kept the cold at bay while they pushed the Camaro onto the frosty embankment. Bethany reached in and turned on the hazard lights, then locked the door. Taylor stepped around the car and walked to the east, the white stripes on her socks gleaming in the moonlight. She turned around. "You coming?"

Bethany glanced back as she hurried to catch up. The hazard lights cast baleful, yellow flashes on the road's gravel shoulder and frosty, dry brush. It felt hard to breathe, like when she was little and Danny used to sit on her chest.

She'd wanted the pretty, yellow Camaro the instant she saw it, and her dad had bought it for her. It felt wrong to leave it, especially when it was the last thing she had left of him. Taylor was right, yet Bethany had a bad feeling that they should have stayed in the car.

Headlights appeared ahead. Bethany's heart shot into her throat. "Oh, crap." What if it was some weirdo who wanted to take advantage of two young girls walking alone along a deserted country road? She dove into the weeds, frost crackling beneath her feet.

"What are you doing?" Taylor crouched down beside her until the lights flashed past.

"We don't know who's in that car. It could be creepy people who want to get us."

"Uh… oh-kaaaay."

They walked on, and thankfully encountered no more traffic. It seemed like hours later when unmoving lights appeared ahead, indicating habitation. Soon after, a flashing yellow light at an intersection illuminated a green sign reading *Hollowville Corp Limit.* A sandblasted wood sign proclaimed a welcome. "Thank God," Taylor said. "My feet are freezing." Bethany's were, too.

There wasn't much to Hollowville but a cluster of houses, a post office, and a couple of businesses. The false-front buildings with high, arched windows bespoke old Americana, but the facades and trim looked clean, cozy, and new.

The girls approached the nearest, a low, shed-like structure bearing pristine, white siding and a neon sign with the words Rub-a-Dub's Pub. Strains of a jukebox blaring country music came from within. Taylor paused at the door. "This is probably our best bet for a phone."

"Uh... I'm underage." Bethany's voice wavered.

Taylor gave her a stern look, pulled out her cell phone, glanced at it, and dropped it back into her purse. "You want to go back to the car? 'Cause I sure as hell don't." Despite her bravado, Taylor shivered. Bethany shook her head.

Taylor yanked the door open.

Bethany tried not to stare at the flannel-shirted men around the pool table and the bar, though several of them let their gazes rest on her longer than they should have. *Jail bait!* she wanted to shout, though she doubted that would deter them. Taylor marched to the bar, seemingly oblivious to the stares.

A sixty-something woman with a cigarette dangling from the corner of her mouth approached. "What c'n I getcha?"

"Um, nothing, please, our car broke down and we were wondering if we could use your phone."

"Sure, hon." The barmaid reached under the bar and grabbed a phone.

Taylor took the handset, and Bethany handed her her motor club card, glad to let her friend take the lead in giving the operator their information. A minute later Taylor slammed down the phone in disgust. "Three hours before they can get anyone here."

"We've already missed the rehearsal," Bethany moaned.

"Tell you what. Chad has a friend who lives around here. Real close, I think. She'll pick us up and let us crash at her place for the night, then we can still make it to the wedding tomorrow."

Bethany squeezed her lips together. "Okay." Once they had a plan, she'd call her mom to let her know what happened—and when they'd be there.

Taylor punched in a number. "Hey Chad?"

She explained the situation, then grabbed a napkin. "Yeah, Bethany and I'll just wait here. What's her name again? Florence Allen—"

"Florence Allen?" the bartender shrieked. "You're friends with Florence Allen?"

The nearest man at the bar jerked straight on his stool. "Ain't that that witch?"

"Look at 'em," someone hollered from behind them. "I bet they're witches, too!"

The phone slid out of Taylor's hand and clattered onto the bar. Bethany backed into her friend as she searched the gathering crowd.

"We don't want no witches in here!" a woman yelled. The man at the bar rose and loomed in front of the girls, baring his teeth in a snarl.

Taylor squeezed Bethany's arm. "We're out of here!"

Amidst shouts and catcalls, Bethany shoved her way past the on-lookers. She glanced back as she flung the door open to see the barmaid talking on the phone and a couple of the men pushing their way through the crowd, coming after them. "That one's even dressed like a fuckin' witch!" one redneck hollered, pointing at Taylor. The girls bolted outside.

The post office offered the nearest concealment. Of the same mind, they both ran for the small, low building and crouched behind a dumpster beside it. The clouds had thickened, obscuring all but a faint circle of the moon, but a light on a high pole illuminated most of the parking lot. No one came after them. Bethany tried to catch her breath. "What the heck's going on?" What was this Saturn Society of Taylor's, and was Florence Allen a part of it?

"Fucking narrow-minded assholes," Taylor muttered.

"Now what do we do?" Bethany leaned against the post office wall.

"I don't know." Taylor pulled her sleeves down over her hands. "I left my fucking gloves in there, too."

Bethany scrunched her neck down so her coat collar came over her chin. "I'm fr- freezing. Maybe I should go back in and get—"

A car rolled into the lot and parked in front of the dumpster, blocking any escape. Bethany felt as if she'd been lassoed, and who-ever held the rope was pulling it tighter. A man climbed out of the car.

In the dim light cast by the parking lot lamp, a star-shaped badge gleamed on the breast of his brown coat. "A cop," Taylor said.

Bethany let out a breath. "Thank God. Maybe he can help—"

He strode around the dumpster, his shoes loud on the pavement. "Now just what're you two young ladies doin' here, hidin' behind a trash bin?"

"Um, we..." Bethany began.

"We just wanted to use the phone in there," Taylor said. "Our car broke down, and—"

The man extended a hand to help her up. "Why don't ya come with me'n we'll see what we kin do about that." He spit a wad of tobacco out the side of his mouth and opened the back door of his SUV—a Mercedes, Bethany noticed. She chewed her lower lip and glanced at Taylor. The other girl shrugged, and climbed in. Bethany followed, ignoring the crawly sensation in her belly that something wasn't right. *You're just freaked out because of your car, and those weirdoes in the bar.* The sheriff hopped in and put the SUV into gear.

As they drove off, Bethany realized what was weird. Maybe the sheriff wasn't driving a cruiser because he was off-duty. But if that was the case, why would he be wearing his badge? And how many small-town, rural cops made the kind of money to afford a vehicle like his?

Sixteen

Bethany lifted her head from a blanket that stank like dog pee. Her mouth was dry, her head muzzy, and her vision cloudy. She blinked.

Concrete walls. Rough canvas beneath her hand—she was lying on a metal-framed cot. Just enough dampness in the air to make it cold and clammy. Gray, steel door. Musty, old basement smell. Toilet through a doorway in the corner with rust stains around the base. Sharp, bright sun slashed through a dirty, glass block window high above.

Where the heck was she?

A scary feeling rose in her belly, like she was on a roller coaster about to go over the big hill. A roller coaster that was ramshackle and broken down, about to fall—

"Bethany?"

Bethany turned toward the voice. Taylor sat on another cot across the small room, her coat draped over her shoulders like a cape.

"Whash..." Bethany swallowed, trying to wet her tongue. "What's up?" Her scratchy, dry throat roughened her voice. "Where're we?"

"Someone's basement. Locked in." Taylor shook her head. "I think we were drugged. Maybe it didn't hit me as much since I weigh more."

"Tell me 'bout it," Bethany croaked. Being drugged would explain why she felt like crap, why her mouth was so dry and why her mind was foggy. Her tummy felt yucky. And hungry. Which explained her mental la-la. "There anything to eat—"

Somewhere outside the room, a door squealed. Slow, even footsteps approached. Taylor moved to Bethany's side as keys rattled in the door and it swung open.

"Well, well." The sheriff tugged his pants up at the waist, grinning. "Did you girls sleep well?" He fingered the gun in his holster. So much for trying to make a run for it.

"Yeah, too well—" Bethany began.

"Why are you keeping us here?" Taylor sprang to her feet. "Who are you? What did we do—"

"Sorry 'bout that, but I got my orders." He dropped a plastic grocery bag on the floor. "Here's something to eat—"

"Orders from who? My boss—" Taylor began, but he backed out the door and slammed it shut. A click and a snap told them he'd locked it. "Hey!" Taylor yelled. "Come back here!"

"Please!" Bethany shouted. "I need my medication!" She could eat the whole bag of food, but without her insulin she'd starve. "Sir! My purse! Please!"

The footsteps returned. "What kinda medication?"

"She's diabetic!" Taylor yelled. "If she doesn't get—"

The door swung open a handbreadth. He tossed the two purses in, then pulled the door shut and locked it. "Don't bother tryin' yer cell phones," he snarled as his footsteps receded.

"Hey! Wait a minute!" Taylor yelled. But the footsteps faded, and a door down the hallway slammed shut. Taylor clenched her fists. "Fucking bastard."

Food. It was all that mattered at the moment to Bethany. She grabbed the grocery bag and pulled out a plastic-wrapped sandwich and started to peel away the cellophane. "I wouldn't," Taylor said. Her stomach growled in disagreement.

"Why?" Bethany emptied the bag. Three more sandwiches, two bottles of water, a couple bags of Doritos, and two bruised apples. She raised her sandwich to take a bite.

"It could be drugged."

Bethany put down the sandwich. Ham and cheese. With mayo. Her mouth watered. She could practically taste its salty goodness. "I don't have a choice. I have to eat."

"Check your phone," Taylor said.

Bethany set the sandwich down and did as she asked. "One bar on the battery." Her lip trembled. "But no service." She put the phone back into her purse.

"I didn't really expect there to be, but it was worth a try." Taylor dug out hers, punched a button, then put it away.

Bethany grabbed the sandwich and ate. It tasted fine. Delicious, in fact. But one thing was for sure, that guy was no sheriff. Unmarked car. He hadn't read them their rights or told them why they were being held.

She had only enough insulin to last a day. If she didn't get more soon, being abducted and held for ransom—or whatever the guy was doing with them—was the least of her troubles.

They spent the afternoon talking about anything and everything—except Bethany's dad. Taylor swore she knew nothing more than she'd already shared, even though Bethany pushed until Taylor got snippy and quit talking.

They beat at the door every now and then, and tried the glass block window, too, but it might as well have been solid steel for the good it did.

They played tic-tac-toe and hangman until they used up the notepad in Bethany's purse. She tried not to think about her mom or Aunt Lisa and Uncle Charlie, or Mark, or her friend Angie from school. Or Timmy, the slightly-mentally-challenged garbage man, who worked Aunt Lisa's neighborhood and always told her how pretty her car was, if she was outside when they came for the trash. Or her car, left on the side of the road.

A door slammed from somewhere above.

Taylor jumped up and pounded on the steel door. "Hey!" Bethany joined her.

A couple minutes later, the so-called sheriff opened the door, gun drawn. "Settle down, ladies, if you want your dinner."

Bethany backed away. Taylor squinted at the white plastic bag on the floor behind his feet. He waved the gun. "You, back up."

Scowling, Taylor did as ordered. He held out the bag.

"About fucking time." She snatched it from his hand. "Now how about letting us go?"

"No can do." He fingered his gun. The room's bare bulb cast a shiny spot on his receding hairline.

"Can't I at least call my mom?" Bethany hated how whiny she sounded.

"Yeah, people are going to be looking for us," Taylor said.

The sheriff pointed at Bethany with his thumb. "Oh, they're lookin' for her all right. You, I don't know."

Taylor started to say something, but Bethany cut her off. "My family's got money, if that's what you want."

"Oh, I like money, all right. Way more'n your mom's got, 'specially with your daddy's bank accounts all frozen."

"Who—" Taylor began.

"Sorry, girls, that's all I can say." He pulled the door shut, then the lock clicked.

Taylor pounded on the door. "Hey! Come back here!"

By the time she gave up, Bethany had already pulled the two Styrofoam food boxes out of the bag and started eating. Roasted chicken, mashed potatoes, and mixed vegetables, obviously from a restaurant.

With a sigh, Taylor grabbed the other box and sat on the cot beside her. "Well, I guess it's better than typical prison food."

"Mm-hmm." There were two packages of chocolate chip cookies, one of which Bethany shoved into her purse for later. She'd need her insulin soon, so she dug for that.

Her fingers brushed her almost-dead cell phone. Two Jolly Ranchers. Two pens. Makeup. Her wallet. That flare thing Taylor had ripped off. She'd ask what the heck Taylor'd been thinking, after she got her insulin. She kept digging.

Her stomach slid down past her butt. Where was her insulin pen?

Hadn't she grabbed an extra one when they were at that truck stop? "Crap, crap crap—" Her fingers lit on a long, plastic cylinder, and she let out a breath.

Taylor looked up, a bite of chicken halfway to her mouth. "Beth?"

Bethany laid her purse down, insulin pen on top. "Nothing. I just couldn't find my meds."

"How long will that last you?"

Bethany swallowed. "Tomorrow morning." She made a fake laugh. "I hope that dumbass sheriff guy brings more with breakfast, or you might be eating lunch with a dead chick."

"Mom! There's a dead wild lady in our cellar!"

Violet's eyes slid open to a bright shaft of sunlight spearing through a narrow window above, and dry, cold concrete beneath her. Heat radiated from a round, squat tank—a boiler. Something warm and heavy lay in her arms—

Isaac!

She tried to push herself up, but the effort was too great. Recovery. Where was she? What on earth had happened?

The memories filtered slowly into her recovery-addled brain as she heard the little boy yelling for his mother again, from farther away. Those men from the Order. Going to their encampment to get sent home, then—

She'd been shot. By Tony. Which explained the soreness that blossomed beneath her ribs as soon as the thought passed through her mind. She vaguely recalled waking into someone's back yard, chilled to the bone, and climbing into the cellar door, drawn by the warmth.

Isaac. Still alive, and still in her left arm, clutched against her side. Thank heavens. But why on earth had Tony—

Footsteps clunked down a wooden staircase. She forced her head to the side to see a woman's feet, in brown, lace-up shoes and tights,

the little boy pulling at her skirt—

It worked! She'd gone home, although by Tony's bullet, instead of the Order's technology—

"There she is!" The little boy rushed forward pointing. "She's got a baby!"

Violet tried to think as they approached at a run. Where would she go? What to tell them?

"She's not dead!" The boy jumped. "Look at her clothes! She's an Indian. Or a caveman!"

The woman crouched over her. "Miss? Are you all—"

"Please..." Violet's voice came out a croak. "I... I live at..." Every word was an effort. Not finished recovering yet. She'd slip back asleep soon, had to get to safety...

Then she remembered. The Saturn Society, of course. Mr. Everly would take care of her and Isaac. "One... forty... Harrison Street." Hopefully, it was nearby. "Please...call..."

The boy frowned at his mom. "Isn't that where—"

"You live with *colored*?" The woman drew back, her brows pressed down.

Colored? What on earth? The only person she knew who said that was Stephanie's ninety-four-year-old grandma—

Then it dawned on her. "Please... what's the date?"

"December tenth," the woman said.

"What... year?" Violet managed. So tired...

The boy looked at Violet, his nose wrinkled and eyebrows askew. "Nineteen thirty-nine?"

Bethany lay curled on her side on the cot. Her head felt like King Kong was using it to play dodge ball. The morning sun shining through the glass block window stung her eyes, and her skin felt clammy and yucky,

(Dying)

and she couldn't think straight. "C'n you get my..." Her words trailed off. What was she going to ask?

The girl leapt up and crouched by her side. *(Weird black dress. Dusty and dirty.)* "Oh, God, what's wrong, Beth?"

Beth. Me. "I... feel like sh...."

"Oh, God. That fucktard phony sheriff hasn't been here yet. I swear, when we get out of here, Chad'll make sure he gets locked up for life." She sat on the edge of Bethany's cot and squeezed her hand. "Oh, man. You're all sweaty... You want some water?" She grabbed an empty bottle from the bag and hurried into the bathroom.

"Food." King Kong was taking a jackhammer to Bethany's head. She rolled onto her back, hoping that would help, but it didn't. Everything was all blurry, like when she looked through her dad's glasses. Where was her dad? And the guy who looked like him, who'd killed...

That boy. Someone she knew. Someone she liked. Not a boyfriend.

A door slammed somewhere... wherever they were.

Time stretched into a long, thin line, like a tightly-pulled rubber band. An ant crawled along a crack in the cinderblock wall. Finding food?

A man's voice echoed from a distant corridor. Not talking to her, or the other girl. Someone else.

Bethany's friend jumped up—Taylor, that's who she was—and ran to the door. "Hey! We need some fucking food! My friend's sick—"

The man laughed. "Heh, you keep 'em occupied at the bar, and I'll get the girls moved to our alternate location—"

"Hey!" Taylor screamed. "Get off the fucking phone! My friend's dying!"

"...catch you later, Bill." The lock clicked and the door swung open a crack. "Whad'ya mean, she's dyin'? It ain't been that long since you ate."

"She's diabetic," Taylor snapped.

"Yeah, so?"

"She can't go without food as long as you or me!"

Plastic crinkled. The door clicked and swung open. The sheriff tossed another plastic grocery bag in, then shut the door. "That'll have ta do you for now."

Taylor banged on the door. "Hey!"

Footsteps returned. "What!" the sheriff guy yelled through the door.

"She needs her insulin! From the car!"

"Sit tight, I'll go get it," the man grumbled.

"Or you could just let us go!" Taylor yelled.

"Sorry, ladies, not gonna happen. I'll be back with 'er stuff soon's I can."

"Make it fast!" Taylor grabbed the bag and ripped open a box of doughnuts. She pulled Bethany upright, then knelt by her side, holding the sugary snack to her mouth. "Here, Beth."

Bethany took a bite, then took a sip of water. "Ask him... how long."

Taylor beat on the door again. "Hey!" She pounded and yelled until the guy returned.

"What now? I was walkin' out the door!"

"How long's this gonna take? 'Cause she needs her medication now!"

"Half hour! Now shut up!" His footsteps retreated. "Dumb bitches," he grumbled.

Bethany ate. Felt a little better. "My purse," she croaked.

"What do you need?"

"Drugs. Headache."

Taylor grabbed it and dug in, shoving a red tube aside. *Red Emergency Flare. Have to ask her...*

Taylor pulled out a medicine bottle and handed Bethany two tablets. By the time Bethany popped the pills, she forgot her question.

After they ate, she lay on her cot. If that dumbass fake sheriff didn't hurry back with her insulin, a lot more than her head would be hurting.

Taylor paced back and forth as they waited. "Half-hour, my ass."

"Ugh," Bethany groaned. She was starting to feel nauseated already, from eating without insulin. No energy, either. The guy was taking For. Ev. Er.

Taylor stopped beside her. "You gonna make it?"

"Depends... if he gets here soon."

Taylor walked back to the door, pressed her ear to it, then walked back to the window and stood on her tiptoes to peer out. "Can't see shit through that," she grumbled as she returned to Bethany's side.

She knelt beside the cot. Bethany fought the urge to puke. *Great.* Taylor grasped her hand. "Beth? I'm going to try something that might save us. Might make this never happen."

"Huh?" Bethany wrinkled her nose. How the heck would Taylor do that? And if she could, why hadn't she done it already?

Taylor squeezed her hand. "You gotta promise me you won't tell anyone, okay?"

"Ohhhhh-kaaaay." Whatever. Jeez, she felt like crap. "What's—"

"I need to concentrate. And then I might disappear. But if this works, we'll know not to get off the highway in that traffic jam, and none of this'll happen."

"Wha...?" Taylor totally wasn't making sense. How could she—

Taylor stood, mumbling to herself. "...write Chad a letter, to be opened this year—no, I'll write it to myself, duh, and read it before we leave—"

"Huh?" Bethany choked back another burst of nausea. If she didn't get insulin soon... "What're you going to do? It's not like you can go back in time." She managed a snort.

Taylor grabbed her skirt in both hands. "Actually, I can."

"Come on, buddy, let's go." Strong hands gripped Tony's wrist and pulled. "Come on, wake up."

"Ugggghhhh...." With his other hand, Tony fumbled at the cracked, vinyl seat as the guy pulled him out of the old car in the junkyard where he'd taken refuge.

His eyes slid open as someone grabbed him under the arms, and he found himself staring into a blue-jacketed chest with a shiny badge.

Fuck. He twisted in the person's grasp, but could barely move. *Still in recovery.*

"Something's wrong with him," the guy holding him said.

"Whacked-out on something, no doubt," the cop grumbled.

They dragged him the rest of the way out of the old junk car. He squeezed his eyes shut at the harsh sunlight. His deerskin boots scraped the pavement as they dragged him away. "Check out that getup," the guy who found him said.

"That's fucked up," another guy said. "Like he's a caveman or something."

The first officer snorted, then a car door clunked open and they dumped him onto the back seat, face first.

"Wait, he's been shot," the first guy said.

"Where? I don't see—"

"In the back. See the bullet hole?"

"No blood... looks like a cigarette burn to me."

"I don't know, better be safe than sorry."

The first officer sighed. "Okay, let's take 'im to the Valley."

Miami Valley Hospital, thank God. With luck, he'd be able to recover and warp out before anyone recognized him.

Bethany woke to rough, rusty metal beneath her hands. Cold. Couldn't... lift head. No energy. Everything blurred. Loud rumbling. Floor vibrated, big bumps made her head feel like it was exploding.

(Red and white striped socks near her face)

That girl, her friend.

"Hey," the girl said. "You okay?"

It took several seconds before Bethany realized her friend *(Taylor)* was asking her a question. "Uh... no."

Muzzy head. Blood sugar... too high. She'd eaten, hours ago. No insulin. That was why... could barely think straight.

Rumbling went down in pitch, got quieter, picked up again. Muted sunlight. Dirty window... back of a pickup truck with a cap. "Where... insulin?" she mumbled.

"That fucktard said your car was gone." Taylor's hands twitched in her lap. "He said he'd stop and get insulin at the hospital, wherever the fuck that is."

Hospital? Bethany tried to say, but only a gurgle came out.

She'd be dead by the time they got there.

Taylor fumbled in Bethany's purse. Bethany managed to focus her vision enough to see the other girl pulling at something in her hands. "What're... you doing?"

A red-white light flared, so bright it hurt Bethany's eyes. She squeezed them shut. "What's...?"

"I don't know if this'll work, but..."

Smell of something burning. Smoke. Not exhaust. Bethany coughed, the acrid, chemical smell gagging her. Sizzling sound. The smoke thickened.

Bright light. Hissy-crackly noise.

Dying?

Lightheaded.

(Fading)

Someone screamed through a coughing fit. (Taylor)

Not moving anymore.

(Peaceful)

Someone yelling... getting quieter.

A door slammed. *(Somewhere far away)*

Bethany opened her eyes. Nothing but white fog. Gaggy, chemical smoke. She coughed, couldn't stop, then everything faded.

Her eyes fell closed. Foggy brain. Thoughts swirling, going away. Nowhere. *So this is what it feels like to die.*

A hacking cough broke through the fog. "Bethany! Sit up!"

No way... *(can't)*

Bright light. All around, everywhere. Bethany walked toward it. Couldn't remember getting up, though the haze was clearing from her brain. Whoever was screaming at her, she was leaving. She couldn't hear them anymore. *Sorry.* It didn't matter. Nothing mattered but getting to that white light. One step. Another. Her feet were getting lighter, it was getting easier—

Something grabbed her armpits and yanked her upward. A tingle shot through her, arcing through her body like the time she'd plugged in a lamp only halfway when she was five and touched the hot plug. Along with dizziness. If she'd been standing, she would have fallen.

She jerked, blinked, and the white light went away. Her eyes opened. "Huh?" She coughed on the smoke-filled air.

"Look outside!" Taylor grabbed Bethany's shoulders and hauled her up to the truck cap's dirty window as something clunked from the front of the truck. Shouted curses came closer. Bethany tried to focus. From what she could see, it was an old, dead gas station that hadn't served a customer in years, probably decades. Brown stained the boxy, old-style gas pumps—rust. The cashier's office and garage doors were boarded over, and lines of bright color were probably graffiti.

"Look at the mural on the wall!" The mural was faded, but Bethany could make out a bald eagle, with an American flag banner in its talons bearing the words *1976 America's Bicentennial.* "Think what it might have…" (cough) "…looked like then!" Taylor urged.

"Why?" Bethany managed.

"Just do it!" Taylor coughed again. "Think about it all cleaned up, with customers in old seventies cars…" She trailed off to hack up another cough. "Old fashioned gas pumps with dial numbers. A car in the garage. People with bell bottoms. Hurry!"

Footsteps and swearing announced their captor walking around the back of the truck. "Close your eyes!" Taylor ordered. "Come on, Bethany, think! It's our only chance!"

She vaguely remembered Taylor saying something crazy about time travel. *Yeah, right.* It hadn't exactly worked yesterday. But she clamped her eyes shut and thought. In her mind's eye, an old Ford LTD like her grandpa used to have trundled up to the pump. A guy with a big moustache and sideburns like she'd seen on some of her

aunt's Nostalgia Channel shows started to swing the big door open—
no, her mom told her they used to have people working at the gas
station pump the gas for you. So she pictured a guy in a blue me-
chanic's jumpsuit walking toward the car, the eagle mural brightly
colored behind him—

She lurched as dizziness and a sensation of falling hit her. She
clutched for the side of the truck bed—

Gravel bit into the ankle and hand she'd landed on. She opened
her eyes.

Asphalt pavement. Loose gravel along its edge. The smell of gas-
oline, exhaust and—

A car horn blared behind her. Someone yanked her arm and
pulled her aside. "Bethany! Move!"

She tumbled off the road onto something cold and wet—snow. As
she tried to lurch to her feet before the snow soaked through her
jeans, she caught sight of the gas station.

It was almost like she'd imagined. Only instead of a dark green
LTD at the gas pump, it was a weird-looking little economy car, with
the word Gremlin X over the back fender. And the gas station at-
tendant wore brown coveralls and shop coat, not blue. But he had the
'stache and sideburns. The eagle mural gleamed in bright colors.

Beside her, Taylor picked herself up off the ground. Her mouth
slipping open, Bethany's eyes followed her. "Taylor? Wh- what happened? Where are we?" Her tummy had settled a little bit, like she'd
gotten some insulin, but not enough.

Taylor brushed off her skirt. "Same place we were a minute ago."

Bethany's eyes darted from the old car to the gas pump, which
had funny, black numbers that scrolled down, instead of red, digital
numbers. Neither it nor the car looked old. The eagle mural sure
didn't. The guy collecting money from the customer kept glancing at
Bethany and Taylor. "But... Where's that sheriff guy? And—"

"We're not in the twenty-first century anymore, Toto." Taylor took
her hand and pulled her up. "Welcome to 1976."

Bethany snatched her hand away. "Nuh-uh. I'm fucked up from
needing my med—" She wobbled and started to pitch forward.

Taylor grabbed her arm, steadying her. "We need to get you to a hospital." She steered Bethany toward a blue phone booth next to the driveway—an old-fashioned one you could actually step inside, with a door that shut, like in the movies, though Bethany had never seen a real one like that. Taylor shoved her inside, then slipped in behind her.

Bethany slumped against the wall. Whatever it was that had happened to her had fixed her blood sugar, but only temporarily. The world grew foggy again as Taylor grabbed the phone. "Yeah, I need to make a collect call. The Saturn Society, in northern Tennessee..."

Violet woke to blank white walls, and a faint tapping... wind, blowing barren tree branches against the windows. *Windows?* She pawed the cloth beneath her hand. Sheets. Soft, *wonderful* sheets. And warmth. No ever-present smell of smoke, but instead, the faint scent of lemon furniture polish—

Her heart nearly stopped. "Isaac?" She pushed herself upright and frantically patted the bed. Where was he? And where was she? "Isaac!" As if the baby would answer.

She gazed around the room. A small hospital ward, with four, brass beds, yet no medical equipment.

Her heartbeat slowed to normal. She knew this place. The recovery room, in the Dayton Saturn Society House. Isaac was probably elsewhere in the House, since there were no cribs or cradles in the recovery room. "Mr. Everly?" she called. Then another possibility struck her. She clutched her breast. What if they hadn't found Isaac with her? "Taylor?"

Footsteps approached. Short, sharp clicks. Not Mr. Everly's relaxed stride, or the clomp clomp of Taylor's granny boots.

The chocolate-brown face that appeared in the doorway was definitely not Mr. Everly's. Violet tried to stand, but her legs were too weak. "Mr. Pippin?"

"You're awake at last."

He walked around the bed, and she realized what must have happened. She hadn't returned to 2004, but to decades earlier. Not 1959, for this Mr. Pippin moved with greater ease, his hair unmarred by gray. This hardened face was not the kind man she'd met in 1959. "Y- yes." She drew her finger around the neckline of her... nightgown? Where on earth had that come—*It doesn't matter.* "My baby—I had him with me—"

"The child is in the parlor with my housekeeper."

Violet's eyes fluttered closed. She let out a breath. "Is he all right? Oh, mercy, he must be hungry—"

"Like you, he just woke from recovery."

Violet stretched out her arms, as if Mr. Pippin held the baby. "Please, let me see—"

"After I get some answers." He sat on the next bed, his posture stiff. "Starting with where you've been for the past six years."

"Please, let me at least—"

"Where. Have. You. Been." His brows pressed into a frown that brooked no argument.

"Where I've... why right here, in Dayton. With the exception of the past six months—"

"Don't lie to me!"

"But I have! I swear!"

"You have not been in Dayton. We'd have found you." He drummed his fingers on his knee.

"But I have! I live in—" Of course. Why hadn't she realized? "What year is it?"

He gave her a hard look. "1939."

Violet drew back as the memory trickled into her brain. *1939.* That the little boy had told her that, when she'd woken briefly while still in recovery. "My word. No wonder you didn't find me."

Mr. Pippin's brow lifted. "When—"

"The twenty-first century."

His face darkened. He spoke quietly, his words sharp. "Do not think to ply me with such nonsense, Charlotte, or you'll only—"

"What?" Heavens, was it true? "What did you call me?" She fought to take in air, as if it wasn't Mr. Pippin she spoke to, but the strangler who looked like Tony, and his hands once again clamped around her throat. Heavens, was it true then? Was *she* Tony's Charlotte?

"Your. Name." Mr. Pippin spat each word. "Unless you've conveniently forgotten that, as well as the impossibility of jumping into one's future—"

"But it's true! Please, Mr. Pip—"

A baby's cry drifted from downstairs, pushing aside Violet's fears and questions about her past. Her breasts grew heavy, and yearning for her child mingled with relief that recovery hadn't taken her means to provide for him. "Please, let me feed my son..."

With a huff, Mr. Pippin rose and left the room.

Violet stood, taking care to do so slowly so she didn't get dizzy. *Charlotte.* She was the woman Tony had told her about. And he'd known all along. How on earth could she have turned him in to the Society? The man she loved? Who'd saved her life? Each thought burned like a brand down her throat. She couldn't have. No matter what. Whatever had transpired between her and Tony *before*, she'd loved him, of that she was certain. But why had he kept the truth from her? She would have never—

The baby's cries grew louder, drawing her to the door. But as she approached, two big, muscular men dressed like gangsters blocked her way. "Excuse me," she said.

The men remained, an impenetrable wall.

"Please, I need to get my son—"

"Mr. Pippin says you stay here," one said. Violet started to protest when they stepped aside for Mr. Pippin and a young, colored woman in a black and white maid's uniform.

And Isaac. The woman smiled as she held him out to Violet, and some of the heaviness in Violet's heart lifted. But as she reached for the baby, the maid drew back with a sharp gasp. "Lawdy be, Mary mother of God!" She thrust the baby at Violet then crossed herself.

"What?" Violet clasped Isaac to her chest.

Mr. Pippin's gaze darted from Violet to the maid. "Miss Meri—"

"Look at her hands, Mista Pippin! She bears the mark of the Lawd!"

"Miss Meriwether, that's enough." Mr. Pippin returned his attention to Violet. "Ah, yes. The scars." He grabbed Violet's hand, nearly causing her to drop Isaac. "Do tell, how on earth—"

"It's no divine intervention." Violet tried to hold the now-squalling baby and pat him with one hand. "Please, if I could just feed him, I can explain..."

The thugs withdrew, though Violet suspected they lay in wait outside.

She frowned at Mr. Pippin as she started to unbutton her night-gown—

She looked down. Where had the gown come from?

She glared at Mr. Pippin. The maid handed her a baby blanket, still muttering about the marks of the Lord. Violet dropped the blanket over her shoulder and Isaac, then unbuttoned her gown. "Leave us," Mr. Pippin ordered the maid.

"Yes, sir." Miss Meriwether slipped out. "Mary, mother of God," she muttered as she scurried away.

Violet sat on the bed to feed the baby, hoping Isaac's hunger and her determination to care for him would overrule Mr. Pippin's presence that could make her too stressed to nurse.

He sat on the next bed, his expression demanding answers.

"I was injured." Violet stroked the baby's hair as he fed. "By men who wanted to kill me, in a most horrible way, by staking me to the ground—"

"To when did you go back?"

"I- we're not sure. At least four or five hundred years, possibly twice that. These people were more primitive than the native people— Indians—we read about in history books, and their village was surrounded by a fortification mound..."

Mr. Pippin nodded, his jaw tight. "You and the child were in recovery for three weeks." He gazed at her hands on the baby blanket. "Those marks... were they what brought you back?"

Violet looked down at Isaac, trying to take comfort from his nearness and his gentle suckling.

Tony had shot her. To save her.

She swallowed. "My... husband. He had a gun. He shot me." She reached behind her back and pressed her fingertips to the round scar that had already healed. "He saved me from... a more painful death." Memories flashed through her mind of Tony's flight from the 1959 motel. It was best that she not speak of him. Better yet, change the subject. "This nightgown—where did it come from?"

"Miss Meriwether dressed you. The Society provides for its own." Mr. Pippin glared. "Even the prodigal daughter."

Violet started to protest, but shut her mouth. If she tensed, it would slow her milk, and she wasn't sure she should tell Mr. Pippin about her memory loss. Not this stern, hardened man. Stick to something safer. "How... who found me?"

"A family found you in their cellar, a few streets over. The mother was afraid to get a doctor—couldn't afford one, just as well for us, though she'd hoped to profit from the marks on your hands."

Violet stared down at her hand cradling Isaac's head as the vague memories filtered into her brain.

"Had to pay that woman a handsome sum." Mr. Pippin snorted. "She'd considered charging admission to see your stigmata, and with you quite unconscious! I couldn't believe..." The anger dissipated from his face. "After six years..." His face hardened again. "You will stay here for now. Do not try to leave, or—"

Violet pointed at the door. "Those men." Isaac sputtered, and she rubbed his back. "Who are they? And why—"

"Paid help. Be assured, they won't hesitate to kill you. And if they do, it will be for good."

Because this was her natural time. She forced herself to stay calm, though Isaac turned away from her breast. Beneath the blanket, she switched him to the other side.

"Who is his father?" Mr. Pippin asked.

"My *husband*—" she emphasized the word, for some reason not wanting him to think her a loose woman—"Is from the twenty-first century." Mr. Pippin glanced at her left hand. "We hadn't the means to buy a ring." She felt the need to explain. "Like many people in this time..."

Anger welled inside her like a leaden balloon. Tony had known who she was all along. And he'd kept it from her. Isaac drew away, sensing her tension. It would be no use to encourage him to eat more, so she slid him from beneath the blanket and lifted him to her shoulder.

"What is this man—your *husband's*—name?"

Violet patted Isaac's back slowly.

"Make no mistake, Charlotte," Mr. Pippin continued. "You have two choices. Cooperate with me, and your life will be pleasant, if not happy. Refuse, and you may never again see your son."

Violet's hand froze on Isaac's back, and the baby squirmed. "Co-operate with you in what?" She resumed patting.

"The father's name."

No good. He undoubtedly knew, and was testing her. If she lied, she feared he'd make good on his threat. "Tony Solomon." Isaac hiccupped. Her patting had grown too forceful. She made herself ease up.

"He will come for you."

"He won't. He knows me only as Violet Sinclair, from the twenty-first century." Or so she'd thought. "What- why do you need my help?"

"The man is a menace, and his machinations in the past endanger the very fabric of the universe. He'll return, and when he does, you will lead him to me."

She opened her mouth to protest, but stopped. Even though Tony had deceived her, she couldn't give him over to Pippin. Surely she hadn't before, at least not by her own choice. Tony had misunderstood something. Made a mistake. She would never have betrayed him like that. And she wouldn't now.

"Give me your word." The flush rose in Mr. Pippin's face. His hands twitched on his knees, and in that moment, any doubts Violet held fled. He wouldn't hesitate to make good on his threat and take Isaac—and do worse to her—if she refused to go along with his plan.

She glanced at the door, feeling the thugs' presence. She wouldn't disagree with Mr. Pippin. Not when he held her and Isaac's lives in his hands.

Tony's lies by omission didn't matter. All that mattered was Isaac. "All right. If Tony comes back to this time..." She swallowed. "I'll bring him here. Whatever it takes." An eerie feeling of déjà vu slipped over her, as if she were watching a movie she'd seen before but only barely remembered.

She'd done this, said this *before*.

Seventeen

Bethany woke to white. Fluorescent light over the bed where she lay. The smell of cleaning stuff. The crackle of a cheap TV.

Hospital. Her arms and legs felt rubbery, too heavy to move. And boy, was she thirsty. Luckily, a glass and pitcher sat on a table beside her bed.

She flexed her hands beneath the white sheet. Whatever the heck had happened, she'd gotten food and insulin. Her medic-alert bracelet had probably saved her life.

Beyond the table, someone lay in the bed beside her. As she watched, a hand with chipped, black nail polish reached for a television set the size of a shoebox mounted on the bedrail. "Taylor?"

Her friend peered around the set. "Hey! How do you feel?"

Bethany frowned. "Hung over." Taylor arched an eyebrow. "Well, what I imagine it would feel like. I can't drink, you know."

"But you're okay."

"I think so. Just really tired." Bethany pushed herself into a sitting position, her strength slowly returning. "I can't believe these weird little TVs—"

A nurse bustled into the room. "Oh good, you're awake." She rushed to Bethany's side "How're you feeling, hon?"

"Uh, okay I guess. Just tired." Bethany eyed the nurse's white uniform. Something right off of the Nostalgia Channel. All the nurses she'd ever seen wore scrubs, with puppies or smiley faces or some other cutesy print. Or bright colors, like purple or teal.

"You had us worried, young lady. But it looks like your sugar's stabilized." She looked at Taylor. "Your aunt called, she's on her way." She took the girls' blood pressure and marked a couple of things on clipboards attached to their beds, then left. *Weird.* Didn't they use computer tablets, like the hospitals at home?

Something wasn't right, but Bethany couldn't figure out what, and still hadn't when a woman wearing a beehive hairdo and an orange, polyester pantsuit strode in. She adjusted the canvas tote bag strap on her shoulder as she stopped between the two beds. "Taylor?" She looked from one girl to the other.

Taylor lifted a hand. "Mrs. Allen?"

Bethany studied the woman as she walked to Taylor's bedside. They spoke too low to hear over the buzz of Taylor's TV, but Bethany thought she heard Taylor say something like "twenty-first century."

Mrs. Allen's clothes were whacked. Retro seventies stuff might be in style, but the woman had taken it to an extreme. As far as Bethany knew, polyester pantsuits were not something that had come back. Especially in a color like rust orange.

And her hair. She'd seen old pictures of her grandma, with her hair all puffed up on top of her head like that, but... ew. That was something that shouldn't come back either. She was probably Bethany's mom's age, but she could be a poster girl for *What Not to Wear.*

What she didn't look like was a witch. What were those people at that bar thinking?

"This is Bethany," Taylor said.

The woman turned to the other bed. "Bethany." She grabbed Bethany's hand, and a smile lit her face like she was greeting an old friend she hadn't seen in years. Weird as the woman looked, maybe everything would be all right. "How *are* you, dear?"

"Um, I don't mean to be rude, but... do I know you?"

"Oh! Ah... I suppose not." She gave Bethany's hand a squeeze, then dropped it. "My name's Florence Allen, but everyone calls me..."

Bethany couldn't stop herself from cringing.

"What's wrong?" The woman slid the tote bag off her shoulder and fidgeted with the strap.

"Uh... you're not too well-liked at Rub-a-dub's Pub, are you?"

"Rub-a... oh, that's in Hollaville, I'll bet?"

Bethany gave a slow nod.

Mrs. Allen laughed, though her smile had grown strained. "I'm afraid I'm not too popular around those parts, but... no. I sent in letters to the Society newsletters remindin' people that our kind should avoid—"

"Our kind?" Bethany squeezed the sheet. "What do you mean—"

"Uh, I don't think she understands what happened," Taylor said.

"Oh dear." The woman looked back at her. "Do you want to explain, or should I—"

"Welcome to 1976, Bethany."

Bethany wrinkled her nose. "Huh?"

"You're a time traveler now. Cool, huh?"

Bethany looked around. "Oh, yeah, hah, hah. Come on, where are we?"

Taylor hesitated. Mrs. Allen spoke. "This is your first time, isn't it, dear?"

"First time for what?" She'd been in the hospital before for sugar complications, but hardly remembered. She'd been only five at the time.

"Going back in time," Taylor said.

Bethany studied Mrs. Allen's authentic-looking, retro pantsuit. Thought about the nurse in her starched uniform. She vaguely remembered a doctor coming in to check on her earlier, while her mind was still hazy. She'd noticed his cheesy haircut with the big sideburns and thick moustache. Right up there with the guy at the gas station with his big 'fro.

Oh, God, what had Taylor said? She'd ordered her to think. *1976.*

"Nuh-uh. Quit messing with me." Bethany wasn't sure, but she thought she'd prefer Mrs. Allen to be a witch. Witches, at least, were real. "Come on, now what—"

"I'm not messing with you. Look around." Taylor waved at Mrs. Allen, at the bedside telephone with a dial, at the little TV clipped to her bed that looked like it should have been old, but wasn't.

"I want to call my mom," Bethany said.

Mrs. Allen touched Bethany's forearm. "My dear, it's 1976. Your mother's only a child now."

Bethany snatched the phone off her nightstand, never taking her eyes off the woman. "I'm going to call her." She punched in the number.

Mrs. Allen shrugged. "Well, if you insist..."

A harsh tone shrilled in Bethany's ear. "We're sorry, but your call cannot be completed," a recorded voice informed her.

Aware of Taylor and Mrs. Allen's stares, she hung up and tried to call collect by dialing zero, since she didn't have her calling card with her. When the operator asked for the number, Bethany gave her mom's cell phone number. "What did you say the area code was?" the operator asked.

"Nine three seven," Bethany said.

A pause. "Ma'am, there is no nine three seven area code."

A chill trickled down Bethany's body. "Uh, I'll have to go look up the number again."

She met Mrs. Allen's kind gaze as she hung up the phone.

The woman inclined her head to one side. "It's hard for a lot of people to accept."

"This is so a dream." Bethany smacked her arm. "I'm going to wake up now..." Nothing happened, so she slapped harder. Again, until it stung.

Taylor giggled. "You're as bad as your dad—"

"My dad?"

Taylor shrugged. "Sure. All those times he disappeared—"

"Let me guess. He went back in time?" *Ha-ha. Yeah, right.*

Mrs. Allen put a finger to her lips. "Shh! Keep it quiet—"

"Well, yeah." Bethany glared at Taylor. "They'll send us to the nuthouse." She turned to Mrs. Allen. "You're not really Taylor's aunt, are you?"

With a tight-lipped smile, the woman shook her head. "Like Taylor, I'm part of an organization called the Saturn Society. The Society exists for people like us to help each other."

Crap. Nuts or not, the woman sounded serious. Bethany turned to Taylor. "You mean... like that sign on your house?" She squinched up her nose. "And my dad can do this?"

Taylor nodded. "He came to us almost two years ago."

"What happened to him? Do you know anything? I swear to God, if you do—"

Taylor held out her hands. "If I'd told you he'd gone back in time, would you have believed me?"

"I'd think you were crazy." Bethany studied her for a long moment. "So where is he now?"

"Actually *when* is he, is the question. We don't know. He actually did come to the House the night I called you—"

"He did? How? Why'd you tell me you didn't know anything? Where'd he go? Why—"

"He jumped in time! I couldn't exactly tell you then—"

"Because he was running from the law?" Bethany clutched her sheet.

"That, and other people were after him. People we think framed him—"

"I knew he was innocent! I knew it—"

Mrs. Allen held up a hand. "Girls, this conversation would be best continued at the House—"

"Mrs. Allen?" A young man wearing a crew cut, white shirt and black horn-rimmed glasses walked in. "The ladies' paperwork is ready." He gave her a wink.

"Thank you, Henry." She gathered her purse and stood as the man silently disappeared. "I brought you some clothing. Hopefully, it'll fit." She dug into her voluminous tote bag and pulled out a folded pair of jeans. "If you girls are feeling up to getting dressed, that is..."

"I think so," Bethany said.

As Taylor nodded and threw off her blanket, Bethany glanced at the TV. A newscast, and the man was talking about President-elect Jimmy Carter.

Another chill raced down her body. *Holy cow.* If this was a dream, it was way more detailed than any she'd had before. She swung her legs over the bed.

"Take it easy, honey," Mrs. Allen said. "Recovery can take a while to wear off—"

"Recovery? You mean from my sugar?"

"From time travel," Taylor said. "It's a psychic thing, that's why I told you to think about what things would've looked like in 1976. Pretty easy, but after you jump, it takes a while for your energy to build back up, especially when you're almost dead, like you were. You go into a deep sleep, and your body repairs itself. Almost like hibernation."

"Oh man..." Bethany stared at the wall, her gaze unfocused. "Just like my dad."

"It's a lot to take in all at once," Mrs. Allen said. "Are you sure you're all right? You can stay here another night if you—"

"I'm okay." Bethany planted her feet on the floor and stood. Her knees wobbled, but she forced them straight. She reached for the folded clothes Mrs. Allen held out, glad to see it was simply a pair of jeans—boot-cut ones—and a sweatshirt.

"We've made arrangements to obtain your insulin and testing kits, though I'm sure it won't be exactly what you're used to," Mrs. Allen said.

"Uh huh." Bethany pulled the curtain around her bed, still not sure she wasn't dreaming. Or dead. Or really messed up in the head because her sugar had gotten so screwed up.

In a daze, she dressed, then followed Mrs. Allen and Taylor to the parking lot. It looked weird to see Taylor in jeans and a flannel shirt instead of a ruffled black dress, though Bethany noticed her friend had put on her own red and white striped socks. "How did they let us just walk out like that?" she asked once they were out of anyone's earshot.

Mrs. Allen smiled. "That's Henry's job. He... fixes the paperwork, digs into the computer if necessary, to make it so that you can leave with me. And arranges for the Society to get the bill."

"You mean this Saturn Society pays my hospital bills?"

Mrs. Allen laughed. "Your parents can't exactly pay, can they?"

Cars Bethany's dad would have called boats filled the parking lot.

Holy crap. If it was really 1976, her parents would really be little kids, like Mrs. Allen said.

The woman led them to a huge, old, olive green Oldsmobile. Or maybe not so old, Bethany decided as she opened the door to a backseat big enough to be a bed. A big collie lying on the seat lifted his head and stood. "Wellsy!" Mrs. Allen shooed him over to the side. "One of you'uns'll have to ride shotgun."

Taylor opened the front door and climbed in.

Bethany looked from the dog to Taylor, then back again. Wellsy's tail swept back and forth across the vinyl seat, and he looked up at her, a thin half-circle of white showing in his eyes.

"Aww." Bethany leaned in and petted him, then slid onto the seat beside him. Old seventies cars didn't have child-locks, did they? If this Mrs. Allen turned out to be some weirdo like that fake sheriff guy, Bethany could jump out and run.

"How old is this car?" She shut the door. "My uncle would love it. He collects old muscle cars."

"I bought it brand new a year ago," Mrs. Allen said with a laugh.

Wellsy sniffed Bethany's hand as she brushed the vinyl seat. Not a crack marred its smooth surface.

As Mrs. Allen drove away, Bethany searched for modern cars. But there were none among the old Chevys, Fords, and Dodges. And only a few Hondas and Toyotas. "There's some snacks in the Kitchen Sink—my bag."

"You wouldn't happen to have a Mountain Dew in there, would you?" Taylor asked.

"As a matter of fact, I believe I do," Mrs. Allen said. "Help yourself. I need to get gas, then we'll head for the House and get something more substantial to eat. If good old home cooking's still in style in the twenty-first century?"

"Oh, yeah," Bethany said. Taylor dug into the bag and pulled out a green soda can, then passed the bag over the seat to Bethany.

After leaving the small town, then driving almost-deserted country roads for a good half-hour, houses and businesses started to appear. Mrs. Allen turned into a gas station. Bethany had never heard of the name on the sign—Boron. And she'd seen no cars newer-looking than the one they rode in.

Mrs. Allen got out to pump gas. "Dratted self-serve," she muttered.

"Hey Beth," Taylor said. "Check it out." She pointed up and out the window.

The price on the sign was $77^{\underline{9}}$. "Nuh-uh," Bethany said. "They left off the dollars."

Taylor shook her head. "Look at the pump."

Bethany studied the boxy, old-fashioned looking gas pump. Like the ones at the gas station where they'd escaped that sheriff guy, these didn't even have credit card scanners. As Mrs. Allen stuck the nozzle into the gas tank, Bethany saw the numbers on the pump move.

Not digital readouts, but printed numbers on cylinders that rotated, just like Taylor had told her to imagine. "Oh my God." She really was in 1976. "Whoa. This stuff's for real. I really can travel in time."

Mrs. Allen and the Boron station faded from her sight as possibilities flitted through her mind. "I could go back and ace that science test, now that I know the right stuff to study. I could go back and... and be home when my mom was fooling around on my dad, so it wouldn't happen." Taylor shot her a wary look. "I could go back and tell Danny to leave work early, so that—"

"Beth," Taylor said quietly, "don't. Don't even think it. It's too dangerous—"

"We could go back and not stop in Hollowville. Get the car checked out—"

"No," Taylor said. "We. Can't. That disappearing bridge we saw in the news a while back?"

Bethany's throat got tight. "But you were going to go back, and write a letter to yourself..."

"Yeah, and I couldn't. It didn't work. There's a reason..."

Mrs. Allen got into the car. "Ready to go..." She trailed off. "Girls, what's wrong?"

"She wants to go back and change stuff."

"It's very difficult to jump within your own life," Mrs. Allen pointed out. "And deliberately changing things—that's what causes things to happen like, let's see..."

Taylor turned around "Remember on the news a couple months ago, when they found what looked like tracks from a prehistoric beast up in Minnesota?"

"Uh huh," Bethany said in a small voice.

"Going back and deliberately changing something is what makes things like that happen," Mrs. Allen said. "It's sort of like ripples or gaps in the flow of time."

"So the disappearing bridge—that happened because someone was messing in the past?"

"You can be sure of it." Mrs. Allen drove away. "Learn, observe, and preserve... that's the Society's motto. And this is why."

Bethany tried to let everything sink in as they rode into the mountains, up switchback curves and finally, over a steep, narrow bridge. She gazed into the valley far below. "My dad would be totally freaked at this."

"Your dad?" Mrs. Allen glanced at her in the rearview mirror. "Why, silly me, I didn't even realize, even with your last name. You're Tony's daughter, aren't you?"

Bethany drew back, her head pressed into the seat. "You know my dad? In 1976?"

Tony woke on a soft, clean mattress. He was warm. Indoors. A place where the smell of meatloaf mixed with chicken mixed with potatoes mixed with vegetables. Muted light filled the room, some from a big window beside him, other from recessed lighting. A curtain blocked his view from the rest of the room, but a faint crackle of television came from nearby, along with someone paging some doctor...

Hospital.

So tired...

Recovery.

Vague memories filtered through his mind. Dying, after Keith shot him. Waking up in an old car in a junkyard, hoping no one would find him. Being nabbed by the cops, taken to the hospital. Family stopping by—his parents with lawyers, hushed conversations with doctors. Lisa and Charlie had come by, too, but someone at the door—a guard placed by the cops, he assumed—wouldn't let them in. He didn't let Everly in either.

But Bethany hadn't come. Neither had Keith Lynch.

Isaac. The boss he'd always liked and respected... his son. Tony squeezed his eyes shut. *God, let him have gotten away. Or killed.* If Keith had died in that time, would it have been permanent?

Better that than the Void.

At least he'd saved Violet—or rather, Charlotte. Even if she was working with the Order. Even if she'd betrayed him again. He could only assume she would have returned to 1939, her natural time. He could only hope their son had gone with her.

He had to find them. Take Isaac away from her, without winding up on Pippin's Treatment table.

There wasn't a damn thing he could do for Isaac in the twenty-first century, in the hospital. Thankful his strength was returning, he heaved himself out of bed and paced to the door and back. Had to find something to wear besides a hospital gown—they'd probably burned his dirty, smoky furs, and leathers. Worse, he couldn't see a damn thing—his glasses must've come off after Keith shot him.

He reached for the nurse call button, then froze.

What the hell was he thinking?

He crept around the bed, and peered around the curtain. The other bed was vacant, but in the hallway, a dark-blue-clad cop standing with his back to the door confirmed Tony's suspicions.

Tony paced to the window and gazed over the new wing by the parking garage, then slid back onto the bed, placing his weight on it slowly, so the bed wouldn't creak. He had to come up with a plan before someone came in, discovered he was awake, and carted him off to the slammer.

He eyed the phone on the nightstand, thought about calling his family, then quickly discarded the idea. His sister still thought him a murderer. *What the fuck.* He couldn't do anything hiding out in the hospital playing dead.

A whispered call to directory assistance got him the Society House. Everly knew he was innocent, and he'd said the Society would provide legal assistance.

The phone rang six times before someone answered. "Saturn Society," a woman said.

A chill coursed down Tony. Alpha! He slammed the phone down, bringing quick footsteps into the room. The brawny, uniformed guard peered around the corner at him as he grabbed the police radio from his belt.

"No one was home." Even that little lie twisted Tony's gut.

Within minutes, doctors, nurses, and medical assistants arrived to question, poke, and prod him. No sooner had they left than light, sharp footsteps approached his door. "No visitors," the guard said.

"I'm his daughter—" Tony's heart jumped into his throat. Not Bethany. Alpha!

"His daughter's missing," the guard said. "And you're not her."

Tony squeezed the nurse call remote, his gaze darting about the room. Bethany, missing? How could this happen? Dread crawled down his gut. Was Alpha behind it? Or maybe Bethany's death was one of those things that was meant to be, like Charlotte had tried to tell him...

"You're wrong," Alpha said. Something made a light snap and a *pfft*, then a muffled thud. She'd knocked the guard out, with one of those pen things like those guys that had taken Violet had used on him. Someone in the hallway shouted as Alpha's footsteps came closer.

He dropped to the floor. *1939.* His mind filled in how the hospital had looked in 1933. He hadn't been there, but he'd walked past, seen it. The wing he was in was new, had been a parking lot back then. He imagined it filled with twenties- and thirties era cars, and across the alley bordering it, a row of frame houses. Laser fire sizzled above his head as the dizziness overtook him.

Violet tugged at the window sash as soon as Mr. Pippin's goon shut the door to the little guest room in the Society House—the same one Fred where would stay when it was Mr. Everly's House, decades in the future.

The darn window was as stuck as it had been the night before.

She peered out. The only life down below was an old man bundled in a heavy coat, shuffling down the alley. Parked cars that looked like they belonged in a gangster movie sat in driveways. So strange that this was her time, yet it all felt familiar. It must be cold outside, for frost sparkled on the cars' windshields in the early morning light filtering through gray clouds. Violet couldn't tell for sure, as she wouldn't be permitted to go outdoors, even if she asked.

She rubbed her stiffened hands over her nightgown, then hurriedly dressed, gave her hair a quick brushing, then opened the door.

The hired man sat in a wooden folding chair, reading the *Dayton Journal*. She leaned into the hallway. "Excuse me, Mr.... Thompkins?"

The man grunted, so she supposed she'd heard his name correctly. "Could you please have my son brought up? I'm sure he's hungry."

As if on cue, the baby wailed from somewhere downstairs. "Miss Meriwether!" Mr. Thompkins bellowed.

In seconds, the young, black maid appeared, and handed Isaac to Violet, with a sad yet understanding expression that plucked at Violet's heart as she gathered the baby into her arms. "Thank you," she choked out.

Mr. Thompkins scowled at the maid, and she fled back downstairs.

Violet withdrew into the guest room and started to push the door shut, but Mr. Thompkins stopped it with his foot. "You know that ain't allowed."

"I... wasn't thinking." She stifled a yawn as she pulled a clean receiving blanket out of the bureau and sat in the rocker to feed Isaac. Even with her back to Mr. Thompkins, she could feel his gaze on her.

As much as it annoyed her, she couldn't blame the man. Jobs were hard to come by, and Miss Meriwether had told her that Mr. Pippin was paying Mr. Thompkins and his other two hired men a very generous wage to keep Violet in their constant sight whenever Isaac was with her. Aside from dying in the past, it wasn't possible to jump in time while in view of others, and Mr. Pippin knew she'd never leave without her son.

While she'd bathed the night before, the two men had stood right outside the bathroom door, Mr. Pippin unwilling to take even that small chance that she'd try to leave the House.

He hadn't believed her when she'd told him about her amnesia, grumbling about "helping the enemy escape." So different than the kind man who'd helped her in 1959.

Between that and her worry over Tony, she hadn't even been able to enjoy the warm bath she'd longed for for months. The clean clothes, warm radiators, indoor plumbing—all the things she missed so much—none of it mattered when she lived in constant fear that Tony would indeed come for her—and Mr. Pippin would destroy him as he'd done to Fred.

Her hold on Isaac loosened as a wave of dizziness struck. *Tony?* She clasped the baby close, though she knew she was sensing someone else's jump—the second she'd felt that day.

The vertigo passed. Was it Tony, coming for her? Her fingers twiddled in Isaac's blanket as she prayed he wasn't. Mr. Pippin suspected the first jumper was Tony, and had already left to search, aided by his other two men. Mr. Thompkins remained, ready to stop Violet if she did anything untoward—like try to leave.

But the sensation of the displaced energy was stronger this time, as if the jumper was really close. Maybe even inside the House. Violet rose, placed Isaac in the little cradle Miss Meriwether had bought for him, and ventured into the hall.

Mr. Thompkins sat in a wooden folding chair, newspaper in his lap. When Violet moved toward the recovery room, he rose and followed.

A woman with long, golden hair sat on one of the beds, her head bowed. Her wide-brimmed hat hid her face, but Violet recognized her form beneath her period-appropriate, shirt-waist dress and matching jacket. "Alpha?"

The woman looked up. "Violet? My God, how are you? Where have you—"

"I'm... all right. As you can see—"

"Your baby... did—" She put two fingers to her lip, as if she'd made a blunder in asking.

"He's fine." Violet moved to the woman's side and turned down the bed sheets behind her. "Six weeks old—well, in chronological weeks, to him." She helped the woman slip her blazer off, then held out her hand for Alpha's hat.

"Oh my. You've been... in this time all along? You stayed such a long—"

Violet curled her fingers around nothing. "No, we went back quite a bit further—"

"What about Tony?" Alpha stifled a big yawn as she removed her hat.

Violet's hand froze in mid-air. "I don't know what happened to him." She took the hat and whirled around to hang it and the jacket on a wall hook.

"You didn't translocate together?"

Violet slowly placed the jacket on the hook, then turned around. "Not this time." She forced herself to smile. "But I'm sure he's fine. Now let's make you comfortable." If Tony had been the other jumper, hopefully, Alpha would help her convince Mr. Pippin to spare him the Treatment.

Alpha wobbled as she leaned down to slip off her black leather pumps. After she slid under the covers, Violet pulled them over her. Alpha's eyes slid closed.

Violet slipped out of the room, Thompkins on her heels, satisfied that she'd been able to do something Mr. Pippin would find helpful.

That was the other part of her plan. Do everything she could to ingratiate herself to the Watchkeeper, so that if Tony came to this

time, she'd have regained the Society man's trust. Trust she'd take
advantage of—for Tony.

The fog slowly lifted from Bethany's mind as she took in the four,
old-style hospital beds covered with homey quilts, the plain calendar
tacked to the log wall, and the sampler beside the doorway leading
into a little bathroom. Then she remembered where she was. The
recovery room, in Florie's—as she'd insisted they call her—Society
House. The last few days' events filtered through her mind. The
hospital. Florie. And the surreal weirdness of being alive in 1976.
Learning all about being a responsible time traveler. Then seeing
glimpses of the present—modern cars, a Wal-Mart, the satellite dish
on the back of Florie's House... things that indicated the Pull, and the
end of her stay in the past.

An ache spread through her. She had to contact her mom. And
Aunt Lisa. She longed to hear even Mark's voice.

And of course, her dad's, though who knew when—or if—that
would happen. She'd tried to get Florie to tell her what she knew of
her dad, but the woman wouldn't spill a word, claiming the Society
Code forbade it, and it was for the best. Taylor stood by her earlier
claim that she knew nothing more. This time Bethany believed her.

Hopefully, she could get her car back.

Waiting for her vision to clear, she sensed another presence in the
room. Taylor was still asleep in the next bed. It wasn't her. It wasn't
Florie either, yet was someone familiar.

She sat up and turned around. A warm, brown gaze met hers
from beneath a fringe of graying, brown hair. Her face squinched up
at the man sitting on the bed beside her. "Mr. Lynch?" She pushed
herself upright, not prepared for the dizziness it brought and slid
back to the pillow. "I mean, Keith?"

"Take it easy, Bethany."

"Wh- what are you doing here? I mean-" She brought her hands to her face. "I don't know what I mean. This is all so weird."

A slow smile spread across his face. "I wouldn't know. I've been able to do it all my life."

Bethany pushed herself up, slowly this time. "You mean... you're a time traveler, too?"

"It isn't exactly something you talk about at the company holiday party."

She let the idea roll around in her mind. First her dad, now his boss? And *her?*

A week ago she would have said time travel wasn't possible. She looked at Keith, her face twisted in confusion. "So are you in the Saturn Society, too?"

"Yes, though I keep a low profile, even within the Society itself."

"No shit," Taylor said from the bed on Bethany's other side. "You've never been to our—hey!" Her gaze fixed on Keith. "You're the guy who broke into our House last summer! I saw you! You got a lot to answer for—"

Toenails clicked on the hardwood floor, then a slightly-gray-haired Florie strode into the room, a big Rottweiler at her side. "My, my, such commotion. Is everything all—"

"You always let crooks into your House?" Taylor demanded.

Florie drew back. "Who's a crook?"

Taylor pointed at Keith. "He broke into—"

"I had to sneak into the Dayton House this spring," Keith said. "Someone placed a hypnotic chip into their TV set, and I tried to get it out, but..." His eyes met Bethany's. "I tried telling you about it, too, but...Must be one of those paradox things." He turned up his hands. "At least your dad's safe. And his... girlfriend. And—"

Bethany's mouth made an O. "My dad has a girlfriend? Who—"

"Her name's Violet," Taylor supplied. "She was at the house with him. And went back in time with him, we assumed."

Keith nodded.

Her dad had a girlfriend, and he hadn't even told her?

No way. No frickin' way. "Let me get this straight. My dad can do this... this time travel thing, and so can his girlfriend. Now I can, too.

What about my mom? Can she—"

"No. Just you, your dad, his wife—"

"My dad's married?" Holy crap, what other secrets had he been keeping from her? And why? The realization stung, like when her mom used to give her her insulin shots before she knew how to do it right. "I thought you said—"

"I'm not sure if he is right now," Keith said.

Bethany stared, unseeing, her mouth open.

"Don't worry, Beth, she's cool," Taylor said.

Keith looked at her gratefully, then turned back to Bethany. "Your brother can do it, too."

"But I don't have— oh my God, what else do you know about my family? And how? Are you like, from the future or something?" Her belly was getting shaky, sort of like when she needed to eat, but not quite.

He gave her a reassuring smile. "Not exactly, but I've been to the future. That's why I'm here." His voice sounded like he was about to tell her something really important. He looked her in the eye. "Your dad and your baby brother need your help. I don't know exactly what you're supposed to do, but—"

"Wait a minute." Bethany touched his arm. "I have to know. If you're from the future, what happens with Danny's murder? Do they ever find out who did it? 'Cause even with that tape, I know my dad didn't—"

"Your dad didn't kill your cousin, Bethany. But if you don't go back to 1939 and help him, he won't be around to prove his innocence—"

"1939? I can't go there! Did they even have insulin back then?"

"They did," Florie spoke up. "But you don't need to worry about that. We'll set you up before you go."

"But how? I didn't think other stuff went back with you."

"We didn't jump naked, did we?" Taylor asked. "If you keep something close to your body, it'll go too."

"And I have just the outfit for you to wear to that time period," Florie said as she walked out of the room.

Bethany looked at Keith, at the doorway, then at Taylor. "I still don't know about this." Taylor shrugged.

"Please, Bethany," Keith said. "I can't tell you how important this is. Things are happening in the future that, if your dad and brother aren't there to stop it...." His gaze settled on her intently, and for an instant she saw her dad's blue eyes instead of Keith's. "You know the smallpox epidemic they had up north?"

"Did they ever find out how the virus spread? Did someone break into the CDC, or—"

"Time distortions," Taylor guessed.

"Exactly," Keith said. "They're caused when someone makes a change in the past. Something that shouldn't be. With enough of these changes, the time distortions, or holes, as some people call them, grow larger. Create ripple effects. And the next thing we know, the very structure of the universe is at risk."

"And my dad and my brother stop these people?" Bethany was skeptical.

"Not single-handedly, but they're instrumental to the cause. Please, think about—"

Florie reentered, a dress draped over one arm, clutching a vest in her other hand. She held the vest out. "Look, it has pockets sewn all over the inside. Perfect for your things."

Bethany leaned forward. The tiny pockets bulged with vials, test kits and syringes. "You just assumed I'd go? I haven't even talked to my mom yet! Aren't people looking for me?"

"Oh, you'd better believe it," Florie said. "But the Society folks've been working it, keepin' things low-key, helping your mama. I'm pretty sure they got her into our family program—"

Bethany's eyes widened. "What?"

"An educational and counseling program for linear family members," Taylor explained. "Basically, damage control if you disappear. Especially if the Society person's a kid."

Keith flashed her a smile, but it looked strained. "See, everything's all set."

Bethany drew back. "I still don't know about this..."

Florie took a step backward, holding the vest close. "Well, it *is* your choice. But I'll vouch for I- Mr. Lynch. He's been a friend to the Society for many years. If he says—"

"Wait a minute," Bethany said. "You told us you've lived in this House since you were a little kid, in the twenties. If I go back to 1939, you'd be here, right?"

"Ye-es, that's right." Florie spoke slowly.

"So, you already know if I go or not," Bethany pressed.

Florie chewed the insides of her lips. "Well..."

Bethany whirled around, searching Taylor's face for a clue.

Taylor shrugged. "You gotta do what you gotta do."

Bethany rose and walked to Florie, who silently handed her the vest and dress. "The rest of your outfit's in the guest room."

She followed the older woman there, and returned, decked out in a shirtwaist dress, thigh-high, knitted stockings, tights, and boots that wouldn't have been out of fashion in the twenty-first century. "I still don't know about this," she muttered.

She walked to the bed where Keith still sat, a worried look on his face. "You're not telling me everything, are you?" she asked. "Some-how... this is personal, isn't it?"

Keith sighed. "Yes." The dog hopped up on his bed and sat beside him, obviously well-acquainted with him.

"Look, if I'm going to risk my butt going back over sixty years—"

"Your baby brother."

"Yeah?"

"I'm him."

Bethany's mouth slid open, then snapped shut. "Nuh-uh."

"Uh-huh. My given name's Isaac. Isaac Solomon. And right now, if you don't go back there and help, I might not be—"

Bethany held up a hand. "Why can't you go back yourself?"

"I already exist in that time." Keith rose and walked to a window, gazing out over the bleak, leafless trees. "Yeah, it's possible to warp into your own life, but it's difficult. You have to be in the exact physi-cal location you were at the time you're trying to warp into. It's not exactly pleasant, either, having two of yourself in the same body."

"Which is a baby at that time," Bethany guessed.

"Yes. Which is why I need you—"

"Okay. I'll do it. What do I need to do once I get there?"

Keith let out his breath and looked up at the wall calendar. "Your dad will be arriving by train on the twenty-first, which should give you just enough time to recover." His gaze flitted to Taylor, then Florie before landing back on Bethany. "You need to go pick him up at the station in Hollowville, and make sure he gets here safely."

Taylor tilted her head. "If Florie lived here then, why couldn't she do it?"

Florie's hand tightened on the straps of her tote bag where it went over her shoulder. "I think I've tried, hon. But something must've stopped me. Or otherwise fouled things up."

Bethany turned the vest over and slid an insulin pen out of its pocket, replaced it, and checked two others. Some were long-acting, some were quick. Florie'd also included a tube of cake-decorating frosting in one of the narrow pockets, and both regular pockets contained cookies, wrapped in foil. She'd thought of everything.

Bethany pressed her fingers to the foil wrapping the cookies. "Okay, so me and Florie pick up my dad—and you—at the train station, and get you back here. Then what?"

Keith's mouth twisted. "That's the part I don't know. It's… different every time, and I can't remember anything clearly enough to describe what comes after…"

"Well, yeah, that part hasn't happened for you yet," Taylor said.

"Yes, sort of," Keith agreed. "The only thing I do remember is, there's a woman from the future who intends to harm your dad and me—"

"You mean kill him?" Bethany asked.

"No, she won't kill him in that time, because all it will do is send him back here."

"Oh, yeah." Taylor had explained that to her.

"She's tried to kill him before, many times. Even in this time. But we've always managed to prevent it, or go back and change it—"

Bethany jerked straight. "But isn't that really dangerous?" She searched their faces.

"Yes," Keith said. "But sometimes, the risk of not making the change is even greater."

"So how will I know this woman?" Bethany said.

"She's tall, slender, and physically fit with long, blond hair like yours." He pointed to Bethany's head. "She's had many names. I've known her as Rhea, and I've also heard her go by Jennifer Warren—"

"Alpha!" Taylor jumped up. Bethany looked up sharply. The blonde she'd seen that time at Taylor's house talking to Chad.

"Yes, that's another one. If you see her, avoid her at all costs. Especially if she has a little silver case that looks like a flip phone, or a makeup compact."

"What is it?" Bethany asked.

"A weapon. One that makes people wish for death." He glanced at the wall clock. "If you're going to make the jump and recover in time to meet the train…"

"Okay." Bethany slipped the vest on with trembling hands.

"You'll do fine, dear," Florie murmured. She and Keith slipped out of the room, the dog on their heels.

Bethany sat on the edge of the bed, her breaths fast and shallow. "I don't know if I can do this. What if last time was just a fluke, because I was sick?"

Taylor sat beside her and laid her hand on Bethany's forearm. "Just think 1939, 1939. Imagine the room like it was then."

Bethany squeezed her eyes shut. *1939, 1939.* The room would look no different. Except maybe that cross-stitch sampler on the opposite wall would be brighter. Maybe—

The dizziness hit, and she almost fell over. Then it passed. She opened her eyes.

The room before her lay unchanged. Outside the window, snow blanketed the ground.

Something rustled beside her, and her head whipped around. "Huh?"

Taylor gave her a lopsided smile. "I couldn't let you go alone."

Eighteen

At the sound of Mr. Pippin's Packard, Violet lifted Isaac to her shoulder and dashed to the window. The car's headlights pierced the night, preceding the vehicle into the driveway from the alley.

Mr. Pippin and Mr. Franco climbed out, then Mr. Pippin jerked the door to the back seat open. The hired man pulled out a cloth-covered, man-sized lump. Violet clutched Isaac tightly against her chest. Could it be…? Hefting their burden like a giant sack of potatoes, the two men carried it to the house. When they passed beneath the porch light, Violet recognized the shock of dark hair at one end where the sheet had slipped off.

Tony!

She laid Isaac in his cradle and crept to the doorway, listening to the footsteps plodding up the stairs. Mr. Thompkins rose from his chair as the two men rounded the corner, coming toward her. Violet moved to the doorway. "Mr. Pippin! What on earth—"

"Stand back, Charlotte," he barked. "This does not concern you."

She stepped back as they hefted Tony down the hall, into...

The conference room?

"I want the new lock installed on this door tonight," Mr. Pippin told Mr. Franco. "This man is a dangerous criminal, and must not go unguarded. Is that understood?"

The man mumbled his agreement, then Mr. Pippin's footsteps clacked toward her again.

She ducked inside her room, and pretended to check her hair in the mirror. Miss Meriwether had taken her shopping and to the beauty parlor, with Mr. Thompkins in tow, of course. Violet's new, tidy curls hadn't made her feel much better at the time, but now that Tony was here, she was glad she looked nice—

Tony! What would Mr. Pippin do to him? And when?

The footsteps slowed by her doorway, but didn't stop.

She slid the new barrettes from her hair and readied herself for bed. Somehow, she had to free Tony, before Mr. Pippin did something terrible, like turn him into a drooling idiot like poor Fred.

The next morning, a new, brass doorknob gleamed on the conference room door. Violet turned the knob and pushed, on the off chance that Mr. Franco, who didn't seem particularly bright, had left it unlocked. No such luck.

She bent and peered through the keyhole, but could see nothing but the window opposite. As she went downstairs to get something to eat, trucks pulled into Harrison Street, and men set up scaffolds against the House's front wall. "What on earth are they doing?" she asked Miss Meriwether.

The housekeeper waved. "Mr. Pippin say they don't need no windows in that conference room, so they be brickin' 'em in. Lord knows why." The woman held her hands up, then resumed washing the breakfast dishes.

In the twenty-first century, the conference room's windows were bricked-in.

Mr. Pippin was taking no chances.

Violet whiled the day away listening to old news on the radio, feeding and holding Isaac. She loved how his eyes followed her when he lay in his cradle, and how he tracked the movement of her hand above him while she held him on her lap. She loved the relaxed, contented feeling she got when she fed him, as if all were right with the world.

As if his father didn't lie captive down the hall, waiting to die—or worse.

That night, she retired early. After feeding Isaac at two a.m., she slipped out of her room.

She tiptoed past the conference room, past the recovery room. Somehow she knew which spots in the floor squeaked—from *before*, no doubt—and managed to avoid them. Mr. Pippin had sent his men home since installing the new lock on the conference room. He'd even permitted Isaac to spend the night in Violet's room. With Tony captive, she was no longer a threat—or use—to Mr. Pippin.

When she reached Mr. Pippin's suite at the other end of the hall, she stopped.

The door was shut. When she pressed her ear to it, she heard nothing but Mr. Pippin's light snores.

She slipped inside. Moonlight filtered in through gauzy curtains.

Plain and simple. A star-patterned quilt covered Mr. Pippin's sleeping form. Only a hurricane lamp and a small, wooden box graced the dresser.

A likely place for him to put the new conference room key.

A memory trickled into place that Mr. Pippin was highly intelligent, but not imaginative. Or was it something she'd learned about him during her stay in 1959?

She crept to the dresser, and lifted the box.

The lid wouldn't open.

She held it close to her, eyeing the patterned blocks. Between some were hairline gaps. It was one of those puzzle boxes.

Fine, she could figure it out. Turning on her heel, she tiptoed for the door—

"What do you think you're doing?"

She jumped and spun around.

Mr. Pippin was climbing out of bed, his striped nightshirt tails sliding through the sheets.

Her heart hammered. "Um, uh, how did I get here? Where am I?"

He snatched the box from her hands. "Do you think I am so foolish to believe your sleepwalking charade?"

She forced her voice to steady, hoping she sounded appropriately confused. "I- I don't understand. How did I get here?"

He slammed the box down on the dresser. "Out." He pointed down the hall, following her. Halfway there, he knocked on another, closed guest room door. "Miss Meriwether! Up!"

He stopped at Violet's room. "Inside," he ordered as a door squeaked from down the hall.

Violet stopped in the center of the room and whirled around. Mr. Pippin stood so that his face was inches away from hers, pointing as he spoke. "Did you forget our agreement?" He didn't wait for her to answer. "If you want to keep your child—"

"Sir?"

Mr. Pippin turned to the maid in the hall. "Miss Meriwether. Take the child. You will care for him for the time being—"

"No!" Violet shouted.

"—then return here, and keep watch over Miss Henderson. Apparently she cannot be trusted." He stepped back as the woman crept into the room and scooped the baby into her arms, giving Violet a wide-eyed, sympathetic glance as she passed.

Tears formed in Violet's eyes. "Isaac..."

Mr. Pippin carried the cradle out behind the maid. Violet fought the tears. She couldn't show any sign of weakness, or he'd have that much more the upper hand.

Mr. Pippin turned back to her. "Cooperate, and you'll be allowed to care for your son. Try something like that once more, and you'll never see him again." He waited until Miss Meriwether departed down the hall, then followed without so much as a good night.

Bethany woke in bed with a man.

She shrieked—or tried, but nothing came out, her mouth was so dry. Though his eyes were closed, the man's face mocked her as she struggled to move, her arms like lead weights filling her sleeves—

Just. Chill. Forcing herself to calm down, she looked around, and her panic dissipated.

The man—no, more like a boy, not much older than her—wasn't in her bed, but the one beside it. Behind him, a cross-stitch sampler on the log wall told her where she was. The Saturn Society House, in northern Tennessee.

As the fog cleared from her brain, she let her gaze wander back to the guy in the next bed. *Kinda cute.* Beneath longish, brown hair, and a light beard, his angular features had a youthful softness, emphasized by the sunlight spearing in through the lacy, white curtains. *Actually, he's* really *cute.*

The sheet had slipped down enough to reveal an old-fashioned-looking, drawstring-neck, white shirt—though maybe it wasn't old-fashioned in 1939. She glanced at the pegs on the wall across the room. The fringed, buckskin jacket hanging beside her and Taylor's coats sure didn't look very 1939.

She turned around. Taylor lay in the next bed. Her pointy shoes sat beneath it, and one red-and-white-striped-stockinged foot stuck out from under the covers. The slow rise and fall of her chest told Bethany that like the cute guy, Taylor was still in recovery.

Bethany stood—slowly, she reminded herself—then traipsed to the doorway and stuck her head into the hall. It, too, looked the same as it had in her time, and in 1976, except—

A kerosene lamp graced the doily-covered stand at the end of the hall instead of a telephone. "Hello?" she called.

A female exclamation came from somewhere in the House as a chair scraped the floor. A girl about her age emerged from the living room, followed by a woman in her late thirties or forties. In their plaid, cotton dresses, and the older woman with her hair pulled back, they looked straight out of *The Waltons*, that old TV show her grandma loved. Margaret LeBeau, Bethany recalled from when she'd first jumped into 1939, before she slipped into recovery. The woman had helped her off with her shoes, and assured her there would be food available when she woke from recovery. She hadn't seen Florie.

The older woman nodded to the girl. "Hello," the girl said, "I'm Florence LeBeau, and this is my mother, Margaret. Welcome to our House—"

Bethany's eyebrows shot up. "Florie?"

The other girl's expression echoed hers. "Have we met?"

"Uh, yeah. Or we will. Or..." Bethany looked down. "Jeez, this is all so confusing."

"It's all right," Mrs. LeBeau said. "You're new at this, aren't you, honey?"

Bethany nodded.

"Can I get you something to eat?"

"That would be wonderful." Bethany patted her vest, reassured by the cylindrical lumps where her supplies were.

After the best chicken sandwich she'd ever eaten, she wandered back to the recovery room with Florie. The other girl—how weird that she was Bethany's age!—moved to the bed where the guy still slept, and checked the pitcher on the nightstand.

Bethany peered at her friend in the first bed. "What about Taylor? Why isn't she awake yet?"

Florie tore her gaze away from the guy long enough to answer. "Recovery time can vary. She'll probably wake within an hour or so."

"Oh. Okay." Bethany chewed the insides of her lips. "Where's the bathroom?" The door off the recovery room was gone.

"Bathroom?" Florie's soft, Southern accent made the statement sound extra-apologetic. "Oh, you mean the privy? I'm afraid we don't have indoor plumbing yet."

After Bethany donned her shoes and coat, she followed Florie to an outhouse behind the House. A bad feeling settled over her, like the snow that coated the ground and fell in big, clumpy flakes on Florie's dark hair. These people looked way too old-fashioned. And didn't people have indoor bathrooms and phones in 1939? Maybe everyone didn't have a phone, but the Society had plenty of money, according to the Florie she knew. "What year is this, anyway?" Bethany asked.

"1939. Not what you'd been looking for?"

Relief washed through Bethany. "Yeah. But... you don't have a phone? Or a bathroom?"

Florie laughed. "There aren't any phone lines out this far. Lawsy, we just got electricity a couple years ago. The Society's payin' for us to build an indoor privy, we're just waiting on the money." She stopped a few feet away from the wooden booth. "You looking for anything special here'n this time period?"

"My dad." Bethany's voice hitched. "He's here in this time somewhere, and he's in trouble."

"Ma said y'all were from the twenty-first century—your daddy's Society, too?"

"Yes." Bethany almost could smile. They were *Society*. It sounded so uppity—and weird. "I need to go to Hollowville to pick him up at the train station, whenever the train from Dayton arrives."

"Ohio? There's only one train from up'n those parts, and it won't get here 'till three. We've got plenty of time."

When Bethany returned to the House, Mrs. Le Beau stood in the foyer, handing a set of car keys to Florie.

Florie glanced down the hall toward the recovery room. "Why don't you take her? I'll stay here in case our other visitors wake up."

"Oh, no you don't. You've done spent enough time moonin' over that young man, and we don't even know when he's from." Mrs. LeBeau thrust the keys at Florie. "Besides, you've been wantin' to do more driving." She looked up as Bethany crossed the room. "I'll bet Miss Solomon knows how to drive, don't you?"

Bethany hesitated. "Uh... yeah. But probably not your truck." If they even had automatic transmissions in 1939, the farm truck would be stick. "My dad was going to teach me, but..." She turned up her hands. "That was before he disappeared." Soon, she'd be reunited with him—she hoped.

Unless something happened to screw everything up.

Sadness flitted across Florie's face as she took the keys from her mom and slipped her coat on. "Let's go, then."

The heaviness lifted from Bethany's heart. At last, they were *doing* something.

The truck looked like something from a gangster movie, and tingles raced over Bethany's body as the reality of what she'd done sank in. *I've travelled back in time, almost a century!* And her dad was here, too.

The door creaked as she opened it and climbed in. Florie started the vehicle, then trundled down the gravel drive toward the bridge.

Bethany flinched as the truck rolled onto the rickety-looking, wooden framed structure, and kept her gaze forward. "So... what's the deal with that guy in the recovery room?" She tried to get her mind off the creepy bridge that seemed to go on and on.

"He appeared early this morning." Florie steered the truck over the end of the bridge with a big bump. "He said... he's from the year 1756. Just a couple years after our House was first built."

"But I thought... Taylor said it's not possible to jump into the future."

"That's what we thought, too. Mama thinks maybe he was confused, and said the wrong thing, like maybe he was coming back from a trip to 1756. I'll be real interested to hear his story when he recovers."

"Yeah, if he came from two hundred years ago, that'll be awhile, won't it?"

"Yes, if he's from our time. If he's really from the past, we have no idea. I just want to be there when he does wake up."

"He's pretty hot," Bethany said. That was probably why Florie'd wanted to stay with him, rather than drive her into town.

Florie gave her a perplexed look. "He's feverish? He was fine when I checked—"

Bethany laughed. "No, in my time, if a guy's hot, it means he's good-looking."

"Oh." Pink tinged Florie's cheeks. "Well, he's certainly that, then. So is an unattractive person cold in your time?"

"No, that means they're unemotional."

"That's no different from now."

"But *cool* means something's good."

"Words and phrases sound very confusing in your time!" Florie downshifted to navigate a tight curve Bethany was pretty sure hadn't been there in 1976. Of course, by then, the road was paved and wide enough to for two cars to easily pass.

After what seemed like hours, they finally approached a little town nestled in a valley.

Bethany's belly went queasy when she saw the town's sign. Welcome to Hollowville, Tennessee. She couldn't stop herself from making a face.

"What's wrong?" Florie asked.

"Last time Taylor and I came to Hollowville, we weren't very welcome. Do the people here know what you—or your mom—can do?"

"You mean time travel? Of course not. It's Society policy to keep it quiet. Why?"

"When Taylor and I came here before—in our time—we called yo— the Society, and as soon as we said the name, people started going off on us, calling us witches." Her hands twitched in her lap.

Florie touched Bethany's forearm. "As far as anyone else knows, we're just ordinary farm folk. Well-to-do ones, but nothing different aside from that." She parked the truck in front of the train station, which looked like little more than a small house with white, wooden siding and a long porch across the back.

Bethany gazed around the town as she climbed out of the truck.

On the biggest building, a two-story, white wood structure, hung a sign identifying it as the Hollowville General Store, with Post Office in smaller letters beneath the name. The other big building had a triangle marquis sticking out from above the doors, with a light bulb-framed sign that read *The Wizard of Oz in Technicolor.* "Whoa," she breathed. Gangster-movie cars and trucks, as well as boxy, older, Model-T type cars, parked around a snowy town square, with an American flag in the middle that whipped in the wind. It was like something from a TV show.

Florie tapped her on the elbow. "Don't gawk," she whispered. "Y'need to look like you fit in."

Bethany shut her mouth, but she couldn't stop smiling, especially since it was Florie herself who'd explained—or *would* explain—the Society's policies to her, almost forty years in the future.

They clomped up the wooden steps into the train station.

The single room was bare except for two benches that looked like church pews, a wall clock that said two-thirty, and a potbellied stove, where a guy wearing a green visor stood warming his hands. Beside him, faded poster pictures with old-fashioned-looking scenes of New York, Chicago, and California broke the plain white of the walls. A brighter white rectangle showed where another poster had hung until recently, beside a window with a sign above it that read Tickets.

Florie marched up to the man. "Excuse me, sir, when does the train from Dayton, Ohio arrive?"

"Ain't no trains from Dayton." The man glanced at the white rectangle. "They jus' changed all the schedules, lemme see what else we got." He scurried through a door beside the faded area, then appeared in the ticket window, unfolding a poster. "Nothin' from up north 'till tomorrow. From Cincinnat-uh, at two-fifty-five."

Bethany's lip quivered. If there was no train, then where was her dad? Keith's instructions had been very clear. Then something else occurred to her.

She stepped away from the ticket window. "What day is it?" she whispered to Florie.

The other girl cocked her head. "Wednesday."

"I mean the date."

"December twentieth?"

Bethany palmed her forehead as relief settled over her. "We're a day early."

Florie thanked the ticket seller and they exited the station. "We can go to the general store and ring the Dayton House, see if your daddy's there," she suggested.

"That's cool," Bethany said.

Florie arched an eyebrow, then smiled. "Oh yes, that means good."

In the store, shoppers clogged the aisles, and eleven people waited in line for the cashier. "Where's the phone?" Bethany asked.

Florie pointed at the counter. "It's different in—where you're from?" she whispered.

Better not tell her about cell phones. Bethany nodded and went back to sneaking glances at the other customers and what was in their baskets and cloth satchels. One shopper paid, and the line crept forward. "Is it always this crowded?"

Florie shook her head. "There's a big snowstorm comin' in tomorrow, so everyone's stocking up. Ma came out yesterday and got gas for the generator, plus we got canned goods from the summer."

It seemed to take forever before Florie finally reached the counter and greeted the cashier. "I need to make a phone call, please."

"Sure thing, Miss LeBeau." The white-aproned man pushed the telephone—a strange-looking thing with a big dial on front—across the counter. "Where're you calling?"

"Dayton, Ohio." She reached into her pocket for a couple of bills and dropped them onto the counter. The woman in line behind them stared with wide eyes, and Bethany realized what was pocket change to her was a lot of money to most people in 1939.

Ten minutes later they were headed back to Florie's House, with good news. Florie had reached the Watchkeeper in Dayton, a man named Theodore Pippin, who'd told them that Tony Solomon was indeed in this time, and was still in recovery. Florie offered to put Bethany on a train or bus, which sounded cool but kind of scary. Bethany had never traveled alone in her own time, much less decades before she'd be born. There was a bus heading north, but not until the next day, and her dad would be in Tennessee by then. So they decided to return to town the next day, and if her dad somehow wasn't on that train, Bethany would leave for Dayton then.

As soon as they got back to the House, Florie bolted for the recovery room, anxious to check on the cute guy, no doubt. Taylor had already woken from recovery. She'd changed into a 1930s dress, and sat at the trestle table in the dining room eating stew with Mrs. LeBeau. Bethany explained that they'd arrived a day earlier than planned. "My dad's in this time, in Dayton. The guy who runs the House said he should wake from recovery soon."

Taylor stopped with her spoon halfway to her mouth. "What was this guy's name?"

"Pippin," Bethany said. "Like the guy in *Lord of the Rings*—"

"Oh, God," Taylor said.

"What?" Bethany's good mood trickled away.

"No one told you about the Black Book," Taylor said. "I didn't even think about it, since they stopped printing it long before our time."

Fear seeped down Bethany's spine. "What's—"

"A Society publication that lists those who break the Code," Mrs. LeBeau squeezed the cloth napkin in her hands. "Usually by bending the past to suit their own wishes. Those in the Book who are caught are dealt with rather harshly, a new treatment called a... lobotomy."

"We have a guy living at our House who got that," Taylor said. "He went back to the twenties, to get his great grandpa to buy all the right stocks and stuff—and got caught. He's majorly fucked up—" Florie's eyes went round "—pretty much a drooling idiot. But he never travels in time, that's for sure."

Bethany gulped in a breath. "That weird guy moaning and groaning that you had to go take care of, when the cops were there?"

"Yup."

"Some of us don't agree with the punishment, or think it's a good thing to track folk from the future," Mrs. LeBeau said. "But Mr. Pippin is one of the Book's staunchest supporters."

Taylor swallowed, squeezing the napkin in a fist. "Beth, your dad's in the Book."

"Why? Daddy would never—"

"I don't know. But if Pippin has him, he's in big trouble."

Bethany swallowed. "But Keith said Daddy'd be on that train for sure. He must get away from that Pippin dude somehow."

Possibilities turned over in her mind. Florie'd told her it was an all-day drive to Dayton. But even if they took the truck and left right away, there was no way they'd get there before morning, especially with the snowstorm coming in. And that was if Mr. Pippin didn't do something to her dad before they arrived.

They ate in somber silence until Florie jumped up. "May I be excused, Mama?"

Mrs. LeBeau tipped her head at Florie's half-eaten stew with a questioning look.

Florie shuffled her feet. "I just thought I'd better check on Mr. Allen."

Mrs. LeBeau let out a sigh. "Make it snappy." The girl dashed away.

Bethany and Taylor looked at each other. Bethany raised an eyebrow. "Mr. Allen?"

Tight-lipped, Taylor moved her head in tiny, quick shakes.

"Oh, yeah." Bethany took a bite of biscuit. The Society Code. If that guy was how Florie would become *Mrs.* Allen, they'd better not tell, or it might change something.

"You know something about our other guest?" Mrs. LeBeau asked.

"We may have heard of him," Taylor said.

"Or maybe not." Bethany reached for the butter. "It's not exactly an unusual name."

Mrs. LeBeau held up a hand and nodded. "Say no more."

Florie returned to the table. "No change."

"I could've told you that," her mother said.

The rest of the meal passed in silence as Bethany tried not to think about her dad, or that creepy guy moaning and yelling that time at Taylor's House. The guy who'd gotten the lobotomy treatment from that Theodore Pippin. The bite of biscuit lodged in her throat. She coughed.

"Bethany?" Mrs. LeBeau jumped up, but Taylor patted Bethany's back. The biscuit went down.

"You okay?" Taylor asked.

Bethany nodded as she dabbed her mouth with her napkin. "Just worried about my dad."

"How much do you trust this Keith fella's word?" Mrs. LeBeau asked.

With shaking hands, Bethany lowered her napkin to her lap. "With my life. I guess Daddy's, too."

Violet thought she heard footsteps in the locked conference room when Mr. Thompkins brought her back upstairs. Later, Mr. Pippin walked past with Mr. Franco, who bore a tray containing a sandwich, a bowl of soup, and a bottle of milk.

She leaned out her door, earning a scowl from Mr. Thompkins. Mr. Pippin unlocked the conference room door and slipped inside. Mr. Franco followed, then the door shut. Violet strained to hear, but the heavy door muffled Mr. Pippin's words, though she thought she heard him say something about another attempt to escape. She couldn't hear Tony's response at all. A few minutes later, Mr. Pippin and his man emerged, minus the tray. Mr. Pippin continued to the recovery room, but the others went back downstairs.

In the hall, the phone rang. Mr. Pippin rushed from the recovery room to snatch it up. "Hello?"

Violet tiptoed to the door and listened.

"Tony Solomon?" Mr. Pippin said. "Yes, he's here. I'm afraid he's still in recovery... his daughter? I had no idea others in his family had the gift..." Violet's ears perked up. *They did?* "No, keep Bethany with you," Mr. Pippin said. "I have a guest slated to arrive shortly who can watch my House. As soon as Solomon wakes, we'll head for Cumberland Gap and meet you." He hung up and returned to the recovery room.

Violet drew away. Tony's daughter was a time traveler, too? And she was at the Cumberland Gap House? Florie's?

She remembered their hostess's vehement response at the mention of Theodore Pippin. Did Florie's aversion to Pippin have something to do with Tony? Or Bethany?

She peered at the conference room door down the hall and clenched her jaw. Mr. Pippin had gotten another phone call during dinner, from a Dr. Caruthers, whom Mr. Pippin said was "quite fond" of her. The name didn't sound familiar, but names never did. What troubled her more was that the doctor was due to arrive in the morning to "take care of" Tony.

Somehow, she had to spring him before then.

She stepped into the hallway. Mr. Thompkins shot her a look. "I need to use the necessary," she said.

"Go ahead," he grunted. He didn't rise from his wooden folding chair, so she made her way to the washroom, glancing in the recovery room as she passed. Alpha's feet formed motionless bumps in the second bed, but that was all Violet could see of her.

Water ran in the recovery room's tiny bathroom. Mr. Pippin must be refilling the water pitcher they always kept at a recovering traveler's bedside. Good.

In the washroom, Violet made a pretense of using the toilet, then ran some water while she slid one of the barrettes from her hair.

She hurried past the recovery room, then stopped in front of the conference room. Mr. Thompkins barely glanced up from his newspaper. She loosened her hand. The barrette fell to the floor with a click.

"Just what are you doing, Charlotte?" Mr. Pippin said from behind her.

She jumped. "I... I was only wondering how our visitor is doing, sir." She leaned toward the recovery room door and kept her gaze on his face as she surreptitiously kicked the barrette, praying it went under the conference room door.

"Our guest in the recovery room has not yet awoken. Our other guest..." —he glanced at the locked door—"is none of your concern."

"Oh, but he is." A quick glance down revealed that she hadn't kicked the barrette quite far enough. "I told you how frightening it was, being pulled into the twenty-first century." She kept his gaze while she shifted her foot. "What I didn't tell you was that it was his fault that I went there in the first place. He grabbed me, wouldn't let me go, and when the Pull took him..." She made an exaggerated shrug as she kicked the barrette. "When I woke, I was all alone. I had no idea where I was. Or when. No one knew me.

"I've seen the time bubbles, Mr. Pippin. I've heard the horror stories. An enormous bridge, disappearing. Entire communities stricken with smallpox, which had been eradicated in that time. All because of time distortions. His meddling..."

His face softened. "Charlotte, I appreciate your concern. But fear not, he'll be dealt with as soon as Dr. Caruthers arrives."

"Thank heavens," Violet said as he walked her down the hall. "I was tiring of the charade. I declare, the only good to come of it was Isaac. I fear if left to his own devices, Tony Solomon would take even him away from me."

Mr. Pippin made clucking sounds of sympathy. "I guarantee you he won't, my dear. Now back to your room, I hear the babe starting to fuss."

As she slipped into her room, Violet glanced back at the conference room door. *Please let him find the barrette...*

A sliver of moonlight escaped Violet's slightly ajar door when Tony approached.

He stood in the hall, watching the sleeping guard and the lump in Violet's bed at the same time. Without his glasses, they were just blurs, but neither moved beyond the slight rise and fall of breathing, so he crept inside.

His heart swelled at the sight of Isaac in a handmade, wooden cradle, his face to one side, arms stretched over his head. Tony's gaze lingered on Violet. *Totally Charlotte,* especially with her short, brown curls and 1930s night gown. She lay on her side, angelic in sleep. His heart clenched, and longing to lie down beside her swept through him.

Appearances lie. Especially after what he'd heard that afternoon, on top of what she'd told the men from the Order.

He squatted down carefully, so that the bottles in the duffel bag he'd stolen from Pippin's coat closet wouldn't clank. One bottle of corn syrup, he'd swiped from the larder. The other was half-full of milk, left from the prior morning's delivery. It would have to do until he could purchase proper baby formula with the money he'd snagged from Pippin's wallet.

The slacks he'd swiped from the recovery room's closet stretched across his ass as he crouched beside the cradle to slip the sleeping infant into his arms. He prayed they didn't rip. Too small, but it was either that, or a twenty-first century hospital gown. Luckily, he'd found a pair of stiff, lace-up shoes he'd been able to stuff his feet into.

He slid his hands beneath Isaac's head and legs, and slowly lifted him, blankets and all. Amazingly, the baby didn't wake. Tony clutched the sleeping infant to his chest. As he tiptoed to the door, Isaac made a tiny hiccupping sound. Tony pressed himself to the wall, barely daring to breathe.

Violet shifted, but didn't wake. Tony let out his breath and crept out the door.

Nineteen

It was still dark when Tony reached the train station. The weather was mild, but still cold enough that his face was numb from the wind. No surprise, considering it was just after four A.M.—the coldest hour of the day.

He shifted his arm over the duffel bag, concealed beneath the overcoat he'd stolen from Pippin. He ought to feel bad about taking it, but couldn't dredge up the guilt. Not when the guy wanted to do worse than kill him, and probably Isaac, as well.

Isaac gurgled, the first sound he'd made since Tony had taken him from the House. It was almost like the infant knew his safety— maybe his life—depended on his silence.

Tony wrapped the coat more tightly around the baby, then yanked the door open with his free hand. Warmth billowed out as he walked in, his pilfered shoes clacking on the tile.

He blinked in the bright light, and gazed in amazement at the station that was razed before he was born. The huge clock above the arched windows read four twenty, big enough he could read it even without his glasses. Few commuters shuffled between the ticket sellers and the gates, but traffic would undoubtedly pick up soon.

He forced himself to stop looking over his shoulder and act like he belonged there as he approached the ticket seller's window.

"Where to?" The man didn't look up from beneath his green visor.

Shit, he hadn't thought that far ahead. "Sir?" This time, the ticket seller looked up.

"Uh, what's the first train you've got heading south?"

"Schedule's posted right behind you."

Tony glanced where the main pointed, but all he could make out was a white rectangle with blurred, gray lines. He turned back to the ticket seller. "Uh, I can't read it. I lost my glasses a couple days ago, and..." He shrugged. "No money to buy new ones." That, at least, was truthful.

"Oh." The man looked down. "We've got a five-oh-five to Cincinnati, and from there, you can get to just about anywhere south."

"Okay." Tony shifted Isaac on his left arm while he dug into the coat's voluminous pocket for the wad of cash he'd also swiped from Pippin.

Isaac cooed.

The ticket seller eyed Tony's chest curiously.

Shit. Well, no point in trying to hide him. Tony leaned over so the coat gapped open. "Does he need a ticket?"

"Babes in arms, no." He leaned forward. "My, that's a little one."

"Um, yeah, he's six weeks old." Nervousness trickled over Tony like a colony of ants. What if Violet and Pippin had already reported him to the police? "His mother... died a few days ago. I'm, uh, taking him to some relatives who can help take care of him."

It wasn't totally a lie. Violet was dead—to him, at least. If there was anyone in this wretched time who'd give him sanctuary, it was Florie. And being with the Society made her a sister of sorts, didn't it?

Still, lying to the guy made him want to sink through the elegantly-tiled floor. He couldn't meet the ticket seller's eyes as the man handed him his ticket.

As Tony fumbled with the money,, Isaac's little noises became whimpers. Tony paid for the ticket, then made his way to a wooden bench.

He unbuttoned his coat enough to lay Isaac on his lap, just like he used to with Bethany. He rocked him side to side, but Isaac's whining turned into full-out crying. He held the baby against his shoulder and swayed back and forth, but Isaac wouldn't be consoled.

It had been hours since he'd heard Violet's voice from down the hall, her words soft and gentle, as she undoubtedly fed Isaac.

Guilt tore through him. He shouldn't have taken the baby. He wasn't suited to care for him, what the hell was he doing—

Saving him from the Society, and Pippin. And from a mother who couldn't be trusted. Tony tried to ignore the squeeze around his heart as he dug through his duffel bag.

He poured some of the corn syrup into the milk. Thank God he remembered hearing his grandma talk about doing that to feed his mom, when she'd been unable to nurse. Only Tony didn't know how much corn syrup to put in the milk. He swirled the milk bottle around to mix the stuff, then held Isaac in his left arm while he tipped the bottle to the baby's mouth.

At first, Isaac tried to suck the edge of the bottle, but after it dribbled down his face, he caught on and slurped as fast as Tony tipped the bottle up. Smart kid. Or just a really hungry one.

Tony's stomach grumbled. He glanced at the clock. Five minutes to five. His own needs would have to wait.

Charlotte—Violet—had to have known who she was. She'd made up the whole amnesia thing so she could pick up where she left off in 1933. The only thing that didn't add up were the years she'd spent in the twenty-first century before she'd found him.

And the barrette. Was it possible she'd dropped it on purpose?

He hadn't allowed himself to think as he used it to pick the new lock on the conference room door. It was a chance he couldn't take. Not after what she'd said to Pippin. She'd probably dropped it while twirling her hair.

A man hollered that the train for Cincinnati was leaving. *Shit!* Looping the duffel bag's strap over one arm, Tony hurried toward the gate, baby in one arm, the bottle in the other.

"Excuse me, sir!" a man called from behind him.

He glanced backward. The ticket agent had emerged from his booth and waved frantically at Tony.

Fuck! Tony bolted for the train.

Violet woke before dawn. Enough light seeped into the window from the nearby streetlight that she could see it was a few minutes before five. Odd. Isaac usually cried for a feeding well before then. She crept to the cradle.

It was empty. Not only was Isaac gone, but the blankets were missing, as well.

Her breath hung up in her throat. Tony! He'd taken the baby.

Don't be silly. Her stomach settled a bit. She hadn't slept well, tossing and turning with worry over Tony. Chances were, Miss Meriwether had heard the baby fussing. She'd taken him out to calm him, no doubt.

But as Violet walked into the hall, her heart lodged in her throat. The conference room door lay ajar.

Hesitantly, she peered inside. A pillow and a wad of blankets lay on the floor. But no one was in the room. A quick survey of the second floor confirmed that Mr. Pippin and Alpha still lay abed, and it was Miss Meriwether's day off.

She stole through the House, searching, though she already knew what she'd find.

Isaac was gone. And Tony had taken him.

Violet threw on her coat and strode for the front door. She didn't know where Tony had taken Isaac, but she couldn't very well search for him, trapped in the Society House. But as she reached for the doorknob, a rough hand latched onto her shoulder and hauled her backward.

"Just where do you think you're going, Charlotte?"

"I- Isaac…" She whirled and faced Mr. Pippin. "He's gone! And Tony took him."

He pushed her toward the stairs. "Back to your room! Now!"

Though she couldn't imagine him striking her, she hurried upstairs. She'd have to figure out another escape, before Mr. Thompkins returned.

In her room, she fought the urge to cringe as Mr. Pippin paced back and forth. "You planned this!" He pointed at her.

"I didn't!" Violet took a step backward, stumbling as her leg smacked into her bed. "Why would I let that man take my baby?"

"Your feelings for him are no secret," Mr. Pippin snapped. "And don't try to tell me that you were sleepwalking. I wouldn't put it past you to let Solomon take the child if that would cast doubt on your allegiance to him, until you could sneak out and join them."

"I never—" She fell onto the bed as vertigo struck her.

After it passed, she rose and faced Mr. Pippin, who was pushing himself off the wall. His eyes met hers. She followed him into the recovery room.

The air in her lungs thickened into a sluggish, viscous mass. "Tony," she whispered. He'd gotten a haircut. "But how—"

The misplaced gleam in the blue eyes behind the man's glasses told her this wasn't the man she loved.

"Decided to come back and turn yourself in, have you?" Mr. Pippin rushed to the bed where the man sat.

"Where's—" Violet began.

"I'm not the one you seek."

The man's British accent and deep voice were a stab in Violet's gut. "You!"

His lips spread into a leering grin. "It'll take more'n a pair of scissors to off me, lady."

"What's—" Mr. Pippin sputtered. "You- you're not—"

"Despite my appearance, I'm not Tony Solomon." A wicked gleam sparkled in his eye, sending a chill through Violet. "But I'll gladly help you catch the blackguard—"

"He's a murderer!" Violet found her voice. "This man tried to kill me! He killed—"

"Enough!" Mr. Pippin glared at her, then spoke quietly. "This man is undoubtedly a relative of Solomon's. No doubt burned by—"

"Yes, yes, a distant cousin," the lookalike agreed. "The lady has things quite confused. It's Solomon who's the murderer, not I. Why do you suppose he's in the Black Book?"

"Yes, of course," Mr. Pippin said. The man started to slide off his boots. "Make yourself comfortable, then. If there's anything—"

"I'll be sure to inform you," the man said.

Mr. Pippin ushered Violet out of the room. She tried to argue. "But he's—"

"Enough! Now back to your room while I try to find out where the miscreant went. Unless there's something you're not telling—"

"No!" Violet stumbled as he pushed her inside and slammed the door behind her.

She sat on the bed, defeated. The empty cradle and her breasts, heavy with milk, mocked her.

Isaac was gone. Tony, too. He must have heard her in the hallway speaking with Mr. Pippin, trying to convince the Watchkeeper she was on his side. Tears sprang to her eyes. Why hadn't she kept silent?

Violet paced across the tiny guest room, which seemed to grow tinier as the morning went on. She cried. She expressed milk into a cup like she'd read about in her books before that horrible man who looked like Tony tried to kill her and she'd been whisked away from everything she knew. Somehow, she'd get out of there and find him. When she did, Isaac would need to eat.

She tried to lose herself by listening to the radio, but it worked for less than five seconds.

If she'd only been there a bit longer, she might get the Pull, and return to the twenty-first century, where Tony would surely take Isaac. But he wouldn't have the Pull yet either. There was no escape that way.

She listened for Mr. Pippin's footsteps. At least she was safe from the killer in the recovery room for the time being.

The front door squealed. Someone came in, a man, though his voice didn't carry well enough for her to hear.

But Mr. Pippin's did. "...watch the House for me," he said amidst shuffling sounds of the man taking off his coat. "I regret that I need to leave you when you're fatigued from driving, but I must drive to northern Tennessee. Margaret LeBeau is hosting a young girl who's new to our ranks, and none other than Solomon's daughter. I have no doubt that's where he's headed."

"Not to worry; I spent the night in Columbus." She'd heard this other man's voice before. "Go get him, and we'll get the job done."

Arrows pierced Violet's heart. Tony! But her grim resolve returned. She didn't care about Tony. A man who'd steal a baby away from his mother deserved whatever Mr. Pippin would dole out. But Isaac... would the crimes of his parents make him guilty by association?

She searched the room, though she knew there was nothing there to help her escape, not even a hairpin. Mr. Pippin had made sure of that, once he found her barrette on the conference room floor.

Heavy footsteps trod the stairs. "I'm packed and ready to go, all you need to do is watch over the folk in recovery," Mr. Pippin said. The man mumbled an assent. "And Charlotte. She's in the room at the head of the stairs. She must be watched closely."

The footsteps reached the landing then drew closer. "She helped him escape again?" the other man said.

His voice made her skin feel as if it had suddenly shrunk.

She knew this man from *before*, and it hadn't been pleasant.

"She denies it, but..." Mr. Pippin's voice faded as the footsteps moved down the hall.

The floor creaked outside her room. Violet stared at the gap at the bottom of the door.

That man was out there. Dr. Caruthers, who'd phoned Mr. Pippin the day before.

Footsteps neared again, then something thunked on the floor, probably Mr. Pippin's suitcase. "I suggest you ring my men to help keep an eye on Charlotte," Mr. Pippin said. "Fellow in charge is Alfred Thompkins, the information's on my desk—"

"I'm sure I'll manage just fine," Dr. Caruthers said.

Mr. Pippin grumbled. "Miss Meriwether's due at six. She'll help with the cooking and cleaning, but if you choose not to engage Mr. Thompkins, be sure to attend Charlotte yourself, as I've no doubt she could overpower Miss Meriwether. She's... changed since you last saw her."

Violet wadded her skirt in her fists. The idea that she'd use force against the kind housekeeper! But if she had to, to get to Isaac, she would.

"Nothing to worry about, old boy." The doctor's voice grew slimier every time he spoke. "I'm sure Charlotte and I will get on just fine."

Violet's lip curled.

The footsteps retreated, then the front door slammed. Violet moved to the window to watch the maroon Packard trundle out the alley.

Scarcely a minute passed before feet trod the stairs and a key rattled in the door.

Her gut twisted as the door swung open. "Hello, Charlotte." The doctor stepped inside.

Violet forced herself to stand, put herself closer to his level, instead of flinching and curling into a ball like she wanted to do.

Average height, neither heavy nor thin, his vest concealed the typical physique of a middle-aged man who did little to exert himself. His light brown hair was slicked back in the manner common to the time. His blue eyes sparkled.

She didn't want to respond to him at all, but not doing so would show her unease. "Hello." Her voice was flat, emotionless.

His gaze dropped to her breasts and lingered. "Teddy's right, you have changed."

She lifted her chin. "In what way?"

"You don't look happy to see me." He drew a finger up the underside of her chin.

She fought the urge to recoil. "Should I be?" The tension in her gut dropped lower, making her squeeze her legs tightly together.

"Ah, well, no matter. I'm glad to see you, my dear. I hope that soon you and I will once again be doing the Society's great work together, like the time you brought Fred Cheltenham to justice. It was one of your finest moments."

Her fingers clawed at her skirt as she remembered what Tony had told her about Charlotte, before she'd learned that was *her*.

She'd brought Fred to his doom. Nausea rose in her belly. "I- I'm afraid I don't remember."

He looked her in the eyes. "Then you also don't remember that we were to be married?"

She couldn't stop her mouth from sliding open. Time crawled to a halt as she processed the implications. "No..." she whispered. She would have never married this man.

"You wound me, Charlotte." He pressed closer. She stepped back, falling backward onto the bed.

"No—" He stifled her protest in a kiss so forceful her head pressed into the mattress.

She clawed at his face. He drew back enough that she could twist away. "No! I would have never—"

As he grabbed her hands, his fingers slid over the scar on her right palm. He drew back, still clutching he wrist. "Well, well, what's this?" He turned her hand over, studying it. "Teddy was right. Though I doubt it's a sign from God, as that silly maid says. But I bet you and I'll have a divine time." His hands clamped around her wrists, and he pinned her to the bed. Déjà vu burst through her. Terror. She'd known this man, she was certain. Intimately. And not by her choice.

He sank onto her, his weight crushing her tender breasts, and invaded her lips again, his tongue swirling against her teeth.

She clamped her jaw down.

He jerked off her, screaming. "Bitch!"

She sprang from the bed as he lunged at her. Her leg shot out, her foot catching him in the solar plexus. She fell back on the bed as he backed up a step, then launched himself at her.

She rolled away and jumped to her feet. He crashed onto the bed, but recovered quickly.

He swore as he advanced on her. She danced away, but he caught her wrist and yanked her to him. "Think you can get away, huh, bitch?"

She twisted in his grasp, ignoring the pain in her wrist as he clamped down harder, and brought her knee up into his crotch.

He let go, doubling over in pain. "You goddamn whore! I swear, I'll..."

As he straightened, she took a step backward and—

Hellfire! He'd backed her into the corner. But when he came toward her, she lifted her leg and thrust her foot at him with all her strength, connecting at his crotch.

Something crushed beneath her toe. The doctor howled, clutching himself, and fell to the floor in a ball. "You... you bitch!"

She leapt over him and bolted for the hall, almost colliding with Alpha. "Violet?" the woman asked. "What's wrong, I just woke—"

"That man tried to rape me! I've got to get out—" She shoved her way past and ran for the stairs.

"Violet, wait!" Alpha called.

Hurtling down the stairs, she spied a man's coat on the rack in the foyer. Something in the pocket jingled as she grabbed it, threw it on, and rushed outside. Dr. Caruthers's, she realized.

A shiny, dark green Cadillac sat in the gravel parking area, next to the garage. She thrust her hand into the coat's pocket and came up with a ring containing over a dozen keys. Hopefully, one would start the car.

A yank on the car door revealed it was locked. She glanced at the House as she fumbled through the keys, expecting the doctor to come running after her. But as her hand lit on one bearing a GM emblem, the House's back door flew open and Alpha burst out. "Violet! Wait!"

Violet jammed the key into the car door and turned it, tugging the door open as Alpha reached her side. "I tied him up with the sheets." Alpha ran around the car to the passenger side, her unbuttoned, period-appropriate, fur coat flapping as Violet climbed behind the wheel. "He'll eventually get loose... let's get out of here!"

Violet hesitated. A brief thought flitted through her mind that she shouldn't take the woman, but she dismissed the silly notion. If not for Alpha's intervention, Dr. Caruthers could have recovered and reached her while she hunted for the car key.

She flipped the lock on the passenger door. "Get in." The car started with a roar. Alpha had barely shut her door as Violet threw the car into gear and rumbled down the alley, tamping down her misgivings.

Alpha had helped her. Returning the favor was the least Violet could do.

Twenty

Bethany prayed Mrs. LeBeau's truck would make it to town. The clattering engine sounded like it was on its last legs. It had run fine the day before, but the temperature had dropped overnight, and Florie hadn't been able to start it until her mother dragged out the battery charger and they'd let it sit for a good hour.

Snow fell in fine, white flakes that blanketed the driveway, and made it seem even bumpier than the day before. Trying to avoid jostling Taylor in the ribs, Bethany gripped the purse Florie had given her in the twenty-first century. She stared out the window at the snow-covered fields and woods as they bumped and bounced down the mountain road, praying her dad was on the train—and that he'd escaped the Society House in Dayton. "I hope we find my dad before that Pippin guy."

Florie whipped the wheel around and corrected the truck out of a slide. "Ma says if that Mr. Pippin fellow knows where he went, he'll come after him. But hopefully, your daddy got enough of a head start."

Bethany frowned. "But it's only like a five hour drive—"

"Hello, Beth." Taylor knocked on Bethany's head. "Cars don't go as fast as they do in our time. Especially with no I-75."

"Oh, yeah."

"What's I-75?" Florie's face lit up in curiosity.

"A big high..." Bethany trailed off when she caught Taylor's warning look.

"I'm sorry, I shouldn't have asked. I know better," Florie said.

"No problem," Taylor said. "But you have to be more careful, Beth. Florie's one of us, but…"

"What's the big deal about a road?" Bethany could see the dangers of telling Florie her future husband lay in the recovery room, but the interstate? "I get the idea, but what could she do?"

"I'd invest in property," Florie said.

"Yeah, but who has the money in this time?" Bethany asked.

"The Society," Taylor said. "Though maybe that's okay." Florie had told Bethany about the stockpile of cash every Society House had in a safe or vault. Money in all denominations, from as many historical periods as they could get, so they could take care of their own, contemporaries and otherwise.

Bethany wondered where they got that money, but Taylor's answers had been vague. *Investments, I guess.*

"I doubt Theodore Pippin would think it's okay." Bethany twiddled her fingers in her purse straps, thinking of the drooling, brain-damaged guy at Taylor's house.

That was what would happen to her dad if Mr. Pippin caught him.

They passed a man walking alongside the road, his head bent against the flying snow. The wind whipped his shaggy hair and a flap of cloth sticking out of the duffel bag he held against his chest. "Man, it would suck to be that guy," Bethany said, trying to get her mind off of her dad and Pippin's Treatment.

"I'm guessing *suck* means it's bad," Florie said. "But he doesn't look like he's looking for a ride. If the poor fellow's still walking when we head home, we'll stop just to make sure."

"Hopefully, he's not going far," Taylor said.

Bethany turned to look at the man's receding form as they continued closer to town. In her time, she'd never have considered picking up a hitchhiker, especially a scruffy guy like that. But it was probably common in this time, and the poor man probably wore too-short pants because they were all he had. She faced forward, trying to think positive.

They could play Good Samaritan after they found her dad.

Tony kept his head lowered against the snow. He glanced up every few seconds to confirm he was still on the road, though he could see little beyond a less-white, blurred stripe narrowing into the horizon.

He turned to look behind him, where a truck had passed a few minutes earlier, heading toward town. He didn't recall any other residences in Florie's House's immediate area, but it hadn't occurred to him that the truck might be her until it had disappeared into the swirling snow.

The wind gusted, with nothing to break it in the empty fields bordering the road. Tony clutched the duffel bag to his chest, strap looped over his arm. Isaac was blessedly content, oblivious in his makeshift cocoon.

Tony tried to ignore the hollow gnawing in his gut. He hadn't eaten since the chicken sandwich he'd grabbed when the train stopped in Lexington. His stomach had given up growling, but lethargy threatened to claim him if he stopped telling himself to keep moving. Good thing that farmer had let him hitch a ride, and had even given Isaac some milk. But the way the snow was collecting on the road, the man's dilapidated, old truck had done well to make it to the farm down the road, much less another mile or so to Florie's house. The farmer had apologetically offered to let Tony and Isaac bed down in his barn, as his house was full of family, visiting for Christmas. Tony had declined, anxious to reach Florie. Now he questioned the wisdom of his choice.

He glanced up. Woods lined the road ahead, but through the trees, he thought he saw a thin, horizontal slash across the valley—Florie's bridge. If he cut through the woods, he should be able to reach the shortcut he'd found that day he'd gone running. He walked faster, hoping the trees would cut the wind.

His ears pricked at the buzz of an engine approaching from behind. Hopefully, whoever it was could give him a ride and make it through the snow to Florie's.

He turned to face the oncoming vehicle. Hope thudded beneath his ribs. Was it the truck he'd seen heading to town? But as the vehicle drew nearer, he could tell it was smaller. A reddish-colored car. He stuck out his thumb.

The car drew near and stopped. As the driver stepped out, Tony registered the details through his blurred vision.

Maroon car. Black man. Gun…

Pippin!

"Fuck!" Tony bolted for the woods.

No one had seen Bethany's dad. The ticket agent at the train station told them only one person had gotten off the train that afternoon, and he couldn't give them more than a vague description. "Fella needed a haircut," he said. "Clothes were too small. Oh, and he was carrying a baby, inside his travel bag."

A sparkly sensation built in Bethany's chest. "Was he wearing glasses?"

The man shook his head. "But come to think, he acted like he couldn't see real well, eyes kinda squinty."

"That guy we passed on the road!" Bethany's heart beat in her throat. "That was him!" She ran for the door, her boots banging on the worn, hardwood floor. "Hurry!"

Florie and Taylor scrambled out behind her, and the three leaped back into the truck.

The drive back to the House was slow with the blowing snow reducing visibility to almost nothing but a wall of white. Bethany squeezed her right hand with her left, then switched to clutching her left hand in her right as she scanned the swirling whiteness ahead. They were about halfway back to the House when a dark square shape loomed at the side of the road. An abandoned car.

Florie stopped behind it. "Must've run out of gas. That's a mighty nice car to just leave." She stopped behind the car. "I wonder if someone needs help."

Taylor, sitting in the middle, peered around Bethany. "It has Ohio plates—"

"Oh God!" It had to be Theodore Pippin's car. Bethany slammed her hand on the door handle and jumped out. Tracks in the snow led into the woods.

Faint, clicking sounds came from the maroon car. On impulse, Bethany took the few steps forward and touched its hood.

Still warm.

She was dimly aware of Taylor getting out of Florie's truck. "Bethany! What are you doing?"

There were two sets of tracks. Men's, judging by the size. And they were nearly on top of each other, as if one man had followed the other.

Bethany's voice was choked. "They ran into the woods!" She took a step in the direction the tracks went.

"Beth, if Pippin finds out who you are, he'll be after you, too—"

"I have to find my dad!" And the baby brother she'd never met—well, at least as a baby. And never would, if she didn't find him now.

"Let's go back to the House and get my mom," Florie said. "There are neighbor men the Society pays to help…"

Bethany glanced back. "We might be too late!" She walked, trying to place her feet in the tracks, but they were too far apart. That Pippin guy had been running after her dad.

"Bethany, wait!" Taylor hurried to catch up.

"That car's still warm, they can't be far!" They couldn't risk taking the time to go for help.

"But—" Florie shouted. "Bethany! At least take my satchel!"

Taylor dashed back to the truck and grabbed it. "Stay here!" she told the other girl. "If we're not back in a half hour, get help!" She caught up as Bethany ran into the woods.

Violet's hands ached from being clamped around the steering wheel for so long. Her back, shoulders, and arms ached, too, not to mention her breasts. She'd driven the whole way to Tennessee from Dayton. Alpha didn't know how to drive, as it was an unnecessary skill in her time. Violet hadn't pressed for details. She'd driven all day, stopping only for gas, a hurried meal, or to visit the washroom. Caruthers would eventually get loose and follow, and every minute they delayed gave Mr. Pippin that much more time to catch up to Tony and Isaac, and do something terrible to them.

"Welcome to Hollowville, pop three hundred thirty-eight," Alpha read on a sign.

"Population," Violet said. "Thank heavens." She guided Caruthers's Cadillac down the main street and pulled over in front of a frame building, with a hand-lettered corner window proclaiming it as Curly's Tavern.

"What are you doing?" Alpha stretched.

"I'm going to explode if I don't express some milk." She hopped out of the car.

"I don't see why…"

Alpha's voice faded as Violet hurried to the tavern's door and went inside.

She couldn't let her milk dry up. To do so would be to admit defeat, give up hope of getting Isaac back.

She would get him back, even if she had to kill Tony for him. The thought made her stomach turn in on itself, but her resolve held firm. *Whatever it takes.*

Fifteen minutes later, she climbed back behind the wheel, handing Alpha one of the Cokes she'd purchased inside. "Good thing I brought money, huh?" the other woman asked as she raised the bottle to her lips.

Violet pulled her gloves back on, thankful the bartender hadn't noticed the scars. "Yes, and I thank you again. We wouldn't have gone far without stopping for gas." She started the car. "The bartender says the House is about seven miles east of here."

Though much had changed, the town itself and the now not-so-old barns and farmhouses sparked familiarity from her prior visit to the Cumberland Gap Saturn Society House.

A few miles down the road, they encountered a maroon car, pulled off to the side. A maroon car she recognized. Violet's heart pounded. "Mr. Pippin," she whispered.

"There's no one in it," Alpha said.

Violet stopped the car, fear stealing her breath.

Several sets of footprints led into the field, and tire tracks in the snow indicated a second car's arrival and departure. "He's found Tony." Violet could no longer feel the steering wheel beneath her hands, or the gloves encasing them. The whole world blurred into white. Her breath rattled in her ears. *He's found Tony. And Isaac.*

Alpha climbed out of the car. The creak of the door opening yanked Violet out of her trance. Alpha dug into her pocketbook and pulled out something that looked like a smartphone. Violet stared curiously. How on earth would such a thing be of use in 1939?

The device beeped, and something blinked on its display. "He's out there, all right."

"Mr. Pippin?"

"Tony."

"How can you—"

"This is a tracking device. He went into the woods there." She pointed.

Get away from her!

Violet stopped. Why had she thought that?

She hurried into the woods, glad she'd had the presence of mind to grab a coat from Mr. Pippin's ample stock. Alpha followed, blundering through the brush like a lumbering bear. *Stop!* The little voice inside Violet's head said. *You can't trust her!*

Violet slowed. Why on earth not? Yes, she'd had misgivings about the woman since they'd met. But there was no logical reason for them. Besides, Alpha's tracking device was her best chance of finding Tony quickly.

The path forked. She hesitated.

"To the right," Alpha instructed, peering at her tracker.

Don't! the little voice said.

And why not? Violet argued with herself.

Tony'll die—no, worse!

Absurd. She moved on, though the voice—almost like another presence within herself—urged her not to.

Tony had told her about something like this. Was it herself, from the future?

Whatever it was, she'd known this presence *before,* and it wasn't always benign, judging from the nausea that welled up in her belly the instant she acknowledged it.

Alpha had helped her. She'd bound Dr. Caruthers and brought money so Violet had been able to get gas and food for the long drive. She'd saved Tony's life numerous times. There was no reason Violet shouldn't trust her. She tuned out the little voice.

Alpha's tracking device beeped. "They went off the path here." Alpha pointed at footprints, barely visible in the snow-covered undergrowth.

A brief twinge shot through Violet. Once they found Tony and Isaac, she had to see the tracker. Alpha would probably refuse, but Violet had to ask. "How does it work?"

"The injections I gave you are also homing devices. I can even track across time—"

"Why didn't you come after us?"

"I can't go back that far," Alpha said. "I was just glad this could hone in on you, tell me you and Tony were all right."

"The splinter came out of my hand," Violet said.

"Yes. I feared... something had happened to you." Something in her voice rang false, though Violet couldn't put her finger on what. She concentrated on moving forward, hoping when she found Tony, he'd still have Isaac. Still be all right.

Tony ran through the woods, clutching the duffel bag to his

chest. *Just a little farther.* If he remembered correctly, Florie's House was just past that rise over there... His breath came in short gasps, growing more labored as the incline steepened. *Just over that hill...* Thin branches he couldn't see smacked his face, but he ignored the stings. He stumbled, barely catching himself on a sapling. He looked behind him. Pippin's crashes through the underbrush a ways back were growing louder, amplified in the snow-silenced wood.

Tony moved on, thankful his experience in prehistoric times had strengthened him, leaving him in the best physical shape he'd ever been in. But his lungs burned. His legs cramped, finally forcing him to slow to a walk.

He glanced back. Nothing but swirling white. The world was silent except for the crunch of his footsteps on the snow and frozen ground.

He studied the woods. The deciduous trees were giving way to pines. He'd been running uphill for a good while. He crept between the trees, searching for a place to rest where the pines had blocked the snow and he left no tracks. Finally, he spotted some older pines whose lower branches had long since fallen, leaving room for him to huddle beneath the remaining boughs.

Something made a light snapping sound in the distance, but when it didn't repeat, he dropped to his knees and crawled underneath the pine tree's sheltering boughs.

He slipped Isaac's bag off his shoulder and laid it on the dry ground close to the tree's trunk. Isaac made a little gurgling noise as Tony unzipped the bag and lifted him out.

Isaac squirmed inside his blankets, making baby noises. Tony held him close to his heart. "It's okay, buddy. It's going to be okay." The baby shifted, and Tony thought he caught a whiff of something besides pine in the crisp, cold air. As he laid a kiss on Isaac's forehead, a thin cry rose from the baby.

Damn, he didn't want to take the time to change a diaper now, but if he didn't, Isaac would raise hell and lead Pippin right to him. Tony laid the baby across his knees, then dug a diaper out of the duffel bag. Thankfully, the Society had supplied Violet with a good stash.

As Tony peeled the blankets away, the baby's whimpers escalated into a full-blown wail. "Man, you've got a set of lungs on you." Tony pulled the dirty diaper from beneath him, using a clean corner to wipe Isaac's butt as best he could. "I know, it's cold," Tony murmured as he slipped the clean diaper beneath the baby—

A gunshot cracked the air, the bullet thudding into the ground but a few yards away.

Without bothering to fasten the diaper, Tony tossed the blankets back around Isaac and shoved him into the duffel bag. "Shh!" he urged the baby.

Another shot. Closer.

Shit! Tony staggered on up the hill, looking backward every few seconds to search for Pippin... was that something behind him?

In the shadowy underbrush to his right, something moved.

Footsteps. Puffing breath. Snapping twigs. "Give it up, Solomon!"

He barely saw Pippin's legs in the shadows beneath a huge, old pine tree before the man crouched and rolled under it, then launched himself at Tony. "Arrrgh!"

Tony slid aside to evade the tackle, barely keeping hold of Isaac. Grabbing the duffel bag's straps, he raced down a rise, narrowly missing smacking into a tree. Night was falling, further reducing his lousy vision.

Pippin's footsteps kept pace with Tony's, only yards behind. Tony pushed himself faster, but Pippin didn't falter. *Please, let me be going in the right direction*, Tony prayed. Florence Allen was his only hope. He blundered on blindly as darkness descended. Pippin grew closer. "Give... up... Solomon!"

Tony forced a burst of energy into his legs, though he could see no more than a few yards in front of his face.

He ran on, Pippin's footsteps and panting breath a demonic tempo he had to match.

Until the ground disappeared from beneath his feet.

Twenty-one

Violet stumbled through the wood. Her feet were soaked through from the snow. Dusk was falling fast, and she could see only a few yards ahead. The penlight built into Alpha's tracking device did little to help. The only sound besides their footfalls was its occasional blip.

She moved faster, pushing herself until she started to stumble. If Mr. Pippin reached them first... She tried to make herself slow down, at least enough that Alpha's light would illuminate the woods before her. She'd be little help to her son if she fell and busted her fanny.

"Violet, take it easy." At Alpha's voice, a chill rushed down Violet's throat, though she didn't know why. *Because she's going to kill them!* the other voice in her head said.

Because Tony and Isaac are in danger, she corrected. *Things will be all right.* Alpha's voice held no worry or fear, especially considering that Tony was vital to Alpha's vision of her time. The other presence in Violet's mind disagreed. *Turn back now!*

She couldn't. Not until Tony and Isaac were safe. Maybe Alpha masked her emotions in times of stress. Or maybe she already knew everything would work out. But Violet couldn't leave. Not when her son needed her.

When the tracking device beeped in a different tone, Alpha sucked in a thick breath.

Violet slowed. "What is it?"

"He's hurt."

"What?" Violet forced the word through her throat. If Tony was hurt, what about Isaac?

Tony came to with a blazing headache like he hadn't suffered since his fall and sacrifice in Chichén Itzá. Pain all over his body clamored for his attention, but his left side drowned out almost all of it. He'd surely broken some ribs—

A baby's cry broke through his mental fog.

Isaac! His bumps, bruises and cuts forgotten, Tony rolled onto his belly and lifted his head to look at the overhang he'd jumped off. All he could see was a darker patch of gray that ended twenty feet or so above him.

Slowly turning his head from one side to the other he listened until he pinpointed the baby's location to the right and slightly below him, several yards away. He groped the nearly indistinguishable ground before him, barely noticing the freezing, wet snow, and started to push himself up.

Pain burst through his left arm, and his vision went white as something snapped. "Fu-uck!" Goddamn arm was broken, had to be. He rolled off it and caught his breath as shades of gray came back to his vision.

Slowly, he placed his right arm beneath him, testing to see if it would hold his weight. It was sore, but nothing like his left, so he maneuvered his legs beneath him—

More crushing pain, from his left ankle. "Owww, shit!" He swore, and rolled onto his belly, slowly, testing for more injuries. Nothing worse than a few more bruises and scrapes made themselves apparent, so he lurched onto his knees.

Isaac's cries had died off to hiccupy whimpers. Tony crawled on his knees toward the noise, pulling himself through debris, brush and weeds with his right arm. He estimated he was halfway to the child when Pippin's voice reached him through the darkness. "Solomon... I have... the child."

Tony froze. "Give him to me, damn it."

Pippin spoke through labored breaths. "He appears... unhurt."

A thin strand of relief punctuated Tony's fear and pain. He pulled himself toward the voice. The shades of gray took on shapes, a stand of pines, a rock outcropping, and the darker form of a man sitting against it, the duffel bag at his side. Tony's bad ankle bumped a protruding boulder he hadn't seen. He flinched, biting back another curse. "Give me... my son. Bastard."

Pippin pulled the duffel bag onto his lap, wincing with effort. The baby quieted. "I'll not hurt this innocent child." Pippin's voice was strained. He'd been injured, too. "If you do the right thing... and agree to your penance... for interfering in the flow... of time."

"Go to hell." Fucking bastard. Even hurt, holding a defenseless baby, Pippin didn't stray from his obsession.

Pippin made a harrumphing sound, though it was strained. "It's not my immortal soul in danger. Though if you make it right, there's chance yours may yet be redeemed—"

"Don't talk religion to me, you fucking fanatic." Tony's arm had gone numb, but his ankle still hurt like hell. "Give. Me. My. Son."

Pippin shifted as Tony wrenched himself near. "I will give you the child on one condition." Tony hesitated. "You'll agree to return to Dayton with me and accept your just punishment for your deeds."

Tony's mind rolled over the possibilities. "You're out of your fucking mind," he said as an idea occurred to him.

Pippin rose to the bait. "Then you leave me no choice. Come closer... and I'll take this child... and you'll never see him again." In the darkness, Tony could barely see him cross one extended leg over the other, emphasizing his finality. "Justice... will be served... if I have to carry you there myself."

He'd given Tony the perfect opening. Tony sighed, trying to sound like he meant it. "Okay. But only for... my son." He dragged himself closer. "Just promise me one thing. If there's any way... to get him back to the twenty-first century... get him... to my sister. Lisa Vogel."

"If it is in my power, I will do so," Pippin agreed. "Charlotte has no fitness as a mother, and I will see to it the child is taken care of... elsewhere."

The denouncement of Violet's character sent a leaden ball into

Tony's middle. He pushed away memories of the birth, and the happy days they'd shared in the weeks following. She'd proven her questionable character more than once. He couldn't—wouldn't—let her raise his son.

So why the hell did he feel like the lowest scum of the earth for not arguing the fact?

Between the two of them, they managed to collect enough deadwood to start a fire. Pippin had a tinderbox, which he carried instead of a lighter because it was less anachronistic. He couldn't use it with a broken hand, so he held it in his good hand while Tony struck the flint.

Pippin held the milk bottle Tony had stolen while Tony scooped snow into it, then poured in the last of the corn syrup once the fire warmed it. "I see my larder... came in handy," Pippin remarked. He shifted Isaac to Tony's lap.

"I stole to feed my son." Though why he cared what Pippin thought, he didn't know.

"A forgivable offense." Pippin lay back against the outcropping, the pain from his injuries evident in his tight voice. Even in the dim firelight, and without his glasses, Tony could see the man's ashen skin. "You are not a man without honor."

"Which you would have found out if you'd bothered to talk to me before you tried to stab me!" Tony recalled his first encounter with Pippin in 1933.

The first time Charlotte—Violet—had betrayed him.

"I did try to talk to you," Pippin said.

The milk bottle slipped in Tony's hand, but he caught it.

Pippin was right. He had tried to talk first, that night in the Gibbons Hotel. Tony had refused, having already judged the man. He'd let fear rule him.

Isaac turned away from the bottle with a hiccup. Tony set the bottle down, slid his good arm under the baby, and managed to turn him over, laying him across his knees. He patted the baby's back. "If I'd come peacefully, would it have made a difference?"

Isaac finally burped. Pippin didn't answer for a good minute.

"No."

"And even though you say I'm not a man without honor, you still intend to take me back to Dayton, and give me..." He couldn't say it. "Turn me into a mindless zombie."

"It's what I must do," Pippin said slowly. "You have no idea, the trouble you've wrought, changing the past—"

Something crashed through the brush above. Tony's gaze shot up, searching the gathering darkness as something fluttered in his belly. Were they saved?

A female voice. Indistinct, yet familiar. "They're down here!"

Recognition slid into place, and hope avalanched into his feet.

Alpha. And she'd brought friends.

Bethany crept to the overhang's edge. *Whew.* If she hadn't seen that orange glow from below, she and Taylor would've run right over the ledge. She crouched low, the snow chilling her legs, bare except for her stockings. Why hadn't she gone for help, instead of running after the tracks like a moron? Slowly, she leaned over.

A campfire blazed on another ledge twenty or thirty feet down. A man leaned against a big rock, the firelight gleaming on his black forehead. A second man huddled across the fire from him. The guy they'd seen walking.

Taylor crouched beside her. The men looked up.

"Daddy!" Bethany yelled.

The scruffy man from the road frowned, his features barely visible in the dim light. "What the—"

"Up here!"

Taylor raised up. "Over there!" She pointed to the left.

Bethany followed her to a spot where a water run-off cut the overhang's face. Grabbing branches, saplings and protruding rocks, the girls carefully climbed down.

Bethany skipped through the snow to the man with unkempt

hair. "Daddy!"

His face registered shock. "What the hell?"

She dropped beside him and threw her arms around him. "Daddy! Finally! You're—"

"Bethany?" Of all people, the one he longed to see more than anyone. Not someone to fear. "I can't believe— I thought you were someone else. But how—" He started to hug her, then let out a yelp.

"What?" She shifted to avoid his injury.

He pulled away. "My arm. I think it's broken..."

She wrapped him in a loose embrace. He pulled her close with the other arm. Her voice hitched as she buried her face in his shoulder. "I never thought I'd see you again." She was dimly aware of Taylor introducing herself to the other man, telling him she lived in his House decades from now.

Bethany's dad pulled back from her, giving her a long look as if drinking her in. "I was afraid I'd never see you, either. I—"

Something gurgled in his lap. Bethany drew back. "The baby!"

Her dad drew out of her embrace and tried to slide an arm under the infant. "Bethany, this is your brother, I—"

"Oh, my God." A jolt spread out from her chest, like the time she'd walked into an electric fence. This was Keith Lynch? She reached for the baby, then hesitated. "Can I—"

Her dad leaned back. "Take him."

Bethany slid her hands beneath the tiny baby and lifted him, supporting his wobbly neck like they'd taught her in babysitting class. "Oh. My God." She settled him in the crook of her elbow, sliding her fingers beneath the blanket that covered his head and pushed it back. "He's beautiful," she breathed.

"His name is—"

"Isaac." Bethany stroked his silken cheeks, marveling at how the baby's round, dark eyes already held a resemblance to the man he would become.

"How—"

"Keith told me. He said you're in great danger."

Her dad looked across the fire. Bethany followed his gaze, and

Taylor and the other man stopped talking.

Her mission from Keith tugged at her brain. She had to get her dad and the baby out of there. She scanned the ridge above. All was silent. Nothing moved in the darkness beyond the firelight.

She dug into the blanket to put her finger in the baby's tiny hand. He never took his big, dark eyes from her face. "I can't believe— How old is he?"

"About six weeks." Her father's brows drew low. "What are you doing here? I mean—am I in— Is this—"

"I'm... I'm like you, Daddy." She glanced over at Taylor and—she assumed—Theodore Pippin. Both watched silently, the latter's face exuding masked anger, Taylor's face...

Sad. Wistful.

"Taylor and I got to be friends after Danny..." Bethany trailed off, her voice choked.

"You know I didn't do it." Her dad's face twisted.

"I know. No one believed me but Taylor. I mean besides Grandma and Papaw—"

"But Lisa thinks I did it. And so does your mom."

"Well, the security video..."

She didn't want to talk about it anymore. She started to lean in for another hug, but caught herself before she grabbed his bad arm. "You're hurt, we've got to get help."

"Pippin's hurt, too." He glanced across the fire, then met Bethany's eyes. "There's a woman named Florence Allen. She runs the Society—"

"We're staying with her."

He stared ahead, his eyes unfocused. "There's another woman. Named Alpha. From the future—our future. She's about five-ten—"

"I know, she's dangerous—"

"Take the baby. And go—"

"But I can't leave—"

"Beth, my fucking arm feels like it's going to fall off—"

"Okay," she said quickly. Her dad never swore in front of her unless something was really bad.

"Take that bag over there, it's full of blankets and diapers. Put Isaac in it—"

"Okay." She rushed to grab the bag as Taylor met her. "We've got to get help!"

"No shit, Mr. Pippin's lost a lot of blood..."

Bethany hurried to her father's side and gave him a quick kiss on the cheek. "Daddy, I love you."

"I love you, too." His voice was strained. "Please, hurry..."

"Here." Taylor dug into Florie's bag and pulled out a half-loaf of bread and a foil wrapped package. Bethany guessed it contained leftovers. Taylor dropped it into her dad's lap, then scrambled for the slope.

Bethany stared at the baby in her arms. "How'm I supposed to—"

"Put him in the bag," her dad said. "Like a carrier."

She did, fastening all the buttons except the one over the baby's face. The whole time, he stared up at her with those big, round eyes, not making a sound. As if he knew what was going on. "It's okay, Isaac," she murmured as she looped the straps over her shoulders and followed Taylor. Once they crested the ravine, they could follow their own tracks back to the road.

Only when she got there, the tracks had disappeared. The overhang had sheltered them from the brunt of the snow, which was now coming down in force.

Obscuring their only way to know how to get back to the car.

Violet kept moving, changing course only at Alpha's terse instructions. Thick clouds blocked most of the moonlight, and Alpha's penlight illuminated barely enough to keep Violet from running into trees. "Bear to the right," Alpha said.

Don't listen! the voice inside Violet's head urged.

Nonsense, she argued, but her misgivings grew. What if there was something to it? What about the numerous articles she read about how intuition had saved people from being victims of crime or alerted them to an impending disaster?

She followed Alpha's direction. Her misgivings were not to be trusted. How she knew this, she had no idea, but somewhere hidden in her subconscious, was knowledge that she'd listened to that little voice before—and the results had been disastrous.

She saw the tracks in the snow the instant Alpha's penlight struck them. "We're almost there," Alpha said.

Violet pushed her weary legs faster, ignoring the numbness. Snow had filled the tracks enough that their outlines were indistinct, but logic told her they'd lead to Tony.

The niggling little voice in her head agreed. *Don't go!*

Why on earth not? she argued. Why couldn't she shake this annoying presence who kept denying what her own intelligence told her?

Stop, stop, stop, the voice chanted. *Go somewhere else. Anywhere!* Impending doom settled in, dug itself deeper into her consciousness.

The penlight illuminated a sharp drop-off. A faint, orange glow from beneath it broke the murky darkness.

Stop! the voice warned. "Of course I'm stopping," she muttered. She drew up to the edge of the drop-off and gazed down as Alpha shone her penlight below.

A campfire blazed on a ledge probably ten feet across. A man lay beside it, dark stains marring the snow at his side. Tony! Violet's chest tightened, her heart lodged in her throat.

Mr. Pippin huddled against a man-sized rock formation across the campfire. He, too, was injured, judging from the awkward angle of his leg and the blood-stained snow beneath it. Alpha peered down beside her. In spite of the heat that wafted up with the smoke, ice formed over Violet's heart.

There was nothing there that could be mistaken for a baby. "Tony!" she shouted.

Both men looked up. Terror washed across Tony's face. "Get Isaac! Bethany took him! To Florie's!"

Alpha slipped off to the left, where a steep trail led down the face of the drop-off, and started down, grasping small trees and protruding rocks.

Alpha would take care of Tony and Pippin. Violet needed to find her son. She started back the way the footprints had led when the voice shouted into her consciousness, louder than ever. *No! Go to Tony!* the little voice urged. *He needs you more!*

She gritted her teeth and stepped away from the ledge. Her baby needed her more. Tony had taken him. He was not on her side. He was an adult, he could handle—

Tony's shout from below made her stop. She crept back to the ledge and peered over.

Alpha was pointing her tracking device at Tony, who was trying to scramble under a tree. A beam of white light blazed from the device, enveloping him, masking his shriek in a sizzle. His form faded, then disappeared.

Alpha half-smiled, half-grimaced at Mr. Pippin. "One less enemy for you to worry about."

"What do you mean?"

"He's gone. For good."

Bethany's legs hurt, her chest hurt from hard breathing of such cold air, and she felt light-headed. The straps of the duffel bag cut into her shoulders. Her feet and hands were numb, and her stomach had been growling since they left the train station. It had stopped snowing and the cloud cover had dissipated, but her vision was getting blurry. Even with the light of an almost-full moon, she could barely discern where the creek was. When they'd started following it, the flatter whiteness coating it had been obvious, even in the snow. Now she couldn't tell where the land ended and the ice-covered creek began.

She needed something to eat, and soon. "Taylor..." she puffed, "gotta stop."

Her friend stopped. "What's— Oh man, you need to eat, don't you?"

Bethany managed a nod, and collapsed. She barely noticed the cold, or the wetness seeping through her coat. Taylor rushed to her. "Here, let me get the baby..." Bethany could barely feel her slipping the straps of the duffel bag off her shoulders.

Bethany's gaze followed the dark blur of the bag. "How's—"

"He's fine. Sleeping." Taylor held the bag to her chest while Bethany fumbled with the buttons on her purse.

Her fingers wouldn't work. Taylor ran to a nearby tree and hooked Isaac's bag over a broken-off branch. "Here, let me help."

She dug through Bethany's purse until she found the folded napkin containing cookies from Mrs. LeBeau. Bethany shoved them into her mouth as quickly as she could, barely tasting the sugary oatmeal. "I'm gonna need my test kit, too."

"Got it." Taylor resumed digging in the purse, but her head jerked up. "Who the fuck?"

Coming over the rise behind Taylor were two women. Bethany had never seen the big-chested one with short brown hair, but the sight of the willowy blonde made her stomach plunge down to her toes.

The woman Keith had described. That she'd seen before... at Taylor's house!

"Isaac!" The brunette broke into a run, heading for the duffel bag.

"Violet?" Taylor said.

The blonde—Alpha, Bethany recalled—dug into her purse and pulled out a shiny, silver flip phone. The other woman turned around. "No!" She threw herself at Alpha's feet, and the phone went flying.

Taylor picked it up. "Violet? What's—"

Both women tackled her, ending in a pile.

As they both scrambled for the phone, Bethany tried to shake the fog off her mind and ran for the duffel bag. The baby's thin wail reached her as she grabbed the straps and yanked it off the branch.

Alpha had reclaimed the object, but couldn't get up with Taylor and the dark-haired woman—the one Taylor had called Violet—clawing at her. "Bethany!" Violet shouted. "Run!"

Clutching the bag and baby to her chest, Bethany ran.

She didn't know who this Violet was, or how she'd known her name. She had no idea where she was going, or what she'd do once she got there. From the scuffling behind her, Taylor's footsteps crackled on the leaf-strewn, frozen ground behind her, and her friend quickly caught up.

"You can't get Tony back!" Alpha yelled from behind them. "He's gone forever!"

At the woman's words, Bethany gasped. What did she mean by that?

No time. She pushed herself faster. The creek tapered to a narrow thread, a steep cliff wall rising beside it. The other side was another steep drop-off of a good thirty feet or so, a continuation of the same ledge where her dad and Pippin had taken shelter.

And it was getting narrower.

Footsteps pounded the snowy ground behind her as the ledge thinned to a point, forcing her to stop.

The cliff rose on her left, a steep wall of barren dirt. At its foot, the creek formed a deep pool before it tumbled over the cliff face in a frozen waterfall.

Bethany looked down, and her breath cut off as if she'd swallowed a balloon. The bottom of the cliff was at least as far as the street from the fourth floor windows at her mom's old office at LCT. "Oh shi-it."

Taylor drew up beside her. "We are so screwed."

"Bethany!" the woman called Violet screamed.

Bethany glanced back to see Alpha point the metal thing at her. "Jump!" Violet shrieked. "You can't die!"

"Go!" Taylor pushed her toward the edge. Taylor took her hand, and together, they jumped over the cliff.

Violet surged forward as Alpha approached the edge and turned the tracking device *(It made Tony disappear!)* toward the bottom. "No!" Violet launched herself at the woman.

Stepping backward to avoid Violet, Alpha stumbled. Her foot slipped on the icy ground, and she tumbled into the creek. The ice cracked as she crashed through it. Screaming, she sank into the water, her arms flailing at the ice's broken edges.

Violet crept to the creek's edge. The old, familiar fear of water rose like a tide within her, but she pushed it back. Alpha's hand clamped onto a thick chunk of ice. Violet lifted her foot and brought it down. Alpha lost purchase, and slipped back into the icy water, her screams lost in a thick gurgle.

Violet stood staring down at the broken ice. She'd stomped with enough force to push Alpha beneath its unbroken surface, her body a dark mass. Violet stared, stunned, watching the movements grow slower. From somewhere far away, Isaac cried. Her breasts grew heavy and moist. A burst of dizziness washed over her, making her wobble, but she didn't take her eyes off Alpha until the dark shape went still.

Robotically, Violet moved to the ledge's edge and peered over. Moonlight washed through the clearing above the creek at the bottom of the waterfall. Broken chunks of ice indicated where someone else had met Alpha's fate—Taylor. She'd been the one who already died and warped. Beside the creek, Bethany lay in a heap, her legs twisted beneath her. A few feet away, Isaac lay in a pool of blood.

Violet knew she should be upset—no, beside herself—but something had shut off her emotions and she could only observe in strange detachment.

Another burst of vertigo slammed her, and she stumbled away from the drop off.

She crept back to the pool. The dark spot beneath the ice grew lighter, then disappeared. The vertigo left her.

Alpha's demise brought Violet's emotions back. Terror wrapped her chest in a vise, driving her to the cliff's edge. "Isaac!" The baby's cries had subsided to choked sobs. She glanced down the cliff face, but the only way down was to jump. Moonlight struck Bethany's motionless form, and Violet watched in stunned silence as Tony's daughter faded, shimmered, and disappeared.

Death in the past returned one to his own time, but what about someone who'd jumped into the future?

Mr. Everly's words echoed in her mind. *Never heard from again.* She didn't get the Pull. Tony's daughter and Taylor would return to the twenty-first century, but Isaac's natural time would be at least a millennium ago.

His cries grew thinner as she picked her way along the narrow ledge, searching for the nearest place she could safely descend. Minutes ticked away, every breath lodged in her throat. By the time she found a water runoff she could slide down, Isaac had gone quiet. She made the trek around the pond that took forever, but when she reached him, he lay silent and still.

"No!" She scooped up the tiny form, but no breath issued from his nose, no pulse beat beneath the fingers she pressed to his neck, then his chest. "No..." she sobbed. She laid him across her legs and tried to breathe life back into him, the way she'd learned in that class she'd taken at work, but after what seemed an eternity, Isaac remained motionless, breathless, lifeless.

She crumpled to the ground, sobs wrenching through her throat. Her son was dead.

And it was all her fault. She'd failed him, her friends... and Tony.

She was still sitting there, clutching the baby's body to her chest, her own grown numb, when a scruffy, brown and white puppy led Florie and Margaret LeBeau to her.

Twenty-two

Violet sat in Mrs. LeBeau's claw-foot tub in the odd washroom with no toilet. She couldn't get warm, even though Florie had poured in such hot water she feared it would scald Violet.

Between the poor visibility and slippery roads, it had taken Florie an hour to drive back to the House for her mother, then back to find Violet and Mr. Pippin. Mrs. LeBeau had driven into town to fetch a doctor to set Mr. Pippin's broken leg, though she and Florie had wrapped it enough to staunch the bleeding. Violet barely remembered helping the two women hoist him up the ravine with a rope tied under his arms.

She barely remembered the impromptu funeral they'd held for Isaac in the woods behind the House. She'd let them, knowing that if anyone else found out about the baby, there would be questions she couldn't answer.

She barely remembered anything else, except that flash of light from Alpha's hand.

Tony disappearing.

Isaac's cries from the ledge below. Then silence.

Bethany and Taylor's broken bodies beside the pond, before they disappeared. The mild sadness she felt at having put them through so much was dwarfed by the loss of her son.

And the man she loved.

It's all a dream. Any minute, her alarm clock would buzz, and it would be time to go to work, where she might see Tony in the hall and say hello. She'd dreamed their date, dreamed they'd made love, dreamed up her pregnancy. There was no Tony lookalike who'd tried to kill her, no running to Tennessee or escaping into the distant past. No prehistoric village. No—

Someone knocked on the washroom door. "Violet? Are you all right?" Florie called.

Of course she wasn't. But she couldn't ignore the kind, young woman. "I'm fine." Her voice sounded distant, detached, even to her.

She'd grabbed a knife from the kitchen, considered ending it all, but the perceptive girl had seen and taken it from her. This was the sixth time she'd checked on Violet, aware that it didn't take a lot of water to drown in.

Violet had considered that, too.

She traced the scar on her right palm, then went over the one on her left, vaguely recalling that Tony said the Society would pay for plastic surgery to remove them if she wanted.

But he hadn't had any of his removed.

Neither would she. It would be a penance of sorts, something she'd bear in memory of Tony, a reminder that he'd saved her life twice, and how she'd failed to do the same for him.

Everything she'd suffered had been for nothing. Six months of the hardest life she could imagine in prehistoric America, giving birth under the most primitive conditions, trusting Tony, only to find her trust had been misplaced. All for nothing.

Because she'd made the wrong choice.

The water had cooled enough that it no longer drove back the chill. With a sigh, she stepped out and dried off. If she couldn't live with herself, she'd have to find some other way, some other place, to end it.

Mr. Pippin lay on the sofa in the parlor, listening to the news on a staticky radio that sat where Violet remembered the television set in the twenty-first century. His dark skin was no longer ashy, no doubt due to the liquor Mrs. LeBeau had given him, but his eyes turned her way as she entered. He lifted the bandaged hand that hung off the side of the couch in a feeble attempt to motion her to his side.

She perched on the edge of the wing-back chair beside him, unable to stop from wringing her hands. Mr. Pippin spoke in a ragged voice. "I regret... the loss of your son." He took a heavy breath. "Miss LeBeau... told me what happened."

Violet looked down, willing the tears to stay at bay. She twiddled her fingers, forcing the detachment back into her mind. "It's my fault. I should have known what she was. Should've listened to myself—"

"You did what you had to."

"I let her escape! And she's a far worse enemy than Tony ever thought about being."

"You had no way of knowing that."

"Part of me did know."

"What do you mean?" Mr. Pippin's voice grew stronger.

"It was as if there were two of me in my body. The one in control, and the other one. The one I wouldn't listen to."

Mr. Pippin closed his eyes. "You did the right thing. Hard as it is to believe—"

"How could that be the right thing? Letting her take Tony..."

"As much as you refuse to admit it, Charlotte, your—" his lip twitched "—husband is still an enemy."

"Which I still don't understand. Or why you're so bent on capturing him."

Mr. Pippin turned his head to look at her, his eyebrow cocked. Violet swallowed. Pans clattered in the kitchen. "Please, Mr. Pippin," she said. "I really don't know."

"How can this be—"

"I told you. I warped into the future. I don't know why or how, but I did. And lost my memory. Alpha—that woman—told me that's what happens when you jump into the future. As if it's time's way of ensuring we don't go back to our own time with knowledge to tamper with things."

"Despite your wishing you hadn't trusted her, she sounds wise." His hand bumped the side of the couch and he flinched.

"She made Tony disappear, with some futuristic device! She said he was..." Sobs threatened, but she swallowed them. "Gone forever." She pulled the detachment back in by focusing on Mr. Pippin. He had to be in serious pain, with that leg and his hand. "If only I'd listened to that little voice..."

Florie slipped in from the hallway leading to the recovery room, where Violet recalled there was a young man, still in recovery.

A grimace flashed across Mr. Pippin's face. The liquor hadn't completely dulled his pain. "You truly remember nothing of your life before... your disappearance in 1933?"

Violet pressed her lips together. *In for a penny....* She shook her head. "Nothing before waking up in the back of a pickup truck in the twenty-first century."

"Incredible," Mr. Pippin breathed. "I should like to hear this whole story." Florie stepped closer.

After the way he'd treated her? Violet's jaw clenched, as if withholding information would be a sort of revenge for his threats to take Isaac from her, and the way he'd coerced her to agree to help him take Tony captive.

Yet Mr. Pippin had been kind to her in 1959. And she was certain that when she'd known him *before*, he'd been kind to her then as well.

So she told him her story, from the time she'd arrived in the twenty-first century, until her ill-fated date with Tony. She left out the fact that she'd met Mr. Pippin in 1959, fearing it was something she shouldn't reveal. Talking helped get her mind off her loss, though it was hard not to think about Isaac when her breasts felt like a pair of concrete balloons.

Florie moved to the sofa, shifting the doily on its arm as she sat.

"Amazing," Mr. Pippin mused. "Had I not seen for myself, I would not believe it. All these years, the Society has taught that it's not possible."

"What... how did you meet me? What was I like before?" Violet asked.

"You were nine years old, and terrified." His voice grew steadier. Perhaps the liquor was taking effect. "You'd acquired the gift by drowning. In the Great Flood of 1913. Solomon saved you."

Violet put a finger to her upper lip as she drew in a sharp breath. "He was... the one who..."

"I assume he gifted you, yes. When you took to disappearing, your father was beside himself. Enough that he allowed a colored psychiatrist—" he emphasized the word— "to treat you."

"You're not, are you?" Violet asked.

"No, dear. Educated, yes, but not in the medical arts. I leave that to Dr. Caruthers—"

Violet gasped. "He's a horrible man! Why, he..." She trailed off at Mr. Pippin's puzzled look.

"He what?"

"I... I don't know. I didn't like him very much, did I?"

"No, you always made that quite plain. Much is the pity, I think he fancied you." Mr. Pippin chuckled. "But you were always caught up in your studies, your job—"

"What did I study?"

"Physics. Chemistry. You worked in research for a company that made kitchen appliances, until they went out of business."

"Mercy!" Violet put her hand to her lips again. Tony hadn't told her any of that. "What about my family? They must have been well-off, to put me through college—"

"The Society put you through college, my dear." His face took on a bemused look, though he gritted his teeth when he tried to shift position on the couch. "Your mother passed away when you were just a tot, long before I met you. Your father was a kind man, loved you and your sister and brother, as a good father should. Didn't cotton to associating with colored folk, though. Nor to wasting money on a girl's education—which was why the Society paid for college. He saw the foolishness of his ways soon enough, but by then was in debt so deeply he was scarcely able to keep a roof over his head, much less repay us as he'd have liked. A proud man, your father was."

"He's dead, then?"

"Going on eight years, now." His face twisted in sorrow. "I'm sorry, Charlotte."

Violet stared at her hands in her lap. Oddly, she felt sad, but not the heart-wrenching grief she should have felt for a father she'd loved.

She couldn't remember him. Couldn't call up an image of what he might have looked like, whether tall or short, heavy or thin. She caught no fleeting impressions of evenings spent at a home she also couldn't remember, nor any of the things families did together. Nothing.

Mr. Pippin's face twitched.

"Mr. Pippin? Why is Tony an enemy? What did he do?" Was Tony's suspicion true, or was there something more?

Mr. Pippin spoke slowly. "He changed the past for his own gain."

"But what did he do?"

The Watchkeeper gazed up to his left. "The Book doesn't specify. Those who are like us in the future, in their wisdom, include the ones whose actions present a threat. His crime most likely occurred in a time that is yet in our future."

A flash of the blond girl with Taylor flickered through Violet's mind. Bethany. The girl who'd taken Isaac. Who, while leaping with him to his death, at least saved him from Tony's uncertain, and probably dire fate. "I see," Violet said. "But why is this so terrible?"

"You're aware of the... ripple, so to speak, that occurs when another person jumps into or out of time?"

"You mean the energy displacement."

Mr. Pippin forced a tight smile. "In some ways, you haven't changed at all. Yes, if that's what you prefer to call it. Study has revealed that when one goes into the past and willfully changes it, these... energy displacements... tend to be far stronger. Far more reaching."

Realization and horror trickled through Violet. "Like the bridge in my— in the twenty-first century that disappeared."

"Exactly. Objects, plants, animals, even people... can fall into such a ripple, be taken from one time and thrust into another—"

"Mercy!" Violet's fingers flew to her mouth.

"You really don't remember, do you?" Pain had crept back into his voice.

Violet shook her head helplessly.

Mr. Pippin stared at the ceiling, his gaze vacant. "My lovely wife... we'd just built the House, there in Dayton. She was planting a rose bush in the front flower bed while I washed the windows. Then...

I felt the time bubble. Nellie Mae disappeared before my eyes."

"She didn't warp?"

"Nellie was linear, Charlotte. She couldn't have."

Florie scooted forward on the sofa. "Is it possible that she was sent into the future?"

Violet's eyes went wide.

The Watchkeeper lifted his good shoulder in a sluggish shrug. "There's no way we can know. If it happened like it did for you," his gaze flicked to Violet, "she wouldn't know either."

"But it's possible." Florie darted a glance toward the kitchen, where the banging of pots and pans told Violet that Mrs. LeBeau was preparing supper. Florie leaned forward and spoke quietly. "Mr. Allen... the gentleman in the recovery room..." She glanced at the kitchen again, then locked stares with Violet. "Before he fell into recovery, he told Mama he's from 1756!" She fixed a stare on Mr. Pippin. "We're pretty sure he's not gifted. He could've been brought here by one of those time disruptions!"

Mr. Pippin's face twitched. "Interesting..."

"So perhaps whatever Tony did to get into the Black Book wasn't so bad," Violet said.

Mr. Pippin's face hardened. "Changing the past for our own, self-ish purposes is never acceptable. Particularly when much of the illicit activity is for financial gain, investments, and the like." His face twisted. "I lost my wife to greed, pure and simple."

Violet bowed her head. "As I lost Tony, and my son. To that woman's greed for power." A sob escaped her. "If only I could change it."

Mr. Pippin stiffened. "You mustn't! That's the very sort of activity that results in—"

"But what do I have to lose?" Violet turned her palms up, the scars a stark white.

"You will become an enemy, just as Solomon was. Then Dr. Caruthers and I shall be forced to render you harmless... do you not know what happened to your father?"

Violet shook her head, shamed that she knew nothing of the man.

"When the market crashed, he lost everything. Lived on the

streets, as a beggar, until he sneaked into a church and..."

Violet leaned forward. "And what?"

"He hanged himself."

Violet made a choked gasp. Something twisted around her heart. Though she couldn't remember the event, she suspected she'd had something to do with it.

"He left a note," Mr. Pippin said. "All it said was, 'I should have listened to you, Charlotte.'" His eyes grew hard. "You went back. Relived a day of your own past, urged him to sell his stocks.

"I di— how did you know?"

"It's my theory. One you never disputed when I suggested as much." Grim smugness settled onto his face. "In another timeline, one you didn't alter, your father didn't kill himself."

Violet looked down at nothing.

"I didn't add you to our list of Enemies because I was not completely sure. But do this and I'll be forced to hunt you—"

"Why?" Violet asked, though she knew. She couldn't remember Mrs. Pippin, but chances were, she'd been as kind and lovely as Mr. Pippin described. "Mr. Pippin.... is this something your wife would have wanted? For you to prevent me from doing the only thing I have left to live for? Maybe all Tony did was save a child's life. And you would punish me for doing the same for my son? Would Nellie Mae approve?"

He spoke quietly, thoughtfully. "No one has ever asked me that." He settled back onto the sofa, as if deflated. "It's fate. That's all I can be sure of."

"Fate?" Violet asked. "Or is it simply a future no one had the courage to change?"

Tony could feel nothing. Could see nothing. Could hear nothing.

Am I dead?

As soon as the thought occurred to him, the answer came.

No. And yes.

When he'd fallen, cracked his head and nearly died—when he got the time travel ability, the accident that started it all, he'd seen a long tunnel in a blaze of white.

He hadn't seen it this time. Everything around him was... not white. Not dark. Just... nothing.

His broken ankle and all the scrapes and bumps he'd gained, falling over the cliff... gone.

No pain. No sensation of gravity, of whether he was sitting, standing up, or lying down.

Was he breathing?

He thought for a moment, then realized he had no sensation of drawing air in through his mouth or nose, no feeling of his chest rising and falling. No feeling in his chest at all, no sensation that he even had lungs. Did he even have a physical body?

He tried yelling. *Violet!* But there was no sound. No feel of air rushing out his mouth, no vibrations.

It wasn't her fault. She'd told him there was something she didn't like about Alpha.

She left me. But he'd told her to go after Isaac. *God, please, let her have saved him.* The thought of his son, existing in this... this nothingness... He waited for his chest to tighten up, but it didn't.

He doubted even God heard his non-voice, his thoughts.

The idea that he was completely alone, in nothing, sank into his consciousness. There was no time here, wherever here was. He was stuck here. For good, maybe.

He'd never know what happened to Violet. Whether or not she'd managed to escape Alpha with their son. Never would know that as much as Tony wondered where her loyalties lay, he still loved her.

He wanted to cry, but he had no tears, and no eyes from which they could fall.

Violet's heart beat faster as Mr. Everly's SUV ate up the miles on I-75 and drew closer to Dayton. Closer to the house where she'd lived for years. Closer to Timmy and Stephanie, whom Violet hoped would take her in again.

She had to focus on getting her old life back, put aside the memory of the husband and child she'd had for those few short weeks. Had to keep moving forward, keep her head down as if she were walking into a hard rain.

Unwilling to return to Dayton with Mr. Pippin and risk Dr. Caruthers's wrath, Violet had stayed with Mrs. LeBeau and Florie in 1939. Each day she tried to warp back to the twenty-first century until, two weeks later, she'd succeeded. After she woke from recovery, Florie—how strange to see her as an octogenarian who looked sixty, if that—had assured her that she'd found Taylor and Bethany two weeks earlier, in the ravine behind the House. The girls had recovered quickly, and Bethany's mom had arrived the next day, after the Society had done some major damage control with the media. Taylor had left with Mr. Everly.

She'd apparently filled him in on what happened in 1939. "I can't believe I trusted her," he said for what must've been the fiftieth time since they'd left Florie's.

"She had me fooled, too." Violet shook her head as she stared, unseeing, out the window. "She had everyone fooled, Tony most of all. I've asked myself a hundred times, and logically, I can't come up with a single clue she gave us, and yet..."

Mr. Everly drove onto the bridge to Cincinnati, across the Ohio River. "And yet what?" His jaw was slack, lacking the happy-go-lucky smile he'd constantly worn before.

She frowned at her hands in her lap. "It was like there was, I don't know, another presence in my head. That didn't want to trust her. Mr. Pippin said I jumped into myself, from the future."

"Jesus Christ." Mr. Everly shivered—maybe from the cold, although it was warm inside the Jeep. "He's probably right."

Violet picked at a hangnail on her thumb. Mr. Everly swore beneath his breath. Her head whipped around. "Missed the exit." He pointed behind them. "No big deal, I'll just get off at the next." They'd crossed into Cincinnati, so it wouldn't take long.

He smacked the steering wheel. "Damn, I can't believe I was so gullible..."

Violet stared out the window. Thankfully, Mr. Everly was quiet the rest of the way to Dayton. He turned off the interstate at the exit Violet told him. "You're sure you want to do this? You can come back to the House you know."

"I have to know now." He'd warned her that a lot could change in six months, especially when one threw time travel into the mix. Violet could fill in the blanks. For all she knew, her friend could be dead. Or in jail. Or have disappeared off the face of the earth.

Violet had seen the news at Florie's, and one of the prevalent threads each day was the alarming increase in missing persons. Disappearances that couldn't be explained with something logical like the kidnapping operation whose clutches Bethany and Taylor had fallen into.

Mr. Everly turned down Stephanie's street. "Which house?"

"The fourth one, on the left." Violet's trepidation grew as he stopped in front of the red, brick ranch house. Tears threatened but she tamped them down. "Thank you. For everything."

"It's what we're here for."

She gave him a short nod. "Goodbye, then."

Mr. Everly didn't say anything, so she got out of the car and strode up the walk to the front door. There were lights on in the living room, and in Stephanie's bedroom window. Violet glanced backward. Mr. Everly sat in the car, waiting.

As she knocked on the door, her misgivings solidified. Where were Stephanie's holiday decorations? She, Stephanie, and Timmy had always spent the weekend after Thanksgiving putting up the Christmas tree in the front window, and lights around the front door. If she hadn't seen decorations on other homes as they drove, she'd have no idea it was even near Christmas.

The door opened, and a young man with pierced eyebrows and spiked, orange hair leaned out.

Violet's chest constricted, cutting off her breath. "Yeah?" the man said.

"Ah... is Stephanie here?" She prayed it was a new boyfriend, though he was rather young and not her friend's type.

"Stephanie? I don't know no Stephanie."

Violet's heart plummeted. "She... used to live here. About six months ago."

The man shrugged. "We've lived here since August—"

"Stephanie sold to you?"

"I dunno. We rent. Not from any Stephanie, though. Some older guy."

Violet forced her chin up. "I'm sorry to bother you."

She blinked back tears as she returned to the Jeep, thankful Mr. Everly had waited. He and the Society could be all she had left.

She flung the car door open and plopped into the seat. "You were right."

"I'm sorry." Mr. Everly put the car into gear.

Violet bowed her head, pressing her fingers into her eyes. Lord have mercy, she was so tired of crying. Surely Steph and Timmy simply lived somewhere else. She'd look them up on the Internet as soon as she got the chance.

"You know you'll always have a home in the Society House," Mr. Everly said.

"It appears I'll have to take you up on it. Though I won't be able to pay anything until—"

"Violet, the Society doesn't charge rent. You can live at the House as long as you want."

"Oh, no." She wrapped her arms around herself and pressed her back into the seat. That pitiful Fred—the one she'd led there so that horrible Dr. Caruthers could...

"You don't have to stay in Dayton," Mr. Everly said. "You can go to any House you want, as long as they have room. We take care—"

"I don't want to take charity, but it appears I have little choice. But I *will* pay the Society back. After I get a job."

"It's not necessary, but if that's what you want, that's fine."

"Can you take me to LCT?"

"Where?"

"LCT? Downtown?"

"Never heard of it."

Her apprehension returned. Everyone had heard of LCT.

"I used to work there. And... I think my boss had an idea of what was going on. He told me to take off as long as I needed, that he'd have a job for me whenever I was able to return."

"Your boss knows about—"

"Not the Society. At least, not as far as I know. He knew that people were after me—"

"Oh yes, the bodyguard."

They drove downtown. Even if Mr. Lynch wasn't in, she'd feel better. As if she could do at least one little thing toward getting her life back.

Violet's spirits lifted a little as Mr. Everly turned onto Seventh Street and the twenty-three-story LCT building came into view. "Where to?" he asked.

Didn't he know? "The big building there."

He stopped at the curb, and Violet's heart bottomed out.

There was no LCT logo over the front doors. Inside were signs for a bank, a travel agency, and two restaurants.

Not the LCT lobby. "Could you stay while I go check on something?" Barely waiting for his answer, she threw open the car door and burst into the building.

A directory graced the walls above the elevator banks. She scanned them, then read over them again, more slowly.

LCT wasn't on the list.

Perhaps they'd relocated? She stepped in front of a man walking toward the elevators. "Excuse me, sir, do you know where LCT is located now?"

"No idea." The man sidestepped her and moved on.

Dread swelling beneath her ribs, she asked a teller at the bank. "Never heard of it," the woman said. "I've worked at this branch for fifteen years."

Violet thanked her, then trudged toward the doors.

She couldn't breathe. Couldn't think. Couldn't feel. Nothing was right. Woodenly, she climbed into Mr. Everly's SUV.

He looked at her questioningly. She could barely force the words through her thick throat. "It's not there."

"We can search the Internet when we get home. Maybe they set up in a different location than before you made your jump."

"I'm not very optimistic. I'm afraid..." She jerked her head up. "I've changed something. Something big."

LCT didn't exist. And it was all her fault. She'd let Alpha take Tony. His existence was somehow tied to the company.

And he was gone, forever. So was Isaac. Her chin bumped her chest. "This is horrible. Nothing makes sense anymore. And it's all my fault."

The first thing she noticed when she walked in the Society House's front door was the sound of laughter, so incongruous with her situation it sounded alien. Then she realized it came from the television in the parlor—the same set that had precipitated her and Tony's trip to prehistory. "Good heavens, no one's watching that, are they?"

Mr. Everly preceded her into the parlor. "It's okay. After you warped, we dug into it—found some kind of digital device that must've played the virtual landscape you saw. We turned it off when I almost warped, and took it out." He shook his head. "I still have no idea how it got there."

"Alpha," Violet said.

He stepped around the corner into the parlor. "Have a seat while I go make up the bed in the other third floor suite." He motioned her in and lifted his hand in a wave to Taylor and the girl sitting on the sofa. "Violet's going to be staying here for a while." He disappeared up the stairs.

Violet and the blond girl stared at one another. Tony's daughter, heaven help her. Violet felt as if she'd swallowed a bucket of rocks. What would she say to her?

The girl's blue eyes were round, and full of... accusation? Or apprehension? Had Tony told her of her—as Charlotte's—betrayal?

Violet opened her mouth, but the words wouldn't come. Surely Bethany blamed her for her father's death.

The girl's chin trembled. Violet forced calmness into her voice. "You must be Bethany."

Tony's daughter tried to speak, but her lip quivered, then she lowered her face into her hands. "I'm sorry! Oh, God, I'm so sorry! I swear, I didn't mean to kill your baby, Daddy told me to take him, I thought he'd come back here with me—"

Taylor laid a hand on Bethany's wrist and the girl's wails turned to sobs.

Revelation gripped Violet's heart. Bethany blamed herself for Isaac's death? "You didn't know he was born in the past." Violet squeezed back her own tears. "It's not your fault."

Taylor flinched. "I'm the one who told her to jump."

Bethany scrubbed at her eyes with the back of her hand. "But I was holding him. I should've been more careful, should've found another way—"

"There was no other way," Taylor said in a choked voice.

Violet swallowed. Isaac was dead. "Better a quick death than..." Than what happened to Bethany's father. But Violet couldn't tell her that. It was better that she didn't know.

Bethany rubbed her lower eyelid, wiping away mascara smudges. "What happened to my da—" The television caught her eye, and her face went slack. "Oh my God."

The newscaster wore a somber expression as he made a sweeping motion at the empty plains in the background. "Yesterday, there was a railroad track here," he said, "and a train that carried hundreds of people every day. Today, it's as if that track—and the train with three hundred fourteen passengers—never existed." Behind him, a photo showed a sleek passenger train zipping through the European countryside—a marked contrast to the video on the newscaster's left of an unblemished, plain.

Soldiers led a line of fur-clad people to waiting military vehicles. The photo of the train switched to a slideshow of portraits—the people being moved by the soldiers, Violet guessed.

Their fur and leather clothing bore a striking resemblance to that worn by the prehistoric villagers from centuries—or even millennia— ago.

"...these individuals do not speak German, Dutch, Italian, Greek, or any of the other languages people have used in an attempt to communicate with them," the newscaster said. "No one knows where they came from—or who they are."

"Holy cow," Bethany said. "They look like cavemen."

"Lord have mercy," Violet said.

"Time disturbances," Taylor said. "Just like the smallpox epidemic."

Violet turned sharply to her. She'd heard about the epidemic on the news at Florie's. Thousands of young people had been stricken, mostly concentrated in the Midwest. Anyone born after hospitals had stopped vaccinating babies for the disease was susceptible. "How do you know?"

Taylor shrugged. "That's what the Society scientists say. The CDC's stores haven't been messed with. No one has traced a path for it to have come from anyplace where it still exists."

"It could be a government cover-up," Bethany said.

"I don't think so," Mr. Everly said from the doorway. He pointed at the television. "Those people are from the past. Society sources have already confirmed it. That—and the train, and the smallpox—is exactly the kind of crazy shit that happens when we change the past." His gaze landed on Violet. "Especially for our own gain."

Somehow, Violet made it through the next few weeks. She never found Stephanie, and no one made further attempts at her life. Maintaining the Society Intranet and helping other Houses with computer issues kept her busy.

Nights were the hardest. Lying alone in the dark was when she couldn't stop thinking of Tony, missing his warmth and conversation, or waking in the wee hours to feed Isaac, only to remember she'd lost him, too.

The news was the worst. She couldn't escape it, especially since events suspected to have been triggered by time distortions were highlighted on the Intranet. An airplane over the Pacific Ocean, gone one second when it had existed the one before. People drowning in the ocean—the mere thought of falling into that endless water sent chills rushing through Violet. A long-extinct volcano flared to life in southeast Asia, engulfing cities of millions. A dinosaur appeared in the middle of downtown Dallas, wreaking havoc like a real-life Godzilla. Floods and famine wracked northern Europe, where an ice age had inexplicably, suddenly returned.

Staggering numbers of people had gone missing. Others had appeared in odd costumes, sometimes speaking languages no one knew—or claiming they'd come from the future.

It really hit home one winter morning when Mr. Everly woke her up at six-thirty A.M.

"Wha…?" Violet tried to clear the sleep from her brain.

"Tornado. Touched down in Vandalia. Basement, now!" He left to rouse Taylor and Bethany, who'd taken to spending the night at the House more often than she stayed at her aunt's house.

"Tornado? In January?" Bethany mumbled.

"Alpha's behind it, you know," Violet said as she threw on her robe and hurried down the stairs. Taylor gave an emphatic nod.

Fred groaned from the second floor as Violet and the girls clomped past. "Nooooooooo!" The one word he could clearly say resonated from down the hall.

"Come on, Fred, you gotta go." Mr. Everly's voice faded as they reached the first floor, but Fred's protests grew louder. "Noooooooo! Bayyyyy… hurrrrrrrrr!"

Taylor yanked open the basement door, flipped on the lights, and started down, Bethany on her heels. Violet hesitated as her insides shriveled. The basement always made her feel like that, as if she were the doomed female character in a horror movie, about to descend to her death. She was even wearing a nightgown.

A flashlight, that was what she needed. As she hurried to grab it from the drawer in the dining room credenza, Fred clambered down the stairs. "Urrrrrrgggghhh!"

"No Fred, this way!" Mr. Everly yelled.

Her head jerked around as he grabbed the brain-damaged man by the arm and tried to drag him through the kitchen to the basement door.

"Nooooooooo!" Fred flung his arms out and braced himself in the doorway.

Mr. Everly tugged at his arm. "Fred, we've got to take shelter, come on!"

"Noooooooo!" Fred's vacant eyes narrowed as his gaze landed on Violet. "Herrrrrrr! Sharrrrrr.... Noooooo!" Violet cringed.

"Come on, Fred!" Mr. Everly pulled harder, but the impaired man seemed to have taken on super-human strength. Mr. Everly grasped Fred's arm with both hands, but as he shifted his grip, his hand slipped, and he stumbled backward.

Fred bolted for the front door and was out in a flash.

Mr. Everly picked himself off the floor and hurried to the entry. Violet gazed out from behind him.

The light reflected by the snow-covered ground held a greenish cast. Wind battered the road sign at the corner. Beneath the sound of the rushing wind, a tornado siren howled from somewhere in the distance.

Dawn was just near enough that she could see Fred's footprints veer off from the shoveled walkway and cut across the yard to disappear over the plowed drifts alongside Harrison Street. But Fred was nowhere in sight.

Mr. Everly reached for his coat, swearing under his breath. As he shrugged it on, Violet touched his elbow. "Chad..." She swallowed. He'd told her to call him that, many times, but still... "I don't want to sound callous, but..." She peered through the open door. Still no sight of Fred. No sounds other than the wind, the siren, and a banging shutter on the house across the street. "If something happens to him... maybe it's kinder."

Chad looked outdoors once more, then gave her a thin-lipped nod as he pulled the door shut. "He won't go in the basement. He does this every time, but I have to try. I'm responsible for him."

"You did what you could." They hurried into the kitchen, and to the stairwell. Violet squeezed the flashlight as she preceded him down the stairs, her knees trembling. What was it about the basement that troubled her so? Was it the same thing that made Fred run away in terror?

At the bottom of the steps, Chad motioned toward the far end of the low-ceilinged cellar. "The old coal storage room is the safest place."

They walked past a modern, gas furnace, ducking beneath the ducts. Nausea rose in Violet's stomach as she moved toward the light spilling from the open, solid wood door he indicated. When she walked through into the narrow, wood-paneled room, the gag reflex kicked in fully, and she ran to an enameled sink in the corner and vomited. Nothing came up but spit and bile.

"Are you okay?" Chad took her arm as she turned away from the sink and led her to two old, quilt-covered trunks, where she sat beside Bethany.

"I… I think so." She wiped her mouth with the back of her hand.

Something bad had happened here, *before*. Something very bad.

She gazed around the barren, wood paneled walls. Were those dark stains near the floor blood? "What… was this room used for?" she asked Chad. "Other than storing coal, I mean."

Chad's gaze slid from her, to Taylor, and back. "We believe this was where Theodore Pippin and Dr. Ben Caruthers from Cleveland performed lobotomies. Which would explain Fred…"

Heaven help me. Tony had told her she'd worked in the Society House as Mr. Pippin's assistant, back when she'd been Charlotte. And Dr. Caruthers certainly knew her. Violet's stomach turned in on itself. Had she helped them perform those vile deeds?

Beside her, Bethany flinched. "Ewwww…"

Breathe in, breathe out. Violet watched Taylor, who had a cell phone out and watched its screen intently.

Violet turned her hands over in her lap, traced the scar on her right palm. Whatever part she'd played in Dr. Caruthers' horrific experiments, she was not that woman now.

She traced over the other scar, vaguely aware that the wind had grown louder, like the roar of rain pummeling the House's roof. Something rattled in the dining room. *I'm not that woman now. Not that woman—*

"What happened to your hands?" Bethany leaned over and stared, then met Violet's gaze. "I mean if you don't mind—"

Violet swallowed, her mouth dry. "It's all right." Better that than think about what might have happened in the very place where she now sat. "Your father had a gun. There was an accident." She'd told Bethany, Taylor, and Chad about her and Tony's experiences in prehistoric times. "One of the village leaders was killed, and they blamed me." She turned her right hand over, and traced the scar on its back. "I was executed. Or would have been if your father hadn't saved me..." The wind increased in intensity, so loud she couldn't hear herself speak. Chad said something—she could see his mouth move, from where he sat on the trunk across from her, but she couldn't hear him, couldn't hear anything except the roaring wind.

Bethany curled into a ball, hugging Violet's arm. Taylor leaned against Bethany and wrapped an arm around the younger girl, holding the cell phone in her other hand. "It's right on top of us," Violet thought she heard Taylor say. The cell phone's screen showed a mass of green, spinning in a big circle over a mostly-obscured map.

The lights went out as the wind roared on. Violet had heard people say being very close to a tornado sounded like a freight train, and it did, on and on. From upstairs came a loud crash. Banging. Things falling. And Fred was outside in that, somewhere.

It would be kinder. Had she really said that? She slid her arm from Bethany's hold, and flicked the switch on the flashlight she held on her lap. Its beam flickered, then cast a wan circle on the ceiling.

She beat the light against her palm, and it got brighter. *Yes, kinder.* Death had to be preferable by far than to live with what had happened in this room, locked inside oneself.

Something loud crashed outside. Beside her, Bethany shivered, then finally, the roaring wind subsided.

Violet leaned around Bethany to peer at Taylor's phone.

"Looks like it's passed," the other girl said.

"I'm almost afraid to look." Chad stood, his downcast expression emphasized by the dim glow of the flashlight. "Not to mention Fred..."

Once he opened the door, Violet practically raced across the cellar. She couldn't get out of there fast enough, no matter what unpleasant surprises awaited.

Upstairs, Chad picked up broken glass from the kitchen floor— antique, china plates that had been displayed on a rack above the doorway. "Don't want anyone to step on this," he mumbled.

Violet knew he was really delaying the inevitable necessity of searching for Fred.

The four moved though the dining room, grabbed their coats, and filed out the front door.

"My word." Violet followed Chad off the porch and gazed up at the House.

Half of the third floor was gone—mostly Taylor's room, but there was a gap over the corner of Violet's, too.

"Fucking tornado in January?" Taylor kicked at a snowdrift. "At fucking six-thirty A.M.?"

"It's just wrong." Bethany crept to her friend's side and hugged her.

Violet's gaze drifted down the street, in the direction Fred's tracks went, and her hand flew to her mouth. "We were lucky. Look..." Two doors down, on the other side of the street, the rising sun illuminated an empty space where two houses had been leveled, and an entire wall was missing from a third. A car that was normally parked down the street lay on its roof in the middle of Harrison Street. All around the neighborhood, people emerged from houses with shouts of outrage, shock, and disbelief.

A young man and woman—U.D. students, probably—crept up the stairs to all that was left of one of the destroyed houses.

"It's just wrong," Bethany said.

"Yeah, who the hell ever heard of a tornado in January?" Taylor's gaze followed Chad, who strode across the street toward the newly-homeless couple.

"Just wrong," Bethany repeated. "More time anomaly stuff, you think?" she asked Violet.

Violet shivered. "I would bet on it—"

"My car!" Bethany disappeared around the side of the House.

Although the yellow Camaro was pretty, Violet had initially found the girl's attachment to the vehicle rather strange—then she'd learned it had been a gift from Tony. *All I have left of him,* Bethany had said. Lucky for her, the local police had recovered it after the kidnapping, and a shop had replaced the cut fuel line.

Across the street, the woman had started crying. Her husband—or boyfriend—held her and patted her absently as he listened to whatever Chad was telling him—probably offering help, or a place to stay at the House.

It was all Alpha's fault. So wrong...

Bethany returned, her breath forming white puffs. "It's okay." Her mouth slid open as she spied the scene across the street. "Oh, wow..." She shivered.

"We should go inside," Violet said. "You're freezing." Come to think, so was she, wearing only slippers on her feet.

"I'm not cold." But Bethany retreated up the walk and followed Violet and Taylor inside.

Bethany stopped in the foyer and drew herself up straight. "This should have never happened. It's just like that train in Europe, or the plane, or those cave-man people."

"Not like we can do anything about it," Taylor said.

"But we can," Bethany said. "Or at least, I can." She looked Violet in the eye. "I'm going back. Next year."

Violet clapped her mouth shut as her stomach slid up to her throat. How many times had she thought that very thing? Then dismissed it?

"Beth, I don't think—" Taylor began.

"I can change this. I can make sure her baby doesn't die."

"Yes." Violet's voice came out a whisper.

"But you could screw things up even more," Taylor said.

"More than this?" Bethany waved toward the door. "A tornado in January? Disappearing bridges? A hurricane in Scotland? In the winter?" She crossed her arms over her chest. "I'm going to do it. And you can't stop me."

"Actually, I probably can, but…"

Violet's resolve settled like a warm, home-cooked meal. "You're right. It's all wrong, too wrong. I'm going to go back, too. In December. And maybe between us, one of us will make our last-year's selves listen."

Twenty-three

Violet sat on her bed, squirmed, and smoothed her skirt again. Mr. Everly had gone to bed an hour ago. Finally, Taylor's footsteps clomped up the stairs to the third floor, and the door to her suite across from Violet's clicked shut.

It was time. A year ago—or nearly seventy, if one went by the calendar—she'd nursed her son and put him to bed in this very House, unaware it would be the last time she held him.

She closed her eyes, and exhaled with a shudder. The good Lord willing, she'd see Isaac again when she woke from recovery. And Tony would be locked in the conference room.

She closed her eyes. *1939, 1939...*

Nothing happened.

What? Worry trickled down her neck like a drop of sweat. She tried again. *1939, 1939...*

Nothing. Then she remembered.

Silly goose! You have to be in the same exact place!

She tiptoed downstairs, thankful they had no visitors and the guest room at the head of the stairs was vacant, as it had been since that freakish, January tornado, after which Fred's body had been found on Fifth Street, over a mile away.

She slipped inside, and sat on the bed. Imagined her former self, frightened for Tony and of Mr. Pippin, her breasts still capable of producing milk. She imagined her baby lying in the cradle at her feet, already asleep, his precious, soft hands in little half-fists at his head, which was turned to one side. She imagined the faint crackle of the radio in Mr. Pippin's suite—now Chad's—down the hall as the Watchkeeper caught his last tidbits of news before he retired. Imagined the vanilla scented pipe he sometimes smoked, and the fragrance of the fried mush Mrs. Meriwether often cooked for breakfast.

The dizziness struck instantly.

Bethany parked in front of the Cumberland Gap Saturn Society House and got out of the car before she was tempted to turn back and go home.

She'd told her mom she was going on a holiday trip with Taylor.

She'd told Chad, her aunt, and everyone else that she was going to visit her mom.

Her mom was caught up enough in her own life she wouldn't notice when Bethany didn't call. Her aunt might notice, but Chad would figure out what she'd done, and he'd cover for her. It was what the Society did.

As she knocked on Florie's door, she hefted her purse over her shoulder. It bulged with cookies, a jar of glucose tablets, and enough insulin and test kits to last three weeks.

Florie opened the door, and her eyes went round, though pleasure overtook her surprise. "Bethany! How good to see you!" Rufus nudged his nose under her elbow.

She led Bethany into the living room, where she'd apparently been on the computer using a Society chat room. "Sit down, relax. Just let me tell Candace goodbye... we were chatting about the horrible things going on—she lost a sister in that tunnel collapse down in Georgia, bless her heart. Lordy, I don't know what the world's comin' to." She typed a few lines then dashed into the kitchen. "Would you like a Coke, dear?" she called.

"Diet, if you have it."

"Sure thing, hon, that's what I meant." Bethany's gaze floated around the room, taking in the familiar landscape paintings and cross-stitch samplers. It seemed like only yesterday that she'd last been there, not a year ago—or nearly eighty.

Florie reappeared with two glasses and sat in the wingback chair opposite Bethany. "So what brings you here?"

Bethany sipped her drink while she tried to figure out what to say. "Um..."

Her dad would say just tell the truth. "I want to go back."

Florie lifted an eyebrow. "To...?"

"Last year. I mean, 1939. Like last year."

Florie slowly set her glass down. "Are you sure? Sometimes... things don't work out as we expect."

"Yeah, that's what Taylor says. But..."

She thought of that adorable little baby. She thought of Violet, always sad. She thought of the man who'd met her here at Florie's, begging her to go to 1939—what was his name? She couldn't remember. Couldn't even remember what he'd looked like, it had all gone hazy, but he'd been someone important.

She'd let him down. She'd let everyone down. Herself, Violet, and most of all, her dad. "I have to." An airy-scary feeling rose in her chest, like the first time she got behind the wheel of a car, or the time she'd sneaked and kissed a boy behind Danny and Mark's garage when she was ten.

"You know who Theodore Pippin is, don't you, dear?"

"Yeah, he was there with Daddy." Right before he'd disappeared. "Taylor says to stay away from him. 'Cause if I do this, I'm an enemy. Like my dad. And he'll make me like that guy that lived in our House in Dayton."

Florie's lips thinned. "Then you know the risks." She led her to the recovery room. "You got everything you need?"

In response, Bethany opened her purse. Rufus sniffed at it, undoubtedly hoping for a bite of cookie. "All right, then." Florie gave a sharp nod and left the room, Rufus on her heels.

Bethany sat on the second bed from the doorway, the same one where she'd sat and talked to... whoever that guy had been last year.

She glanced at the clock. Just a few minutes after two.

That seemed about right. Taylor'd said it would be hard to jump back into her own life. She'd need to be in the exact same physical location she'd been at the time she wanted to jump back to, because she'd be occupying the same physical space she had a year ago.

Bethany studied the cross-stitch on the wall, the same one that was there in 1939. She looked out the window and imagined it snowing, as it had been then.

1939. Take me back to 1939. It felt silly, like she should be clicking her heels together and saying there's no place like home—

The dizziness hit, and the bed dropped from beneath her.

Violet stood before the mirror in the ladies' room at Curly's Tavern. Everything was as she remembered. The confrontation with Caruthers. Alpha's unexpected help. Their flight to Tennessee. They'd finally reached Hollowville, and her breasts felt ready to burst if she didn't express some milk. Thankfully, Alpha hadn't protested too much, though she fidgeted and picked at her nails as Violet got out of the car.

Violet unbuttoned her dress and pushed up her brassiere, flinching at the ugly bruises Caruthers had inflicted. Mercy, she wished she'd not had to relive that part, but she'd feared that if she drove to Tennessee while in the twenty-first century, she wouldn't have been able to put herself in the exact right place at the exact right moment to be able to make the jump.

Twenty minutes later, she buttoned her dress and rinsed out the lavatory. It was an odd sensation to feel her old-self's sadness at washing her baby's sustenance down the drain. *You'll see him soon*, she promised her former self. *If all goes well*—

It *would* go well. She couldn't let herself think otherwise.

Her trepidation grew as she and Alpha headed out of town toward the Cumberland Gap House. She couldn't stop herself from glancing over at Alpha every few minutes, thinking of the woman's subterfuge, her lies, and tricks. She sensed her former self's protests. *There's no reason not to trust her. She helped you. She saved Tony's life many times.*

All for her own reasons, her now-self argued. Fear crept through her, raising the hairs on her arms. What if she couldn't convince her former self not to trust Alpha?

She forced herself to keep breathing when a dark speck appeared in the snowy road ahead. Mr. Pippin's maroon Packard, abandoned. "Mr. Pippin's," she whispered.

"There's no one in it," Alpha said.

Violet stopped the car, her heart pounding in her throat.

Several sets of footprints led away from the car, and tire tracks in the snow indicated a second car's arrival and departure. "He's found Tony." Violet's heart lodged in her throat.

Don't do it! Don't lead this woman to Tony! she screamed in her mind.

Her former self didn't listen. She watched her body shut off the car, open the door, and get out.

It all happened exactly as Violet remembered. She watched as her former self followed the tracks through the woods, then followed Alpha's directions when falling darkness and snow made the tracks indistinguishable. She begged her former self to lead Alpha away from Tony, but the stubborn woman she'd been refused to listen to her now-self's urgings that defied logic. Finally, the orange glow from Tony and Mr. Pippin's fire appeared over the edge of the drop-off.

Fresh footprints led away. Bethany and Taylor's, Violet's now-self realized. Would her former self mention them to Alpha, and give away the girls'—and Isaac's—whereabouts?

Despite the cold and falling darkness, the trek through the field and wood was easier than Bethany remembered, maybe because she'd been there before. Weird, it felt like there were two people in her brain—yet they were both her. The other presence—herself, from last year—seemed only slightly aware of her current self's presence.

Like the night her friend Ashley had almost been killed by those older guys they'd met at that party.

Bethany would've been with them if her dad hadn't shown up and almost passed out, making her leave with him. And then she'd called Ashley, just because... "Holy cow!"

Taylor stopped. "What?"

"Uh... man, it's cold." *Better not tell her.*

Taylor gave her a no-shit look and moved on.

But Bethany was pretty sure what had made her call, and then contact the police when her friend hadn't answered. She'd known what was about to happen to Ashley, because she'd gone back from sometime in the future. She'd made her earlier self make those calls, and saved Ashley from a horrible death.

It didn't take long to reach the ledge where her dad had taken refuge with Theodore Pippin, and she soon had the baby in the duffel bag, slung over her shoulders like a backpack. She led Taylor away, careful not to raise the other girl's suspicion. Wrenching herself away from her dad was harder than before, knowing that no matter what she did, she might never see him again.

"You have any idea where we're going?" Taylor asked.

"Florie's House is this way," she heard herself say upon prompting from her now-self. "I have a good sense of direction."

"You didn't when the car broke down."

"I was freaked out!" *Time to eat,* Bethany urged her younger self, remembering how she'd almost forgotten until she grew faint. Her younger self obeyed, and slowed. "Taylor... I need to stop."

"What's wrong?"

"I need something to eat."

"Can't you wait?"

Her old-self considered. *No!* she urged. "No."

Just like before, Taylor held Isaac, asleep in the duffel bag, while Bethany dug for her cookies.

"Here, let me..." Taylor reached for Bethany's purse.

Bethany hesitated. *Do it,* her older self urged. "Okay."

The duffel bag slipped in Taylor's other hand. "Uh..."

"Hang him in that tree over there," Bethany said.

Taylor gave her a weird look but did it.

As soon as Taylor got the cookie out, Bethany stuffed it in her mouth as fast as she could. *Hurry!* her older self urged. *Daddy needs you!* "We have to go back," she said.

"Back where?"

"To my dad—"

"He told you to get the baby out of there!"

Leave him—he'll be fine, older-Bethany said. She licked the crumbs off her freezing hands. "Leave the baby here—"

"Are you crazy?"

"Taylor... he'll be safe here, I'm sure. He'll be all right." She had to explain. "It's like there's... I don't know, someone else inside my head. Only it's me. Telling me that I have to—"

"Oh, God."

"What?"

"You've warped back into yourself."

Bethany could feel her younger self's confusion. "Huh?"

"You've warped back from sometime in the future. To relive this time, do things over—"

"Holy cow."

"I've never done it, but I've heard people in the Society describe it exactly like that."

"What should I do?" Bethany asked. *Listen to me! I'm you!* she shouted to her younger self. *Save your dad to save Isaac!* "This little voice in my head keeps saying if I don't go back to my dad, terrible things will happen. I feel all... weird and jumpy inside, like I don't know..."

Taylor stepped close, her face serious. "Beth... changing the past can be dangerous."

"I know, Florie told me. Learn, Observe, Preserve and all that. But I'm afraid if I don't—"

Hurry! she urged herself. *Or you'll be too late!* "Stay here with the baby. I'm going back for my dad."

Bethany rushed back down the trail, thankful the snow had

stopped and the clouds had parted to allow the moon to light the way, hoping it would be enough.

Violet stared down at the footprints. Her former self started to mention it to Alpha. *Don't worry about the footprints!* her now-self urged.

All right, her former-self agreed. Her now-self saw the logic filtering through. The footprints were too small to be Tony's. *Bethany and Taylor's,* her now-self realized. Since her former self remained focused on Tony and Isaac, she paid no mind to the other Violet's thoughts and continued toward the orange glow rising over the drop-off.

Stop Alpha! she screamed at herself.

Why? She felt the hesitation in her former self's thoughts, but her feet kept walking. *There's no reason to think ill of her.*

She stopped at the edge and peered down. Tony lay on one side of a campfire, Mr. Pippin slumped against a rock formation on its other side. "Tony!" The now-Violet sent her former self a wordless urge to watch Alpha.

Both men looked up. Terror washed across Tony's face. Violet scanned the ledge.

Isaac was not there. Fear shot down her throat. "Where's—"

"You're not getting my son!"

"But..." Violet sensed her former self's confusion. *Bethany took him, he'll be fine.*

Alpha crept toward a steep trail leading down the drop-off, and started down, grasping small trees and protruding rocks. *Stop her!* Violet screamed. Her former self stood rooted to the spot, her thoughts focused on Isaac.

Her body turned to follow the footprints away, toward the baby. *No!* she screamed at herself. *Tony needs you more!*

She clenched her jaw and stepped away from the ledge. Violet sensed her former self's anger at Tony, and the logic filtering through that Alpha would take care of him—

"Violet!"

Violet's head whipped around. The voice didn't come from the gully. It sounded like Alpha, but Alpha was down there—

"Violet!" The girl burst out of the woods and barreled into Violet. Tony's daughter Bethany. "Stop her!" Bethany bolted for the water run-off and climbed down.

Violet lurched to her feet only to crash to the ground as her foot caught on a root.

The seconds blazed by in a blur of sensation. The cold, wetness of the snow soaking through her clothes, her body sliding along it, the rush of air as she slipped over the edge. Rough dirt and rocks as she slid down the path.

The solid smack of the ground as she hit it. A dozen aches and pains bursting through her. Tony's shouts. Alpha's shrieks—or Bethany's? They sounded almost alike—

Another scream. Violet heaved herself to her feet, ignoring pains all over her body. *Tony. Tony, get to him, now!* she urged her former self. *Stop Alpha!*

Time ground to a near halt. In slow motion, Alpha drew her tracking device from her purse and pointed it at Tony like a weapon. *No!* Violet's later-self screamed, pushing her former self's logic aside at last. With the last of her strength she launched herself at Alpha's feet as the woman pressed a button on the object.

As Alpha went down, light burst from the weapon, striking a tree. Screams sounded, as if from a deep pit.

Something sizzled, and vertigo swept over Violet. In the firelight, the tree shimmered, faded and disappeared. Violet's dizziness went away.

Realization struck her former self. It was the interdimensional containment device she'd heard those men from the Order speaking about. *She made the tree warp into the Void!* Ignoring painful bumps and bruise, Violet pushed herself up.

Alpha scrambled for the device, which had landed near the fire. As her fingers lit on it, Violet hurled herself onto the woman.

Alpha clawed at her legs, writhing beneath her. Violet pitched sidewise, grasping at Alpha's arm, but the woman shoved her toward the campfire.

Violet lurched for the containment device, but Alpha anticipated the move and jumped on top of her, crushing her to the snowy ground. She punched Violet's face, then got up to roll Violet over. Violet tensed, resisting. Alpha punched her again, and pain flared in her temple. From the corner of her eye she saw Tony trying to pull himself to the women. Bethany crouched at his side. Theodore Pippin lay motionless on the other side of the fire.

Violet struggled, trying to dislodge Alpha, trying to reach the silvery, phone-like device glinting in the firelight. With a shriek, someone else launched onto the pileup.

All Violet felt was a sudden weight added to Alpha's. Stars burst in her vision, as if a great hand were forcing her into the ground. She couldn't breathe, the weight of the two attackers too much—

The pressure lifted. Violet raised up to see Tony's daughter pulling Alpha's arm. Alpha beat at her with the containment device. Bethany yelped, and a realization struck Violet.

She sounded just like Alpha. She looked like her, too. Same thick, straight, blond hair. Same strong yet feminine features. Same willowy build.

If Alpha was from the future—

Alpha flung Bethany away. The girl bumped into Violet, knocking the wind out of her, but Violet recovered enough to grab the girl before she lost her balance and fell into the fire. Alpha raised the containment device, and everything again slipped into slow motion.

Tony lay behind Violet.

She was his only hope—

Use Bethany! her newer self ordered.

Her former self hesitated. Alpha's thumb pressed down—

Violet grabbed Bethany by both arms and yanked her around so that she stood between Alpha and Tony, with Bethany as a shield. If she was wrong, Alpha would send the innocent girl into the Void along with Violet, but—

Alpha froze, her finger poised above the button on the device.

It was all Violet needed. She threw Bethany at Alpha, and the containment device flew from her hands, landing at Violet's feet.

Violet picked it up. Alpha grabbed Bethany, clasping her to her chest as Violet had.

"Use it!" Bethany shouted.

Violet turned the containment device over in her hands. How did it work?

Do it! her now-self screamed.

She lifted the device, pointed at Alpha.

Alpha grabbed Bethany, holding the girl in front of her. "It won't work! It'll only work for him! Or her!"

Logic kicked in for both Violets. It had worked on the tree.

"Do it!" Tony yelled from behind her.

Bethany twisted aside, and in that second, Violet pressed the button.

As she remembered from before, light burst from the device, enveloping Alpha, Bethany, and the campfire. The dizziness struck, and Violet's world rocked.

A second later, the vertigo subsided. Bethany stumbled and fell forward, crashing to the ground beside Tony.

Alpha was gone.

Violet tried to catch her breath. She'd done it. Saved Tony. Eliminated the threat—the real threat. But where was I—

"Witches!" A voice shouted from above.

What? Violet picked herself off the ground, wiping melted snow and dirt from her face, and gazed up at the rim of the drop off.

Into the face of Dr. Caruthers.

"Witches!" A second man appeared beside him, the firelight glinting off his wire-rim glasses. "She made that woman disappear!"

British accent. Violet's lungs turned to ice.

The murderer with Tony's face peered over the embankment. Dr. Caruthers climbed down the water runoff. Others followed.

"*They're* witches!" Mr. Pippin pointed at Violet from behind the campfire.

Shouts rose from above. More angry people.

Violet stepped backward. Where had these people come from? And how—

The man who looked like Tony leered over the ledge. "You'n I'll have us some jolly good times, lady." His face stretched into a sick grin. "But I promised the good doctor he could have you first."

Dr. Caruthers leapt at Violet, firelight glinting on the polished silver, Saturn Society knife in his fist.

Violet swung her arm up, pointed the containment device at him, and pushed the button. The world went white as the light enveloped him. For a long second, nothing existed but that whiteness, and his fading scream. Then silence.

"Witches!" someone shrieked from above. "She made him disappear!"

"They're all witches!" Mr. Pippin shouted. "Especially him!" He pointed to Tony.

A man crawled down the water runoff, then another swung over the edge to follow amidst more shouting.

"Stop!" Bethany shouted from behind Violet. "Unless you want the same thing to happen to you!"

The man climbing down the slope froze, his gaze fixed on Violet.

Bethany's presence nudged Violet into action. Violet brandished the device. "Leave us! Now!"

Grumblings rose from the group at the top of the ravine. The first man withdrew. "You, too!" Violet yelled at the men halfway down the slope. She glared at them until they scurried back to the top, waited a few minutes, then climbed up to make sure they'd left. Pounding footsteps retreated.

"Lying cowards!" she yelled after them.

"Vio—" Tony's call cut off in a strangled choke.

She whirled around.

The lookalike killer had climbed from the upper ledge and held a knife to Bethany's throat.

"You bastard!" Bethany twisted in his grasp. "You killed my cousin!"

The man laughed. "And a thrill it was, to feel his young life slip from beneath my hands. Just like yours soon will."

Tony struggled to pull himself toward the man, the sweat on his forehead glistening in the firelight. "Fucking... bastard... leave... my daughter... out—"

Laughing, the man tossed Bethany like a rag doll. She stumbled into Violet, whose breath left in a whoosh as she tumbled to the ground. "Run away, girlie," the man said. "I'll get you when I can get you for good." He leaped onto Tony and grasped his neck. "Now him... as many times as he's died in the past, this just may be his last. Wouldn't't'cha love to find out?"

"No!" The man squeezed harder. Tony made gagging sounds as Bethany leaped for him.

"Stay away, and I may let him live a bit longer—"

"Violet!"

Her head whipped around. A woman in full, black skirts with a lumpy backpack slung over her shoulders clambered down the water runoff. "Taylor?" Bethany said.

Violet glimpsed the baby's face poking out of the unbuttoned end of the duffel bag in the woman's arms. "Isaac!"

"I couldn't just leave him." Taylor slipped the bag's straps off her arms and handed Violet the baby, then her eyes went wide as she took in the scene by the fire.

The killer laughed. "Say goodbye, ladies!" He squeezed Tony's neck as if he was gripping a weight. Tony gurgled, his arms flailing.

"No!" Bethany and Violet screamed in unison.

Bethany lurched toward the man, but Violet hung back, fearing he'd come after Isaac. Taylor grabbed Bethany's arm. "Let him!" her friend whispered. "He'll go back—"

"But he said—"

"You've been a thorn in my side far too long, Tony Solomon," the lookalike muttered. "Kill you here, we'll go back together—"

Bethany ran toward him, but tripped over a root and crashed to the ground. Violet clutched Isaac as a dizzy spell assaulted her. Taylor grabbed the rock outcropping where Mr. Pippin lay.

When the dizziness passed, both Tony and his double were gone.

Violet sank to the ground, defeated. Isaac cooed as she clutched him to her.

She was dimly aware of Bethany sobbing a few feet away, and Taylor's murmured words as she tried to console the girl. Mr. Pippin slumped against the big rock, unconscious. From the distance, Violet heard Florie calling.

The girls and Mr. Pippin would be all right. But she could do something more.

Once one had done it, jumping to the future had fewer limitations than jumping into the past, Alpha had told her. She didn't need to wait for the Pull that would never come, and she'd been in 1939 long enough to have built up strength.

She glanced into the duffel bag, the baby's face visible where the snaps had been left open. Amazingly, Isaac had fallen asleep. Slipping the bag's straps over her shoulders so that Isaac's head lay between her breasts, she looked up to meet Bethany's tearful gaze. "I'm going after your father." She crept along the ledge—the drop off there was so far down, she couldn't see it—and slipped behind the rock outcropping where Mr. Pippin lay.

She gripped the containment device in her hand. The woods were unlikely to have changed noticeably. She pictured Florie's newer, steel bridge that would be visible through the trees above the ravine. She barely thought the date—Tony's natural time—before the dizziness swamped her.

"Wot have we here?" a British-accented voice crowed as the vertigo faded.

Violet jumped to her feet and took advantage of the surprise of her arrival. The killer was picking himself up a few feet away from Tony.

She pointed the containment device at the clean-cut Tony, the source of the British voice, and pushed the button, bracing herself for the brightness, but it flared quickly then died. Either its short window of operation had closed, or it wasn't programmed to work in the twenty-first century.

Tony picked himself up, brushing the dirt off his pants. Too small, Violet noted in a detached way. "He jumped," Tony said.

"But I didn't feel—"

"Not in time. Down there."

She crept to the ledge's edge and peered over.

A thin moan reached her from the bottom.

She stepped away, rubbing her hands together. No snow, but mercy, it was cold.

And the fatigue was hitting her.

Tony stumbled, then fell. He sat, staring into space. "Got to... get Florie. Recovery..." He rubbed his left arm, the one he'd broken. Though dried blood crusted his coat, Violet suspected it had healed.

"I'll find her," Violet said. "You'll fall into recovery faster." What the killer had been counting on. The water run-off was grooved a little deeper, but otherwise everything looked as it had in 1939, only it was lit by the full moon instead of a fire. She started to pull herself up when a voice from the gorge's rim above made her slip.

"Violet? Tony?" A graying-brown-haired head peeked over the edge, and a long, black nose followed. Rufus barked.

"Florie! Thank heavens!" Violet called. From the bag at her chest, Isaac gurgled.

"Jest sit tight, help's on the way," the older woman called.

Everything was going to be all right. Violet rushed to Tony's side as Florie disappeared. "Are... are you all right?"

He held up his left arm. "Still hurts, but... yeah, I'm okay." His head jerked up. "Isaac. What—"

"He's right here..."

Tony's head lolled, and she realized he was slipping into recovery.

He blamed her for leading Mr. Pippin to him. How could she ever convince him she hadn't betrayed him, that her bargain with Mr. Pippin was a ruse? She'd never again hear him say loving words to her. But as much as it pained her, she could live with that. She had Isaac, and that was what mattered most. Her son, safe. Warm. Alive. She carefully unzipped the duffel bag.

Isaac's gurgly baby noises were the sweetest thing she'd ever heard. She pressed him against her, drinking in how right he felt in her arms, his sweet baby smell, his silken cheeks against her skin, soft even in the cold. Her eyes misted over.

His gurgles turned to cries. Not wails, but simple hunger.

"Can y'all make it up, or do I need to go for help?" Florie shouted from the ledge above.

"I think so." Violet hefted Isaac's bag against her chest.

"Give me... baby." Tony reached for her, his arms trembling.

Violet hung back. Having been injured, recovery was coming on faster for him, but if she didn't hand over their son, it would deepen his mistrust. Slowly, she slid the duffel bag's straps off her arm and helped Tony slide them onto his. "You first." She pointed to the slope. If he fell, she might be able to catch Isaac.

And hope they reached Florie's house before they collapsed in recovery.

Twenty-four

Morning sun slanted through the white lace-curtained windows when Isaac's cries woke Violet. She blinked. *Where on earth?* She took in the sampler on the wall, the hurricane lamp on the doily-covered nightstand, the quilt-covered beds—Florie's recovery room.

Tony lay in the bed beside her, still in recovery, judging from his extra-slow breathing.

Baby gurgles and coos drifted from a few feet away. She dragged herself out of bed and followed her ears to a small, wooden cradle on the floor. Isaac quieted as soon as her shadow fell over him. Bruises peppered her body, announcing their presence with her every movement. As she gathered Isaac to her, sat on an empty bed, and unbuttoned her gown to feed him, sheets rustled behind her.

Tony's unfocused, blue eyes fell on her the instant she turned to face him. He sat up, his gaze never leaving hers, laced with accusation and hurt that went beyond his now-healed injuries. She tensed and looked away. The bed creaked as he got up. She tried to focus on Isaac, but the baby sputtered and let go. The third time he tried to feed then gave up, she finally forced words through her thick throat. "Please leave, Tony. He doesn't feed well when I'm tense."

She waited until his feet shuffled out the door.

She felt like someone had dropped a skid of bricks on her. She forced her mind to blank so the tension would leave. She couldn't think about Tony. Couldn't think about how he lied, and pretended he didn't know who she was. Couldn't think about him stealing Isaac.

Couldn't think about the times he said he loved her.

She focused on her baby's face, his beautiful, perfect, rosy cheeks, his satiny soft skin, his downy dark hair. The uncanny way he never cried unless he was hungry or had a soiled diaper. The way his mouth opened—almost in a smile, as if he sensed her sadness and knew the one means to chase it away.

By the time she fed and burped him, conversation drifted from the kitchen. Her stomach growled. She didn't want to face Tony, but she dressed and crept out to the living room, where tinsel glittered and colored lights twinkled on a Christmas tree in a marked contrast to the tension in her belly. The faint aroma of pine from the live tree lingered beneath the more pervasive scent of fried eggs and skillet gravy.

Though Florie's cooking was marvelous as it had been before, breakfast was a somber affair. Tony took two bites, then leaned his elbows on the table, forehead in his hands. Rufus nudged his elbow, hoping for a handout, but Tony ignored the dog.

"You all right, Tony?" Florie asked.

He shook his head. "My daughter. I have no idea where she is, or when—"

"Why, she's in 1939. And she's just fine."

He looked up. "How do you know?"

"Where'd you think she stayed?" Florie reached across the table and patted his arm. "Mama and I got there right after the two of you jumped. Us and the two girls hauled that awful Mr. Pippin up all by ourselves." She made a face. "Though I was half a mind to leave him there, after he got the townspeople all riled up that we were witches."

"Bethany'll come back here?"

Florie smiled. "Just after New Year's." She walked to a wall calendar behind Violet and flipped the page up to January. "Right about there, give or take a day."

Tony's narrowed gaze settled on Violet. "How could you," he said through clenched jaws, "use my daughter... like that?"

She recoiled under his glare. "I saved your life!" Even though all had worked out well and she knew she'd done the right thing, her stomach curled in on itself at the chance she'd taken, had her suspicion been wrong.

"She could have been zapped away—"

"All worked out for the good," Florie said.

He ignored her. "She could have gotten sent to—my God." His face went white.

"How could you miss the resemblance?" Violet jerked him out of his trance.

"What resemblance?"

"Bethany. And Alpha."

"Huh?" Florie said.

"Their voices even sound alike," Violet said.

"Yeah, but—"

"Tony, Alpha's your descendant. And Bethany's. That's why she kept saving your life. Until she could be sure Bethany lived. Then you became a liability, so—"

"Holy shit." Tony's mouth fell open. "Keith said Alpha needed her, but I never would have guessed…"

"That's why she couldn't send Bethany to the Void," Violet said.

Tony arched an eyebrow.

"Those men from the Order told me about it. A dimension between our temporal planes of existence, where nothing exists at all. Just empty, wandering souls who are never able to contact each other, or anything of this dimension—"

"Oh, God." His face paled. "I've seen that place. In my nightmares."

"Lordy," Florie murmured. They sat in silence for a long moment until Florie picked up a bowl of biscuits and thrust it at Violet. "Come on, y'all need to eat. Especially you, nursing the little one." Violet took a biscuit and passed the bowl to Tony.

She held Isaac on her lap while she ate. Tony's eyes never left the baby. She knew it was irrational, but she was afraid that if she let Isaac out of her sight, he'd be taken from her again. She wasn't sure by whom. Though her anger at Tony still burned, she knew in her heart he wouldn't try to take the baby again.

"Violet? Tony?" They both looked up at Florie. "I'm going to take Rufus for a walk. If y'all don't mind…" Rufus bolted for the back door, where his leash hung.

"Of course not," Violet said. Tony mumbled an agreement as Rufus bounded into the room with his leash in his mouth, prancing in circles around Florie.

"All right, all right..." Florie clipped the dog's leash on and let him drag her to the door, thanking them as she slipped out.

Tension wound around Violet like a tightening rope, but she forced herself to clear the table. Anything to escape Tony's scrutiny, though it was difficult to work while holding Isaac.

Tony rose and stood beside her. His nearness brought flutters to her belly, as if a colony of sparrows had taken up residence there. She ached to throw herself into his arms, yet beneath the birds, a cauldron simmered, not at what he'd done, but at her body's betrayal—that after all he'd done, damned if she didn't still want him.

She focused on the dishes.

"I'm not going to take him away." His words were cool and measured, barely concealing the hurt and anger beneath.

She dropped a handful of silverware into the sink. "You knew," she said quietly. "All along, you knew."

"Knew what?"

"Who I am. Or was. Yet you pretended you didn't." She gripped a wad of Isaac's blanket.

The baby let out a choked gurgle. Violet realized she was squeezing him and loosened her hold. "You let me go on for years, having no idea who—"

"I didn't know who you were until last year! And even then, it was just a suspicion. I sure as hell wasn't sure enough to say anything."

"But you did know me. And we..." She jerked her head, trying to clear her throat. "We meant something to each other."

"I saved your life! I pulled you out of the flood."

"So Mr. Pippin told me."

"And when I came back, twenty years later, you repaid me by luring me into your home, so Pippin could come after me—"

Violet gasped. "I couldn't have!"

"You did. When I came back a second time..." He paused, clenching his jaw. "I tried to escape. And you killed me."

Violet choked on a breath. Her throat felt like someone had jammed a stake down it. "I know." Her grip loosened on Isaac, and she tightened it just in time to keep from dropping him.

"Give me the baby." Tony held out his hands.

"No! I won't—"

"I'm not going to take him away. Just let me hold him before you drop him."

She handed him the baby. "I couldn't... couldn't have—"

"You did." He shifted Isaac to one shoulder and pulled up his shirt, baring the scar on his stomach. "See this?"

"No..." she whimpered.

"You did it."

No! She sank into a chair, her legs no longer able to support her. Her worst suspicion, reality.

She was a murderer. Or worse.

Mr. Pippin would have wanted Tony alive, to administer that Treatment Tony had told her about. "What if I..." she swallowed, "killed you to save you? From Mr. Pippin?"

Tony looked down, his jaw tight. "I thought of that. But seeing you in the car with Pippin, then what you did at the House when he locked me up—"

"I tried to save you! I kicked my barrette under the door so you could pick the lock!" She spoke with shaky breaths. "Then you took Isaac."

Tony held the baby close, stroking his back. "If I hadn't, Alpha would've gotten both me and him with that... thing."

"Is that why you took him away?"

He looked down, deflated. "No."

Violet watched Tony and Isaac. The way they looked at each other, she could swear the baby knew something of what was going on between them. The connection between father and son was almost palpable. Her throat thickened. She tried to think of something to get Tony's mind off her

(I killed him)
and onto something else. "How is your arm? I heard you, around four A.M."

His eyebrows lifted. "It wasn't my arm." At her questioning look he continued. "Nightmare."

She stiffened. "I didn't know you suffered from—"

"I dreamed... when Alpha came up to me and Pippin back there... that you weren't able to get that thing away from her. And she zapped me with it. Then, there was nothing but... nothing."

"Wha-at?" Violet said weakly. Alpha had overcome *her* instead? Nervousness radiated through her body. That other timeline was already fading into memory, but it had happened. Before she'd changed it.

"I was existing in a...like a vacuum." Tony patted Isaac's back in short, sharp strokes. "I couldn't see anything, but it wasn't dark. Just nothing. I couldn't hear anything. Not even my own breathing. Couldn't feel anything—I don't think I had a body, more like I was just my thoughts. That's it. Nothing else.

"They teach in my mom's church that hell is fire and brimstone, but I don't think it is." He rubbed the baby's back, as if needing the reassurance of human touch. "I think that nightmare, that nothing-ness... that's what hell must be."

Violet swallowed. "The Void."

"Probably."

He'd gone there, because of her. She hoped that timeline would fade in his memory, the way her recollection of it already was. "I sent Alpha there. I would never let something like that to happen to you." The thought of Tony there, in that horrific nothingness, made her choke up. Then she reminded herself of what he'd done. "Even if you tried to take my son away from me. Even Alpha... the only reason she deserves something like this is because she tried to do the same to you."

Though she had a hard time feeling bad about Dr. Caruthers. "I could never do this to..." She wet her lips. She had to admit it. "...someone I loved. No matter what. I can't imagine ever being able to... help Mr. Pippin and that horrible Dr. Caruthers turn you into a bumbling zombie like that poor man at Chad and Taylor's House."

"Yet, you were ready to turn me in to him in 1959." Tony's face remained impassive, but she saw the hurt and anger simmering beneath.

"Because I didn't remember! I was trying to get help! I didn't know anything about that Black Book, or Dr. Caruthers' lobotomies then." She sniffled. "I'm... before all this started, I'm certain that I... cared for you. But I was telling the truth when I said I had no idea who I was before. I won't lie to you now, Tony. I have no idea what my intentions were when I was... Charlotte."

Florie came in from her walk, Rufus bursting into the kitchen to coax someone into giving him a treat. Violet grabbed a dog biscuit from the tin on the counter and handed it to Rufus, then returned to clearing the table and washing dishes.

Somehow, she managed to get through the rest of the day. She stayed away from Tony, except when he asked for Isaac, or when he was already holding the baby, and Isaac needed to be fed.

Every time she approached Tony, her hurt deepened. How could she have betrayed him to Mr. Pippin? If he thought that, it was no surprise that he didn't believe she'd lied to Mr. Pippin in the hallway outside the conference room.

Watching television with Florie helped occupy her, though her thoughts were never far from Tony, especially when his picture—or rather, his lookalike's—flashed on the news.

Rescuers had found the murderer at the bottom of the gorge, injured but alive, thanks to an anonymous phone tip.

"You called, didn't you?" Violet asked Florie.

The older woman smiled.

Violet looked back at the television as the newscaster explained that the unknown man was being held under guard in the nearby hospital. Tony's family had insisted on DNA testing, which had confirmed the John Doe as the murderer. Tony's acquittal was certain, should he even go to court. He'd already spoken to his parents and sister, and Mr. Everly was already en route to pick them up.

A commercial came on, and Violet forced herself to ask the other questions she'd been dreading. "Florie, what's going on with the smallpox epidemic? Are they vaccinating babies again?" Isaac hadn't had shots, of course.

"Smallpox?" The woman's face was blank. "What'n the world are you talking about?"

"What about the railroad in eastern Europe? That disappeared?"

Florie's face blank, she slowly shook her head.

"People showing up, like they're from out of the past?"

"Don't know anything about that, honey."

Violet started to ask about another catastrophe, then realized she'd forgotten what she was going to say. The events were fading in her memory. She'd altered the time stream by saving Tony and relegating Alpha to the Void. The smallpox epidemic, the displaced people, the disappearing train track had never happened.

The news came back on, this time about a kidnapping ring. "Jerry Mercer, twenty-one, has been added to the list of participants in the scheme," the newscaster said. "Mercer was employed at Mad Murphy's Truck Stop and Travel Mart, where he identified the prospects and tampered with their car. Mercer awaits indictment, along with five other residents of Hollowville, who have come forward and confessed to their part in the crime." Mercer's photo disappeared and a drawing that looked remarkably like Alpha flashed on the screen. "Participants claim they were paid amounts ranging from ten thousand to a half million dollars by this woman, who goes by the name Jennifer Warren. Her motives remain unclear." The newscaster concluded by asking anyone with information to call the FBI.

Florie pointed at the television. "That's what Bethany and Taylor got mixed up in."

"Holy hell," Tony said.

"Yup. That's how your daughter got gifted. She ran out of her insulin, and was about to die when Taylor gifted her. Jumped back to '76, got her to a hospital just in time." She chuckled. "That was quite a stunt Taylor pulled, swipin' that road flare."

Tony's mouth curled. "Huh?"

Florie smiled. "Accordin' to Chad, Taylor has a little problem with shoplifting. Turned out to be a stroke of luck for your daughter. Lightin' that flare in the back of the truck was how they got that fella to pull over. Good thing, too, seein' as your daughter was near death."

"Holy shit." Tony looked down, his wide-eyed stare unseeing. "You're sure she's okay now?"

"I said she was, didn't I?"

Someone knocked on the front door. Florie jumped up to answer it. "That must be Chad." She flung the door open. "Come in, come in! So nice to see you... but it wasn't necessary—Taylor'n Bethany aren't due back for another week, and Lordy, you shouldn'ta left your House unwatched—"

"I got Tom from Toledo to come down." He looked up to meet Violet's gaze, and his characteristic grin stretched even wider as he wrapped her in a hug. "You have no idea how we worried about you..." His smile disappeared as he stepped backward. "Jesus, I can't believe I trusted her." He shook his head, gaze downcast.

Talking about Alpha, of course. "You had no reason not to," Violet said in a gentle voice.

Mr. Everly mumbled at the floor. "...can't imagine what might've happened..."

Florie smacked him on the shoulder. "Enough of that! There's no sense in borrowing trouble from another today." He let her steer him to a chair in the parlor.

Violet followed, unable to suppress a shiver. She could imagine, but there was no point in telling Mr. Everly. If she hadn't listened to her future self this time... Images flickered through her mind of destruction, freakish natural disasters, people like the prehistoric villagers appearing out of nowhere. "It all worked out in the end." She sat on the sofa. Tony took the far end, holding the sleeping Isaac against his shoulder.

Mr. Everly's mouth twitched, then his smile returned, although more subdued. He pulled a narrow package from his jacket's inside pocket and handed it to Tony. "I ordered this for you. It came just before Halloween."

Tony laid Isaac across his lap to open the package, and Violet had to restrain herself from jumping up and grabbing the infant. If any kind of parenting arrangement was to work between them, she had to trust him.

He picked at the package wrapping, but his broken fingernails slipped on the tape. Florie dashed to the kitchen. "Hang on, I'll get the scissors."

Tony studied the box. "Saturn Society Headquarters, St. Augustine, Florida, huh?"

"Looks like I need to order one for you, too," Chad said to Violet as Florie returned.

"What?" Violet asked, but everyone's attention turned to Tony as he cut the box open and slid out a polished, silver dagger in a leather sheath. He passed Isaac to Violet, then held the knife inches from his eyes. The Christmas tree lights highlighted the name and date etched in the handle. "I think you've earned that, a few times over," Mr. Everly said.

With a tight-lipped nod, Tony put his Saturn Society knife on the end table beside him.

He and Violet took turns holding Isaac while they told Mr. Everly about their time in prehistoric America, and about Bethany's harrowing experience that led to her becoming a time traveler.

When Violet got to the part about Alpha, Mr. Everly's smile disappeared again. "Jesus Christ." He stared into his lap. "I helped her. Here I thought..." He shook his head, then looked up, his eyes full of pain. "This is my fault. I led her to you. I—"

"You couldn't have known," Violet said. "None of us could."

"I sure as hell didn't," Tony said.

Mr. Everly shook his head. "I know, but—"

"Did you rig the television set?" Violet asked.

"No. But Alpha had the full run of the House. I trusted her..."

Violet pointed up. "It could have been the burglar, right before we came."

"Maybe." Mr. Everly looked up. "If there's anything I can do for you, any time... I know I can never make up for what you've been through, but..."

Violet felt bad for him. "It's not your fault. You had no way of knowing Alpha was their ringleader. She had me fooled right up until the end. Which reminds me..." She dashed to the coat she'd worn in 1939—Caruthers', ugh—and pulled the interdimensional containment device from the pocket. "Is there somewhere we can store this for safekeeping? It's my understanding that it can only be used for a short window of time, and once someone's trapped in here, there's no way out, but as much as Alpha fooled everyone..."

Florie took it. "I'll lock it in the vault, and contact the Society Council, see what we should do long term." She disappeared into the kitchen. A door squealed, and the slap of her walking shoes receded down wooden steps.

Mr. Everly slipped into the entryway and returned with another small package. "I almost forgot. This came for you last week. No idea who it's from, or why they sent it to the House—"

"For me?" Tony asked.

"It's addressed to both of you." He handed it to Violet.

"It's from the office." She frowned. What on earth?

"Open it." Isaac gurgled, so Tony sat him up and rubbed his back while the baby watched with interest.

A brief worry flitted through her mind. What if it was another trick of Alpha's? "I'm not sure I should..."

Tony took it with his free hand and quirked an eyebrow. "That's Keith's handwriting." He gave Isaac a strange look. "I guess I should fill you in—"

She tore the pull strip. A thin, square envelope and a small, brown-paper-wrapped box tumbled into her lap. "A DVD." She picked up the box. *Tony* was handwritten across one side. "This is for you." She handed it to him, then held up the DVD. "I wonder if Florie has a player?"

The other woman appeared from the kitchen. "Of course I got a player. Even with satellite, there's not much worth watchin' on TV."

Violet eyed the DVD warily. "Are you sure we should—"

Florie plucked it from her fingers.

"It's okay, it's from Keith." Tony laid Isaac on his legs, with the baby's head at his knees, and swung his legs from side to side while Florie inserted the disk.

Keith Lynch's image appeared on screen. He sat behind a big, mahogany desk—"His home office," Tony said. Violet drew back. What on earth?

"Hello Tony, Violet," Keith said. "By the time you watch this, I won't be able to talk to you, as I'm only a few weeks old."

"What?" Violet jerked upright.

"I never had a chance to tell you," Tony said. "This—" he pointed at Isaac "—is Keith."

"Son of a gun," Florie said. "And he was here just the other day…"

"My word." Violet pressed her fingers to her chest as her gaze flitted from her baby to the man on the screen. "But why—"

"Shh," Tony said.

Violet stared at the baby. The resemblance was unmistakable, even at only six weeks old. The shape of his eyes, a dark, murky blue that she'd already figured would turn brown, the tilt of his mouth, his left eyebrow that was smidge higher than the right. "I still can't believe it." She tried to pay attention as Keith explained that the rationale behind many of his business strategies had been based on his knowledge of the future. "I realize that Chad and Florie may be watching with you, and that my actions aren't exactly Society-approved, but everything was very necessary." Keith swiveled in his chair. "We're at war in the future. Not countries or political powers, though that will come if we fail to contain those who threaten our way of life.

"You may be acquainted with a traveler from the future, a woman named Jennifer Warren Alpha 8736, otherwise known simply as Alpha. In your time, the Society believes that intentionally altering the past promotes discord and chaos in the fabric of time, creating ripple effects and causing the thread of time itself to unravel. Ms. Warren is the leader of a rogue faction of the Saturn Society, known as the Order of Titan, who refute these facts, believing instead that those with our gift are not the bearers of great responsibility, but are instead entitled to wealth and power and even world dominance."

"Jesus Christ," Chad muttered.

"Approximately two hundred years in your future, Ms. Warren has—or will—build a substantial following, who will use whatever means they can to gain this power. Governments have failed to fight this menace. The wealth the Lynch Companies have amassed will finance efforts within the Society." Keith leaned back and clasped his hands over his stomach. "The fact that you're watching now means that our cause will triumph, and I was able to return to your time to arrange for courier service to get this to you."

"Good heavens," Violet said.

"I've kept my identity secret for many years. Why, you may ask. Tony, until last year, when you acquired the gift, would you have believed me?"

"Fuck no," Tony said. Florie shot him a stern look. Chad's grin returned in full force.

"And after that, you needed time to acclimate," Keith said. "You needed time to learn what you were capable of. And you needed to meet my mother, who for many years, I was unable to locate due to her own forward jump which cost her her memory. For a long time, I feared for my existence, particularly since Ms. Warren tried numerous times to prevent you two from meeting."

Violet turned sideways to meet Tony's gaze.

"But all has happened as it should. Including my sister becoming like us." Keith tipped his chair back. "If Bethany's not with you, tell her I love her, and give her my thanks for saving my life. Oh, and tell Chad and Taylor that I'm sorry for breaking into their House. I tried to prevent that horrible trip back so far that you endured, but I failed, and for that I apologize. I hope I'm worth it.

"None of you ever need to worry about money. In addition to making a sizable donation to the Society, I've set up a family trust. You also have full access to any of the Lynch Company's residential and resort properties." He explained that the documents were in a safe-deposit box in an offshore banking facility, as well as the location of his various cash stashes—in various times throughout the last two centuries.

"Finally, I thank you for a happy, loving childhood. Our home wasn't—won't be—stable, but you always taught me what I needed to know, made sure I never lacked for any need. Because of our... odd... circumstances, I've never been able to say it, but..." He scrubbed his nose with a fist. "I love you."

The screen went blank.

For a long moment, no one spoke. "Wow," Mr. Everly finally said. "I can't believe I trusted—"

"Enough of that!" Florie held up a hand. "I trusted her, too. Heck, she even pulled the wool over Rufus' eyes, and dogs almost always know." At her feet, the dog lay down, his chin between his front paws.

Violet scooted closer to Tony, where Isaac still lay across his lap. "I can't believe... this is *him*." She stroked the baby's arm. "Yet, I can see the resemblance, especially to you." She looked up at Tony. "All this time when people would remark how much you and Mr. Lynch looked alike, I thought it was just a coincidence."

Tony stroked Isaac's cheek. "He's got your eyes."

The baby's eyes were still a newborn's dark blue, but Violet knew Tony referred to Keith, the adult. "He does, doesn't he?"

Tony didn't look up. "Keith—I mean Isaac—introduced me to Dora. Dorothy C. Henderson. Must've thought she was you. Same name and all—well, almost."

"Yet, it must've been meant to be," Violet said. "Or Bethany wouldn't have been there when we needed her."

Isaac had fallen asleep, mesmerized by the side-to-side motion of Tony's legs. Everything had happened as it was meant to.

Except her and Tony.

Tony smoothed the baby's hair. Violet twisted the hem of her skirt, keeping her gaze fixed on Isaac. She wanted to ask Tony what she'd been like before, when she'd been Charlotte, but she couldn't dredge up the nerve.

Chad looked down, his lips pressed tight, then he looked over at Florie. "You know, I saw some fantastic Christmas lights in a little town not too far from here. Might be worth seeing up close. Want to go?"

"I'd love to. With no assistant, I don't have much chance to get out." The Tennessee Watchkeeper glanced sideways at Tony, Violet, and Isaac. "That is, of course, if Violet and Tony don't mind watching the House for me for a couple hours."

"Of course not," Violet said.

Tony looked at Violet, at Isaac in his arms, then faced Florie. "I guess we could."

A stake drove through Violet's heart at the reluctance in his voice.

He didn't want to be alone with her.

Florie thanked them, and grabbed her Kitchen Sink bag, then she and Mr. Everly left, Rufus bounding out the door past them.

The front door shut, and the silence in the House grew oppressive. It was almost a relief when Isaac woke and started to cry. "What's wrong, buddy?" Tony murmured to him. "It's been a while since he ate." He held the baby out to Violet.

As she took the baby and sat in the rocker to feed him, she had trouble relaxing. Especially her mind. Tony mercifully walked away and stared out the window, where fat, white snowflakes caught the glow of Florie's porch light.

He forced himself not to pace, knowing it would make Violet tense.

He tried to figure out how to broach the topic of what to do about Isaac. For the baby's sake, it would be best to come to an agreement over child visitation.

It was not what he wanted.

She betrayed you, he reminded himself.

She had as Charlotte, but had she when Pippin had him locked in the conference room, awaiting the arrival of Caruthers? Or had she dropped the barrette intentionally, as she claimed?

Violet put the baby to her shoulder to burp.

He'd been wrong to take Isaac. She may have lied to him, may have deceived him about everything, may have had every intention of turning him over to Pippin, but she wouldn't harm their child.

An image—or lack thereof—burst through him. Nothing. No light. No sound. No darkness. He pulled away from the window with a shudder.

Violet looked up. "Tony? Is something wrong?"

"Just... for some reason, I started thinking of the nightmares."

Violet's voice was choked. "You... you were there. And it was my fault." On her shoulder, Isaac squirmed, but didn't burp. She rubbed his back.

Tony held out his arms. "Can I?"

She passed him the baby, who burped as soon as Tony settled him against his shoulder.

Tony held Isaac in front of him, smiling at the tiny bit of satisfaction that gave him. His son's eyes were half-closed. Violet followed Tony into the guest room, where he laid the baby in the cradle. "How was I there? And how do you know?" He crouched beside the cradle and tucked the blankets around Isaac, trying not to let his hands shake.

"In... another timeline. I don't remember it clearly now, but... you told me to get Isaac."

"I told you that this time."

"Yes. But in that other timeline... I did as you said. And Alpha trapped you in... in..."

"In the Void." Tony'd tucked the baby in so snugly he doubted he'd be able to roll over. He stood and faced Violet. "You changed the past."

"Yes." Her fingers twiddled with the neckline of her dress, drawing his gaze.

"You always used to fidget with your quarter like that."

"Wha-" Her fingers flew to her mouth. "The Ohio quarter?"

Tony jerked back. "You remember it?"

"Not from before. I had it around my neck. The day Timmy found me." She drew herself up straight. "Tony... what was I like... before?

Mr. Pippin told me a little..."

"Why did you change the past?" Tony didn't like the fear that zipped through him when she'd admitted to it. "Did Pippin know? What about Everly—"

"I couldn't let you stay there!" She turned to the window, her face in her hands. "I have nightmares, too. No, memories. Of a life where all I did was exist. Isaac was dead and you were gone, in the Void. All the while, terrible things were happening in the world."

"What sort of things?"

"Natural disasters, war, people disappearing... I don't remember clearly now, but..." She looked up. "It was all because she'd gotten away. And because Isaac—and you—were no longer in the world..." Her voice hitched. "All because I made a terrible mistake." She scrubbed at her eyes, tears glistening on her fist.

Tony couldn't stand it. He took the three steps to stand behind her, near enough his breath stirred stray wisps of hair. He wanted to take her in his arms, yet something stayed his hand.

Slowly turning, she wiped her face once more and met his gaze. "Tony... do you think the woman who betrayed you is the woman I am now? The woman you pretended to marry?"

He opened his mouth, but nothing would come out, as if someone had shoved a gag in it.

As much as playacting had been his intention when he posed the question, speaking the vows themselves had been anything but. "No." He looked away. "It wasn't pretending to me." He took a deep breath. "I wanted you to give Isaac my last name when we got here, so it would be that much easier for me to get him, but what I said... It was real. As real as you and me standing here. As real as our son lying there." He tipped his head down. "Though after what I did— yeah, I knew who you were from the first time we warped together into 1959. After the motel, I had no doubt. I couldn't figure out why you were hiding your identity." He swallowed. "When you told me about your memory loss, I was afraid it was just another ploy to get me for Pippin. But I—" he dragged his hand over his face, "I never stopped loving you." He turned away and paced. "I... I wouldn't blame you if you never forgave me. Especially after I tried to take Isaac."

"I wanted to hate you," Violet said. "Especially then." Her voice quavered. "But I couldn't. I don't even know what all I did, so I can hardly ask for forgiveness."

He forced the lump down his throat. He couldn't take this. Not when they had a child together, needed to be a family for him.

And most of all, because he didn't want to.

He was sick of being afraid, sick of the distrust. In that instant, he made a choice. A desperate choice. Because in that instant, he saw the future spread out before him.

He could spend the rest of his life in misery, distrusting, fearful, and regretting what he couldn't have. Or he could take a chance—risk it all. He jammed his hands into his pockets. "You don't need to ask forgiveness. If you can forgive me—for keeping you from... you. And for taking Isaac—"

"Done."

As he yanked his hands from his pockets, the small, brown-paper-wrapped package flew out. "What the...?" He scooped it up and ripped the paper off in one swipe.

The hinged box was covered in brittle, textured leather that was peeling off at the corners, revealing smooth, worn wood. He'd seen that box before. How Keith had gotten it, he had no idea. But it was here, now, for a purpose. He cracked it open.

"A ring?" Violet leaned over to study it. "It's beautiful—an antique, I'm sure—"

"It was my grandma's." Tony scowled down at the torn paper. "But how the hell Keith ever got hold of it... It was in my safe deposit box." He slipped the ring out of its velvet cushion and turned it in his fingers. "Mom didn't give it to me when I married Dora because she didn't like her. Knew we were never right for each other. It was supposed to be for Bethany. But apparently Keith—Isaac—has other ideas."

Air rose in his chest, almost lifting him off the floor.

The ring was a sign. "Vio—" he hesitated. "I guess I should ask, would you rather I call you Violet, or Charlotte?"

She stared down pensively. "Charlotte's my real name, but I remember nothing of that life."

"Charlotte... Violet..." He squeezed the ring in his fist. "I love you. As far as I'm concerned, you've been my wife since that day in the woods. But..." He took her hand in his, and held up the ring. "Would you do it over again? Legally, this time?"

She bowed her head, and he couldn't tell if she nodded, but she didn't pull away, so he slipped the ring on her finger.

When she looked up, her eyes brimmed with tears. "I love you, Tony. I'd do it all again. In a second." She reached up and wrapped her arms around his neck, pulling him to her, and when he tasted her lips there had never been anything sweeter.

Finally, he drew back and let his gaze slide over her. Charlotte, Violet, it didn't matter. It didn't matter what she'd done.

She reached for his pocket, where he'd slipped the Saturn Society knife, and lifted it out. "At least that question's answered."

"Huh?"

She ran her finger over the knife's hilt, where his name was engraved. "What name to tell Mr. Everly to put on mine."

Tony took the knife, his finger brushing across the scar on her palm. He set the knife on the end table and took her hand in his other, turning it up, traced over the scar again. "I should probably get those removed."

"Don't." Tony squeezed her hand.

"You saved my life."

Tony pulled her against him. "No, you saved mine." He scooped her off the floor and carried her to bed.

Three weeks later

I still can't believe this is ours. Violet gazed around the Watchkeeper's suite as she nursed Isaac. Chad had moved his belongings out, and she'd replaced the quilt on the antique sleigh bed she and

Tony now shared with the new one Florie had given them for an early wedding present along with a wedding sampler she'd stitched, and two, new still-life paintings Violet had picked out. "Make it your own," Chad had told her. Besides the antique, mahogany furniture that was too beautiful to get rid of, the only thing left from Chad's days there—or before—was Mr. Pippin's little puzzle box on the dresser, where he'd hidden the conference room key.

She especially couldn't believe Tony had agreed to take Chad up on his offer to take over the Dayton House. She wouldn't have agreed to it herself, if not for the fact that Fred had run away screaming when she and Tony had arrived at the Dayton House. His body was found over on the west side a few hours later, an apparent casualty of a hit-and-run. Soon after, Chad had made them his offer, so he could move into Florie's House and better research his next novel.

She couldn't blame Tony for not wanting to live at the apartment complex, considering his nephew had been murdered there, but she suspected it was Bethany who'd ultimately made up his mind. The girls had warped into the Dayton recovery room from 1939 a few days earlier. With Bethany's mom back in Georgia, moving in with her dad seemed the thing to do, and Taylor's attic suite was the coolest bedroom ever.

Pans clanked from downstairs, where Tony was fixing breakfast. The girls were still asleep, although Violet thought she'd heard Bethany get up in the middle of the night, probably to make sure her car was still in the garage behind the House. The girl had the oddest attraction to the bright yellow Camaro, though Violet had to admit it was pretty, and its ride surprisingly smooth. She and Tony had driven it home after Florie had gotten its sabotaged fuel line replaced, and confirmed that Bethany and Taylor drove Theodore Pippin home in 1939 and would return to the present in Dayton.

Violet and Tony had delayed the wedding until the second weekend in January to ensure that the girls would be there. It also gave the Society time to diffuse the rest of the media attention that had surrounded the girls' disappearance, as well as to debrief Tony's family. Despite knowing Bethany was fine, it had been hard for them to celebrate Christmas without her. It was even more so for his paternal grandparents, as he and Bethany had missed Chanukah altogether. But everyone had welcomed Violet into the family, including the grandparents, who'd complimented her for giving the baby a good Jewish name.

Violet lurched to the side as dizziness burst through her. Isaac sputtered and let go. The vertigo passed quickly, and she repositioned him at her breast, but he turned away, finished. As she rose and pulled her robe around her, Tony's footsteps clomped up the stairs and into the recovery room.

Chad. Apprehension bubbled in her belly as she grabbed a burp cloth and lifted Isaac to her shoulder and moved down the hall.

Tony had already reached the recovery room. "Well, this is a switch, me taking care of you. I thought you were in Tennessee?"

"I had an errand to run here." Chad sat on the edge of the nearest bed, and looked up with his characteristic grin as Violet entered the room. He lifted his hand in greeting, then his grin subsided. "Any news on John Quimby?"

"Legal's still trying to delay his court date." Tony helped Chad remove his shoes.

Violet's lip curled at the mention of Tony's lookalike. "As long as he doesn't get the death penalty."

Tony straightened. "Yeah, it doesn't help that the bastard's acting remorseful and keeps insisting that he deserves to die. Not that I disagree, but..." Of course, death was exactly what Quimby wanted, and exactly what the Society needed to prevent. Hopefully, the legal team would succeed, and would also succeed in keeping him out of solitary confinement. Violet had no doubt his next move would be to engage in whatever bad behavior would get him there.

"Enough about him." Chad's grin returned. "I hope I'm not too late for the wedding?"

Tony glanced at the wall calendar, which Violet had just replaced for the new year. "When'd you warp from?" Tony asked.

"1958." Chad's gaze met Violet's.

Her hand twisted in her skirt. Hopefully, he had the news she'd hoped for.

Tony drew back. "I thought you were researching for your book."

"I was. I had a very interesting visit with Theodore Pippin. He's been back to the frontier quite a few times himself." Chad slid down on the bed. "We also discussed Mr. Quimby. Turns out that's not you in Pippin's Book at all."

Tony stiffened. "It's him."

Chad gave a single nod. "Yep."

"How'd you figure that out?"

Chad titled his head. "Glasses?"

"Oh man, you're right."

"What?" Violet studied Tony's face, her brows pressed down.

"You don't remember the picture in the Book, do you?" Tony moved to her side. "I had long hair, and a beard. Like when we first came back from prehistoric times. And no glasses—I lost them right before Keith zapped me with his laser gun and sent me home."

"Mercy," Violet breathed. Tony had gotten a haircut and shaved his beard, and of course had replaced his glasses. He was back to his old self—the man she'd gone on that fateful date with nearly a year before, only leaner, stronger—and no longer distrusting. "But then how did the picture get into Mr. Pippin's Book?"

Chad lay down and pulled the sheet up. "Pippin found the book lying out when he and the girls got home. The page with your picture was lying beside it. I guess the doctor caught the guy messing with the Book, right after Pippin left for Tennessee."

Violet closed her eyes and took a deep breath, clutching Isaac against her. She should be sorry she'd trapped that horrible Dr. Caruthers in the Void, but she just couldn't dredge up any regret. She met Chad's gaze as she patted the baby's back. "Did you... give Mr. Pippin my message?"

Tony drew back, and a flurry of emotions crossed his face.

"Yes." Chad's head lolled to the side, and his eyes drifted closed.

He was slipping into recovery. "Chad!" Violet squeezed Isaac's blanket in her fist.

Chad's eyes opened. "Theodore agreed... not to tell you anything... in 1959."

Violet rubbed Isaac's back in short, irregular pats as she met Tony's curious gaze. "I asked Chad to go back."

"It was... th'least I could do." Chad's speech was starting to slur. "Screwed up... so bad. Can't believe.... trusted her." He didn't have much time.

"So much could have gone wrong," Violet said. "I'm afraid that if one thing were to change, even something as simple as Mr. Pippin telling me... about me."

Tony gave a sharp nod. "Good idea."

"Theodore... thought so, too." Chad's eyes started to shut again, but he forced them open. "And also..."

Violet gave a tiny shake of her head—*Not now!*—but Tony met her gaze, his expression taut. Isaac squirmed and fussed.

Tony reached for him. Violet handed the baby over, and Tony moved toward the door.

"Tony..." Chad said.

Tony stopped in the doorway, his gaze hardened and fixed on Violet. "I thought we decided to trust each other."

Violet wanted to shrink away, but stood firm. "We did, but..." She stared at the hardwood floor. "I have to know."

Tony gave a sharp nod and started to take another step, but Chad spoke again. "Wait."

Violet fisted a wad of skirt. Chad struggled to keep his eyes open. "Theodore said... you killed Tony... so he could escape."

Violet let out a breath she hadn't realized she'd been holding. "Thank heavens."

"I think..." Chad forced the words out. "It's the beginning of the end... of the Black Book." His head lolled sideways and sank into the pillow.

"Thank you." Violet's voice shook as she leaned down and threw her arms around him. "Thank you, so much."

Chad's breathing slowed. He'd fallen into recovery.

As Tony returned from putting Isaac down for his morning nap, she threw herself into his arms. His wrapped around her, and he kissed the top of her head. "It doesn't matter," he said into her hair.

"It did to me." She tightened her embrace. "But thank you for trusting me anyway. No matter what."

Violet shifted her weight from foot to foot, gazing around the Society House's parlor. She forced herself not to pick at the beading on the formal wedding gown Tony'd had her choose. She'd insisted she didn't need anything expensive, but he said he'd seen her eyes light up when she saw it in the store, and it wasn't like they couldn't afford it.

He'd offered her a sumptuous affair like his first wedding, but she'd declined. They'd found a Society woman from Cincinnati who was a licensed minister to come to Dayton to perform a simple ceremony. Though the room was crowded, it held all those Violet held dear. Tony's parents and three grandparents, who'd become like her own. Beside the minister stood Chad, who both she and Tony had quickly come to regard as a friend, and had agreed to be the best man. On the minister's right, Taylor and Bethany, Violet's co-maids of honor, whispered to each other. Both were due to start classes at Sinclair Community College in a couple days, much to Tony's relief. Taylor would keep an eye on Bethany, train her in the ways—and more importantly, the avoidance—of time travel, and hopefully, Bethany's studies would keep her too busy to let her mind wander and jerk her into the past.

Violet had found her friend and former roommate Stephanie, who sat on a footstool between Timmy and her new husband, the police officer she'd met when reporting Violet missing. Behind Stephanie stood Bernie, who Violet recognized from the bagel shop around the corner from the office, where Tony used to eat breakfast every day. Thankfully, Bernie blocked the television from Violet's view. Even turned off, even though Chad insisted it was fine, the thing still gave her the willies.

Finally, her gaze landed on Tony's nephew Mark, his brother-in-law Charlie, and his sister Lisa, who held Isaac. Violet hadn't wanted to truss up the baby in the silly miniature tux Tony's mom had bought, but she couldn't bear to risk hurting her feelings. Isaac didn't seem to mind, his bright eyes darting all over the room.

Violet's heart went out to Lisa for losing her son at the hands of that horrid John Quimby. Tony had considered going back to re-do the night of Danny's murder, but they'd both feared changing the past any further. Violet prayed the prison staff would remain vigilant in not letting Quimby out of other people's sight long enough to warp to another time. It hadn't happened yet—

"Everyone's here now!" Tony called from the foyer as a middle-aged woman Violet had never seen pushed a wheelchair into the parlor. The hunched-over man sitting in it looked at least a hundred years old.

Tony motioned Violet over. "Violet, this is Lydia. She's a distant relative of yours, and this—" He crouched, pulling Violet with him so that they were at the old man's eye level. "...is Dewey Henderson."

"Ch- Charlotte?" the old man whispered.

Violet sucked in a breath. Beneath all the wrinkles, his golden-brown eyes, so like hers, sparkled in recognition. "My- I can't believe..."

"Your brother," Tony said quietly.

"Oh, my..." She took the man's hand in hers. "H- How did you know?"

Dewey spoke softly. "Knew you woudn't'a gone off and left without good reason." He lifted his hand toward Tony. "And that's as good a reason as any—" He broke off when tears spilled from Violet's eyes. "Don't be cryin' girl, it's your wedding day. Now get up there and do what you should've years ago."

She wiped her eyes, trying not to smear her makeup, and made her way to the front of the room where the minister waited.

She began with the traditional wedding ceremony. Violet stood firmly with Tony, until they reached the part where Tony spoke his vows. The minister stepped back, as they'd decided to speak their vows themselves, without having her read them first.

Tony took Violet's warm, dry hands in his. "I, Anton Joseph Solomon, take you, Violet Sinclair, to be my lawfully wedded wife. I promise to love you, honor you, to cherish and protect you, for better or worse, for richer or for poorer, to have and to hold for as long as we both live, for present, past, and future, wherever, and whenever, we find ourselves."

Violet trembled. He gripped her hands more tightly. "It's okay," he whispered. "Just say whatever you want."

For a second, he feared she'd bail out, but when she spoke, her words were steady and sure. "I, Violet Charlotte Henderson Sinclair, take you, Anton Solomon, to be my lawfully wedded husband, to love and honor, to have and to hold, through times of ease and times of trouble, in sickness and in health, as long as we both live. I give you my heart, my trust, and my life, past, present, and future."

Tony barely heard the rest of the ceremony, his world focused on Violet, until his gaze flicked to the alert yet uncannily quiet baby in his sister's lap.

He slid the ring on Violet's finger, tracing his thumb over the scar on her palm, a symbol of everything she'd sacrificed for their son... and for him.

He had no doubt the times of trouble were far from over. Alpha may have been contained, but according to Keith, there were others, and while the battle had been won, the war wasn't over. Between Keith's legacy and the Society, they had plenty of places to live in a variety of eras, but there was a good chance they wouldn't be able to stay in any one of them for long before those others caught up to them.

Order and structure were overrated.

"Tony?" Violet looked at him with wide eyes, and he realized the minister had stopped speaking.

"Don't you want to kiss the bride?" the minister said with a smile.

In answer, he scooped Violet into his arms, crushing her against him, and brought his lips to hers. As he reveled in her softness, her beauty, and her love, Isaac cooed. With a smile, he broke the kiss and sank into his finally-legal wife's golden gaze, ready for whatever, wherever, and whenever life would take them.

Author's Note

Many thanks for allowing me to share Tony and Violet's adventures with you! Your time is valuable, and this is a privilege I don't take lightly.

My goal is for every Mythical Press story to provide an excellent reading experience. To that end, if you've spotted a typo or other error in any Mythical Press book, please let us know so that we may correct it, by emailing publisher@mythicalpress.com.

Research, of course, plays a big role in a story like this, and is particularly challenging when dealing with a prehistoric culture, who by definition, left no written history. While it's well-known that at least one group that was part of the Fort Ancient culture lived in the Miami Valley (the site of today's Sunwatch Indian Village), this group may or may not have been the people who took in Tony and Violet in the story, as the modern travelers had no way of knowing exactly how far back they journeyed in time. Furthermore, there's no consensus among the archaeological community as to what became of the Fort Ancient peoples, as they disappeared before European explorers reached the Miami Valley. It's unclear what relationship they had, if any, to the native peoples who later populated the area. Basic daily life shown in the story is based on what we do know of the Fort Ancient cultures, but only loosely. Any deviations from current knowledge are either literary license, or my oversight.

If you enjoyed *Time's Fugitive*, I'd appreciate it if you could take a minute to post a review on Amazon, Barnes and Noble, Goodreads, or other venues; and recommend it to friends and family who might enjoy it. Reviews and word of mouth are vital to an independent publisher, and your opinions matter! Posts on Facebook, Twitter, blogs, forums, and other social media are also a great way to get the word out and help independent publishers keep producing stories.

To stay informed of future releases, please stop by my website and blog at www.jenpowell.com, or connect with me on Facebook and/or Twitter. I look forward to seeing you there!

About the Author

Jennette Marie Powell is the author of several time travel and paranormal romance novels. A lifelong resident of the Dayton, Ohio area, she likes to dig beneath the surface and find the extraordinary beneath the mundane, whether in people, places, or historical events. While she has no desire to change the past, she enjoys learning about local history, particularly the early 20th century. Her preferred places to time travel are from her computer or Dayton's Carillon Historical Park. By day, she wrangles data and websites between excursions to search for the aliens and spacecraft that legends say are stashed away on the military base where she works.

Jennette lives with her husband, daughter, two Rottweilers, and assorted small critters. When not working or writing, she enjoys spending time with her family, learning about local history, cruising in her Camaro, and riding her Harley.

Visit Jennette at www.jenpowell.com, or connect with her on Facebook or Twitter.